Advance Praise for
A Delightful Compendium of Consolation

"Beguiling storytelling sorcery. Imagine Scheherazade crossed with A. B. Yehoshua. Readers will be so captivated by the vivid characters in this romantic portrait of life in Medieval North Africa that they may not notice how deftly rabbinic tales and Jewish wisdom have been woven into the plot. Delightful it is... also absolutely brilliant."
— **Letty Cottin Pogrebin**, author of *Deborah, Golda, and Me: Being Female and Jewish in America*

"Delightful indeed! An enticing blend of scholarship and imagination. I couldn't put it down."
— **Maggie Anton**, author of *Rashi's Daughters*

"A 'delightful' historical novel, capturing the spirit of this dynamic period: a tale of merchants and scholars, of families, rabbis and students—real and imagined. A world in which Jews and Muslims, even Jews of different religious persuasions, lived together more harmoniously and with less conflict than they do in many parts of the world today."

— **Mark R. Cohen**, Professor of Near Eastern Studies, Princeton University, author of *Under Crescent and Cross: The Jews in the Middle Ages* and, most recently, *Poverty and Charity in the Jewish Community of Medieval Egypt*

A Delightful Compendium of Consolation:

A Fabulous Tale of Romance, Adventure, and Faith in the Medieval Mediterranean

by Burton L. Visotzky

Ben Yehuda Press
Teaneck, New Jersey

Published by
Ben Yehuda Press
430 Kensington Road, Teaneck, NJ 07666
http://www.BenYehudaPress.com

Ben Yehuda Press books may be purchased for educational, business or sales
promotional use. For information, please contact:
Special Markets, Ben Yehuda Press,
430 Kensington Road, Teaneck, NJ 07666.
markets@BenYehudaPress.com.

Cover credit: Hebrew text from an early Judeo-Arabic manuscript of Rabbenu Nissim's DELIGHTFUL COMPENDIUM OF CONSOLATION, courtesy of
the Library of the Jewish Theological Seminary (MS 2472, folios 67b-68a).
Feather and scroll image © iStockPhoto/Jelena Savic. Jambiyya image ©
iStockPhoto/Paul Cowan.

Library of Congress Cataloging-in-Publication Data

Visotzky, Burton L.
   A delightful compendium of consolation : a fabulous tale of romance,
adventure, and faith in the medieval Mediterranean / by Burton L. Visotzky.
       p. cm.
   Includes bibliographical references.
   ISBN 978-1-934730-20-1
   1. Mediterranean Region--History--Fiction. 2. Religious fiction. I.
Title.

   PS3622.I788D45 2008
   813'.6--dc22

                        2007033441

07 08 09 10   / 10 9 8 7 6 5 4 3

Contents

"He did not want to compose another Don Quixote - which would be easy - but *the* Don Quixote. It is unnecessary to add that his aim was never to produce a mechanical transcription of the original; he did not propose to copy it. His admirable ambition was to produce pages which would coincide - word for word and line for line - with those of Miguel de Cervantes."

"Pierre Menard, Author of Don Quixote"
Jorge Luis Borges, *Ficciones*

Editor/Translator's Introduction

Just over a century ago, two learned, widowed, Scots Presbyterian sisters—twins actually—traveled to Cairo and Jerusalem. The two women were accomplished linguists, knowledgeable in Greek, Hebrew, and Syriac. They were very wealthy and collected Bible manuscripts. In May of 1896, they returned to their home in Cambridge, England, and enlisted the aid of Dr. Solomon Schechter, the Reader in Talmudic and Rabbinic literature at the University. Schechter happily deciphered the Cairo manuscript fragment they had put before him; it was the Hebrew original of the apocryphal biblical book of Ben Sirah. As Schechter wrote to them that very afternoon, "I think we have reason to congratulate ourselves... It is the first time that such a thing was discovered."

Schechter subsequently traveled to Cairo himself. There in the old synagogue he discovered a Geniza—a storage room in which aging Jewish manuscripts had been put away. The Jews of that community were loathe to discard sacred texts and so deposited anything written in Hebrew script in that ante-chamber. As it happened, Hebrew script was the regular alphabet of the medieval Jewish community of Fustat or old Cairo. The Jews wrote Hebrew, Aramaic, even Arabic in the Hebrew alphabet. As a result, Schechter recovered texts and documents dated as early as the ninth century and ranging for almost the entire millennium thereafter. When he finished distributing *baksheesh* to the locals, Dr. Schechter succeeded in hauling 140,000 manuscripts and fragments back to the Cambridge University Library.

All told, some 220,000 such manuscripts and fragments from the Cairo Geniza now reside in libraries and rare book rooms all over the world. The texts range from Bible manuscripts, like the fragment discovered by the two sisters, to rabbinic texts, medieval Hebrew poetry, personal letters, business agreements, marriage and divorce documents, etc. As the late Prof. S. D. Goitein of the Institute for Advanced Studies at Princeton described this vast archive, it revealed "A Mediterranean Society."

It was a society made up of Jews, Christians, and predominantly, Muslims. The heyday of the Geniza period was in eleventh and twelfth century Cairo, at the time when Egypt and its Fatimid Empire held sway over the Mediterranean Muslim world. The Jews who left their writings in this depository wrote and received mail and documents from all over the Islamic world, from Spain in the West, to India in the East. The Geniza people, as Goitein fondly called them, loved travel, business, their Jewish life and, like good folk everywhere, a well told story.

And so, these pious Jews circulated collections of rabbinic stories. One of the more famous works of that period was called, in its widely read Hebrew version,

A Delightful Compendium of Consolation. Nissim ben Yakov ibn Shaheen, known as Rabbenu Nissim, was the author/collector of the *Delightful Compendium*. The work itself was composed in eleventh century North Africa, in the Tunisian city of Kairawan. That town was an important caravan stop and boasted a major Talmudic academy.

The Cairo Geniza has revealed many of Rabbenu Nissim's other works. We have, for the first time in a millennium, his own Talmud commentary. We have Nissim's reference work for Talmudic study (*The Key to the Locks of the Talmud*). We even have his scholarly diary (*The Scroll of Secrets*). And we now have the Arabic original of the *Delightful Compendium*. Because Nissim actively had his works copied and preserved them by sending them to the Jewish community of Fustat, we are able to reconstruct his life and works in imaginative detail.

What follow are "newly discovered documents" from among the hundreds of thousands in the Cairo Geniza. They help us illuminate the circumstances of the writing of Nissim's famous book of tales, his family life, and the lives of his colleagues. These texts weave a tale of famous story-tellers who lived and loved and wrote a millennium before our time. These documents have been arranged chronologically wherever possible to tell, as it were, their own story.

Burton L. Visotzky

Part One:
Wandering

Chapter One

Fall, 1031 c.e.

From Dunash in Old Cairo, to Rabbenu Nissim in Kairawan

To the illustrious elder, may God prolong his life and make permanent his prosperity, to Rabbenu Nissim ben Rabbenu Yakov, may his soul rest in peace, ibn Shaheen. In Kairawan, if God wills it.

From Dunash HaCohen al-Tustari, in Misr which is Fustat, during the festival of Sukkot in the year 1343 of the Common Reckoning, in the name of the Merciful One.

Blessed be the True Judge.

I am writing to you my dear friend, teacher, and business colleague, about a matter heavy upon my heart. My darling daughter is gone! Karimah, who walked with us but 18 years, is no longer among us, and now I must learn to live with but her memory. May God have mercy upon her.

I apologize for writing this brief epistle to you in haste to request your assistance in my time of grief. I know that with your vast wisdom and knowledge of rabbinic sources you may provide me with relief that my community here in

Fustat cannot. I wish not to turn to the works of the Muslims for relief after adversity, though such books among them are plentiful.

So I beseech you, Master, to help your friend in his mourning for his loss. Write for me a work of consolation from the tales of your rabbis, as might have delighted my Karimah, were she still among us. Perhaps I might find joy from your letters, which I await always and value as though they were written by my very brother. I shall collect what you send me so that I may find solace again and again, and others, too, might find some consolation. I know my own dear son al-Iskander, who will soon be of the age of commandments according to your reckoning, will wish to hear and read this compendium, that he too might be consoled after the loss of his elder sister.

I am sending you by caravan eight camel loads of flax which I have purchased at a good price. We shall be partners in its profits one-half each. Further, I am sending by ship two small bales of finished silk garments wrapped in leather. Please help me sell this for a consortium of business colleagues here, for which we can offer you a commission of five silver dirhems per gold dinar. Another four larger bales are of pepper. Wait to sell until you get a good price. It would be best to wait until shipping closes for the season, but do not wait too long lest the pepper, which is not of highest quality, lose its zest.

I remind you that you have on account with me 23 and one-quarter dinars. I enclose my own check to the merchants of the Perfumers' Market in Kairawan, who will provide you with the dirhems for your expenses. I also ask you to take what sum you deem necessary to redeem the captives taken for ransom by the pirate ships of the Rum. God willing, the pirates will not harass the very boat which brings you this letter. Let me know what you have spent for this noble act, but under no circumstance pay beyond the common sum of thirty-three and one third dinars per soul, lest those brigands be encouraged. Ransom the women first, of course, and may God preserve their chastity.

Send me a full accounting of the business and of the charity you undertake on my behalf. Send me goods to trade, I will find a fair profit for you, God willing.

To my Master Nissim ibn Shaheen, may God prolong his life and make him always safe and happy, please God

From Karimah
to her brother al-Iskander in Fustat, Fall, 1031

Dear al-Iskander, my sweet little brother, may God lift His face to you and give you peace. I imagine you did not think that I would write to you, but you were wrong. The trouble is there is almost no way to get letters back to Fustat, especially without Daddy finding out about them. Do not even dream of telling him I am writing you or I will never speak to you again.

I am also sending on a letter for you to read to Mommy, but only to Mommy and not to Daddy—I am still so angry at him. But you must also make Mommy promise not to tell Daddy that she is hearing from me. I am writing letters to Mommy so she will not worry too much about me. I am writing you the stories of my travels, but you must not read these to her or she will worry too much. This is just between us, like our adventures used to be.

So swear to me that you will not breathe a word to anyone of what I am writing you—not Mommy, certainly not Daddy, not to Nanny, and not to any of your friends. You are old enough now to keep a secret, I know I can count on you, little brother; you are such a sweet Persian-fruit.

I cannot believe that Daddy was so stubborn. Did he really go into mourning and sit the seven days? Part of the reason we left on Sukkot was so that he would have some time to think and change his mind before he could "mourn"—how can he treat me like I was dead? There is a huge difference between being in love and being dead! I feel so very alive now, maybe alive for the very first time. I am on my own, and not under the stifling gaze of the master businessman of the honorable house of al-Tustari.

Besides it is Daddy's fault that I had to leave, since he would not give his permission for what *he* started in the first place. Was it not *his* business I worked for? Did *he* not teach me how to write and read in Arabic? Did he not make me work like a dog, copying everything under the sun for him? He made me add and subtract endless columns of numbers, it was so boring. Skandi, do not ever learn math. Daddy will make you a bookkeeper.

Anyways, it was Daddy who took me out of the house and made me work in Bahram ibn Abdallah's courtyard. His women stayed veiled while I sat there bare faced. I actually would have felt better under the veil. Daddy always said it was good to have a Muslim to work with because then he could be a partner on caravans riding over Saturdays without having to worry about violating the Sabbath. And it was Daddy who got Abu-Ismail to go on the caravans so Daddy could stay home and do nothing except make me work. So what should I have done when Ismail saw me calligraphing? I thought it was nice that he showed me how to make my Arabic script better. Even Daddy thought it was good that 'Smail taught me how to write certain things so that I could keep better records of our purchases and our properties. So it was Daddy who sat me with the Muslims and then got all upset when I actually noticed that Ismail was a man.

Oh al-Iskander, it is so unfair. Just because I fell in love with Ismail ibn Bahram ibn Abdallah now Daddy wants me dead. He is just so severe with me. But

'Smail is really good to me so Daddy is wrong! It is so romantic that we ran off together. Ismail is my very own king Shahriar, and I shall be his Shahrazad!

I am pretty sure that 'Smail told his father that we left together, but Bahram ibn Abdullah has not said anything to Daddy because he fears for his business. You would think that a Muslim would be just fine doing business with the Caliphate, but everybody worries about crossing an al-Tustari. It would be just like Daddy to punish Abu-Ismail to get even with me.

'Smail and I left the way you and I used to, by crossing over the Nile to the Giza side. Do you remember how we used to go exploring at the pyramids there and pretend to be beggars to see how much money we could get from the tourists? Do not ever tell Mommy about that! 'Smail and I went up the Nile from Giza to the Fayyum. It had always seemed so far away, but when you actually hitch a ride on a barque it is not a long trip at all—at least compared to what we have done since.

We just got to the lowest part, I am not even really sure it is called the Fayyum there yet, but it was enough to remember that the rabbis' teacher Saadya came from there—they revere him so much, but he said such insulting things about our Karaite community of Scripture. I know because one of those rabbinic Jews once paid me to copy a letter this Rabbi Saadya sent and it was just so disrespectful! Anyways, they have the most curious mummy boxes there—they are not at all like the ones near the pyramid. Do you remember when we saw that mummy unwrapped and the skin and bones were so disgusting? We Jews would never treat a body that way, what we do is so much more natural. From dust we come and to dust we return, like it says in Scripture.

The Fayyumis put their mummies in these boxes, but they paint the outside of them with pictures of the dead people inside. The boxes are really old, you can tell, but the pictures of the people on the outside look so real, like they are still alive. It is so odd, they stare at you. I think they use wax to make them more lifelike. Anyways, the painting is fabulous, much better than anything I have learned to do, and much more real looking than the old Misri tomb paintings. The writing on these caskets is strange, it reminds me of the writing at the church in our neighborhood. And one more thing I forgot to tell you is that the pictures show the people wearing beautiful jewelry—you would think that would be an invitation for grave robbers like at Giza, but the mummy boxes did not look like they had been opened.

Once we left the Fayyum and came back across the Nile to head East, 'Smail said that it was not safe for me to travel with him, even if we pretended we were husband and wife. I did not know whether to be happy that he could think of us as husband and wife, or to be sad because I thought he was telling me we could not go away together. I did not want to come home and have to see that look on

Daddy's face when he said "I told you so." But I told 'Smail, I said, "Ismail ibn Bahram, I am going with you wherever you go; no matter what you say!"

'Smail said, "Of course, but it is just that it is not safe with you being so beautiful and desirable. I should call you Wuhshah!" I think I might have blushed when he said that aloud because it was not like him to compliment me. That is when I started to think of myself as Wuhshah and thought that I should not use my old name any more since Daddy wanted me dead anyways.

As it turned out, I was not to be very Wuhshah, since what 'Smail had in mind was for me to dress like a boy. He said this way no one would bother me and we could share a tent. So I put on some of Ismail's clothes even though they were too big for me. I stuck my feet into the extra pair of boots that he had brought—I could see he was not happy to give up his boots like that, but he was the one who said I should have a disguise. Then I wrapped my hair in a turban like his, and drew the end of it down across my face like the Badawi do to keep the sand and sun off their mouths. It was almost like wearing a veil—I felt so Muslim, if you know what I mean. The final piece of my disguise was a *jambiyya* dagger, to tuck into my belt. I know that you play with knives, but even wearing this without taking it out of the sheath will take me some getting used to.

As if all this were not enough, 'Smail said that now I would have to ride, and he meant on a horse! They took one of the horses that had some bundles loaded on it and tried to sit me on them. But I kept slipping off, so one of the servants suggested that he make me a saddle. I asked him, "What is a saddle? I never heard of such a thing in all my life."

He answered, "With your permission I will make you a saddle so that you can ride in comfort."

I agreed, so he took some pieces of wood and shaped them like a chair, which he covered with some cloth. Then he took a piece of leather which had been covering one of the bundles and stretched it over the wood and cloth. Finally, he strapped this onto the horse and I got on once more. But I promptly slid off again. Everybody laughed, even 'Smail, I was so embarrassed! So then he took some straps that had been holding together some of the clothes we were carrying and he looped them over this saddle thing. I found that if I pushed down into the straps the same amount with each foot, I could balance on the horse.

Anyways, there was another piece of thinner leather that they put into my hands and from there it went through the horse's mouth, and the horse drooled all over it. But they showed me how to pull the bridle one way then the other and the horse moved the way I wanted him to! I am sure that judging from the way I rode no one in our party thought I was a boy; but then they knew who I was to begin with. The important thing was that the Badawi not think I am a girl and carry me off and sell me into slavery or whatever it is they do. After all this horse riding I can explain to anyone why I no longer have my signs of maidenhood. It is like those rabbinic Jewish girls claim, "I was injured by a stick." Some stick!

Anyways, I just prayed that no Badawi would notice I was the only one riding with a saddle. They asked me what name they should call me now and I told them to call me Kamar al-Zaman. But when I told them that in private they could call me Wuhshah, they all laughed. I thought that was a good thing and it broke the tension. They all seemed to be so loyal to 'Smail.

Dear al-Iskander, my sweet brother, I will stop my story here and add a letter for you to read to Mommy. Do not read this one to her! Only read her the one I address to her. I shall write to you again and send all the letters at the first opportunity. I miss you.

To my little brother al-Iskandri
Whose mouth is always full of candy
Everybody thinks you're dandy
Even though your legs are bandy!

To al-Iskander ibn Dunash HaCohen al-Tustari, may he grow to Torah and great deeds. In care of the Sugar Factory and sweet shop in the small bazaar of Fustat. For his eyes alone, may the ban of Rabbi Gershom of Mainz be upon you!

From Rabbenu Nissim in Kairawan, to Dunash in Fustat, Old Cairo, Fall, 1031

To my lord abi-Skander, the most illustrious Dunash HaCohen al-Tustari, may God protect you and keep you. May He who created you come to your aid and lessen your sorrows. In Fustat, Misr, if God wills it.

May the Omnipresent bring comfort to you among the mourners of Zion and Jerusalem. I speak to you who, as a Karaite, always mourns Zion and Jerusalem, while yet supporting the Jews there. My dear friend Dunash, we could not dispense our charity to the Karaites or to the rabbinic academy in Jerusalem without your constant support, may God recompense you for your generosity.

You touched me with the letter which you wrote with such a troubled soul, telling with almost audible sighs of your dearest daughter's departure, may she rest in Eden. May God repair the breach and visit you with children who merit long life.

Your letter reawakened my own grief over the loss of my household, now more than a year ago. Although my mourning period has passed my wounds are fresh.

Each time I gaze upon my daughter Ghazal I cannot keep myself from bitterness over the loss of her mother, who left us while bearing the girl into life. As our sages of blessed memory teach: Love and grief upset the normal order.

Sometimes I think that my grief makes me look upon my only child as though she were ill formed by God. The Rock Whose work is pure has given us our lot and we accept it. But I am not alone in noting that our daughter seems short of stature, even for a baby; yet her head seems too big. Perhaps this was responsible, Heaven forefend, in some way for the demise of her mother. But again, perhaps my own sins were the cause of both my loss and my Ghazal's apparent deformity, for though I have so named her, no gazelle is she.

Forgive me pouring out my sorrows to you who need to be consoled. Yet I wish you to understand how well I sympathize with your loss. It is difficult to justify the passing of a girl as pure and innocent as your Karimah, learned and obedient, such a bright light. Indeed, she was near the age of my late wife, as you may well recall. My wife was young, yet is gone. And now your Karimah, though also young, is no longer among us. May they rejoice together in Eden.

I am sending you 12 camel loads of medium size al-Hilwah dates, which the Muslims love because their prophet loved them. Others love them for their sweetness. The season is plentiful again and I know that dates sell better in Fustat than here in Afrikiya. In truth, as God is my help, it is virtually all I have to offer you for sale—it is even an affront that I might ask as great a trader as you to serve as my consignee. Yet I know that you, with the help of God, will bring me a price far greater than I could ever hope for here. I appreciate that you also send me business to profit by, for without your help and that of my patron Shmuel ibn Naghrela, who now is the Nagid of Granada, my students and I would not survive.

Here in Kairawan our venerable Rabbenu Hushiel, Head of the academy, is not well. He grows weaker daily and his son Elhanan, God bless him, frets with frustration at being unable to help his father for all his pain. God certainly tries his righteous ones. Alas, I fear Hushiel soon will meet his reward. I shall miss him, for he was a good teacher and even a surrogate father to me—although I feel sure he will die and still never have learned a word of Arabic. It is good his Hebrew is so fluent.

Hushiel's son, my friend and teacher Elhanan, also has not learned Arabic. But Elhanan is Second and I am not. So Elhanan shall become Head and I will be Second—but please God may that time not be soon. It is right that Hushiel's son now succeed him, even though I am now forty-one and fit.

My dear unhappy friend, I have gone on too long speaking of my own troubles when it was my intention to address your sadness. I shall send another epistle which will be the first installment of the work you requested of me. Let your heart gladden in due time.

Burton L. Visotzky

I pray for this letter and for the fruit that I send, the same prayer which you prayed—that the pirates of Rum not take them captive. I smile, old friend, for I know that your heart was taken captive by your wife and I recall that she comes from Amalfi, a great port of the Rum. Maybe God will grace me with my own pirate from the Rum to steal my heart, may it be so, please God.

To Dunash HaCohen al-Tustari, for whom my love, like old wine, grows stronger with years. By the ship "Ali Abu Dahab" via his family.

From Karimah
to her mother in Fustat, Fall, 1031

To my mother, light of the household, who bore me to life and guides my footsteps upon the right path, from her faithful, loving, and pious daughter. Peace be unto you, my mother and my teacher. To be read by al-Iskander.

From her loving daughter far from home, exiled from her father's house, wandering with Ishmael in the wilderness of Hagar.

Dearest Mommy, I am well and I am happy and I hope you are thinking of me. I am traveling now, unable to come home, you know why. But it is good for me to be traveling, I am no longer a baby and it is time for me to be a woman on my own. I am very happy with Ismail and he is taking good care of me. He does everything that I ask of him. He is a gentleman to me. I can take care of myself.

We are eating lots of fruits and vegetables. We have slaughtered pigeons, but only those which our community considers fit to eat. I am not eating other birds, either according to the rituals of the Muslims or the permissiveness of the Rabbanites. There have been plenty of fish to eat as well. I have been careful to drain the blood in accordance with the ruling of our teacher Daniel al-Qumisi, even though both the Muslims and the rabbis allow fish to be eaten with the blood.

So you see I am scrupulous. I have also taken care to study the locusts which are here in small numbers, thank God not like during the plague of the Egyptians. I have been able to determine that there are kinds which are permissible to our community, but have refrained from eating them so long as there are fruits and vegetables.

I recite the Psalms every day at the time that the Muslims say their prayers toward Mecca. Often I hum them to myself as I travel, for the Hebrew words soothe me and keep my spirits bright. I do not fear of sudden terrors or the time of the evil ones when it may come. I have silver—do not fret. I put my trust in God.

You would be proud of me; I have learned much. I am caring for the clothing. You know I took some clothing with me from the house. Ismail has some clothes that I can wear as well. I wash them clean and when I need to I sew; you know that I can do so well. I practice my writing whenever I can. Unfortunately there are no supplies for drawing or illuminating. Paper and quill are not plentiful here.

I will write again. Pray for me and remember me, your loving daughter. Give my love to Nanny and kiss al-Iskander for me.

From Nissim in Kairawan, to Dunash in Fustat, Fall, 1031

To my sad friend, Dunash HaCohen al-Tustari in al-Kahira, which is the fortress of Misr. From Nissim ben Yakov in Kairawan, in the name of the Merciful.

You mentioned in your letter that it was your desire to read a work which would console you, which would gladden your heart and remove your worries. You told me that the Muslims have a book of relief after adversity and requested that I compile a compendium along those lines, based upon the legends of our rabbis and sages, may peace be upon them, so that you need not read any other similar work.

Although I am not accustomed to this type of work, my desire to fulfill your request and to please you has encouraged me to try my hand. I asked for help from God and requested guidance on the proper path to do this favor. I have placed this task ahead of other matters because of the high esteem in which I hold you.

I hope that the Creator, may He be blessed, rewards me in the World to Come; as our rabbis, peace be upon them, have taught us regarding the reward for those who bring joy to aching souls and troubled hearts.

They tell the story of Rabbi Meir who was sitting and teaching in the rabbinic academy one Sabbath afternoon when his two sons died. What did their mother do? She placed the two of them upon a bed and covered them with a sheet. When the Sabbath was ending Rabbi Meir came home from the synagogue.

"Where are my two boys?" he asked.

"They went to the academy," she replied.

"But I looked for them there and did not see them."

She handed him a cup of wine with which to end the Sabbath and he pronounced the blessing.

Again he asked, "Where are my two boys?"

She told him, "Sometimes they go someplace. They are on their way now."

Then she served him his supper and he ate. After he had thanked God for his food, she said to him, "Rabbi, I wish to ask you a question of Jewish law."

He said, "Ask your question."

She said, "Rabbi, earlier today a man came and left me a deposit to hold. Now he has come to retrieve it. Shall we return it or not?"

He told her, "My daughter, is not one who holds a pledge required to return it to its owner?!"

She said, "I would not have returned it without your consent."

What did she do then? She took him by the hand, brought him up the stairs, drew him near the bed, and removed the sheet from upon them. He saw the two of them dead, resting upon the bed. He began to cry, saying, "My sons, my sons. My masters, my rabbis! My natural born sons, yet my rabbinic masters in that they enlightened me with their Torah."

At that moment she said to Rabbi Meir, "Rabbi, have you not taught me that we must return the pledge to its Master? Thus is it said in the book of Job, "The Lord giveth and the Lord taketh away. May the name of the Lord be blessed".

With these words she consoled him and settled his mind. Thus is it written, "A woman of valor, who can find? Her worth is far greater than rubies."

I offer you this consolation, my friend Dunash; for your daughter, while precious as rubies to you, was but a pledge on loan from God. We must let go and find a way to thank God for the life we were given, while not begrudging God the right to take back the pledge He left with us.

Elsewhere the sages taught:

When Rabban Yohanan ben Zakkai's son died, his disciples came in to comfort him. Rabbi Eliezer came in and sat before him. He said to him, "Rabbi, by your leave, I would say a word to you."

Rabban Yohanan said to him, "Speak."

Rabbi Eliezer told him, "Adam had a son who died, yet he was consoled for his loss, as it is said in Genesis, 'So Adam again knew his wife.' So you too must be consoled."

Rabban Yohanan replied, "Is it not enough that I have my own sorrows, that you remind me of Adam's sorrows?"

Rabbi Joshua then entered and said to him, "Rabbi, by your leave, I would say a word to you."

Rabban Yohanan said to him, "Speak."

Rabbi Joshua said, "Job had sons and daughters and they all died on the very same day. Yet he received consolation for them; as it is said, 'The Lord giveth and the Lord taketh away, may the name of the Lord be blessed.' So you too must be consoled."

Rabban Yohanan replied, "Is it not enough that I have my own sorrows, that you remind me of Job's sorrows?"

Then Rabbi Yossi entered and spoke to him of Aaron's loss of his two sons, and Rabbi Shimeon spoke to him of King David's loss of a son. Each was likewise rejected by Rabban Yohanan ben Zakkai.

Finally, Rabbi Elazar, Rabban Yohanan's favorite disciple, came to call upon him in his sorrow. When Yohanan saw that he had come he said to his servant, "Take fresh clothing and follow me to the bath-house—for it is time to end my mourning. You know that Rabbi Elazar is a great man and I shall not be able to withstand him."

When Elazar entered, he sat and spoke as follows, "Rabbi, I shall draw you an analogy to what this may be likened. It is like a person with whom the Caliph has entrusted an item as a pledge. Each and every day that man would weep and wail and ask, 'When shall I be quit of the responsibility for this pledge and find peace?'

So, you, my Master, you had a son who learned much Torah: he knew Pentateuch, Prophets and the Writings, further he knew the Mishnah and all the other works of rabbinic Law and Lore, and he departed this world free of sin! You should find consolation in that you have returned your pledge intact in peace."

Rabban Yohanan said, "Elazar, my son, you have comforted me in the way in which one man comforts another."

And so I say to you, my dear friend Dunash, may God preserve you and keep you from future sorrows. You had a dear one who was your daughter. She too studied Torah. She read, she recited, she wrote Hebrew and Arabic, and she departed this world free of sin. Do not blame yourself for this loss, nor blame your household. You raised a daughter without sin, there is no blame to be had. God gave you a loan, a precious gem to keep until the time came to take it back. You have returned that pledge intact, so you must be consoled and find peace, my friend.

I pray that your household soon heals from this grievous wound and that you and your dear son al-Iskander, may his light shine bright, find comfort in these pages. Rabbenu Hushiel continues to wane. I shall send more later in the season.

Burton L. Visotzky

To Rabbenu Nissim, may his light shine forth from the rising to the setting of the sun, Rabbenu Nissim ibn Shaheen, in Kairawan, may it be God's will.

From his friend, poor in knowledge but striving for deeds of charity and loving kindness, Dunash Ha-Cohen al-Tustari, in Misr, please God.

How fortunate am I to have received an answer to my humble request in that you have taken time from your busy schedule of teaching and rendering God's law to address my need in my hour of despair. You have blessed me with much sweetness, by both of your letters and the dates which you sent along; for sweet they are called and sweet they tasted. They arrived only partially dried, which was excellent; for Fustat and even the Caliphal mansions of Cairo still have too rich a memory of the recent years when the Nile did not rise. The droughts then keep the prices high even now, so the succulence of the dates which you sent allowed me, thanks be to God, to auction the various loads to different dealers in the fruit market. With each load the price rose yet still higher and so God has blessed you as He has the date orchards of Kairawan. Your profit of seven dinars is enclosed in this letter in the form of a check drawn, as usual, on the merchants of the Perfumers' Market.

You know how I hate to leave my dinars sitting idle, so I beg of you to take your profit and add to it a like sum of my own so that we again may be partners in a venture I wish to propose. I have made an entree into the court of the Caliph al-Zahir, through the good offices of my cousins Sahl Abu Saad al-Tustari and Abu Nasr al-Tustari, may God continue to shine His countenance upon them.

The Caliph Al-Zahir has taken as his concubine the former slave of Sahl Abu Saad. She is a Sudanese, black as the night and as beautiful as she is black, as it is written in the Song of Songs, "I am black and beautiful." Praised be to God, that former slave has borne the Caliph a son, whom he favors. This gives my cousin Abu Saad even more influence at the court than he already had, I expect it shall wax continually. He is so wise and generous.

Of course you know of his generosity, for he contributes to your academy in Kairawan, as well as to both the Jerusalem and Babylonian synagogues here in Fustat. I understand that he also sends money to Jerusalem and to the schools of your rabbis at Baghdad: Sura, and Pumbedita. This from a man who does not pray with your rabbis but rather, like all of our family, counts himself proudly with the Karaite community of Fustat.

In any case, Abu Saad and Abu Nasr, my al-Tustari cousins, called me to their office. It is so odd, for it is at once opulent and yet modest. It is opulent in that they have a huge wooden desk at which they sit and write their accounts. It looks as though it is one piece of wood, although it is impossible for me to fathom how a tree could grow to such dimension. Of course, we never have thick trees here, nor do I suppose are there such thick trees in Kairawan or anywhere else in Afrikiya for that matter. I am told that they had this impressive piece of wood imported especially for them from the Rum, praised be the Creator of such wonders. Yet for all of the magnificence of the desk, the two brothers share it as though they were school boys! I did not dare ask about it, but I suppose it is either a sign of their affection for one another or else a sign that neither would allow the other to sit alone presiding over such an expanse.

Now it is clear that Sahl Abu Saad the elder is the more wily. It was he who was well schooled and well lettered. It was he who inserted his slave into the Caliph's harem. It is he who is now like the very Wazir in his power to influence the Caliph. Yet he does everything together with his brother; and Abu Nasr seems content to rise and fall—God forbid—with his brother's waves of fortune.

So much gossip and I have not even begun to tell you the topic of my letter, which was my very own audience with the Caliph! Of course I have the al-Tustari brothers to thank and God be praised, will spend the rest of my life thanking them for this golden opportunity. Al-Zahir is such a great man of stature, the opposite of his father, al-Hakim. We were silent when al-Hakim became erratic and persecuted the Christians, so we were punished by God for not standing up to al-Hakim. Oh how we suffered from the badges and special clothing he made us wear and the riots he provoked against us. We are still hoping to repair or rebuild the synagogues which were damaged in those awful days.

But now, praised be the Creator for all He sends us, times are much better. Al-Zahir is a man with whom we can do business. He is careful not to make the Jews and Christians in his court too visible, lest the Sunni Muslims have even more cause to complain against him and his glorious Fatimid dynasty. But the parades and public displays are plentiful; in my next letter I shall describe the magnificence of the costume and the glory of the court's clothing.

A word to the wise must suffice for now—there is opportunity for one like me who works in rags to spin gold out of the cloth I trade in. My introduction to the court, thanks be to God, may allow me to gain a royal commission to produce uniforms for the Turkish troops who guard the Caliph. I am thinking that I can send you flax and silk to see if the households of your students in the Kairawan academy can sew garments. I will propose to the court that I first be given a contract for the Kutama guards, for those ferocious Berbers hail from Afrikiya and wish to wear their local Kairwanese costume.

For now, ask your disciples if their households wish extra sewing. We will undertake the weaving here. You can pay them whatever wage you see fitting, we can share the profits half and half. This should benefit you and your academy. As your sages say, If there is no flour, there can be no Torah.

Speaking of which, I am sending with this letter a shipment of 16 boxes of wheat. I am sending it by caravan for I do not wish to risk the salt and moisture that seeps in when things are stored in a ship's hold. Please let me know that it has arrived. Sell it in the winter market at Kairawan. It is good quality wheat, sell it for a good price. You can use part of the shipment to bake bread for the poor of Kairawan.

The caravan is ready, so I am sending this now, with the wheat. I will speak of your kind stories in my next missive, please God, which I hope to send to you soon. I thank you again for sending me such delightful consolations and wish for more; Nissim and the Almighty willing.

From Dunash in Fustat to Nissim in Kairawan, Late Fall, 1031

To Nissim, may his light burn brightly, Rabbenu Nissim ben Yakov ibn Shaheen, in Kairawan, by the Creator of the winds and seas. From Abul-Iskander, Dunash HaCohen al-Tustari, in Misr, which is Fustat. In the name of the Merciful.

I am sending this by boat for I wish you to destroy the letter which I sent you with the shipment of wheat. I was most intemperate in putting to paper both my plans for business and my thoughts about the late father of our Glorious Commander of the Faithful, al-Zahir, may God keep him and enlarge his rule. God forbid that letter fall into the hands of an enemy of the Jews, for although what I have written of al-Hakim may be common knowledge, putting pen to paper was most unwise. Further, I worry about an evil eye lest my plans for a partnership in Caliphal clothing not find favor in God's eyes. So please, exercise care with the letter I have sent you, lest it become a stumbling block before the blind.

I promised to tell you of my meeting with our Caliph al-Zahir, may his rule be extended unto Baghdad. I met him in the library of the Western palace in the very heart of Cairo. But my journey began in Fustat. Of course, it is expected that a man of my rank not go on foot, so I had the servants prepare a donkey for me to ride. It is but three miles north to the palaces in Cairo from the fortress in Fustat, where our home is by the old Roman wall and aqueduct. If protocol had demanded I should have been happy to walk there for this opportunity.

As it was, when I passed the mosque of ibn Tulun I was greeted by representatives of my al-Tustari cousins. They had a horse for me to ride! Of all things, a Jew riding a horse! I confess I sat awkwardly, but we rode slowly and all who saw me knew of my triumph. We arrived at the main street that runs between the Eastern and Western Palaces, the street called Bayn al-Kasrayn. There I dismounted and walked the remainder of the way. I did not mind walking for it was enough just seeing the majesty of the fortresses. In the distance, at the north end of al-Kahira, one can see the huge box-like mosque of al-Hakim.

I had thought we would be granted an audience in the Eastern palace, for the Gold Hall of the women is there, where audiences are often held, and the Iwan palace of the men is also there. Yet before we even reached the parade ground between the two palaces, we turned aside to enter the Western palace. I was dismayed to find myself suddenly accosted by the smells and sounds of the kitchen, for that was the entrance I was brought in through. We passed the piles of garbage with cats and rats burrowing among the spoiled food. I assume that once I entered the palace grounds I was subject to the whims of the Berbers and the Turks, who wished to show me that my cousins' influence was less powerful than I had thought. But it was a minor humiliation, especially after the thrill of riding, however briefly, on horseback.

We entered the Dar al-Hikma, where the Caliph keeps his library. They say there are two hundred thousand books there, praise be to God. One could not read all these works were one's lips to move from dawn until night every day of a lifetime of reading! The books on display there are great works of beauty; the calligraphy is exquisite; and many of the works are illuminated with fine draw-ings and paintings.

I missed Karimah especially then, as I thought how she would have marveled to see the Persian miniatures illuminating the manuscripts. I swelled with pride that our families come from a land where such art is so renowned. I must admit, I even was dazzled by the Quran in its magnificence. Never have our scribes or sages illuminated a scroll with the beauty and detail with which these Muslim artists gave homage to Allah. Of course, I know that you will tell me that it is what is in the books which is important and that we should not look at the vessel but at what it contains.

The Commander of the Faithful sat enthroned in the House of Wisdom. Those walls which were not covered with shelves of books and scrolls were covered with tapestries and brocade drapes. The floors were covered with thick carpets. There were gold curtains separating one section of the room from another. The Turks were there in their finest robes, each gowned in fine brocade shot with threads of gold. The Kutama, as I have written you, prefer their Berber costumes. They bear terrifying arms as part of their attire. Each Berber wears a form of pantaloon covering his privates and legs. The pantaloons are held up by a silver buckle with what appears to be a hand with a pointing finger at its end. It struck me as not unlike the silver hands which you use in the synagogue to point at the Torah scroll. I wondered if, God forbid, the Berbers had expropriated those items for their pantaloons when the synagogues were destroyed in the riots not so long ago.

I entered and, as instructed, kissed the ground in deference to the Commander of the Faithful. He said I should be given a tour of the Eastern palace and then he withdrew forthwith. I understand that even so brief an audience was exceptional given al-Zahir's sensitivity to those who say he is under too much Jewish influence. Ever since he took his Sudanese wife, my cousins' influence has waxed; yet our public visibility has waned. I do not know if this is good or bad, I put myself into God's hands.

I write on a second sheet, having erased an alphabet I cannot read, to describe for you the beauty of the clothing I saw within the palace. Surrounding the Caliph were mamelukes bearing his symbols of authority. They held his sword—so many jewels you could not believe. Each of these eunuchs was dressed in beautiful buqalamun cloth which shimmered in the light. I saw with my own eyes that this cloth changed color depending upon which direction the mamelukes turned! I assume that it was some silk shot with alternating colors, the woof a constant color and the warp alternating between contrasting hues which then came to prominence as they turned this way and that. In any case, the effect was dazzling.

I, of course, have no pretensions to weave or supply anything that fine. I should be happy to be able to make cloth as white as the turbans they wore. I will, by the way, be sending you some turban cloths in a separate shipment—these must not be sold for less than 150 dirhems each. Of course, I will pay you the usual commission of five dirhems per dinar. The turbans I am sending are 18 to 21 cubits in length.

The Caliph's guard each wore a much longer turban, perhaps as long as 25 or 26 cubits. But the Caliph al-Zahir, himself, Commander of the Faithful, had a winding of majesty that was wrapped around a most beautiful ruby in its center. He looked like some character from the 1001 Nights, so magnificent was his bearing. I could imagine a Jinn had conjured a ruby of such amazing size. Who can find its worth?

I have written so very much I am surprised, but the thought of having part in this clothing enterprise has turned my head from my sadness and sorrows. Let me close by thanking you for your kind attention to my needs. Your stories speak to my sorrow, and I believe your advice is good. I try not to blame myself for what happened to Karimah, for you are right, I did teach her Hebrew writing and how to read from the Torah, even how to read the works of the rabbis. Perhaps my guilt was that I taught her Arabic and allowed her to read the works of the heretics. Perhaps I should never have allowed her to draw pictures or to paint. Surely I was wrong when I asked her, a girl, to do sums and keep accounts. As it says in Psalms, "All the glory of the princess is within." Perhaps I should have kept her as the Muslims do, in the house and out of sight. My Muslim partner keeps his women veiled even in the house. I, who am there almost daily, have never seen his wife's face. And yet they saw the face of my Karimah. That is my shame and guilt, no doubt.

But I confess to you, may God forgive me, that more than I blame myself or my household, I blame her and, I am ashamed to admit, I remain angry with her for leaving us. She was so young. My misery is abject. God help me, what am I to do?

Write to me, dear Nissim, of things that will lift my spirits and explain the mysterious ways of our Creator, may His name be blessed. I send this on the last boat of the season. From Dunash most wretched in Misr, to Nissim, in Kairawan, by boat.

Burton L. Visotzky

Chapter Two

From Nissim in Kairawan,
to Dunash in Fustat, Late Fall or Early Winter, 1031

To my dear friend Abi-Skander, may the Lord bless him and watch over him, Dunash HaCohen al-Tustari, may the Lord shine his face upon him and show him favor, in Misr, God willing.

My dear Dunash, let me assuage your fears by returning your letters to you. I did not wish to destroy them since they contained God's holy name. I know it is your custom in Fustat to "put away" letters and sacred books no longer fit for use. Or you can store these letters in such a place that they cannot be read by any eyes other than your own. But please, have no worries on my account. I do not repeat gossip, for our sages have taught that an evil tongue brings destruction to three - the one who speaks it, the one who hears it, and the one of whom it is spoken. Or as they say elsewhere, Why are fingers shaped like pegs? So that a man can stick them into his ears to avoid hearing unseemly things.

You responded to my letter of consolation by blaming yourself. I confess that I sometimes blame myself, or my daughter, or worse, her mother for her passing. And I understand well your anger at your daughter, for it is a feeling I share. Needless to say I do not wish this known, any more than you wish to have your letters shown to others. Certain things are meant for private conversation and should not be public, ever.

I wonder if we might not be better off turning our anger toward God, may His name be praised. For surely the Creator of Heaven and Earth can endure our anger better than can our children or our household or those whose memories we seek to preserve.

Did not our sages teach us that at the hour that the Blessed Holy One said to Moses our master, "The time has come for you to depart the world," that Moses cried out and wept, saying, "Master of All Worlds, did I labor for naught? Was it for nothing that I worked like a horse on behalf of your children? Now shall my end be the grave and my finale be the dust?! Let me suffer, but do not turn me over to the bonds of death!"

The Blessed Holy One said to him, "Moses, I have vowed that no kingdom may overlap another, even a hairsbreadth. Up till now you were Caliph over Israel. From this point onward it is Joshua's turn to rule."

Moses replied, "Master of the Universe, in the past I was master and Joshua my disciple. Now let me be the disciple and he shall be Head, just that I might not die!"

God replied, "If you think you can do so, go ahead."

So Moses went to Joshua's entranceway to serve him as a disciple. Moses assumed a bowed posture so that Joshua did not even notice his presence. When Israel arose to greet Moses in the morning as was their custom, they could not find him. They asked, "Where is Moses?"

They were told, "He stands at Joshua's tent." The Jews went to Joshua's and found Moses standing in servile posture.

They asked Joshua, "What have you done that our master Moses stands in service upon you?" Joshua's eyes were opened and he saw our master Moses serving him!

At that moment Joshua prostrated himself. He wept and said, "My Father, my Father, My Master, My Rabbi. My father, in that you raised me since I was a boy, and my rabbinic master, in that you have taught me wisdom. Rabbenu Moshe, what is this you have done?"

Moses replied, "Leave me be, for thus has the Blessed Holy One told me to do to Joshua that I may not die."

At that moment all Israel wished to stone Joshua, but God's Pillar of Cloud interposed between them. They asked Moses, "Complete the Torah for us, master."

But the tradition escaped him and he could not reply. Moses fell to his knees and prayed, "Master of the Universe, better my death than life like this!"

When the Blessed Holy One saw that Moses had reconciled himself to die, He offered a eulogy for Moses, our master. Then Moses wept and asked Israel for forgiveness. They in turn asked him to forgive them for all that they had troubled him. Finally Moses mourned his own death and gave up his soul to God.

You see, my friend, it is natural to be angry at flesh and blood at the time of death, for Israel sought to stone Joshua when they learned of Moses' coming demise. And is not Moses himself angry at the Blessed Holy One? Yet our sages teach that God interposed the cloud, which is soft and billowy, so that it can absorb anger or any stones which may be cast. God can endure our anger and forgive us. Indeed, our sages teach that at the time of death we must learn to

Burton L. Visotzky

forgive the one who leaves us and in turn seek their forgiveness of us, too. So I will try to forgive my wife and my daughter, and you, beloved friend, forgive your daughter for her departure from you. We must heal and give praise for God and his mysterious ways, for all His ways are just.

Is it not said of Rabbi Beroka that once when he was in the bazaar Elijah appeared to him? Beroka asked him, "Is there anyone in this bazaar meant to inherit the World to Come?" At first Elijah said no, but then there came a man wearing black shoes, who was not wearing ritual fringes upon his garments. Elijah said, "This one will be in the World to Come."

Beroka ran after him and asked, "What is your business?"

The man replied, "Leave me today and come back tomorrow."

The next day Beroka asked him, "What is your business?"

He said, "I am a jailer. I keep the men and the women in separate cells and place my bed between them to protect their virtue. And when I see a Jewish woman who has attracted the amorous attentions of the men, I will risk my life to save her. Once there was a betrothed girl who had been jailed for non-payment of the poll tax. The gentiles were planning to take advantage of her. I spilled the dregs of my wine upon her dress and told them she was menstruant. Of course, they stayed away from her then."

Rabbi Beroka asked, "Why do you not wear ritual fringes and wear black shoes?"

He said, "I pass among the gentiles dressed as one of them and they do not know that I am Jewish. That way if I hear of evil plans against the Jews, I can notify the rabbis that they may pray for God's mercy and annul the evil decree."

Rabbi Beroka asked, "Why did you ignore me yesterday and tell me to return today?"

He replied, "Just then I had heard of a decree against us and so I decided it was better to act first to notify the rabbis and only then speak with you later."

Just then two more men passed by in the bazaar and Elijah indicated that they, too, were destined for the World to Come. Rabbi Beroka approached them and asked, "What is it that you do?"

They replied, "We are clowns, who bring laughter to the sad. Also, when we see two people angry with one another, we make peace between them."

So shall I, dear Dunash, try to bring happiness to you and those who read my stories, and to bring peace to troubled souls. I will write you stories and the deeds of our sages to illuminate the mysterious ways of God. I will tell you stories that not everyone knows, so that you and all who read this book might benefit. I place my hope in God, that I may not be shamed.

I have received the turbans and the wheat. We have distributed the bread to the poor and have ransomed two more captives from the slave market at the usual price. The garments you sent us are now sold, as is part of the flax. I will take the remaining linen and ask the wives of the boys in the academy if they can sew Kutama uniforms. I am still holding the pepper and the bulk of the wheat until the winter market, as you recommended. We put our trust in the Lord.

Your generosity to me and to my academy is overwhelming—may God grant you reward and length of days. I pray that the book brings you as much consolation.

From Karimah
to her brother in Fustat, Winter, 1031 - Spring, 1032

To al-Iskander ibn Dunash HaCohen al-Tustari in Misr, with the help of God. From his sister, who has entered the wilderness of Sin, in the name of the Merciful.

Dear little brother Skandi, I pray you will receive this letter and the other that I wrote to you while I was yet in Misr. I did not know then that my mount would not be a horse for very long, for we traveled east and entered into the Sinai wilderness. When we had crossed over we traded our horses for camels. I received what looked to be a three-legged camel. When I asked the servants about this, they laughed at me and pointed out that the animal was "hobbled." With one front leg tied up the camel could not wander off. So in the end I had a four-legged animal, but its joints seem to work backwards so that rising up and getting off seems like riding in a boat on the waves. I know that you and the other boys have ridden camels, but it was new for me. As mommy always used to say, "It is not proper for Jewish girls to ride."

The animals made funny noises, grunting and gurgling. One of the servants can imitate the camel so well it sounds like they are speaking to one another. But when I tried to offer some greens to my camel, it spit and snapped at me. Without thinking I hit the beast across his snout. His long neck reared back and I feared for my life. But from that point on the camel has been respectful of me. Now everyone has a kind of saddle. It is different from that of the horses, but I blend in better in my guise as Kamar al-Zaman. There are 12 camels in our train, but I am told that is a very small number. If the Badawi of the Banu Hilal or Banu Sulaim clans attack us, they say we will be robbed of everything and I mean everything. We would be stripped naked, which means my disguise and life would both come to an end. So pray for my safety, brother.

The servants now carry swords in addition to *jambiyya* daggers. I will not carry a sword as I cannot use it and it would only bring me danger should I need it. But 'Smail says even a girl can learn to wield a sword, if only I would let my arm muscles grow stronger. It is true that when I began to write with the quill my arm tired quickly and then grew stronger, so perhaps I will yet master the sword. Imagine that!

The Wilderness of Sin is fearsome. I feel like the Israelites at the crossing of the Sea. The very first thing that happened to us was that a wind blew up the dust into a pillar of cloud. I felt protected then by God's Presence, although the sand got in my hair and eyes and in my mouth and even between my teeth. The camels snarled at the sand storm, but it was brief. There are wadis here in the Sinai which during the winter can suddenly run full of water higher than the camel's snout. So we are constantly listening for the rumble of water coming down a wadi. If we hear that we are supposed to ride as fast as we can to the highest ground we can get to. So far it is dry.

One of the intersections of the wadis is called Ayn Mousa; and the Shaykh, our old guide, tells us it was here that the Israelites sang their song. He says that Maryam's well must be nearby, for she, too, led them in song. The wells are just holes in the ground that one is lucky enough not to fall into. One of the camels already lost its footing at such a well, but no one got hurt, not even the camel. The servants, I think, were hoping the camel would become lame so they could eat it. Out here it does not seem as cruel as it sounds. It would be a mercy to the camel and a feast for the servants.

For my part I am doing my best to eat in purity, but there are no more vegetables. We eat dates until my insides churn - not a good thing for traveling on camel back. I have taken to laying nets for the birds and killing them with my *jambiyya* and cleaning them myself. I cook them over the open fire on a stick and everyone says they are delicious! They remind me of the quail that fell for the Israelites, they are so plentiful. Do not tell Mommy what I am eating. I have not yet resorted to eating locusts, but the old Shaykh eats them and some of the servants just catch them and pop them in their mouths. They sound crunchy.

We traveled south and it was truly awesome to look west and see Egypt across the water. I have never felt closer to Scripture or to our ancestors, even though we grew up in Egypt. The next big wadi we came to was Feiran. There were many palm trees, so at least there were dates and lots of fresh water. I bathed in the middle of the night by the moonlight. It was so good to get clean. I think maybe some of the servants might have seen me bathing because they have been calling me Wuhshah since, but Ismail does not think it is funny at all that they say aloud that I am desirable. He is so worried about my being a girl. I do not think he appreciates how loyal and honorable the servants actually are.

Anyways, there were loads of dates at Feiran and I ate too many of them. I became a bit windy, but so did everybody else. One of the servants told us a story about a wedding he had been to many years ago. There was a man, Abu Hasan by name, who had been of the Fazli clan of the Badawi. Abu Hasan's friends prevailed upon him to find a bride. Abu Hasan found a beautiful young bride, as radiant as the moon when it is full. On the night of their wedding all of the Fazli Bedu came to the feast, where they ate goat stuffed with dates, figs and pistachios, and they also roasted a young camel. They drank much wine and recited love poetry far into the night.

When the bride and groom retired to their tent, the guests waited expectantly outside for the signs of the bride's virginity. They listened unashamedly to the sounds of Abu Hasan and his bride. But the food and drink had the better of Abu Hasan and in the midst of their revelry he let flee an enormous fart which billowed the very walls of the bridal tent! The guests laughed among themselves and drifted away; so when Abu Hasan left the tent and found no one outside, he realized that they had heard him.

Covered with shame, Abu Hasan rode his mare off into the night. It is said that he fled all the way to Hind. He stayed there 12 years and when he was gray of head, finally returned to his homeland. He came to his town and listened to the girls at the well. There he heard a girl ask of her mother, "Mommy, tell me of the night I was born." And her mother replied, "My dear daughter, you were born on the very night that Abu Hasan farted." Poor Abu Hasan was mortified that what had been his wedding night was now remembered for his breaking wind. He left that town and never did return.

My little brother, I think I should call you Abu Hasan from now on, instead of 'Skandi. For our part, we traveled through the wadis without further incident or further wind. The waters of the sea receded from view behind us and we moved eastward toward the middle of the Sinai. It is no longer sandy here, but rocky and more mountainous. There are huge boulders, the size of a man on camel back. We are taking the southern route across the Sinai rather than the northern Hajj route. 'Smail tells me there are marvels here which a scribe like me will be happy to witness. Thus far, however, it is but stone and rock.

I am adding a hurried goodbye to my letter as we have come to a walled fortress in the middle of the wilderness. Ismail tells me we are at At-Tur, which the servants call Tur Sina. There is a Christian monastery here of the Greek Rum within the walls. They tell me that this place is safe for Muslims and that the Rum will not harass us, for al-Hakim built a mosque here just before my birth. This is the place of marvels that 'Smail has promised me. Indeed, it is marvelous in this—there is a caravan of forty or fifty camels which is leaving from the monastery and heading toward al-Kahira. I do not think I shall find one of our

Burton L. Visotzky

own among the Arabs, but shall find a trustworthy Muslim to bring my letters to you in the small bazaar of Fustat.

Remember, al-Iskander, do not read these letters to anyone else. Read Mommy only the letter I sent her and tell her that the letters I send to you say the same thing. Be sure that Daddy does not find these letters—put them away in the Jerusalemite synagogue or destroy them. If you tell anybody what I have written, I will find out and never write to you again. I am telling you about adult things and if you want to know more and learn how to grow into a man, you must keep faith with me. Who knows, Daddy may find you a wife soon. Remember that God knows the way of the righteous and will wreck the ways of wickedness.

To al-Iskander ben Dunash HaCohen al-Tustari in the Sugar Factory of the small bazaar of Fustat, God willing. From Wuhshah in the wilderness, encamped beneath the mountain.

From "The Scroll of Secrets" - Nissim's diary, Winter, 1031- Spring, 1032

—*Hushiel is dying. Elhanan has taken to calling himself Hananel. I think he finally understood that the boys in the academy were actually calling him al-Khannan - the shopkeeper—so he has opted for more dignity by moving God's name to the end of his own so that it is now Hanan-el. Now the name can only be understood in Hebrew, just like Hananel himself— no Arabic. Arabic or no Arabic, when Hushiel dies, Hananel will become Head, First.*

I, Nissim ben Rabbenu Yakov ibn Shaheen, whose father founded this academy, will become Father of the Court, no mean achievement, but still only Second.

—*My students Hillel ibn al-Gassus and Mevorach beRav David HaBavli say they would support me to be Head. Better still, my colleague Rabbi Yosef said he would support me. His young pup, Abu al-Maali, who wishes to become Yosef's son-in-law, will surely support me, as long as he can turn his head away from Yosef's daughter, Mulaah. Too much is unclear. Yet my ambition is clear enough.*

—*The Midrash Leviticus Rabbah teaches in the section, "After the death of Aaron's two sons," (Leviticus 16:1):*

Why did Aaron's two sons, Nadav and Avihu, die on the same day before the Lord? Rabbi Levi taught that they were arrogant. What did they say? Our father's brother is a king, our mother's brother is a prince, our father is high priest, we are associate-high priests, who is good enough for us? ... Nadav and Avihu used to follow behind their father Aaron and their uncle Moses and say to one another, when will these two old men die so we may have our turn ruling over Israel?

Rabbi Pinhas said, It was sufficient that they even thought such—that is why they died on the self-same day.

—I have committed the sin of envy and have lost my household for my hubris. My daughter is deformed because she reflects my deformed, prideful character. I shall not challenge Hananel, he is my teacher and my friend. He is more worthy to inherit his father than I am mine, peace be upon him. I will be Second and seek to restore my father's honor in my humility rather than through pride, envy, and gossip. I will serve my disciples rather than compromise them. I put my trust in the Lord.

From Nissim in Kairawan, to Dunash in Fustat, Spring, 1032

To my friend Abi-Skander, may he grow and prosper and not know sorrow any more…From Nissim in Kairawan, in the name of the Merciful.

Our Master and Head, Rabbenu Hushiel ben Elhanan of the Rum, who came to us as a captive and rose from the dust to head our academy after the passing of my revered father, has joined him in the academy on high, may his eternal rest be Eden. Rabbenu Hushiel was a true beacon of Torah who illuminated not only the Talmud we studied with him, but the lives of all with whom he had contact. I feel as though I have again lost my father, for Rabbenu Hushiel was, these past twenty-five years, my father in Torah.

It is fitting that my teacher, Hushiel's dear son, my esteemed colleague Hananel ben Hushiel, for thus is he now known, Rabbenu Hananel has become the Head of our academy in Kairawan, may his light illuminate us all. In his generosity he has raised me to the role of Father of the Court, Second in the academy. My friend Dunash, rejoice for your friend and client Nissim, may God protect me and make me worthy of this honor.

I wish to continue writing stories to bring delight to you and to all who read them, please God. Today I will recall the legends of our sages that show that God will bring just reward to those who wait patiently for His judgment to unfold. Though many years may pass, each finds reward at the hands of the Almighty. For many there is recognition in their lifetimes and for others there will be a share in the World to Come.

Our sages tell us of the great Rabbi Aqiba who had lowly beginnings as a shepherd for the wealthy Ben Kalba Savua. That rich man had a daughter named Rachel who cast her eye upon the shepherd and she proposed that he marry her. When Aqiba saw her beauty, for she was beautiful both on her outside and her

Burton L. Visotzky

inside, he assented. But this angered Ben Kalba Savua, who could not see that Aqiba was a fit son-in-law for such a one as he. So Ben Kalba Savua swore he would give his daughter no part of his wealth should she stay with Aqiba, but stay with him she did.

Aqiba and Rachel lived with but a pile of straw as their bed. Once a man knocked upon the door of their hut and said, "Sir, my wife is giving birth and she has nothing to lie-in upon." So Aqiba and Rachel shared their straw and so they realized that they were better off than others. Rachel urged him to study Torah, and with her consent he went off to the academy of Rabbi Eliezer and Rabbi Joshua for 12 years until he had mastered Torah. Ben Kalba Savua derided him to Rachel saying, "What kind of husband have you who deserts you now for 12 long years?" But Rachel replied, "Were it up to me he would stay and study yet 12 more."

When Rabbi Aqiba heard this he returned to the academy for 12 more years. At the end of that time he returned home to his Rachel with twenty-four thousand disciples accompanying him! The people of his town came out to acclaim him. Rachel, too, came to greet him, wearing a shabby garment that she had kept as fresh as she could in all those years of poverty. The disciples saw her as a beggar and wished to push her out of the way. But Rabbi Aqiba stepped forward and raised her up, telling them, "All that is mine and all that is yours is because of her!"

Then Aqiba gave his Rachel a tiara of gold, shaped like the city Jerusalem saying, "This, for my Rachel, who suffered with me for Torah."

It is also taught by our rabbis that Rabbi Hananiah ben Hakinai and Rabbi Shimeon ben Yohai were among the disciples of Rabbi Aqiba. They studied with him for 12 years. Rabbi Shimeon wrote and so knew what was transpiring in his home, while Rabbi Hananiah ben Hakinai did not write and did not know. His wife finally wrote to him and said, "Your daughter has matured, come home and arrange a marriage for her."

But Rabbi Hananiah did not reply. Rabbi Aqiba heard about this by the Holy Spirit and announced to his disciples, "Any one who has a daughter of marriageable age, go now and arrange for her!" Rabbi Hananiah realized this was meant for him, so he went to his master, sought his permission, and went home. When he arrived he went to his house but could not find it, for she had moved to a different location!

What did he do? He went to the well and listened to the girls as they filled their buckets. He heard the girls calling, "Daughter of Hakinai, take your bucket and be on your way!" So he followed the girl to her home and walked right in the door after her. When his wife laid eyes on him, her soul fled her body!

Rabbi Hananiah ben Hakinai prayed to God, "Master of the Universe, is this the reward this poor woman gets after waiting 12 years?" At that moment, her soul was restored to her body.

Rabbi Shimeon ben Yohai said, "There are four things the Blessed Holy One hates and I don't love them either! They are a man who holds his penis when he pisses, and one who makes use of his bed while naked, one who speaks of matters between him and his wife, and one who enters his house suddenly—need we mention one who enters another's house unannounced?"

So you see, dear Dunash, there is reward for the one who waits with patience and that the one who is impatient suffers. Alas, that neither of us had the reward of Rabbi Hananiah ben Hakinai, for our women have perished, yet have not been resurrected. We must wait until the World to Come, when all the dead shall rise again and then shall we be reunited.

Since I have written to you of Ben Kalba Savua, the father-in-law of Rabbi Aqiba, allow me to also tell you how he got his unusual name, for you know that his name could be translated as "satisfied son of a bitch." If I may be permitted, dear friend, there are rich men who are so designated. But our Talmud teaches that he came by his name from his hospitality, for all who entered his home hungry as a dog would leave wholly satisfied. Now Ben Kalba Savua was a patron of our revered master, Rabban Yohanan ben Zakkai, as were his two equally rich colleagues, Ben Tzitzit HaKeset and Naqdimon ben Gurion.

Of the former it is told that he got his nickname, which means Son of the Fringed Pillow, because the ritual fringes upon his garments would drag upon pillows his slaves would place before him, so his feet need not touch the ground.

I will save recounting how Naqdimon ben Gurion got his name for another time. Instead I wish to tell you of another of Rabban Yohanan ben Zakkai's patrons. I tell you this story for it shows us that God also punishes corruption in its time. This patron, a woman named Martha bat Boethius, was so wealthy that she bribed the King to appoint her husband as High Priest, even though he had married her when she was a divorcee, which the Torah forbids.

In the end, when Jerusalem was besieged by the Romans, she sent her servant to get fine flour. He returned to tell her, "There is no fine flour, but there is white flour." She told him, "Go, bring it to me." But by the time he got there, it was sold out.

He returned to tell her, "There is no white flour, but there is whole wheat flour." She told him, "Go, bring it to me." But by the time he got there, it was sold out.

Burton L. Visotzky

He returned to tell her, "There is no whole wheat flour, but there is barley flour." She told him, "Go, bring it to me." But by the time he got there, it was sold out.

She said, "I will go myself to see if there is anything to eat." She removed her sandals as a sign of piety and went to forage in the streets. But she stepped upon a piece of dung and died. Rabban Yohanan ben Zakkai eulogized her, "Most tender and delicate of women, whose foot never touched the ground."

My friend Dunash, God rewards and punishes each according to his or her deeds. In this I have complete faith. Each of us shall achieve our desired position in life; each shall be rewarded according to our just desserts.

From Nissim in Kairawan, to Dunash in Fustat, Spring, 1032

Dear partner and friend, upon whom I wish God's blessings as we prepare to rejoice over the deliverance of the Jews of Susa long ago and drink a cup of wine on Purim. Praise to Esther and Mordechai and cursed be Haman and all our enemies. Because we are in the days of Purim festivities, I wish to relate to you stories of our sages' miraculous deliverances and acts of God's salvation. "The winter is past and the rains are gone, let the song of the dove be heard in the land."

I wrote you last of Naqdimon ben Gurion, one of the three rich men of Jerusalem who supported our master, Rabban Yohanan ben Zakkai. Like in the days of the Caliph al-Hakim, there was a drought in Jerusalem and there was no water to drink for those who would make pilgrimage to the Holy City. Naqdimon went to a certain one of the Caliph's courtiers and bargained with him for 12 cisterns worth of water for the pilgrims. That Wazir agreed and they set a date for repayment. Their agreement was that should Naqdimon not be able to repay the water, then he would pay a penalty of 120,000 dirhems of silver.

On the day that the water was due, that Wazir sent a message to Naqdimon, "Either send me my water or send me the dirhems which you owe me."

Naqdimon sent back to him, "What is your hurry? All the day belongs to me."

Then again, in the afternoon, the Wazir sent to him, "Send me my water, or the silver that you owe me."

But Naqdimon replied, "There is yet sun in the sky."

In the late afternoon that Wazir sent to him, "Now send me my water, or the silver that you owe me."

But Naqdimon still replied, "I still have time in the day."

The Wazir sneered at him saying, "It has not rained all year, shall it rain now?!" The Wazir went to the bathhouse joyfully, thinking that he would come out a rich man. The fool did not know that God's salvation comes in but the blink of an eye.

While the Wazir went into the bathhouse, Naqdimon went into the house of God. He wrapped himself in his cloak and prayed, "Master of the Universe, it is known unto You that I did this not for my own honor, nor for the honor of my household, but for Your honor, that there might be water for the pilgrims to this Holy House."

The sky immediately knotted with clouds and the rain began to fall until the water filled 12 wells and more. When the Wazir came out of the bathhouse, Naqdimon asked him for the silver he now owed Naqdimon, because of the excess water!

The Wazir came to Naqdimon and said, "I know that your God disturbed the very order of the universe on your behalf—but I will still get my silver from you. For behold, the sky is dark now, so the day has ended and these rains have fallen on my time, not yours! Pay me the silver that you owe me!"

Naqdimon told him to wait but a moment, and he returned to the Holy Temple where he beseeched God, "Master of the Universe, let it be known that you have loved ones in this world."

At that the wind blew and the clouds parted and the sun broke through to shine yet on that day. And thus is he called Naqdimon, for the sun broke through (*naqad*) on his behalf.

We see that God rewards those who benefit the community. In fact, the Muslims tell a similar story of the Prophet bringing rain in the Hijaz. Take heart Dunash, for your beneficence also is worthy of miracles. Yet, no matter how deserving we may feel ourselves to be, we must not anticipate the rewards that God may give us. We should not dwell upon what we lack, but rather thank the Lord for those gifts which are given to us. Praise be God's name, day by day.

I am enclosing a poem reflecting on death. It was written by the Nagid Shmuel ibn Naghrela, when he learned of my teacher Hushiel's death, may he rest in Eden. "God is righteous in all His ways; He is gracious in all His deeds."

Poem by Shmuel ibn Naghrela, Nagid in Granada

When death calls will you have the power?
Or in hell will you weakly cower?
Just wait a bit as grandees gather
Unto your home, beneath your bower
Where they will wash and oil and lather
And place your corpse upon the tower
They shall dress you in your shroud
Lay you there with faces dour
The cry will sound throughout your rooms
A cry of woe, of voices sour
A man shall lead them in their tears
As they you in the grave do lower
Many shall stand around your grave
And one of them shall plant a flower
They'll turn home in disheveled state
Their eyes aflow for this brief hour
And on the morrow your estate
Their lawyers to divide empower
Cry for yourself alone today
And let your heart fear being nowhere.

From Dunash in Fustat, to Nissim in Kairawan, Spring, 1032

My dear friend and teacher, Rabbenu Nissim ibn Shaheen, Second — how it gives me pleasure to address you by your new and well deserved title. I express my sincerest condolences to you on the loss of your teacher and Head, Rabbenu Hushiel, peace be upon him, for we in the Karaite community knew of his wisdom and gentleness. He did not attack us like your Rabbi Saadya al-Fayyumi, but worked for the welfare of all Israel. May the Merciful bind him in the bond of eternal life and may he rest in Eden, may God will it.

I thank you, as always, for your installments of what is truly a delightful compendium of consolation. Your stories have caused me to acknowledge my errors towards God and towards my household, may God forgive me. I feel now that my mourning is coming to an end with the arrival of Spring. I know my daughter is gone, but as the flowers bloom I have faith in the resurrection when we shall all be reunited.

I am proceeding with our plan to manufacture the Kutama uniforms with the help of the households in your academy. This will insure a steady, if small, income for the families who study in Kairawan. I await your shipment of the trial pieces of linen to be able to set a fair price for the consignment. Send them by caravan.

I have made a contribution in your name to the building fund of the Shami synagogue which your Jerusalem compatriots here are seeking to rebuild. You know that the riots under the last Caliph severely damaged the main room, although the ante-chamber and the exterior walls remained intact. The structure is sound, but needs new accoutrements within. It will take a while to replace the furnishings and avoid the attention of the Muslim authorities who continue to complain about new synagogue buildings. Our case is that this is repair, not new building. Yet I feel certain that at some point they may try to stop the building project. But we try to live within the law of the Muslims as Dhimmi—and we know that as a protected people we are subject to the whims of the Caliph, as was the case with al-Hakim. So far his son, the glorious al-Zahir, has been very good to us, may his mother be blessed.

The rabbanite leaders of the Jerusalem community have been making the rounds collecting for the repairs. Rabbi Ephraim ben Shemariah, the Head of our Jerusalem faction, has sent his two sons-in-law begging for cash for the rebuilding fund. They are promising to publish the names in a donor's Tome of Honor, like in the old days. Of course it is really the cantor, the fellow who came from Tyre to sing here, he's the one who runs the entire enterprise. His name is Abu Ali Yefet ben Daud, but everybody calls him Husayn, and pretty he is. The women all think he is wonderful and long to hear him sing. The truth is that I like him, he's charming but in the end, all business. He runs the synagogue and Jerusalem community's affairs while that Rabbi Ephraim, who is the actual Head, sits in his perfumer's stall in the bazaar, catching up on the gossip from his home in Gaza. At least his perfumes hold their scent, given what he charges for them.

Although I do not pray there, I hope the synagogue is quickly rebuilt. The community of Jerusalemites here in Fustat is more vibrant than the one in Jerusalem itself. At the rabbanite synagogue they claim, although who can believe it, that they built the building on the very spot where Moses' mother placed his basket in the bulrushes. That is as likely as the legend the church just down the road tells, that there is the spot that Jesus slept when he fled to Egypt during some persecution back then. In any case, the members of the synagogue have also put it about that Jeremiah preached there and that Ezra the scribe wrote the Torah scroll that they read from there. I have even seen them kiss the Torah scroll and bow to it, although you surely know that our Karaite elders disdain that practice.

Since I mentioned the Coptic church, perhaps I should tell you a bit more about it, for I think you must not have any Christians in Kairawan. The Jerusalem synagogue is within the old Roman fortress wall here and there are many churches nearby. One of them actually hangs from the old Roman wall—it is dedicated to Maryam—not our prophet, but the one they call mother of God. I assure you this is really what they say.

They have other churches to their martyred saints, holy men like our rabbis of old, who were put to death for their beliefs. There is the church of Mari Jirjis and another to Mari Serjius. But what interests me is that they are building a new church, even though they claim it is merely replacing the churches which were destroyed in the riots under al-Hakim. They fared worse than we did in those days. The Copts were the first to feel his scourge; some of their churches were wholly destroyed in those dangerous times. It will be an interesting test case for us and for the Jerusalem synagogue if the Muslim authorities let this new church be built.

You know there also is a synagogue in the neighborhood for the Iraqi rabbinic Jews. I do not understand why they cannot unite together with those who follow the academy in Jerusalem, like you have done in Kairawan. And, of course, our Karaite community has its own gathering house. I will not tell you about the mosques nearby, but there is one mosque of 'Amr ibn al-As which is almost four hundred years old, dating back to the time of their prophet.

Send me more stories, please. They are most helpful to me and to others, too. I have been copying them, separating the stories and their explanations from the more private parts of your letters. I give them to my boy who has more copies made and they circulate in Fustat. You know that your wisdom has always been respected here in matters legal and Talmudic. It seems now you also have a growing reputation as a story teller of great skill and wisdom.

God bless you, Rabbenu Nissim, and may He make your work light upon your shoulders.

Chapter Three
Spring, 1032

From Karimah
to her brother in Fustat, Spring, 1032

Dear Skandi, the mountain called at-Tur is the mountain we call Horev and Sinai. It was here that Moses went up to receive the Ten Commandments. I am so excited to be here I do not know where to begin to tell you about this place. Let me start at the foot of the mountain or should I say mountains, and then I shall work my way up.

When we got here I thought the walled buildings in the small valley at the foot of this grouping of mountains were a fortress and they are that. But it is a Christian monastery, with monks who speak Greek. It is something like the Coptic churches near our home, but different, too. I realize now that the writing I saw on the painted caskets in the Fayyum was most likely this Greek. It is a language of the Rum. These monks illuminate their books like the Muslims do. Especially they illuminate the first letters in the book. It looks so odd to see a big letter with a picture around it.

The monks claim the library here is one thousand years old! I am not sure I believe that, because it would mean some of the books have been here since before the destruction of the Holy Temple in Jerusalem. I was introduced as Kamar al-Zaman and the monks believed that I was a young man. So they allowed me into their library and one of the monks was very kind to me. He showed me how they write and showed me that they have Arabic texts as well as Greek texts. They had a third set of texts in an alphabet that looked somewhat like Arabic and a bit like Hebrew but was neither. I asked about it and the monk seemed very pleased.

He explained it was Soori or sometimes he said Sursi. He read it aloud and it was Aramaic! I surprised him by translating what he had read into Arabic. He became very interested in me then and showed me how to write out that alphabet. I learned it quickly since it was like Hebrew and I could read the texts which, it turned out, were Sursi translations, much like the rabbis' Aramaic translations of the Bible.

The monk was very enthusiastic. He asked me many questions and it was hard for me to pretend that I was Kamar al-Zaman. I told him I had studied among

Burton L. Visotzky

the Jews of al-Kahira and could write Hebrew as well as Arabic. He asked me to show him and I wrote out from memory a short poem of Shmuel ibn Naghrela and another by ibn Labrat. I wrote the first and last stanzas of one of his wine songs, the one that begins, "I said, 'Do not in bed recline / rather, rise, drink aged wine" and ends with the lament "how can we drink blood of the fruit / when we are exiled beneath the boot?" Of course the monk had no idea what I was writing, he was just so happy to be watching me write in Hebrew.

Then we were shown their chapel which had decorated pictures of that man, Isa, and the mother with her baby. The pictures have lots of gold on them, but the brushwork is very good despite all the gilding. The chapel of the icons is at the center of the fortress. Behind the church there is a raspberry bush which one of the monks assured me was Moses' burning bush. I tried to look impressed, but he reminded me of when we used to pretend we were beggars for the tourists to see just how much nonsense they would believe about the pyramids.

Ismail and the servants were very excited about another item in the monastery. It was a letter from the prophet guaranteeing the monks their safety in gratitude for their hosting him. Mohammad's hand print was at the bottom of the letter. I suspect this letter has kept the monastery safe for much of the time it has been here. 'Smail and the others said that seeing a letter which the prophet himself had put his mark upon was one of the high points in their lives. It made them vow to make the Hajj to Mecca which every Muslim is supposed to do in any case.

There is a mosque within the fortress walls that was built there a few years ago by al-Hakim. I assume al-Hakim had it built there because of the letter from the prophet. There seems to be some kind of arrangement now so that the Christians are protected by the Muslims and the Muslims are protected by the Christians. But if they are both protecting one another, who are they afraid of? All I can imagine is that they fear the desert-dwelling Badawi, especially the Banu Hilal; but there are other Badawi who live within the walls of the monastery! I asked them what their job was and they said they tended the gardens. I asked if they grew vegetables and they said usually, but there had been no rain yet this season so there were only dried fruits to eat. Here we go again.

We were to camp outside the gates of the monastery during the night and before I left, the monk who had shown me the library gave me an Arabic poem he had written out for me. I will copy it for you here:

Travel, that you find new friends for old ones left behind
Work hard, for fruits of life are gained by sweat, you'll surely find
The one who stays at home does not win fame or peace of mind
So leave your place of birth and wander far from your own kind
I know when water pools too long it grows brackish for to drink

And only when it flows it's fresh and otherwise does stink
And if the moon were always full and never did she shrink
A man would not watch out for her nor pay her mind nor think
Unless a lion leaves the cave, he'll never prey to eat
Unless an arrow leaves the bow, its enemy won't defeat
And gold while still aground is naught but dust beneath the feet
Acacia is mere wood until it's burned to produce heat
So labor hard and bend your arm to God's enduring will
And travel cross the world to find Him inside your heart still

I thought the poem was really sweet. I read it while the sun was setting and we were finding a place to camp. There was a small building up ahead of us and I went there to see if it was suitable for sleeping in. It was full of bones! There were arm bones in one pile and leg bones in another pile and a separate pile of skulls. The most disconcerting thing of all was that there was a skeleton displayed like a person dressed in a monk's robes. I screamed and ran out. When I came out the Badawi from the monastery were laughing. They said that the monks kept the bones of all the Christian brothers who had served there.

I asked them about the dressed up skeleton and they said he was Brother Stephen. He used to be the Abbot—that is like the Hebrew Abba—he was the father in charge of the brothers of the monastery. Stephen used to stand at that spot and examine people who wished to come into the monastery to determine whether they were pure enough to spend the night among the holy brothers. I guess I failed Stephen's test.

We ate dates and locusts for supper, for there were no birds to be had at the mountain. We slept in the open that night after hobbling the camels far off so they would not bother us while we were trying to sleep. When we got up the camels were still there and the sun was just rising. It was very, very cold and there were clouds covering the top of the mountain. We decided to climb up the mountain, which was not all that hard to do. Given how cold it was, the exercise helped keep us warm. When I got to the top of Mount Sinai the clouds were upon it like when Moses went up, "darkness, cloud and fog." No quiet voices, and thank God, no storm like in the days of Elijah, only the sun barely breaking through.

I did not find it very transforming. No beams of light on my face; we were just cold and hungry. We worried about the camels and the Banu Hilal Badawi and the monks, too. I am not sure why, but that mountain put a sense of dread into each of us. We hurried down and ate a quick breakfast of dried dates and figs with some water from the well there. The monks had already tried to tell us it was the well where Moses had met Tzipporah.

I will end this letter here brother, for we are moving on. I will hold it with me and send it to Fustat when I have the chance, please God. I expect there will be others to add to it. Be good, young Abu Hasan. The wind of the mountains calls your name.

From Nissim in Kairawan to Dunash in Fustat, Spring 1032

To Abi-Skander, may you grow in strength, in the name of the Merciful, with thanks for your most gracious gifts to the academy and the students and their families here in Kairawan. Dear friend Dunash, you are a most venerable patron. "A man's gifts spread a place for him, they place him among the great." This letter accompanies the garments for the Kutama which I trust will meet your specifications. The wives of the students here immediately undertook to sew the linen. As you so correctly apprehended, they were accustomed to sewing garments of this fashion, for Kutama cloth is a common pattern in the Maghreb. I am sending them in caravan, but wrapped in soft leather binding so that they remain supple. I expect that they will need pressing upon arrival at Misr, as the linen wrinkles easily. I assure you, even though the gentiles do not require it, that there is no admixture of any wool with the linen cloth.

Thank you, too, that you thought of me when you contributed to the Jerusalemite synagogue in Misr. You certainly know how assiduously I have worked to raise funds for the academies of Jerusalem and of Iraq, how tirelessly I write to my colleagues in Spain to the West and in Fustat and elsewhere in the East, so that these great centers of learning may continue to flourish. You have correctly surmised how important it is to me that the synagogues which maintain their traditions also survive. So I thank you, for I know that the Karaites of Misr also suffered in the troubles under al-Hakim and it would have been enough for you to support your own. But you know I have never hesitated to approach you for funds for the rabbanite community, for I know that your generosity extends to all Israel.

This time, dear Dunash, you have outdone yourself, for I did not even ask and yet you donated. I am happy that you donated to honor me, but happier still that you honor the whole house of Israel in the diaspora by your gift. I pray your speculations regarding trouble with the Muslim authorities do not come to pass, God's will be done. I also pray that should the synagogues of Fustat have difficulties in being rebuilt that you and your relatives, God protect them, will make appropriate gifts to the authorities to help the cause.

I wrote to you some time ago about Rabbi Beroka and his encounter with Elijah, may he be remembered for good. He was not the only one of our sages who had encounters with Elijah. They say that Nahum of Gamzo was accustomed to work miracles. Whatever befell that sainted man, he would say, "May this too (*gam zo*) turn out well."

Once when the sages of Israel wished to send a gift to the king of the Rum, they said, "There is no one better for this than Nahum of Gamzo." So they filled a sack with gold dinars and with costly garments and gave it to Nahum to bring before the king. That night he stopped in an inn and the people there stole everything from his sack and filled it instead with dirt. The next morning he took his sack to the king of the Rum and offered it to him as a gift.

The king greedily opened the bag and found dirt inside it. He said, "The Jews mock me! I shall kill them all!" Nahum said, "May this too turn out well."

At that moment Elijah, may he be remembered for good, appeared among them in the guise of a courtier. He said, "Perhaps this dirt is the dust of their forefather Abraham; which when he threw it became spears and arrows!"

The king had a city he had been unable to subdue. He took that dirt and tried it and defeated the city. When the dirt was found to work, they filled Nahum's sack with gold dinars, costly garments and precious gems; far more than he had been sent with. He was accompanied on his journey home with a royal escort. When he arrived at the inn, the people there who had robbed him asked, "To what do you owe this honor?"

Nahum replied, "I merely brought there what I took from here." Those scoundrels tore down the very inn in their haste to fill sacks full of dirt from that place. When they brought it to the king of the Rum, of course it did not work. Then the king had those thieves crucified.

It is also said of Nahum that he was blind in both eyes and his hands and feet were but stumps. His body was covered with boils. He lay on a pallet bed the legs of which were placed into bowls of water. When his disciples asked him why the bed was arranged so, he explained, "This way the ants cannot crawl upon me."

His disciple Rabbi Aqiba said, "Rabbi, since you are totally righteous, how did it come to pass that you are in this condition?"

He told them, "Once I was journeying to visit my father-in-law and I was bringing him a donkey laden with fine things to eat. I passed a pauper, who begged me, 'Rabbi, give me sustenance.' I told him, 'Just wait until I unload the donkey, lest he suffer from an uneven load.' Yet by the time I unpacked the donkey, the poor man had expired. I then and there fell upon him and prayed, 'Master of the universe, may these hands which had no mercy upon Your creature be cut off, and may these legs which had no mercy upon Your poor creature be cut off. And may these eyes, which could not see how needy he was, be blinded.'

Burton L. Visotzky

Yet I could not still my conscience until I prayed, 'And may my entire body be covered in boils.'"

Rabbi Aqiba said, "Woe to us, Master, that we behold you thus."

Nahum replied, "Woe to me, if you had not seen me thus!"

Such is the piety of the great rabbis of old, that they truly were wholly righteous and generous of spirit. For this reason the blessed Elijah would appear to them. And Elijah, may he be remembered for good, does appear to the righteous to teach them of the ways of Heaven. From Nissim, Second in Kairawan, praised be to God.

From Dunash in Fustat
to Nissim in Kairawan, Spring 1032

Rabbenu Nissim, esteemed friend and scholar extraordinaire, upon whom God has bestowed wisdom and understanding that he may share it with God's humble creatures among whom is Dunash, his friend.

Thank you for the lovely stories of the miracle worker who, with the help of God, brought rain to Israel in their time of need. The Nile is high this year, thank God, but not too high, which is even better. But I know whereof you write, dear Nissim, for we have endured drought here in Misr, much as our ancestors did in the time of Joseph. We suffered thirst under our evil Pharaoh, I shall not mention his name, almost seven years of drought and famine, as in biblical times. But our Pharaoh, may his name be wiped from memory, did not have a wise Joseph, or at least refused to listen to the Josephs of his court. Instead he persecuted the people Israel, much as that evil Pharaoh of yore. But now there has arisen a new Pharaoh, who knows Joseph, so that Israel flourishes in his reign and the Nile overflows and all is well under God's heavens.

Indeed, my friend Nissim, I wish to tell you of the Nile and its abundance and of al-Zahir and the various ceremonies which the Caliph performs in relationship to the rise of the Nile, for they are glorious and involve the wearing of many festive uniforms, may God grant us the right to manufacture them and make a profit. But I get carried away as usual and before I tell you of either the Nile or of al-Zahir I must remark upon the disconcerting poem you forwarded to me and to tell you of my own household and an incident with a new slave, for I had thought to have my own Joseph as it were, yet my wife worried lest I become the wife of Potiphar. I know that I have the sexes confused, just as I had the Pharaohs reversed when I wrote above, but so be it, the world is not the Bible, nor is my life the life of the people Israel, but yet they reflect one another and as is often the case with a reflection, if not always, that which is reflected is the reverse of what it mirrors.

First, first. The poem which ibn Naghrela wrote is painfully cynical; it reminded me of the works of Ecclesiastes. And, as it is written there, "of the making of books there is no end and too much reflection wearies the flesh." I appreciate your sending it to me and I will circulate it here and send it on to the East, but you must know that such a poem brings no consolation. The message of the Nagid was that of Ecclesiastes, "all is futile." I suppose we must hear this and perhaps it is even appropriate for the death of one as accomplished as Rabbenu Hushiel, may he rest in Eden. But I prefer your stories of consolation to the reminder that we, too, shall die. We are not getting younger, friend—despite our desires to pretend so.

My wife would have me believe that the trouble that occurred in our home was precisely the result of my unwillingness to accept that I am no longer young and that, like Father Abraham, I wished to prove it with a young slave. I, for my part, have only this to say: I wanted my household to have new assistance now that Karimah is gone. With our daughter no longer among us, I thought that my wife would appreciate help in the kitchen as we begin to prepare for Passover. I know there is much work making everything fit for the holiday.

I had thought, it is true, that after the festival I might teach the new slave to write and read and do sums that I also might have some assistance in my business correspondence and bookkeeping. Finally, I assumed that our al-Iskander, may he grow to be strong in the ways of God, would appreciate a new playmate in the house, especially as he is at such an awkward age.

In any case, with good intentions and a heart full of the love of God, I bought a new young female slave for the household. She was about 14 or 15 years of age and, as the Psalmist says, "Who can understand errors? May You cleanse me of hidden guilt." My mistake was that the girl was very pretty. I suppose I should have known better. The girl endured hardship at the hands of my wife and, as with our matriarch Sarah and her maid Hagar, I was commanded to expel her. It troubled my heart to do so, but I was informed that although our marriage contract may not have stipulated that my wife had rights of approval over any new slave I brought into the home, if I wished to continue having my rights as a husband, the girl had to go. This is what comes of marrying a wife from the Rum. So I sold the slave girl back at a slight loss.

I had wished only to make my wife's life easier for Passover and instead incurred her wrath. I had wished only to ransom a captive and instead took a monetary loss. I had wished only to provide my son a companion and instead became a fool in his sight.

I feel like my trading partner Yefet HaLevi, with whom I trade indigo. He always has first quality Nil, for that is what indigo is called in the trade, but my dear friend Yefet is such a very temperamental fellow. His moods swing up and down, perhaps because he knows how much corruption there is in the Nil trade. I find myself now sometimes elated and other times depressed. I suspect it is not merely the incident with the slave girl, although business is just fine, thank God. The holiday season for some reason always leaves me a bit sad and this year all the sadder. I know that I promised you a long letter about the Nile, dear Nissim, and instead I am writing you about the trade in Nil. I shall write you, God willing, about the River in another letter.

In the meanwhile, please continue sending me installments of your stories and other news. I await your letters, brother, although I know your responsibilities do not make it easy for you to take the time to write to one as unimportant as I, a mere trader.

From Dunash HaCohen al-Tustari in Misr, God be praised. To Rabbenu Nissim, Second in Kairawan, if God wills it.

Fragment of a letter from Dunash in Fustat to Nissim, either Winter, 1031 or Spring, 1032

...[The Nile] is the true brigand of Egypt: feared yet desired. We are fearful if she does not rise at least 16 cubits on the Nilometer, for then there will be famine, for the fields will not yield their fruit. All are desirous that she rise, but not more than a finger's breadth below 20 cubits, for above that and we would be flooded even in the city. When the Nile is lush, her waters flow through the irrigation ditches which line her. This way we can in part control her wrath and help our crops. Yet it is the canals which really help control the rise of the Nile.

The Great Canal of Cairo runs parallel to the Nile, ingeniously connected to two reservoirs. Just to the east of the two reservoir pools is the mosque of ibn Tulun. Once the Nile rises above the 16-cubit mark the Caliph cuts the Canal, which is to say opens it for the season with great pomp and ceremony. The original canal was cut just after the Muslims took Egypt. Back then the canal was used to help transport goods and provisions to the Hijaz for Mecca and al-Medina and they called it the canal of the Commander of the Faithful. Now we just call it the Great Canal of Cairo, to distinguish it, I suppose, from those canals in other towns along the Nile.

The Muslims, of course, imagine that the canal goes back to Abraham. I do not think this is written in their Quran, but they say that when Ibrahim sent

Hagar and Ismail to Mecca, they thirsted for water. According to them, Ibrahim then had the canal cut to send water to them. Of course, this is not in accordance with the Torah, which tells us that Abraham had sent Hagar away, like a divorcee. When the lad Ishmael thirsted his mother prayed and an angel of the Lord showed them a well. There are Muslims who verify this story and say that the well is the one at Mecca called Zamzam. I understand, my master Nissim, that they also hold that the well called Zamzam is connected in some way to Kairawan, but I do not know how.

In any case, enough legend, for the reality of the procession to cut the Grand Canal of Cairo and the festivities which accompany it is legendary enough. The costumes are spectacular. All of the regiments march out bearing arms to accompany the Commander of the Faithful. The Turks and the Kutama lead the way, although a few years ago, early in al-Zahir's reign, he was yet young, this caused some commotion. The troops are fed on this occasion, and the black African troops rioted for they did not get enough to eat. In the end a dozen more camels had to be slaughtered to feed them. But since that time the Turks have had a greater role in protecting the Caliph and the other troops have had their role diminished. This has led to fewer Kutama in the Caliph's court; I think he does not trust the Berbers.

Following the array of troops, there come the bearers of Fatimid pennants. The standards have silk banners attached to them with writing upon them—verses of the Quran and praise of the Fatimid dynasty. The Emirs and the mamelukes follow, surrounding those who carry the emblems of the Caliph: the flywhisk, the inkstand, the jeweled sword of the Commander of the Faithful. Then the parasol bearer walks, and behind him the Caliph rides on horseback. He wears a turban of white shot with gold, white silk robes shot with gold, even the parasol that day is shot with gold thread. The embroidery and weaving is fabulous. It has been rumored that some of the work is imported from the Rum.

The Wazir and his entourage follow the Caliph; also expensively appointed. Did I mention the costumes of the Turks and Kutama are not their usual uniforms but special parade dress? Add to them some cavalry riders, and this is almost 8,000 uniforms in fancy dress. I do not know what the five hundred or so lancers and another five hundred archers wear, for they march bearing their coats of mail. I could not see what they wore underneath.

All of these troops organize in the Eastern Palace and march through the golden gate, out of the walls of al-Kahira. Once they are outside of the fortress walls, they march in very tight formation to protect the Caliph. They turn toward the canal and bring the Caliph's retinue close to where the water would flow. There is much shouting at this point, across the Nile toward the island Roda that sits within the great river. Runners race down Roda to the Nilometer and back again, shouting the cubits marked off on the Nilometer.

Satisfied that there have been at least 16 cubits of rise in the waters of the Nile, the Caliph then throws his spear. It is immediately retrieved by the mamelukes, for the spear is silver and costly. But this is the signal to "cut" the canal, and the dams are opened and the water flows through the Grand Canal of Cairo. They say it prevents flooding.

The Caliph and his party head back to the palace where there is much feasting of the troops. This is good for the Caliph, for the distribution of food and the costly clothing secures the loyalty of those who serve him. In the meanwhile, much of the day has passed and the citizenry of Fustat light thousands of torches on the shore beside the Nile and beside the canal. The Muslims and the Copts come out in droves. The Jews come out on the fringes, but the food is not fit for them to eat, although it is, of course, permissible to the Muslims and it is well known that the Christians will eat anything.

So the Muslims and Christians eat and the locals make much music. The singing is raucous and the women ululate throughout the night. Around midnight, when the mounds of food have been eaten, people start jumping into the Nile. They claim that bathing in the Nile on the night of the immersion, as it is called, insures health for the coming year. The crowds reach up the Nile as far as the Sphinx on the Giza side. On our side, we stay up due to the noise and revelry and to assure ourselves that there will not be anti-Jewish rioting. Ever since the last Caliph, we constantly worry about another outbreak. I think so long as the Muslims and Christians can feast together in harmony, we can relax and enjoy the spectacle.

Nissim, my friend, I have gone on about this parade and festival in my excitement not only because once again the canal has been cut and the Nile has risen, but because the uniforms and the costumes of the court need manufacture and it is upon that my heart is set. God grant us success. From Dunash HaCohen al-Tustari in Misr, God be praised.

From Karimah
to her brother in Fustat, Early Spring, 1032

To al-Iskander ibn Dunash HaCohen, please God. From his sister, known as Wuhshah, wandering in the wilderness. Praised be to God Who does good for the guilty, for He bestowed His grace upon me.

Skandi, I have had the most amazing adventure, but you must never ever tell Mommy any of what I am writing to you. You will see that I trust you and am treating you like an adult, for I have no one else to turn to and someone must hear my story. So first, read the following letter to Mommy and then when you are alone and no one can overhear, read what has happened to me, by the grace of God that I am here to tell you.

Dearest Mother, my teacher, my light, in the name of the Merciful, please God.

Mommy, I miss you and I miss the people of our household. Tell al-Iskander who reads this now to stop and kiss your hands for me, and then you kiss him too from me. I am well and have been to Mount Horev where our master, Moses, received the law. We approached the mountain in purity, as the Israelites did before us when they, too, came forth from Egypt. We had a great experience there and I feel transformed by it.

Mommy, I am scrupulous here in the wilderness and eat but doves and fruit. I miss your cooking and only now appreciate how hard it is to plan the meals and instruct the servants what to buy and cook. Here in the Sinai we do our own gathering, like our ancestors of old used to gather the manna, day by day. We gather fruit, usually dates, and spread nets. It is hard to separate the birds one from another but I am most careful. I have lost some weight and look very pretty with some sun on my skin.

Do not worry, I am careful to cover up from both the sun and the eyes of the men. Ismail continues to be very good to me and protects me and makes sure I am well. We are heading up the Sinai towards Ayla and the Holy Land. I will write again when I have a chance, if God wills it.

Your daughter wishes the blessings of God upon you in abundance.

Now 'Skander, give Mommy her kisses and take this letter with you to somewhere very private so I can tell you what befell us when we left the mountain. The same day we traveled eastward. We were hungry and sore from sleeping in the cold and climbing up the mountain. Even though it was late in the day, it was still overcast from the clouds that had gathered above Jebel Mous, which is what the Arabs call Mount Sinai. When we packed to move off, we noticed that one of the camels had its hobble rope cut. We were most fortunate that it had not wandered away. At the time we assumed that the camel had somehow rubbed the rope on a rock for it was frayed. It was the camel that carried the weapons of the servants.

As the day wore on it became sunny, but very moist in the air. The buzzing of the insects was loud and insistent and it was very annoying, we were all bitten up by the bugs that swarmed about us that afternoon. We came to a junction of wadis nearing the eastern shore road of the Sinai when we were confronted by a band of about ten Badawi on horseback. They were armed with *jambiyya* daggers and long, double-bladed, two-pronged swords. Some of them carried lances as well. Two or three had bows slung over their backs with quivers of arrows. It was not promising.

What made matters worse is that we were trying to descend down a narrow pass into the wadi, so that they had effectively trapped us there. It was impossible to get the camels to back up in that narrow a passage, especially with uneven footing when they would have to be backing uphill. The leader of the Badawi rode forward and had the temerity to greet us formally. He said his name was Abu Sin and that he was a Shaykh of the Banu Hilal. This, of course, only made us more upset. He asked us very politely to please share with his men all of our silver and gold. 'Smail asked him what would happen if we did not wish to share. "Then we will take it from you," Abu Sin said. "But if we take it, we will also take your clothing and possibly your lives. It is for you to decide."

I did not see what happened next, because I was in the middle of our little caravan, but I could hear the buzz of the insects growing louder and louder. The wind was blowing harder now and I could not imagine why the insects had not blown away. The sky darkened like when we were upon the mountain, but since we were in a very narrow pass, I did not take notice. The wind and the insects began to sound, as the Psalmist says, "like the voices of many waters, like the breakers of the sea."

The camels in front of me suddenly backed up growling and spitting, I had never seen them so panicked. It was then I saw the wall of water rushing through the wadi, sweeping everything before it, even the boulders were rolled along like marbles. The water hit the Badawi and immediately covered them over, "horse and rider hurled into the sea." The waters came rushing up the narrow path we were on and began to cover the legs of the camels. I leapt from my camel and scrambled as best I could up the face of the rock, grabbing on to branches, stones, bushes, anything to get higher.

The Banu Hilal who had been in the junction of the wadis were no longer visible. Our camels, even though they were on higher ground, could barely keep their nostrils above the water. All of us had run for higher ground but the Badawi were overwhelmed by the water. "The water was like a wall on their right and on their left." The Badawi chieftan swept by me in the water. His leg was at an odd angle and I could see it was broken. I did not wish to see him drown, but I did not wish him to kill me, either. He reached out a hand to me and said but one word, "Please."

I do not know what made me reach out my hand to him, but I held the bushes with one hand while I held him with the other against the force of the flow. He, for his part, held on to me with one hand and his sword with the other. I could see the string of his bow around his neck, cutting in to him, strangling him. But I could not help him, for I could not let my hands go, either one of them. He was turning blue. Finally, I prayed to God not to let me lose a life and pulled him toward me with all my strength. He reached his arm around me and held his body tightly to mine as the waters rushed by us. With my hand now free, I was able to turn his bow so that it strangled him no more. He never let go of his sword, but I knew I was no longer in danger from Abu Sin. I had saved his life and by the code of the Badawi he was bound now to protect me with it.

When the waters stopped rushing by and the sun returned he was like a dead man. Both of my arms trembled for hours afterward from the effort of holding on and holding him. We climbed even higher and at the hilltop in the sun surveyed the damage. We had lost one servant. Some of the Banu Hilal were dead; but others simply had vanished. It was as though the earth had swallowed them. Ismail carried Abu Sin into a tent which we finally opened once we had calmed and fed the camels. 'Smail was furious with me for saving Abu Sin's life and practically spat at me, "He is your baby, tend to him!"

The very first thing Abu Sin said when he opened his eyes was, "Please, bury my men." Then he lapsed back into his swoon; he was very hot to the touch. I kneeled next to him and lifted up his robes a bit to see what I could do about his leg. The sight of it made me dizzy, brother. Nonetheless, I was able to align the bones with one another and bind his leg to his bow. Everything was still wet from the flooding, so I left him, hoping that he would be cooled and his fever might abate. Otherwise, I feared he would be dead by morning.

Everywhere around us things were hanging out to dry. I slept in the open, outside the flap of Abu Sin's tent. In the early morning, before the sun came up, Abu Sin whispered to me. I told him I would not come into his tent. He claimed to be better and said he had no memory of what had happened once the flood began. I told him I had saved his life. He said, "Oh yes, that I do remember and I am obliged to you. Now I would be obliged if you would help me rise and gather my weapons." I was fearful, but he had said he was obliged. He hobbled from the tent and stood leaning on his sword. He asked if I would unstrap his bow from his leg and place it over his neck, which I did, taking care not to rub the bowstring against the raw flesh there.

I could see him grimace as he tried to stand without leaning on the sword. He said, "You must be quick now, for I need to leave with a minimum of commotion." Then he whistled a shrill whistle and his horse came trotting up the hill! "Help me climb upon her," he commanded. He leaned heavily upon me as he pulled himself upon his horse. I held his sword in the meanwhile; it was very heavy in my hand. When he sat straight upon the horse's back, I reached his sword up to

Burton L. Visotzky

him for him to take it. "It is yours now," he said, "you have earned the right to carry a Banu Hilal sword, may Allah protect you."

Just then some of the servants started to come out from their tents. No doubt the whistle and the horse had awakened them. Abu Sin held the reins and turned the horse to go over the hill. Just then, at the last moment, he transfixed me with his gaze and said to me, "Some stick!" At that he galloped off.

I was aghast! He must have read my letter to you about the rabbanite girls. This I could not understand, for I had given the letters to a caravan well before we encamped at At-Tur and the monastery. How could he have known what I had written? And how could he be such a dog!? I guess danger simply makes dogs of men, there can be no other explanation. But how Abu Sin knew what I had written, that is a mystery that worries me. I pray, my dear al-Iskander, that you have received my mail. I would be most unhappy to learn that I am cut off from you, dear brother.

In the meanwhile remember what I have repeatedly written you. Mommy must never see this, nor anyone but you. I am counting on your maturity. Now that I am not at home you are the oldest. Help make Mommy think that everything is all right so that she may not worry. Pray for me Skandi, I do not wish to be Wuhshah any longer.

Fragment of a letter from Karimah to her nanny, early Spring, 1032

...and I again implore you not to breathe a hint of this letter even to al-Iskander, for I have written to him separately and he is too young to know what I write to you here. Oh Nanny, I am so grateful that I can tell you still of the stirrings of my heart.

We had an encounter with Badawi brigands. God protected us by sending a flood through the wadi where we were being robbed. By the grace of God, I rescued the brigands' chief for I could not watch him drown. That man, his name is Abu Sin, had his leg badly broken in the rushing waters. That evening, after the flood abated, I entered his tent to see if I could help his leg mend – it was bloody and deformed. As I knelt next to that man he reached his hand beneath my robes and did to me as the rabbinic sages claim that Abraham's servant did to our matriarch Rebeccah when he checked her virginity with his finger!

Nanny, I am afraid that it made me gasp; it was as though the flood which had flowed through the wadi now flowed through me. I grew faint for a moment and then came to my senses. I lifted my body forward and pressed upon his leg. He screamed and I felt vindicated. He passed out and I then was able to mend his bone despite my shock and anger. Part of me wished that I had never rescued that crude pig and yet the other part of me was disturbed that I could think such evil thoughts. I feel I atoned for my bad thoughts and the pleasure I felt by nursing him and setting his bone. Yet I wonder, why do I think of him still?

I was so shaken that I shared the tent with Ismail that night upon the mountain. In the tent, 'Smail took off all of his clothing and then suddenly fell upon me. When he had finished he stood outside the tent to urinate, holding his cubit in his hand—well, actually not really a cubit at all, more like a digit, but that is what they call it. He said to the Arabs, "I am the conqueror!" and was angry when they laughed. I was furious, but only later realized that they were not laughing at me, but because he had urinated all over the clothing that he had tossed out of the tent. It serves him right.

'Smail must have seen what he did to his clothing because he rushed immediately into the tent and knocked it down upon us both. I had had more than enough that day and told him so. I left Ismail's tent and slept instead outside. The next morning, as the sun rose, that evil Badawi fled. But he gave me his sword then, and told me I had earned the right to carry it. Whatever will I do with his sword in my hand?

O Nanny, I am so confused. That evil man—he even read my mail—made me feel things that I have never felt with 'Smail. What can this mean? Is my heart that of a normal woman, or am I now evil, too?

Nanny, you are far away and I still need your wise counsel. No matter what, I know you will keep my secrets, as you always have. I kiss your eyes and hands…

Excerpt from the "Scroll of Secrets," Rabbenu Nissim's diary, probably Spring 1032

—Dunash has written that he bought a young slave girl who is of "fine figure and good to look at." Alas, the old fool, did he think that his "wife of his youth" would allow him the pleasures of father Abraham at one hundred? Could not this man-of-Scripture remember what happened to our father Abraham and how the episode gave rise to the Arab peoples? No good can come of such dalliances. It is not for naught that our marriage contracts more and more often stipulate that the senior wife must have full authority over the purchase of female slaves. Perhaps Rabbenu Gershom, light of the Exile in Mainz, is right to utterly ban second wives, even if the Torah itself permits it.

In any case, his wife was quite correct to insist that the girl be sold. As God told Abraham of Sarah, "Whatever she tells you, do as she says." At least she did not force Dunash to banish the poor child. On the other hand, I sympathize with Dunash's good *intentions. One needs help in the household, especially when there are young children present.*

—I do not know what I would do without Mulaah bint Rav Yosef's constant help with Ghazal. She is so good with the girl and seems not to mind her deformities. Mulaah insists to me that Ghazal is quite bright, but I can hardly bring myself to look at her grotesque head and tiny body, God forgive me.

Whatever shall I do when Mulaah marries Abu al-Maali, which surely must take place soon? Mulaah is of such good family, if I were not still in mourning I would consider the girl for myself. It would make for a good liaison with the Cairo community, her grandfather having been Head there. He even lived here in Kairawan when his daughter Diyya first came here, poor thing, losing her husband by drowning like that. At least her father Elhanan made sure Diyya collected her marriage price and remarried Yosef HaCohen. We all were so happy when she gave birth to Mulaah. Ah, come what may, I put myself in God's hands. I must wish Mulaah and Abu al-Maali every happiness. Somehow I shall provide for my own poor daughter.

—In the meanwhile, I must rebuke Dunash for his descent into foolishness. What could he have been thinking taking a pretty young girl into his household? She was younger than his own late daughter! Rebuke I must, for our sages say that one who has the power to rebuke and does not, is considered among the cursed. On the other hand, the matter has resolved itself and it is better not to alienate an important donor. The academy here could not survive without Dunash's attentions and business.

Perhaps the stories I am sending him can make my point. Our sages of blessed memory knew very well that one may command the body by means of the law, but that the soul must be drawn by stories. I shall recount to him the potential treacheries of women and the difficulties of slaves. He will attend, for though he is a simple business man, he is engrossed by legends. But then, we all are, for tales teach the truth of God and His presence in the world. As our sages taught, "Do you wish to know the One Who Spoke and Brought the World into Being? Read stories!"

Chapter Four
Spring, 1032

From Nissim in Kairawan, to Dunash in Fustat, Spring 1032

To Dunash, my dear friend and patron, with the joy of the festival upon us, may God bring redemption in our day, too, Dunash HaCohen al-Tustari in Misr, with the help of God. From Nissim ibn Yakov... in the Name of the Merciful.

My dear friend, my best wishes for a joyous Passover to you. I pray that you and your household have been able to prepare for this festival with your own two hands and the help of God Almighty, and without the addition of an extra servant in your abode. I read your rueful letter with sympathy, and yet, as is so often the case, your wife had the correct idea to banish the girl. However painful the episode may have been, as God said to Abraham, "everything she says to you, hearken to her voice."

I embrace you, friend, for I too have lost a most precious household helper even now during the intermediate days of the Passover festival. The dear girl, Mulaah bint Rav Yosef HaCohen has become engaged. I do not know if I ever told you how helpful this young woman has been to me since my own dear wife departed this world, peace be upon her. Almost from the moment of Ghazal's birth, Mulaah has been like a mother to her, "raising her upon her knees," and freeing me from the troubles and worries of raising children.

I have confessed to you how complicated my feelings are for my Ghazal, and I know they are affected by my sense of anguish over the loss of my wife, her mother. But Mulaah has none of these constraints and has spent virtually every day caring for Ghazal, feeding and changing her, while I study and teach in the academy. Without Mulaah I should have no time to write, nor might Ghazal have flourished. Under Mulaah's tutelage, Ghazal has begun to speak words. It is so hard for me to hear the sweet childish babble that comes forth from that distended head and too small body. Yet Mulaah has encouraged Ghazal and so, has encouraged me to think that there may yet be a life for her—I do not know—I put my trust in God.

And now, to my misfortune and to her joy, Mulaah has been formally betrothed to Abu al-Maali. He is a good boy who studies in the academy with me

Burton L. Visotzky

and with Rabbenu Hananel. At first, I had thought that he courted Mulaah as an excuse to be here in my household and have more study time with me. But eventually I was able to see his genuine affection for the girl, who is, I admit, a pearl. Mulaah is not pretty, but a good soul and wonderful with my daughter. Further, she is of very good family. Mulaah is the daughter of Diyya, who was daughter to the late Rabbi Elhanan ben Shemarya, peace be upon him, who served as the Head of the Rabbanite community of Fustat. Did you know him?

Diyya had married in Fustat and she sailed with her husband on business to Kairawan at the time. Tragically, the boat went down and he drowned. Rabbi Elhanan was a good father and traveled here to console the girl who was too traumatized to travel back to Fustat. Diyya insisted on staying here in Kairawan. Elhanan ben Shemarya wrote letters back and forth and was able to guarantee that her bride price was paid by her late husband's family, so at least she was provided for. When Rabbi Elhanan saw she was as settled as could be and still adamant about not returning to Fustat, he traveled back east.

Praise be to God, Diyya found a second husband in Rav Yosef HaCohen. They have been happy ever since. I had thought their happiest moment was at the birth of Mulaah—for it was the first time I saw Diyya without the shadow of her first husband's drowning darkening her visage. But at the second Passover Seder this week, they asked my permission to announce Mulaah's engagement. Of course our sages long ago ruled that one should not mix one joy with another and since we were celebrating the Passover festival, I was initially inclined to forbid the announcement. But then I reasoned that it was the second day of the festival and as it is not commanded by the Torah but only a rabbinic enactment, I was determined to be lenient. I was further influenced by a Talmudic ruling which permits engagements on the intermediate days of the festival, on the principle: "lest another suitor jump to the fore."

In truth, despite my own loss of Mulaah as a nanny to Ghazal, I ruled based upon the glow on her mother Diyya's shining face. I am glad that I told them to announce the engagement, for the joy here in Kairawan was as though the Red Sea had split a second time. Does not the midrash teach that making appropriate matches is as difficult for the Blessed Holy One as was the splitting of the Red Sea? So here is a match made in Heaven: Mulaah and Abu al-Maali. Would that I should ever know such joy for my Ghazal, please God.

I have written you, dear friend, some stories of consolation. I wrote to you of Martha bint Boethius and of Rabbi Aqiba's wife, Rachel. One of the first stories I wrote to you was of that "woman of valor," the wife of Rabbi Meir, peace be upon him. I wish to write you now another tale of Meir and his wife, and, especially, her sister. It teaches us of the degradations of slavery and how a virtuous woman can persist in purity if she has the help of a man faithful to Torah.

Our sages taught that after the sainted Hananiah ben Teradyon was martyred by the Rum emperor, the latter commanded that Hananiah's daughter be sold to the slave market as a prostitute. Her sister, who was the wife of Rabbi Meir, asked her husband to rescue her sister from this disgrace. Meir took 400 dirhems and said, "If she has remained pure, God will help and perform a miracle on her behalf."

Meir came to his sister-in-law in disguise and offered her the 400 dirhems as a fee. She demurred saying, "I am menstruating and unfit." Thus Meir realized that she had remained pure. He went to the guard and offered him the 400 dirhems to release the girl. Meir told him to use half to save her and keep the other half for himself.

But the guard was reluctant to disobey the emperor. Meir reassured him that no harm would come to him and that if he felt threatened he should say, "God of Meir, save me." The guard scoffed and asked, "What proof can you offer that this would work?"

There were ferocious dogs guarding the treasury of the emperor. Meir entered there and as the dogs sprang at him he cried, "God of Meir, save me!" At that, the dogs became docile. So the guard was convinced and released the daughter of Rabbi Hananiah ben Teradyon, may he rest in Eden.

The guard indeed incurred the emperor's wrath and was to be crucified. But when they came to hang him up he cried, "God of Meir, save me." No man was able to harm him. The emperor asked after this Meir and had the guard describe him and had a likeness of Meir drawn. The army was sent in pursuit of Rabbi Meir.

One day, Meir was in the market when an imperial guard spotted him. Meir escaped by hiding in the very brothel where his sister-in-law had been condemned to serve. No one would believe that the man called Rabbi Meir would ever be seen in a brothel, so he escaped. Rabbi Meir and his wife then fled to Iraq where they remained for the rest of their lives.

So you see that women slaves are easily made prostitutes, but that the virtue of Torah can save them. Our sages tell another tale of a prostitute who lived in the islands off the coast, who commanded 400 gold dinars as her price. Once there was a rabbinical student who amassed this fortune and set himself to have her. He arrived at her boudoir, gave over his gold, and her servant admitted him to her presence. He saw before him seven beds. Six were of silver and the topmost was of gold. Each bed led upward to the next by means of a bronze ladder. The prostitute lay naked on the topmost bed and invited him to join her there.

The boy undressed and as he removed his garments his ritual fringes arose against him like witnesses to his depravity and slapped him across the face. He was mortified and sat upon the floor clutching his clothes and weeping. She demanded of him, "I adjure you by the love goddess Venus; I will not let you leave here until you tell me what flaw you see in me!"

He replied, "By the Temple service, I have never seen a woman as beautiful as you! But we have a commandment in the Torah regarding ritual fringes upon our garments, wherein it is written "I am the Lord your God," two times. The first time, because God will pay us our reward for observance of His commandments. The second time, because God will punish us for our sins. These fringes now have risen as witnesses to remind me of this commandment."

She replied, "I shall not release you until you tell me your name and where you come from and the Madressa where you have learnt this Torah." He wrote this down for her and fled back to the academy, grateful that he had resisted sin.

That prostitute sold off all her belongings and divided her fortune. One third she gave to the poor. One third she gave as bribes to the authorities. The final third she took with her to the Madressa of Rabbi Hiyya. She came before him and offered him her fortune if he would convert her. He asked, "Perhaps you have been involved with one of my disciples?"

She admitted the affair and gave Rabbi Hiyya the piece of paper with all the details written on it. At that, Hiyya called the student before him. When the student saw the woman he almost died of shame. But Rabbi Hiyya said to him, "Go now and prepare this woman for conversion. Thus you shall have in accordance with the Torah what you denied yourself when it was forbidden."

Now if this is the reward for observance of the commandments in this world, I cannot imagine how great the reward can be in the world to come!

Dear Dunash, I must attend to the demands of my students and the holiday. I shall write you more just after the Passover festival has ended. Know that your great deeds and support will be rewarded in this world and in the world to come, God willing.

From Nissim in Kairawan,
to Dunash in Fustat, Spring, 1032

"The winter has ended, the rains are gone. The buds are now visible in the land, it is the time for pruning. The sound of doves cooing is heard in our country-side. The fig tree puts forth green fruits, the vines waft forth their fragrance."

We count the days, dear Dunash, as the time of the Festival of the Giving of the Torah sweeps daily nearer. We are now in the third of the seven weeks until the festival, which I count as truly the start of summer. The boats are already in the water, awaiting full loads for passage. The caravans are forming here and no doubt in Fustat.

As I ended my last letter to you with stories of consolation from the works of the sages, so shall I begin this letter. But before I write you of the pleasures of Torah, I attend to the business between us. Please send as soon as possible the cloth for the Kutama garments. The girls here are eager to undertake the sewing and we depend on the profit. As always, master, I am at your disposal for sale of goods here in Kairawan. If you cannot send anything for sale here, I should be delighted and honored to serve as a middle-man for the transport of goods further west in the Maghreb. You know I am in constant contact with Granada and have connections to the court there.

Please do not fault me for presuming, but the lack of boats in the winter months and the paucity of caravans leave our finances thin. I know that you do the majority of your trade with the Taherti family here; they are, after all, full time businessmen while I am but a dilettante. Yet whatever trade I can do with you benefits not only me and my household, but many of the boys of the academy. Rabbenu Hananel has his own contacts in the Rum and prospers from them for his own large household—but of that, more later. He has been my salvation of late, God bless him and keep him. But in you "I have found one man in a thousand."

When King Solomon, of blessed memory, recited the end of that same verse of Ecclesiastes, "yet a woman among them all I have not found;" it dismayed the members of his court. Solomon, who had a thousand wives, taught them that the perfidy of women knew no bounds. He told them that an unfaithful wife was "more bitter than death, she is a trap, her heart a snare, her hands a rope to bind. The one who escapes her God reckons good, the sinner is ensnared by her."

His courtiers thought him too harsh, so he set about to prove to them the treachery of women. There was in his kingdom a woman of exceptional beauty who had a pious and faithful husband. The king called for him and said, "You have a reputation for trustworthiness and piety. I wish to marry you to one of my daughters that you might help me rule the kingdom."

The man, who was as modest as he was astonished by this offer said, "O king, I am but the least in your kingdom." Solomon flattered him by saying, "It is precisely this modesty which recommends you. Here now is a sword, go kill off your present wife that I might betroth you to my daughter."

The man left the king's presence with fear and trembling. He hid away the sword and sought to put the matter out of his mind. But late that night, when he could not sleep for worry, he reasoned, "If I do not obey the king's command he

Burton L. Visotzky

shall have me killed. If I do obey, my wife must be killed. Either way there will be a death." And with that reasoning he resolved to slay his wife.

He took the sword in his hand and went to her bed. He drew off the covers and beheld her beauty. His spirit failed him and he determined not to kill her. "She is my wife and the mother of my children," he said. "Better I should tell the king of my failure and die in her stead, saving mother and child." And so, the next morning he returned to King Solomon and told him that he would not kill his wife, even to become son-in-law to the king. Solomon smiled and said, "For this faith I shall reward you." Thereupon he ordered the man be given 400 gold pieces and be made an advisor to the king.

But the next day, secretly, Solomon called the man's wife to the palace. He beheld her and saw that she was very comely. Solomon said to her, "My daughter, I have heard of your beauty. But I did not believe the reports until I saw with my own eyes that not even the half of it had been told to me. I wish to take you to me as a wife and set you on the throne of Israel. Go home this night and slay thy husband and on the morrow return to be my queen, sharing both my bed and throne." He handed her a sword to do the deed; but she did not know that it was but polished tin and not of iron.

That night she fed her husband well and gave him much wine to drink. She took him to bed and "danced a thousand dances" with him that he would be exhausted and sleep deeply. When he slept, she crept from the bed and took up the sword in her hand. She brought down the sword in one blow upon his neck only to see it crumple there and awaken him. He sprang up to demand why she had sought to kill him. At that the wife confessed how Solomon had tempted her. Her husband forgave her and related his own temptation by Solomon. When the wife realized her husband's faithfulness and her own perfidy, she repented and was pure and faithful to him from then on. As for Solomon, he repeated to his courtiers, "yet a woman among them all I have not found."

It is said of our master, Rav, that his wife contradicted everything he said to her or asked of her. If he asked for lentils for dinner she made him peas. If he asked for peas, she gave him lentils. When Rav's son Hiyya grew up, he observed how his mother disobeyed his father and sought to mitigate the discomfort in the household. One day Rav said to Hiyya, "Ask your mother to cook lentils for dinner." So Hiyya said to his mother, "Father desires peas for dinner." She served him lentils and Rav was pleased.

Another time, Rav asked Hiyya to have his mother make peas. Hiyya said to his mother, "Oh mother, my teacher; my father desires lentils." Of course she made him peas, and Rav was pleased. He remarked to Hiyya, "See how your mother has changed and now seeks to please me." At this, Hiyya admitted his ruse. Rav commended his son for being clever and finding a way to honor his father, but rebuked him for encouraging his mother's recalcitrance.

But there are wicked women whom no rival can restrain. Did not Ben Sirah teach, "A daughter is a deceptive treasure to her father; his fear for her keeps him from sleeping nights." For even a woman who appears pious and prayerful can be evil at heart and seek to harm others.

Our sages gave the example of Yohani bat Ratibi who pretended to prayer and piety. When pregnant women neared their confinement, she would go and offer to pray on their behalf. In fact, she would cast evil spells to try and harm the infant and then she would revoke the spell. Thus these poor women, who saw their children first fall ill and then recover, believed that Yohani's prayer had helped them, when it was really her evil spells which had harmed them in the first place.

Eventually, this evil woman's plots and spells were discovered. She is the reason that the sages frowned upon teaching women to read and write and offer prayers. Has not Rabbi Eliezer said that teaching your daughter Torah is like teaching her promiscuity? Better a wife should be taught obedience and to stay at home caring for the children.

Speaking of caring for children, I have been saved by Hananel's daughters. Our master Rabbenu Hananel has assumed the position of Head since his father's death. He is leading the community admirably and has, for the most part, well adhered to Rabbi Eliezer's dictum; for he has not taught any of his nine daughters to read or write. Hananel still has contacts in the Rum, where his father came from, and these business opportunities have enabled him to support his large family. Alas, he has no sons. There was a brief while that Hananel encouraged me to think about marrying his eldest daughter, but she is too young and it was too early for me after my wife's death. It might have been a good thing to ally our two families thus, but it was not God's will.

Since Mulaah has become betrothed, Hananel's daughters have taken her place caring for Ghazal. There are so many girls in the house I do not know all of their names. Yet Ghazal knows each one by sight and calls them each by her own name. The girls speak Arabic, unlike Hananel. They tell me of Ghazal's progress and needs. I confess for some reason I am more comfortable with this gaggle of girls in my household than I was even with Mulaah. I feel deeply indebted to Hananel and his household, for otherwise I should not know what to do with Ghazal. When the *minyan* of girls—his nine plus my one—takes over my house, there is so much life and vibrancy there. I can teach and write with hope for Ghazal's future, praised be God's name, day by day.

Dunash, I pray that your holidays went well and that this coming trading season be prosperous for you and for all Israel. Write to me, dear friend, and send me business that we might both flourish.

From Karimah
to her brother al-Iskander, Late-Spring to Summer, 1032

To al-Iskander ibn Dunash HaCohen al-Tustari... via the Hajj caravans, with the help of God. From his sister, sometimes Wuhshah, sometimes not, in the Hijaz, may God preserve and uphold me.

My dear Skandi, so much has happened to me in the past few months, I do not know how to begin to tell you everything. I will try and tell you what I can first, first, and then on until I get to the last. The last time I wrote to you I told you of my time at Jebel Mousa and the troubles there. That was, I think, in early Spring, in any case, somewhere around Passover, not that I actually celebrated Passover—do not even think of telling Mommy that!

Actually, I really did celebrate Passover, for did I not leave Egypt and make my way to the wilderness of Sinai and stand at the mountain? In any case there was no bread to eat during that period—no manna either, just dates, locusts and a rare bird. And have I not since left Sin and come first to Ayla and now into the Hijaz? When we left the Sinai after the frightening incident with those Banu Hilal Badawi, God preserved us and led us up the east coast of the Sinai past Laban and Hazeroth and di-Zahav.

Ayla was a wonderful oasis and the sea is very tame there. We were able to bathe and swim; the fish and the coral are beautiful, and praise God, we ate well. I think that Ayla is part of the land of Canaan, promised to Moses and our ancestors. Like Moses, I got to see the land, but not go in; for from Ayla, 'Smail and our party all turned south into the Arabian peninsula to enter the Hijaz, a more fearsome wilderness than even Sinai.

We joined a small caravan in Ayla which was going south for the Hajj. The caravan was much larger than our own, but I understand now that some can be hundreds of camels. Ours was fifty at the most. We headed south by stages without incident. Those who knew the route said it was Allah's protection that the Badawi did not attack us, especially the Banu Hilal. We, of course, had already been attacked by the Banu Hilal, but we could not disagree about Allah's protection, for we had been saved by the flood.

Instead of going on the inland route, we stayed close to the waters of the Red Sea. At al-Jar we halted for a few days. There is a very small port there, somewhat west of al-Medina. But it was a good place to stop, for the boats come down the Red Sea to there from all along the coast of Egypt. There was much trading and the caravan grew in size. I realized that 'Smail had planned this part of the journey long ago, for he met one of the boats there which had extra provisions for us. I was glad to eat well and know that we had weapons and gold to bring forward on our journey—the Hajj route is dangerous.

From al-Jar we moved on to Bir Sa'id, a tiny well which was not more than a hole in the ground. The water was brackish and disgusting, but since the fresh water we had taken on at al-Jar was finished, we drank without complaint. From Bir Sa'id we rode on to Bir Abbas, which had better water but not much more to speak of. By now the caravan was near to one hundred camels and we no longer worried about attack from the Badawi. As we were soon to come to al-Medinah, 'Smail and his servants made it known that they were undertaking the Hajj.

This surprised me, although looking back, I do not see why I could have thought it would be otherwise. Why else venture into the Hijaz? Surely there is little profit in trading there, beyond Hajj souvenirs and the food that the pilgrims require. But we ourselves also required that food, so there was nothing for us to trade—except for this: 'Smail wanted me to trade my Judaism and become Muslim! I told him point blank that I had no intention whatsoever to submit to Islam. I was Jewish and though I may have loved him and gone away from my family and my community for his sake, I was not prepared to renounce my share in the World to Come.

He argued that it was precisely so that I would have a share in the World to Come that I should "embrace Islam and submit—for there is no God but Allah and Muhammad is his messenger." I said I certainly had no argument about the unity of Allah, no Jew would, and I did not doubt that Muhammad was a great teacher, much like the Christian's Isa. But a Jew I was and a Jew I would remain. He said I was as stubborn as the Jews of al-Medinah whom the prophet converted.

By this time we were on the outskirts of al-Medinah, entering the edge of the city through the Bab al-Ambari. Many houses are being built there and 'Smail proposed that we stop for a week or even two so he could find work there to earn more money for the Hajj. He suggested that in the meanwhile, I could rethink my decision to submit.

We could see over the walls into al-Medinah, which was very busy and beautiful. Off to our left we could see the very mosque of the prophet himself. 'Smail thought that should help me to find my way to Islam. I know that the tombs of the holy ones of Islam are in al-Medinah, which makes the city sacred, but I was adamant. I might not be attached now to the practice of our ancestors, but neither could I become Muslim.

Burton L. Visotzky

'Smail was not very nice to me during all of this. He would not share his tent with me because he said he was in purity in preparation for the greater Hajj when we got to Mecca. I know that non-Muslims cannot come into Mecca. So I told him I had no intention of becoming a Hajja, or going on to Mecca, or even staying with him in al-Medinah. I told him I would find my own way home.

I had never seen 'Smail in such a fury, not even when we were attacked by the Banu Hilal. He turned to the servants and said, "She is yours—do with her as you wish. When you have finished, sell her in the slave market so that you may buy Ihram to wear in the Haram al-Sharif." Little brother, I tell you at that moment I very much regretted ever being called Wuhshah, for those servants looked as though each was ready to have his way with me.

I shouted that they were all undertaking to be Hajjis, how could they contemplate such violence and impurity when they were within sight of the tomb of the prophet? This actually worked and their ardor cooled, much as the angel Jibril cooled the flames of the furnace for Ibrahim. Instead of abusing me physically, the servants decided that they would sell me as a slave. They took me to the markets of al-Manakhah, just outside the Misri gate. I do not know what price I fetched, but I know that I suddenly had my wrists bound and I was led to a tent full of women in the area where they hobble the caravan camels. I do not know what smelled worse, the smell of the camels or the smell of fear which was upon each of the women; for we had all been sold as slaves, and God only knew what would become of us!

I was allowed to keep my saddle bag with me, which was good, for my *jambiyya* dagger and my two-edged Banu Hilal sword were still inside it. I intended to defend myself if need be. As it turned out, it was an easy thing to cut the ropes binding my wrists and cut a hole in the tent large enough for me to escape. I thank God for the sisterhood of those women, for any one of them could have sounded the alarm. Instead, they closed ranks around me so my escape was unseen.

I entered into the place where the prophet had prayed. It was dark inside there, yet open enough for me to enter unobserved. I pulled a robe out of my saddle-bag and disguised myself again as Kamar al-Zaman. I pulled my turban's end cloth across my face so no one would know me and found a corner to sleep. I arose the next morning to make my way out of al-Medinah. I did not know where I would go, but I knew I had to flee.

God granted me one final satisfaction there on the edge of Yathrib, where the Muslims first submitted to the message of the prophet. As I was cautiously making my way towards the Bab al-Shami to head north out of the city, I saw one of the new houses going up. Guess who was sitting astride a beam working on the building? 'Smail was splitting the beam with two wedges, sliding backward each time he drove the one wedge further into the beam and then securing it with the other wedge so that the beam would not snap shut. In my disguise I walked beneath the beam and motioned to him to lean down toward me. As I did this, I reached into my saddle bag and grasped my Banu Hilal sword. I was still unsure what I would do to him until I noticed that as 'Smail leaned down, his robe parted so that his "eggs" dangled there in the crack of the beam. At that moment I lifted up the sword and poked the wedge out of the beam. The two sides of the beam which had been forced open by the wedge snapped shut. The last sounds I heard in al-Medinah were Ismail's pathetic cries.

Skandi, little brother, do not think me cruel; I think I gave 'Smail what he deserved. He left me stranded in the middle of the Hijaz, an escaped slave. Besides, he wished me to convert to Islam and in my turn, as it were, I circumcised him. I will write more when I have an opportunity. For now I will try joining a caravan on the Damascus route in my Kamar al-Zaman disguise. If nothing else, I hope to get to Wadi al-Qura where there is a Jewish community.

From Dunash in Fustat, to Nissim in Kairawan, Summer 1032

My dear teacher and friend, Nissim, Second, may God bless you and keep you. I want to thank you for your letters which are as dear to me as the beating of my heart. I take great solace from your writings, even as I take to heart the lessons and gentle chastisements contained therein. You are correct about that girl whom I so foolishly purchased before Passover—God forbid she had turned out to be as promiscuous as the women of your stories or as the foreign woman of King Solomon's Proverbs or Ecclesiastes. Even the quotation from the book of Ben Sirah was apposite, although we make it a practice here to put away his works as they are outside of the biblical canon. Indeed, I was surprised to find you quoting them, as the rabbinical authorities of Fustat have repeatedly issued anathemas against that work. Many copies have been "hidden away" now in the Jerusalem synagogue.

I even pondered the wisdom of your Rabbi Eliezer who has such an intense dislike of women that he could compare teaching them the holy Torah with teaching them promiscuity. As you know, I taught my dear Karimah the Torah and I disapprove of what your Rabbenu Hananel has done to his daughters, for we must educate our children. You know that my wife, raised as she was in the Rum, cannot read or write, but my children, male and female, surely have learned to read the word of God. When Karimah was with us she taught other girls and even her nanny how to read and write. By the way, I knew your girl Mulaah's family here in Fustat. Her grandfather was the leader of the rabbinic community and tried to unite the Jerusalemites with the Babylonians. His daughter Diyya was quite sharp, and if I recall, even pretty. We surely all remember when her first husband drowned; it was such a grievous loss. He was learned in Torah.

Of course I will not say it was learning Torah that made us lose our Karimah. She is gone and we remain. But it is Torah, such as we receive from you, that brings us comfort in the wake of such tragedies. And not we alone, but others find solace from your works. As I have written you, I have the boy separate the personal parts of your letters to me from your delightful stories. These are by now almost a full work unto themselves, which circulate here in modest numbers. Each new installment I send round is eagerly received and you have as many readers of your lore in Fustat as you do of your commentaries and your works of law. Please, dear friend, continue the precious legacy you send us with every epistle. The stories entertain, it is true, but they also teach of the mysterious ways of God, may His name be praised. So, as your Iraqi compatriots would say, "Teach us, O master."

Under separate cover I am sending you two shipments. The first is by boat and contains goods for market. The second, by land, contains cloth for your girls to finish into Kutama garments for the Caliph's Berber troops. Although they will take more time by land, return them to me by caravan, for the possibility of water damage is too great a risk at the margins of profit we are trying to achieve.

By boat: I am sending two baskets of kohl for sale in the perfumer's market in Kairawan or further west in the Maghreb. The total weight is 300 pounds. See, I make you my agent in good faith, my friend and teacher.

I also have sent one small basket of faience beads for the jeweler's bazaar; sell it for the going rate at the Kairawan auction. I include as a covering for this shipment three scraped hides, which may also be sold at market value there. For the above items, I offer a 15 percent commission to you.

I include 200 strung coral necklaces, and 800 chick-pea bracelets—if the latter get wet with salt water, you may as well eat them. I include three jars of rose marmalade from my household to you and the boys of your academy—it is a gift; please enjoy it with your Sabbath meal.

By caravan I am including 85 bolts of pure Egyptian flax for the manufacture of Kutama garments. You should be able to cut 18 garments per bolt, totaling 1530 garments. The more quickly you can return these garments ready, the more business we can pursue. Remember; by no means send them over water.

Finally, I am very pleased to send you six bolts of silk. The silk is suitable for turbans or clothing—whether for men or for women. If you have faith in the needles of your girls, by all means have them manufacture garments.

Please note that from your commissions and profits the following should be subtracted before dividing our profits:

Exit permit............2 7/8 dirhems
Tolls.....................3 dir
Transport...............20 dir
Sales agent.............8 dir
Canvas..................5 dir
Transport from al-Mahdiya for goods by boat.....38 dirhems
Packing.................4 dir
Porters in al-Mahdiya....8 dirhems
Caravanserai dues...........1 1/2 dir
Night watch there............1 dirhem
"Gifts" to port tax farmer.....8 dirhems

From Dunash in Misr, please God. To Nissim, Second, in Kairawan, with the help of God. To be followed by parcels by land and by sea, In-sh-Allah.

From Karimah in the northern Hijaz, to her brother in Fustat, Summer, 1032

My dear al-Iskander —

The kosher butcher here is a pig! But I am getting ahead of my story. I should stop and pray that you and the family are well, Mommy and Nanny and our entire household. I miss you all, especially now that I am on my own, no Ismail ibn Bahram to turn my head, that snake. I cannot believe he could think that I would turn my back on my community that way. I hope his father is proud of him, his son the Hajj who sells girls into slavery and turns them over to other slaves for abuse. I hope he is still aching from the lesson I taught him. I too have learned a lesson, 'Skandi. I am such a romantic fool.

Anyways, I left al-Medinah without ever going there. I was only in the city's outer walls and never got to enter the Bab Misri, which would have taken me into al-Medinah's old city. In my disguise as a man I was able to accompany a caravan north on the Damascus route. When they saw my *jambiyya* and my two-pointed sword, they actually hired me as a guard to ride with the caravan! God be praised, we did not encounter any Badawi on the route; I could not have raised my sword in battle and would have been dead before I could blink an eye. Thank God who protects the simple.

I recalled having once copied legal questions from the Jews of Wadi al-Qura. Although there were no Karaites, there were rabbinic Jews there. When I got to the town I quickly shed my disguise as a warrior—some joke that—hid away my dagger and sword, and made my way into the Jewish community. Basically, the town is so small, well, actually it is not really even one town. Wadi al-Qura has one town on the north end of Wadi Taymah and another even smaller town some hours to the south called Khaybar. Both towns share one community official who serves them as the synagogue cantor. He alternates weeks from one Sabbath to the next in one town or the other and he also serves as their scribe and ritual slaughterer—their kosher butcher, that pig.

I approached him in the hopes that he could use some help copying documents. I was quite correct in my guess that very few people in the town knew how to write, so he actually needed some assistance. With me there, he could sing and slit throats while I did the work of writing and reading to those who received letters and documents. He is a big fellow, taller than Ismail, but fat. He has a thin little beard and fat nose. But even I must admit he has a high, pretty voice. Sweet voice or not, he smelled of mutton.

Since he had dwellings in each town, it meant I would always have a place to stay, so long as I was willing to travel back and forth from week to week. They even had a donkey for me. We agreed that I would be paid in food and lodging so that I would not need to receive charity assistance of bread or clothing. Fortunately I still had two men's costumes. Unfortunately, by his leaning over me and his constant sniffing around me and touching me while supposedly checking that I was writing properly, the cantor learned that I was not quite the man I pretended to be.

No sooner did he discover this than he made his wife complain about having to travel from town to town every Shabbat. She had recently given birth to a baby and said she now wanted to stay put. So that cantor kept his wife in one town and me in the other. This was fine for almost two whole weeks, until he showed up last Friday afternoon and announced we would be sharing the small house together for the Sabbath. I complained that house sharing was not part of our agreement. He pointed out he had no other place to stay and it was his house in any case. Later I learned that this was not even true, the community owned the house. Since it was his custom to do his slaughtering on Friday mornings so people could have meat for the Sabbath, I offered to cook him a bird for "our" Sabbath meal. The old fool actually thought I would be his "rival wife" every other Sabbath.

What I did was take the fresh pigeon he had slaughtered and carefully drained its blood into a cup. Then I stuffed the bird with dates, figs and pistachios—do you remember the recipe? It's the one that gave Abu Hassan such wind! When Friday evening came there was a Sabbath lamp lit, according to the rabbinic custom. Had it been dark like a Karaite house on the Sabbath, my trick would not have worked. I fed him the bird—I'm really getting to be quite a good cook—and I had him drink much wine. In the dim light of the Sabbath lamp, he reached for me and touched the blood that I had poured from the cup into my lap. I did not say a word. He knew he had not wounded me, so he assumed I was ritually unfit. That pig accused me of trying to lure him into sex when I was menstruant. He said the Torah declared this a mortal sin, what kind of a whore was I?

I answered that he was such a powerful man; his mere touch had made my virgin blood burst forth. Then I told him that in the morning I would bring my garment for all the town of Khaybar to see. I told him that I was sure they would rejoice with him over his new co-wife. Well, needless to say, he did not actually want a co-wife, nor did he want his wife in Taymah to hear she had a rival in Khaybar. He begged me to not tell anyone what had happened. I agreed, but only if he would sleep on the floor in the other room. Then he began to threaten me. I knew that the cantor, that pig, would find some way to get even and he was an expert with a knife. No sooner did he walk out than I shut and barred the door to the inner room.

I knew that my brief stint as an apprentice scribe had ended. Unfortunately, I also knew that I could not wait for the Sabbath to end—it was a case of saving a life—mine! I prayed he would not be quick to head to Taymah where his wife and squalling baby awaited him. He could surely spend a few days after the Sabbath in Khaybar writing for the Jews there before heading back north. I wished to head north in any case, so I climbed out the window, took the donkey and as much writing material as I could carry in my saddle bag, and rode off as quickly as I could to Taymah as dawn broke that Sabbath morning.

While I was riding north I realized that the cantor would come back to Taymah as quickly as he could once he understood that I had headed there. He would want to be sure I did not make too much trouble. I did wish to do some damage, if for no other reason than to get even for the ruined garment that pig caused me. But I could not ride a donkey into the heart of the Jewish community on a Sabbath afternoon; they would think I was bewitched or insane. So I found a place outside the town in one of the little caves formed by the wadi and tethered the donkey there. I hid my saddle bag deep inside the cave and slept until Sunday morning.

I entered the town of Taymah and went to the cantor's home in the Jewish section. His wife was there with the new baby. She seemed a bit dazed but not surprised to see me. I realized that she had no idea who I was in my disguise and it would be unseemly for her to invite a strange man into the house. From the veranda I spoke to her through a window and told her that her husband had tried to seduce me in Khaybar. She laughed nervously and said it was of no consequence to her, so long as he did not marry a rival wife. I was about to say to her that his sleeping with me would be the acquisition of another wife by means of sexual congress—when it dawned on me that she thought me to be a young man! Like I said, the kosher butcher is a pig.

Al-Iskander, I will write and tell you what happens after I leave Khaybar and Taymah. The Damascus caravans pass through here, as do many to al-Kahira and Fustat. I know I shall be able to send you more letters along with this one. I wish I could stay here long enough to ask you to write to me, but I cannot remain among the Jewish community any longer here and I do not know where God's hand shall guide me next.

'Skandi my dear brother, I have been away from home more than half a year. Winter and Spring have passed and it is summer in the Hijaz. I miss you and Mommy dearly. I want you to read what I attach to Mommy. I am writing it on a separate page so she will have a letter all to herself. Do not tell her anything of what I am writing to you. Read what is there and if need be, reassure her that I tell you the same. I will tell you the stories of my life as I wander the wilderness and have my adventures.

I will write to Mommy so that she will not cry with worry about me—I know how I am always first in her thoughts. Be a sweet boy and read this to her. You must have grown a full hand's-breadth by now. I will write to you again very soon, God willing.

From Karimah in Wadi al-Qura, to her mother in Fustat, Summer 1032

To the light of my eyes, my mother, my teacher, I kiss your hands, may God bring you to comfortably satisfied old age and rest.

From your daughter, Karimah, in the Jewish community of Wadi al-Qura, thanks be to God.

Dear Mommy, Nanny, and the rest of the household. I am well, thank God, and working here as a scribe and teacher in Wadi al-Qura. This is an entirely rabbinic community. They are very pious and proper Jews. I write for them, copy their letters and rabbinic works. I have copied correspondence between them and the Gaonim of Pumbedita in Baghdad.

There is a very kind cantor here with a sweet, sweet voice. He keeps his voice so by eating figs, dates, and pistachios. Since his young wife recently gave birth, I sometimes cook for him and make him pigeons. He also drinks bees' honey in hot water on Friday evening, so that he can sing the Sabbath liturgy as sweetly as possible on Friday nights. On Friday afternoons, he slaughters for the Jews, usually birds and other fowl. I, of course, will only eat pigeons according to our custom. I confess, I have not told them I am a Karaite, since every Jew here is rabbinic and I do not wish to have an argument with them. Nevertheless, I am scrupulous not to kindle flames in advance of the Sabbath and I try very hard to derive no benefit from their use of such lights into the Sabbath eve.

Between the birds' feathers and the reeds growing in the wadi, there are plentiful writing materials; although it is hard to get a good ink that will not fade. He does not copy Torahs or any sacred texts, so the ink does not really matter. Still, I would prefer a firm, dark ink that neither runs nor pales. I guess I must learn to make do with these hardships.

There is enough work for me to write each day. In the rest of the time, I teach the younger boys to read and write. Some of the mothers are nervous about me having contact with their husbands, so I encourage them to bring their boys themselves. I have convinced one or two of the mothers to stay through the first part of the lessons and I think they understand my plan—that they, too, could learn to read and write! God willing, I will be able to accomplish this goal.

But I do not know if I shall stay here, for if there is a caravan of Jews I may join it and try to make my way to the Holy Land. I should praise God were I able to see Jerusalem and weep over her ruins. Is it not the goal of every one of us of the community of Scripture to mourn for Zion?

Mommy, as you will see, my travel companions are no longer with me. They should be making their way back to Fustat by now, in-sh-Allah. Perhaps you might learn more from them. I am certain they will have a very interesting story to tell. In the meanwhile, I am well, eating properly, and writing daily. Praise be to God who has preserved me and sustained me.

I kiss your hands and your eyes, dearest mother who brought me forth into this world. May God support you on the right and on the left. Kiss al-Iskander for me, and Nanny too. I pray for the health of my entire household. From your loving daughter who misses you, with Heaven's support.

Chapter Five
Summer, 1032

From Karimah in the northern Hijaz
to al-Iskander in Fustat, summer 1032

Dear Skandi, I hope that this letter finds you and the whole family well. I miss you all. I wrote to you that I was leaving Taymah, but as it turned out, I only left their Jewish community. I had to leave them that very Sunday. I walked into the Muslim sector, for unlike Fustat, the Jews and Muslims here have separate sections in the town. This is because the prophet tried to convert the entire Hijaz to Islam and almost succeeded. He converted the Jews in al-Medinah, but not those of Wadi al-Qura. But many of the Arab pagans who had lived and traded with the Jews in the wadi did convert, and the Muslims took their dwellings and moved away from the Jews. As a result, the Jewish communities of Wadi al-Qura just survive, while the Muslim communities of the two towns prosper, because they are on the Hajj route and mark a major point for the caravans.

When I got into the Muslim town, I was not sure just what to do, indeed, I was unsure of everything but the growing hunger in my belly. Just then, a lovely lady dressed in Mosul silks came by and quaintly addressed me, "Porter, do you wish to earn a dirhem? Awake, sleeper, and follow me to find your load!"

I willingly followed her for I had no other plan and hoped to find not only a dirhem's earnings but perhaps a bite to eat, as well. She came to a door where she knocked and a Christian answered, but not like any of the Copts we have in Misr. She handed him a gold dinar and he immediately disappeared only to come back in a few moments with delicious smelling wine. I realized that the Muslims of this town were mostly pious and did not openly sell wine, but that they drank it anyway, buying it from the Christians. I took up the jug of wine and followed her to the next stop.

She stopped at the fruit stalls and bought apples from Syria, quinces from Oman, peaches from Persia, cucumbers from our Nile banks, limes and citrons from the Fayyum, an entire crate of fruits. "Up with your load Porter, make it snappy," was all she said, and so I followed her onward.

Next we went to a Muslim butcher, where she bought mutton, almost ten pounds. I know for I carried it on my back. The butcher wrapped it in a banana leaf and I balanced it upon my back with the crate of fruit and the jug of wine. It was very hot and I was freely sweating, but my hunger and greed for the dirhem she promised kept me walking under the load.

We next stopped at a grocer who carried dried fruits and nuts. She bought pistachios from Aleppo, almonds from Lebanon, raisins from Timnah, all of which were piled into the crate I already had. "Lift up, lift up, there is more, you lazy Porter," said the woman. We went to the confectioner's store where I thought of you, Skandi, and how you love the sweets that were arrayed there: cookies, halava, bird's nests, phyllo fingers and filled flutes, baklawa, semolina cakes, and honey-syruped walnut tarts joined the party. All she said was, "Lift up."

I foolishly said, "Had I known you were buying a banquet I would have brought my donkey." She hit me and said, "Silence you ass, just lift up and follow me. You are the porter, I am the mistress."

Next I stumbled to the perfumer's stall where we bought rose water and sugar, incense lumps and orange-flower musk, violet scent and candles of bees' wax scented with vanilla. "Lift up, lift up," was all she could say to me. Thank God, the next store was the last, for I was staggering under the load. "Porter," she asks me, "do you not wish to earn your dirhem?"

I was tempted to tell her to take her dirhem and her load, but I held my tongue, for my hunger was by now overwhelming. We went to the oil shop, where we bought sun-flower and olive oil, olives green and black, some with red pepper, some with caper berries. There were cheeses from both goats and cows, some yet soft and others hard in little wheels. I liked to die of hunger and hoped for a reward in food when we reached her abode. "Lift up, lift up, now follow me," said she.

We came to a mansion with a front court with columns, leading to a gate of ebony-wood, inlaid with mother-of-pearl. A fountain of cool water was inside the courtyard, where I hoped to wash when I put down my load. I eagerly awaited a vision of the inside of the house when the lady said to me, "Set down, set down, cur, your task is complete." Slowly and carefully I lowered the tower of items from my aching back into her courtyard. When my load was set before her she clapped and a huge slave appeared in the courtyard. He grabbed me by my collar and lifted me off the ground. Then he took me to the gate and threw me out!

"But what about my dirhem that the lady promised?" I shouted. "And I am hungry besides, can you not spare some food, where is your fabled hospitality?" The slave came forward with his fist raised and said, "Do you wish your dirhem? I shall give it to you. Here it is within my fist." He punched out at me, but I rolled away in the dust, picked myself up, and fled to the sound of his laughter. I was still famished and now dirty, sweaty and humiliated. But you know me, brother, and hungry though I was, I was equally determined to get even.

Burton L. Visotzky

I snuck around the alleyways of the town until I was behind that rich lady's mansion. I easily climbed the fence, keeping an eye out for the giant slave, or others like him. What I had not reckoned on were four large dogs in the back garden, each of which immediately bounded towards me. I was tired and knew I would have no chance to fight off the snarling dogs. As they drew near I went limp, resigned to my fate. But the dogs must have scented the food I had been carrying all morning or perhaps the lingering smell of the kosher butcher's trade had permeated my clothing; I do not know. I was blessed by God in that moment, for the dogs each sniffed at me and then licked my hands and arms until they had practically cleaned all the dust off of me.

I noticed then that each dog wore a jeweled collar and I carefully petted the dogs, removed the collars and slid them into my robes. Then I saw that the dogs each had food bowls set behind the kitchen, out of view from the house. I admit it brother, I ate what food was set out for the dogs; but you must know that this was a rich household, for they had mutton and fine cheeses in their bowls. Even more amazing, the bowls themselves were of gold! These, too, went within the folds of my robe. I had my dirhem now!

Unfortunately, my robes were now so full of booty that I could not climb the wall to leave. I explored the garden until I found some tasty looking pomegranates growing there, which I also picked and stuffed into my garments. Now I looked like a short fat man, so lumpy were my robes. But, praise God, there was a wicket door in the garden wall just there. I let myself out the gate and at once saw the giant slave at the end of the alley. I turned the other way and began walking slowly, praying all the while that he would not see me. Blessed be the Lord, for that alleyway had a bend in it, what is called a dog's-leg, and so I was soon out of his sight. At that I ran as fast as I could without dropping my loot. Now that I had eaten, I had strength to run all the way to the cave outside of town where I had tethered my donkey.

I found the animal still tied where I had left it, thank God. It was calmly eating from the bushes nearby, as though nothing untoward had occurred while I was gone. But for me, I had ridden on the Sabbath, eaten unclean foods, milk and meat together, and stolen—from a dog, no less. With those sins on my mind, I went into the cave to unpack from my robes the collars and bowls I had stolen from the dogs. I had just finished placing the last of the bowls in my saddle bag when one of the pomegranates fell from my robe. I rose from where I had been squatting so I could go get it, when I felt two sharp points suddenly pressing at the back of my neck.

The moment I felt those pricks on my skin, I realized that the Badawi sword had not been in the saddle bag. "You should be more careful where you hide this sword," a voice said from behind me in the darkness of the cave. Ahead of me I could see our shadows, there was only one man holding the two-pronged sword to my neck. "This is a valuable sword, you know, it belonged to a great warrior," my captor said.

"Yes," I added with relief, "but he limps now." It was the Banu Hilal brigand Abu Sin who held the sword to me; and I felt sure he would not harm me. He replied, "He limps not at all, and that is thanks to you." He removed the sword from my neck and asked calmly, "Pomegranate?"

I knew I had to appear in control so I said, "Why yes, thank you." At that, Abu Sin poked the tips of the sword into the fruit and with a flick of the wrist had flipped it into the air. I could not see well, for I was looking out of the cave now into the light. I could tell that the fruit did not fly any higher than his shoulder. He turned his hand this way and that and bent down to pick up the fallen fruit. Brother, he handed me that pomegranate neatly cut into quarters. All he said was, "I've missed this old sword."

I felt very confined within the space of the small cave, so I suggested that we might eat the fruit outside in the sun. But Abu Sin would not move from the door of the cave. He only said, "It is too hot out there. And besides, Sitt Wuh-shah, they are looking for you—you are now a brigand, just like me." At that he laughed out loud and even showed his teeth, which were very white. We sat in the cave and ate that pomegranate and then the others. It was like that verse in Song of Songs, "I have given you to drink of my scented wine, of the juice of my pomegranate."

I slowly chewed the seeds of the first, after sucking up the juices. But Abu Sin said, "Do not be so polite, you will regret it later when your belly aches." He took the sword once more and with the tip made two holes in the fruit. Then he rubbed the pomegranate hard between his hands and gave me to drink, just as Nanny used to do for us. At that, I too laughed. When he asked me why, I told him with a smile, "Because you are like my nanny." Thank goodness he laughed and did not take offense.

But Abu Sin again frightened me when he said, "You have been to al-Medi-nah and now come from Khaybar. Where will you go next?" I was stunned that again he seemed to know my past and my every thought. I asked him, "Since you know all this, perhaps you will tell me where I shall go next." And he said, "With pleasure, Sittuna, you shall go to visit the tomb of Haroun the prophet, brother of Moses. It is a holy site; no one will find you there. But it may take us some time to get there, for like me, you must now avoid the authorities."

Skandi, it was only later that Abu Sin revealed how he knew so much, for his Banu Hilal serve as spies throughout the area. They report to the Rum on the activities of the Muslims, and then they report to the Fatimids on the activities of the Rum. The Badawi of his tribe roam throughout all of Sinai and most of the Hijaz. They have penetrated as far north as Syria and also report to the Turks, who Abu Sin says are growing ever stronger. He says it is they and not the Baghdadis whom the Fatimids and even the Rum will have to fear. Abu Sin says that his Badawi are learning the science of sea-chariots; for mastery of the world, whether of Islam or of the Rum, shall be determined by who controls the Great Sea. He does not trust the Berbers either, even though he rides with them. Abu Sin trusts only himself and his Banu Hilal.

I feel like I am drowning in a vast ocean, little brother, with only Abu Sin to keep my head afloat for now. I do not know whether this is good or bad. I have no choice but to trust him. I am giving him these letters to post. He will place them with a caravan of Hajj returning to Fustat and he guarantees they will arrive. I have no doubt that Abu Sin will read them; he's never even heard of Rabbenu Gershom.

From Karimah in the northern Hijaz and southern Trans-Jordan, late Summer/Fall(?), 1032

Dear 'Skander, another letter so you know what I am doing and can read of my latest adventures. I do not know when this or other letters will come to you, for we are avoiding the Damascus caravans—sort of—and keeping to ourselves in the wilderness of Moab. I have spent these last weeks with Abu Sin and become his student. Early on, I had heard his Badawi refer to him as "the philosopher," and now that we are together I was able to ask him if he is THE philosopher Abu Sina. He just laughed and laughed, I thought he might fall down he laughed so hard. By then, I was angry and embarrassed at his laughing at me. "What is so funny?" I kept asking him.

Abu Sin finally calmed down enough to say that his name was Abu Sin, which is a *kunya* that meant he was master of the Sinai wilderness—it is a Badawi nickname. That other philosopher, who is also a physician and an astronomer and a mathematician, is not Abu Sina, but ibn Sina—and his full name is Husayn ibn Abdallah ibn Sina. He is known by the *kunya* Abu Ali, and he lives in the east, in Samarkand. I asked Abu Sin why his Badawi called him a philosopher and he said that his was the philosophy of the sword and that he would teach me.

Brother, he has taught me the art of the sword and it is great. But it is not philosophy. On another occasion, I pressed him on why his troops called him a philosopher. Again, he put me off by saying that when we met up again a few weeks ago, did not we meet in a cave and see the shadows on the wall? I told him that this certainly was no answer, for what did a cave with shadows have to do with philosophy? He started to laugh at me again and I got really angry. Then

Abu Sin turned serious and said, "Sitt Wuhshah, my men call me a philosopher in jest, for that is what the Christian monks call one another. My men call me that because they feel that I live like a monk. They say I am a hermit and accuse me of being a celibate because I do not indulge in their excesses when we attack a caravan that has women in it."

I asked him, "What is a celibate?" Abu Sin told me that it was when a monk renounced sex. "But how could your men have said that of you?" I asked him in amazement. "Because at that time," Abu Sin answered gently, "it was so." He became gruff with me then and said it was time to learn the way of the sword. Here is how he taught me, brother. Do the men teach you this? If not, maybe someday I can teach you, just like I taught you the *alif-ba*.

Abu Sin had me hold the Badawi sword in my right hand, with my arm straight out from my side. In my left hand, I held my *jambiyya* dagger, with that arm extended as well. Once I had set my arms parallel to the ground he said, "Now I shall begin the lecture. But you must keep your arms out, for the moment they begin to fall, I shall stop teaching you."

Dear al-Iskander, it took me a long time to hear his lecture on swords. I had no idea it would be so hard to simply hold my arm out from my body, but the iron of the sword is heavy and the braiding on the hilt dug into the flesh of my hand. "The blade, you will see, is straight, and has two points at the end," Abu Sin began. "There are other straight swords: those with one point at the end, those with no point at the end, those with but one cutting blade and those like the one you hold, which are called two-faced." Here the first lecture ended, for my arm fell.

Later that day we began again. My forearm was sore, but I was determined to keep my arms out straight for a longer period. Abu Sin explained why the straight sword was good for thrusting, but not as good for parrying. He said that most riders prefer the scimitar, which is curved like a bow, for it sliced through the air and so was more effective for Badawi who ride on horseback. His own straight sword was modeled on the Turkish swords. The scimitars usually had only one cutting blade, on the outside edge of the sword. The *jambiyya* is really a small kind of scimitar.

By his third lecture I could hold both hands up for five minutes at a time. Then Abu Sin spoke to me of the parts of the sword: the blade, and the tang or tongue, which is the part below the shoulders of the blade. A sword with only a point and no side blade is called a foil. A sword that grows broader from the point comes to an end at the "shoulders." The tang sticks out from the shoulders, like the head from the body.

The hilt is built around the tang. A hilt is for holding on to the sword and it has a pommel or a little apple, attached to the end for balance. Some hilts have cups or baskets at the shoulders. These protect the hand from the blade of an opponent who seeks to cut the sword out of your hand.

I sound like Abu Sin, but you did not have to hold your arms out while I taught you all this. Anyways, I think all of this new teaching of the sword is really interesting; don't you?

The reason he made me hold my arms out so long is to strengthen them. I can now hold the iron sword for a long time. Abu Sin taught me the various motions of thrusting and parrying with the sword. This part is called technique. So much of the technique has to do with how I move my hips and feet. I find it beautiful to watch him practice. We go through exercises by drawing the sword from its sheath and then thrusting forward, sideways, and the like. Then we practice the upward and sideways and downward parries. Finally we return the sword to the sheath to protect the blade of the sword. I am learning how to hone and polish and keep the iron free of rust and in good fighting condition.

Abu Sin was proud to teach me the Latin terms which the Rum use for the sword and sheath. The sword is called the Bugio, and the sheath is called the Wadjaina. Abu Sin calls his sword by a variety of Arabic names: al-Ahlil, al-Deukkak, Ed-Dommar, and such. The thrusts and parries each have their own name, too. Abu Sin has made me memorize them and when we practice he calls out the name and I perform the gesture, almost as though he were choreograph-ing a dance. He insists that constant practice improves technique and makes me ready for battle conditions. If we cross swords, we always keep them in the sheath to be safe.

The names of some of the moves should amuse you, brother. The thrusts are called: the serpent strikes, the screw of Archimedes, the tail of the ostrich, the battering ram, the camel's hump, driving the peg, the smith's hammer, the bucket in the well, and fitting on the sock. This last technique is a means to put the sword into the sheath at the end of practice. Each of these maneuvers is now second nature to me and I can run through them all in any order without tiring. I am trying to learn on my own when to use them. This, of course, depends on the position of your opponent and whether you are parrying or thrusting.

Abu Sin and I practice constantly. Sometimes I feel as though I am perma-nently sore from all the thrusting and changing of positions. But he says this makes me stronger and I believe him. I am much more confident now, 'Skander, more so than I ever was with Ismail. Abu Sin has taught me to be a warrior. He says the most important thing is knowledge and confidence; if you have those you might never have to draw your sword in battle, in-sh-Allah. It is not as though I want to go into battle, Skandi, but what is the point of all the technique if you can not use it some day?

In any case, I really feel like I finally deserve a Banu Hilal sword. I wear the *jambiyya* and the sword at all times. I am dark from the sun and dress in the robes and turban of the Badawi. Now that I finally really look the part of Kamar al-Zaman, I am more Wuhshah and Sittuna than ever. Nevertheless, I remain your sister, Karimah.

From Nissim in Kairawan
to Dunash in Fustat, Summer, 1032

My dear Abi-Skander, or shall I now call you Abi Yudan? For though you are in fact the father of your son al-Iskander, you are also Father of the Jews, Abi Yudan— by virtue of your beneficence. Your business partnerships have benefited me and my household and the whole academy here in Afrikiya. The boys of the academy are able to study uninterrupted thanks to your gifts and their households flourish for the sewing of Kutama garments.

Even the Taherti brothers, who have now joined in partnership for these Maghrebi garments, have commented on your extraordinary generosity to the rabbinic academy. They remind me that you are not only open-handed to us here, but that you give in equal measure to the teachers of the rabbinic synagogues in Fustat and the Land of Israel and to our sages in the schools of Sura and Pumbedita, in Baghdad. They do not need to add how good an eye you have for the Karaites of the Land of Israel and Fustat and those who remain in Iraq. Dunash, truly you are father to all the Jewish people; God bless you and keep you.

Even as you are always looking for an opportunity to do good and share your business, our sages of blessed memory tell the tale of a thief who was always on the lookout to steal. Once that thief entered the Caliph's treasury and took some golden serving bowls. As he was leaving, he saw purses of newly minted gold dinars, still sewn shut, with the amounts noted on their sides. As these were worth more than the bowls and easier to carry, he put down the bowls and took up the purses of dinars. But then he saw even larger purses, so he put down the smaller and took up the larger purses. He was ready to sneak out of the treasury, but as he neared the door his eye lighted on a box of pearls and precious gems. "Surely," he thought, "these are worth more than all the dinars of the treasury." And so it continued, until dawn came and he had to flee empty handed, lest he be caught. He departed lamenting, "If only I had taken the least valuable object, but now I have risked my life and come away with nothing."

The sages liken this to a fox that saw a beautiful orchard of fig, apricot, pomegranate, and pistachio trees. That fox searched for a way into the orchard to eat the fruit until he found a narrow crack in the gate. He could not squeeze through this crack, but was determined to eat these delicious fruits. So he starved himself until he could wedge his body through the narrow crack and enter the orchard. Once within he gorged himself on the fruits and nuts until he was quite full.

Of course, when the fox went to leave the orchard he was far too fat to climb out through the crack in the gate. So he hid in the orchard, all the while in fear of his life, until he was again thin enough to squeeze through the fissure. When he got out he lamented that he had no more than when he had entered and was as hungry as ever. All he had to show for his adventure was fear for his life.

So it is with those who wish to do evil, who are never satisfied with what they have until they forfeit their own lives. And then there are others, like you, dear Dunash, who give no thought for yourself, but always look to see how you might benefit others. Our sages tell of a great rabbi who had a dream in which he saw himself seated at the banquet of the righteous in the world to come. Next to him was a man who was the butcher of a small town. When this great scholar awoke he was very disconcerted to think that he would spend eternity seated next to a lowly butcher. He determined to visit that small town and confront the butcher.

When he found the butcher, the man was small of stature and wore a blood smeared apron. "How can I help you?" he asked the rabbi. "Do you not know whom you address?" asked the sage. "No sir," said the butcher, "but I should be most honored if I could make your acquaintance over dinner." The butcher changed out of his apron and brought the rabbi home, where he was served a delicious meal of mutton braised in pomegranate juice, garnished with pistachios and almonds.

When the rabbi had eaten his fill, he quizzed the man. "What have you done that you are worthy to dine with me?" asked the rabbi. The butcher thought hard and answered with a frown, "I cannot think what I may have done to have such an honor, O master. But perhaps it is that I give half of my profits to charity and always serve mutton to the poor of my town every Sabbath eve." The rabbi sneered, "Plenty have done so, but have not gained sufficient merit. Have you nothing else to your credit?"

The butcher thought some more and said, "Perhaps this one small thing that I have done. Once a caravan passed through this town and they were selling slaves who had been taken captive. I saw a pretty young woman in the slave line and worried lest someone might buy her who would defile her. So I paid for her ransom and brought her to my home. I bathed her and fed her and taught her to write, so that she might have a trade. When she had stayed with me for some time, I betrothed her to my eldest son, so that neither he nor she might be misled into sin."

Still the rabbi said, "Is that all?" "Well," the butcher continued, "there was more. I planned a wedding banquet for my son and the girl. I invited the entire town and fearing that the poor might be too embarrassed to come, I secretly had garments sent to them so they would be indistinguishable from the grandees of the town. When the banquet began, the entire town sat mixed together and every table rejoiced with meat and wine. All but for one table, who sat there overcome by sadness.

I sat with them and asked how I could cheer them. They said that they were surely well cared for, but there was at the table one who was so sad that he made the rest of them stop rejoicing. I sought him out and even to look at him saddened my heart. I took him aside and asked him why he cried on a day of rejoicing. He said that he had been engaged to the girl who was now to be my son's bride, but Badawi raiders had taken her captive. When he went to search for her, he, too had been taken and then sold as a slave. Now he finally had found his bride, but she was about to marry another.

At that I took my son aside and said, 'Dear son, all I wish is your happiness. I promised you this bride and clothing and jewels for you to start your life together. Just now I have learned that she is betrothed to another! My son, we must do what is right in God's eyes.'

My son said, 'Father, I listened to you at the outset, so I hear and obey you now.'

At that we called all the guests to attention and told them the tale of the two engaged captives. They were joined in marriage that very night under my own roof and the rejoicing went on for all seven days of the wedding week. I provided them with the clothing and jewels that I had intended for my son. They stayed with me for many months and then went on their way. For his part, my son found another bride. We danced at his wedding and the joy was even greater than it had been the first time, for we all knew we had been saved from sin, thank God Almighty."

At that, the dour rabbi said, "Amen and thank God that I am privileged as to have my seat next to you."

Dear Dunash, I consider it a privilege that I am able to write to you and to do business with you. May it be God's will that I could do for Ghazal what that butcher did for his son; setting her on the path of righteousness and please God, rejoicing at her wedding some day. And may you raise up al-Iskander to Torah, to the wedding canopy, and to good deeds—like those of his illustrious father.

To Dunash, from Nissim, in the Name of the Merciful.

Given the season and that your community of Scripture are firm believers in mourning for Zion, my dear friend, I thought it would be apposite to share with you from the Talmud some tales of how the Holy Temple, may it be rebuilt speedily in our day, was destroyed by the Romans.

Nero Caesar was sent against them. As he came he shot an arrow to the east, it fell on Jerusalem. To the west, it fell upon Jerusalem. To each direction of the compass, it fell on Jerusalem. He reasoned, "The Blessed Holy One wishes to destroy His house, but He will blame it upon me!" Nero went and fled and converted to Judaism.

Then Vespasian Caesar came against them. He besieged the city for three years. There were three rich men in the city. One said, "I will supply wheat and barley." Another said, "I will supply wine and oil and salt." The third said, "I will supply fuel wood." There was enough food to sustain the siege for 21 years.

There were zealots in the city who wished to war with Rome. They said to the rabbis, "Let us go meet them in battle." But the rabbis replied, "It will not have the support of Heaven." The rabbis then said to the zealots, "Allow us to make peace with them." But the zealots did not allow it. Then the zealots arose and burnt the storehouses of food and a famine ensued.

The head of those zealots was the nephew of Rabban Yohanan ben Zakkai. He sent to him to come in private. Yohanan asked him, "How long will you kill off the populace with famine?" His nephew said, "What can I do? If I say anything to them they will kill me! But here is what to do. Pretend you are ill and have two of your trusted disciples attend you. Then let them say you have died and place you in a coffin. Allow no one but your disciples to carry you. Have them carry you out of the city. Perhaps a little bit can be salvaged."

Rabban Yohanan ben Zakkai had his two disciples carry him in a coffin to the city gate. At the gate the guards wished to pierce the coffin with daggers. They said, "Shall people say you have desecrated the corpse of our Master?" The guards allowed them to pass. They carried Rabban Yohanan to the camp of Vespasian. He arose from the coffin and greeted the general, *Vive Domine Imperator!*

Vespasian said, "You have doubly condemned yourself to death. For I am not the Emperor, yet you greet me as the emperor. And if I were the emperor, what took you so long to come?" But Rabban Yohanan said, "Surely you shall become Emperor, for only an emperor could take Jerusalem."

At that moment, messengers came from Rome and proclaimed Vespasian emperor. He said, "I must go now, but I will send my son Titus in my stead.

Ask what you wish and it shall be granted to you." Rabban Yohanan asked for a physician to heal the rabbi who had been fasting in the hopes of preventing the destruction of Jerusalem. And he asked that the lineage of Rabban Gamaliel be saved. Finally, he asked permission to study in the town of Yavneh. These were granted to him.

When Titus came he took a prostitute into the Holy of Holies of the Temple, and unfurled a Torah scroll and sinned with her upon it. Then he took his sword and slashed the veil of the Temple. A miracle occurred and blood spurted out. Titus actually thought he had murdered Him. Then he took the curtain and made it like a sack in which he placed all the golden vessels of the Temple to take back to Rome with him in triumph.

When he boarded the ship for Rome, a storm arose. Titus blasphemed, "It seems to me that the God of the Jews only has power over water. He drowned Pharaoh. He drowned Sisera. Now he wants to drown me. One who has victory at sea does not compare to one who has vanquished an enemy in his own palace. If he is so mighty, let him fight me upon dry land!"

A voice came from heaven and said, "O evil one, son of an evil one, descendent of the evil Esau. I have a simple creature called the gnat. Let it join battle with you."

When Titus came to Rome in triumph they presented him with a silver trophy-cup full of wine. As he threw back his head to drink, a gnat flew up his nostril. It bored into his brain for seven years. The constant buzzing drove Titus to despair. One day, he was passing a blacksmith's shop and the sound of the hammer hitting the anvil caused the buzzing to be drowned out. Titus said, "Ah, relief!" At that he hired smiths to hammer before him. To a gentile he paid four *zuz*. To a Jew he said, "It must suffice that you may see your enemy suffer." This worked for thirty days. After 30 days, the gnat buzzed ever louder. When Titus died, they split open his head and found the gnat had grown to the size of a two-pound pigeon.

Thus does God punish the enemies of the Jews. And thus are Jews punished for mindless hatred, foolish piety, and communal dissension. But it need not always be so, for even today there are Jews, Rabbanites and Karaites, who dwell in the Holy City. It is as we are taught:

Once Rabban Gamaliel, Rabbi Aqiba, and their colleagues ascended to Jerusalem. When they came to Mount Scopus they followed the ritual and rent their garments in memorial for the fallen sanctuary. When they came to the Temple Mount, they beheld a fox slinking out of the place where the Holy of Holies had stood. They began to weep, but Rabbi Aqiba laughed. They said, "Aqiba you continually astonish us. Here we are weeping and you laugh?!"

He said to them, "And you, why do you weep?" They replied, "We weep for the place, of which it is written in the book of Numbers, 'If a stranger enters therein he shall die;' and behold, a fox is lurking there. Thus we fulfill the verse of Lamentations, 'for this our heart shall sorrow, Mount Zion desolate, foxes finding footfall there.'"

Aqiba replied, "It is just so that I laugh, for it is written in Micah 'Zion shall be plowed as a field and Jerusalem a heap of ruins.' Until this verse was fulfilled, I feared the next verse could not come to pass. Now that I see Jerusalem in ruins, I know that the remainder of the prophecy is to be: 'The Mount of the Lord's House shall stand firm above the mountains and it shall tower above the hills… Torah shall come forth from Zion and the word of God from Jerusalem.'"

They said to him, "Aqiba, you have comforted us, indeed, you have given us comfort."

So take comfort, my friend, take comfort. May you have an easy fast in memory of our fallen glory, dear friend Dunash, who loves every Jew and works to bring us together. Write to me, I miss you as I would if you were my own brother. Tell me your mind, dear friend, do not hold back.

Fragment of a marriage contract for Mulaah and Abu 'l-Maali, Kairawan, late summer 1032.

In God's name, may we prosper and succeed.

In an auspicious sign, on the 15 day of Av in the year 4792 since the creation of the world, which is the year 1343 according to contracts, that is 962 years since the destruction of the Holy Temple, may the Merciful One rebuild it in our day and in the days of all Israel, I write this contract of marriage in Kairawan, at the well of Barouta, in Afrikiya, to testify how the groom, Abi 'l-Maali ibn Yefet said to Mulaah the daughter of Rav Yosef HaCohen, the virgin, "Be thou my wife according to the prophet Moses, and Israel the chosen one, and I shall work to feed and sustain and support and maintain and earn and honor you, according to the laws of Jewish men who feed and clothe and honor their wives, in truth. I give over to you in honor of your virginity two hundred zuz as your marriage contract, as Moses said to give to the virgin daughters of Israel."

Then Mulaah the daughter of Rav Yosef HaCohen, the virgin, replied and accepted that she would work and serve and honor and be honored by the groom, Abi 'l-Maali ibn Yefet, according to the laws of the women who are the daughters of Israel, who work and serve and honor and are honored by their masters in cleanliness and purity...

2 silver bangles,
silver anklets,
1 copper pail,
1 copper drinking vessel — shallow,
1 shirt of two dinars,
1 wrap of three dinars
3 head coverings at 1 dinar each
colored bedding at 4 dinars
1 large quilt at 4 dinars...
a dinar is a dinar...
if you are taken captive I shall ransom you up to 33 1/3 dinars gold;

I shall not hire female household help, nor shall I take a co-wife without your permission, in return you shall not leave Kairawan for Fustat or anywhere else without my permission... willingly concluded without force or constraint, with legal acceptance of all stipulations of the document, as written and specified before us, who are witnesses,

Hananel ben Hushiel, may I be an atonement for his
resting place, Head, Witness
Nissim ibn Yakov ibn Shaheen, Second, Father of the
Court, Witness
Hillel ibn Gassus, of the court, Witness
Ibrahim ibn Yosef, Head of the Order, Witness

From Nissim in Kairawan
to Dunash in Fustat, end of summer, 1032

To Abi-Skander, businessman and philanthropist, Dunash HaCohen al-Tustari... with the assistance of Heaven.   From Nissim... in the name of the Merciful

My dear patron, whose words I yearn for "as the hart panteth after water." The month of Elul has begun, the sounds of the ram's horn awaken us daily to prayer and repentance, and though you sleep, my heart awakens to you, aching for a letter. I have not heard from you since you so generously sent the shipments to Afrikiya by land and by sea. We have prospered greatly from the business and the garments you had us sew are almost complete. In the spirit of this season, dear friend, I beg your forgiveness if I have offended you. If I have hurt you—intentionally or unintentionally—I offer my contrition. I could not bear to have caused you even the slightest harm. I pray that my words have not pushed you away and that you still desire my friendship and my words of Torah. For I feel our partnership is like that of the sages Rabbi Yohanan and Resh Laqish.

Rabbi Yohanan's beauty was like a new silver goblet filled with pomegranate seeds and surrounded by red rose petals, placed between sunlight and shadow. One day Rabbi Yohanan was bathing in the Jordan river when Resh Laqish saw him and jumped in after him. Rabbi Yohanan said to Resh Laqish, who was then a famous brigand, "May your power be that of Torah!"

Resh Laqish replied, "May your beauty be that of women!"

Yohanan told Resh Laqish, "If you repent from your ways, I shall give you my sister who is even more beautiful than I."

Resh Laqish accepted the offer. When they climbed ashore Resh Laqish went to take up his weapons, but found he no longer had the strength to lift his sword. So he studied Bible and Mishnah and became a great rabbi. One day they were debating the ritual status of "the sword, the knife, the pugio, the lance, the scimitar and the scythe" to determine at what point in the manufacturing process they were liable for ritual uncleanness. Rabbi Yohanan said, "Once they have been burnished in the kiln." Resh Laqish said, "No, but only afterwards, once they have been tempered in the water."

Rabbi Yohanan said, "Well, the brigand certainly should know the business of weaponry!"

Resh Laqish was distressed by this reference to his past and asked his friend, "What have I benefited? Then I was called Master, and now am I called Master."

Rabbi Yohanan replied, "I have benefited you in that I have brought you beneath the wings of the Divine Presence."

Rabbi Yohanan was offended by this quarrel with his brother-in-law. For his part, Resh Laqish actually became ill. His wife came to her brother and asked that Rabbi Yohanan pray on behalf of Resh Laqish. He refused. She implored him that she might not become a widow. He still refused. Finally, she begged him to pray that her children not become orphans. Still Rabbi Yohanan refused. When Resh Laqish died, Rabbi Yohanan was beside himself with grief.

Rabbi Yohanan's disciples sought to assuage his sorrow at losing his study partner. They had Rabbi Elazar ben Pedat sit and study with him. Each time Rabbi Yohanan raised a point, Elazar cited a source in support of him.

Finally Rabbi Yohanan shouted at him, "Do you think you can be like Resh Laqish!? When I would raise a point with him he would offer two dozen objections. Then we would find twenty-four responses to those objections. Thus did we gain knowledge—while you, all you do is offer sources to support my opinions. Don't you think I know that what I am saying is correct?!"

At that, Rabbi Yohanan rent his garments and began to weep uncontrollably, saying, "Where are you Bar Laqisha? Where are you Bar Laqisha?" He cried and cried until he lost his mind. His depression was so acute that the other rabbis prayed that God have mercy on him and take his soul.

I did not mean to be so maudlin, friend, nor to suggest that we are arguing, God forbid, nor that your silence might drive me to distraction. Rather, I wish to illustrate that my love for you is as strong as the love between Rabbi Yohanan and Resh Laqish. Had you a sister to wed to me, as did Rabbi Yohanan for his partner, I should be thrilled to be your brother-in-law.

But know, Dunash, that Rabbi Yohanan had another study partner long ago who was a great business man, just like you. It is told in the Talmud that Ilfa and Rabbi Yohanan studied Torah together and were very poor. Finally they determined that they would go into business and so fulfill the words of Deuteronomy, "that there be no poor among you." On their journey they happened to stop to eat beneath a tottering wall. Just then two ministering angels came by and Rabbi Yohanan heard one say to the other, "Let us throw down this wall upon them and kill them—for they are abandoning the eternal life of Torah study in favor of mundane business."

But the other angel said, "No, let us leave them, for the hour of greatness is nigh for one of them."

Rabbi Yohanan asked Ilfa, "Did you hear anything?"

He said he had not. Rabbi Yohanan reasoned that if he heard yet Ilfa did not, then he was due for greatness and Ilfa was not. So Rabbi Yohanan told Ilfa, "Friend, I must return to my studies. I shall fulfill in my person that other verse of Deuteronomy, 'The poor shall not cease to be among you.'"

So Rabbi Yohanan returned to the academy, while Ilfa left it. By the time Ilfa returned to visit the academy many years later, Rabbi Yohanan had become Head. They said to Ilfa, "Had you only sat here and studied, you would have been First and not him."

At that, Ilfa went and climbed up to the top of the mast of his ship. He yelled, "If anyone can cite a source that I am unable to reconcile with the Mishnah, I will throw myself from this mast and drown!"

Burton L. Visotzky

Just then an old man appeared and quoted a particularly abstruse citation regarding the fulfillment of an inheritance clause in a will. Ilfa immediately solved the problem in accordance with the opinion which holds, "It is a commandment to fulfill the stipulations of the dying."

Dunash, my dear friend, I look forward to hearing from you—for like Ilfa you have become a great success in business, while I remain poor but accomplished in Torah. I know that you are scrupulous to fulfill the stipulations of all contracts which you undertake. Please undertake to write your friend Nissim, who longs to hear from you and receive your forgiveness in this season of atonement.

To Nissim in Kairawan, from al-Iskander ben Dunash al-Tustari in Fustat, late summer, 1032

To Rabbenu Nissim, Second and Father of the Court of the Rabbis of Kairawan, may his light shine throughout the Maghreb and all the Diaspora.

From me, al-Iskander, only son and apprentice scribe of Dunash HaCohen al-Tustari, in Fustat, in the name of the Merciful.

Honored Rabbenu Nissim, forgive my handwriting and my forwardness at replying to you instead of my father, may God preserve him for good, Dunash HaCohen al-Tustari. I have received your many letters to my father regarding his business and especially those letters which tell the stories of consolation after our troubles with my sister Karimah. All of us in the household—I know I speak for everyone because it is I who read to them your stories—all of us in the household have found much relief from your tales.

You may know that the leaders of our Karaite congregation here in Fustat are great men who have mastered Torah and God's law. They have instructed us in the ways of proper mourning and in the rituals which are authentic to Jews since the time of the Torah and Moses our master. They have written great histories such as al-Kirkisani's *Book of Lights*. They have appealed on behalf of Zion, as did our teacher Daniel al-Qumisi. They have even engaged in debate with your teacher of the Fayyum, Rabbi Saadya; for that is what our teacher Salmon ben Yeruham did in his *Book of the Wars of the Lord*. But I must admit that none of our teachers has given the gift of consolation that you have, rabbi. Your mastery of lore unites the Jewish people even when we may differ regarding the law.

I hope I do not offend you by presenting the works of our Karaite masters, for we are faithful to our community of Scripture. But even so, we all, and here I mean even those outside of my household with whom I have shared your works, we all love to read your stories. So allow me to thank you and to say that you are a great teacher of Torah. I hope you do not take offense that one as young as I may take such pleasure from your subtle works which are, perhaps, beyond my meager comprehension. Also please forgive me if I have not used the proper form of address for you, master, for I am not familiar with the customs or titles of the rabbanite community.

I am writing to you because in your letters, particularly the last one in which you have written of Rabbi Yohanan, you ask that my father write to you. You will see that he has not. So I have undertaken to write on his behalf, forgive my broken Arabic and my faulty Hebrew, I write to beg forgiveness that he has not responded for I know that he would have happily responded were he here in Fustat. God forbid that he could be upset with you or with anything that you have said or written to him, which is not the cause for his silence.

My father, may God keep him safe from harm and sorrow, my father has sailed off on a business voyage. The trip itself was meant to be short; otherwise I am sure he would have informed you of his impending absence. He left in the days between Passover and Pentecost shortly after the shipping lanes had opened. He took a barge down the Nile to Damietta and from there filled a large ship for trade with the Rum. It was his intention to head north across the Great Sea to Antalya, but if the winds favored the shore, he hoped to stop in the Holy Land.

The timing was such that he might have even been there for the Pentecost holiday of First Fruits. I know he carried with him funds for our teacher Yusuf al-Basir, for he wished to support him in his disagreement with the other masters of our community regarding the proper lineage for permitted marriages. I have overheard much discussion on this topic which I do not understand—but I am old enough to know when my elders disagree with one another.

Dear Rabbi Nissim ibn Yakov, do not worry. My father, may God bless him and guard over him, my father should return to us any day. I know that he will rejoice at the letters here in my hand from you. I pray he will approve of this letter I am sending you. I am keeping a copy here so he will know everything I have written to you.

My father was supposed to have returned home by the start of the month of Av. He is only one month late. I tell you what I tell the rest of the household: do not worry, God will protect him and watch over him. My father planned to take fabric from the Rum at Antalya, even though he hates to run the risk of ruining it with the salt waters. So it would take time for him to sell the goods he brought from here and then fill a boat there to return here. God willing he shall return to us soon and no mishap has befallen him.

Mother worries about the pirates of the Rum. There have been reports of fighting near Syrakusa in Sikilia between Muslim pirates and ships of the Rum there. God willing, father will be home with us very soon, by the New Year at the latest, please God. Then he will write to you his own good wishes for the New Year. In the meanwhile, Rabbenu, please accept my wishes on behalf of our household.

"Do not be afraid of sudden fright or the disaster which befalls the evil ones. For God shall be your assurance and guard your feet from the trap." From al-Iskander ibn Dunash, may God guard his going out and his return home, in Misr. To Rabbenu Nissim, Father of the Court, Master of the Maghreb, Second in Kairawan, may his light shine forth with the help of God, may He be praised.

Chapter Six
Fall, 1032

Dear Skandi, it has been a year, I think, since I have seen your sweet face or heard your voice—you must have grown so much. I am pretty sure the New Year and Yom Kippur are past and maybe even Sukkot. It is so hard to tell because the only caravans we have contact with are the Hajj caravans coming up from the Hijaz on the Damascus route. There are almost never any Jews on those caravans and so I have no idea what the Jewish date is. I am not even very sure of what the Muslim date is either.

Abu Sin has trained me to ride with his band. I am no longer sore and can ride a horse without a saddle now. Since I dress in the clothing of the Badawi, I can run to the horse and leap on to it. By squeezing our legs or kicking, the horse knows how fast to go. I can ride at full gallop without fear. Like all things which must be learned and are difficult, mastering the horse was a matter of practice and the willingness to fall.

Abu Sin is an excellent teacher. Just like he taught me the art of the sword, he has taught me mastery of horses. I can ride and swing the sword. I can ride and throw a lance. I can ride and shoot an arrow from a bow, but the truth is the arrow does not fly hard or straight when I shoot from horseback. O brother, the real truth is that the arrow never really flies hard or straight when I shoot it. I suppose this is all for the best, because I also cannot comfortably wear the bow around my neck as the others do—my woman's body gets in the way and it does not do me good to reveal it to an enemy.

We ride out against the caravans. Most often, they are expecting harassment and are prepared to pay for our protection while they are in our territory. This payment is good, even generous. But there are those caravans, oddly enough usually small ones, which feel they do not have to pay for security. Once we have visited them they understand the wisdom of having safety. Sometimes, we take their gold and jewels. Some we take the remainder of their possessions. Once a small caravan master insulted Abu Sin and lost his life. I was not there when it happened. I am glad I did not have to see it or to know who of our men actually wielded the sword which ate a life.

The best attack I witnessed was when the caravan defied Abu Sin and we took their possessions and their clothing. Abu Sin said that it was an affront to Allah that we leave them naked, so we let them keep their turbans. They rode off naked, but with turbans on their heads. We laughed and laughed. They were not very happy, but another of our men reminded them that they should thank Allah for their lives. I am not allowed to speak on these raids because then it will be clear from my voice that I am a woman. I do not wish anyone to know this because it would be an invitation for trouble.

We camp near the tomb of Haroun, who you know as Aaron ben Amram, brother of Moses, and father of our family's tribe of Cohanim. I felt like I was visiting the grave of a long lost relative. It was very exciting to see the tomb for the first time, because we came to it from the east. In order to get to the tomb we had to pass through a canyon with high walls on either side. It is precisely the kind of place we have been taught to fear, for we could easily be trapped since there is only one entrance and one exit. I constantly remember the waters which overtook us in the Sinai and keep my ears like a funnel, listening for any sound of water. There are very old channels which drain this passage. It is quite long, probably a thousand footfalls of the horse in length.

The walls are so high that even at mid-day there is only shadow. It is always cool and there is a breeze. On the very hot days of summer we often went to the passage to find relief. What is amazing about this passage is when you come to the end, the stone changes from tan and beige to a bright reddish-pink. As you come out of the gorge into the sun, there before you is a rock face, brilliantly lit, shining like a red pearl. The rock is carved with columns, like those the Romans left. The columns hold up statues and more columns, so that it is as though you are looking at a two-story structure. But it is not a building at all, but a carving into the rock face.

The Arabs among us call this the treasury. Riding past the treasury you can see many, many carvings in the rocks. It is as though there was once an entire city there. There are tombs and arches, more buildings, even statues carved into the red, red rock. The patterns on the rock are fabulous. There is a group of Badawi here called al-Bdoul. They help us by gathering food and water. The tomb of Aaron is upon the highest of the peaks which surround Raqim, for that is the name of this city. There are other statues there which Abu Sin says are of idols that the Badawi worshipped before the Prophet, peace be upon him, taught them the Quran and made them submit to the oneness of Allah.

Abu Sin says that among the caravans there are people he knows and can trust. He will rely on such people to deliver this letter without revealing the place of our encampment. We have left Raqim, so my describing it will not put us at risk.

Since then we came upon a city which was even more fantastic which I will try to describe to you.

Much as the stone and rock of Raqim was pink and red, the stone of this city was black, jet black. The very walls of the city were of smooth black stone. The gates of the city were black as well. Indeed, brother, the entire city was made of this black stone. Further, the very folk of this town had been formed of black stone—but that is not an accurate description. For surely they were once flesh and blood, as are you and I. But somehow they brought the wrath of Allah upon them. Every inhabitant of that city was turned into the same black stone. Perhaps the city itself was once like other cities, but now all had been turned to black stone.

But even so I do not describe it properly, for although the walls and floors and the people of the city were of stone, surely the remains of the city were not. There were goods left in the streets, at the bazaars, in the houses, and all of these were as natural as those you would find in the market of Fustat. We collected silver and gold, beautiful garments with costly embroidery, swords and scabbards encrusted with precious gems. We made our way to the palace and there was the king of that city, surrounded by his Wazir and Emirs—all of them black stone. We took their rings and robes. We even removed the tapestries and the bedding from the harem.

Within the harem we found the queen arrayed upon her divan, wearing a golden diadem, pearls and gems. She and her handmaids were also black stone. We took these jewels and despoiled that city, carrying as much away as our horses could hold. As we were leaving, Abu Sin and I heard a sound like chanting coming from somewhere within the palace. Abu Sin had his men ride on out of the city to protect the spoils, while we went to investigate. We each drew our swords and followed the sound to a small room. When we opened the door, there was a young man, about my age. He was dressed like a Muslim and was flesh and blood, most definitely not black stone. We listened to his chanting, for he had not ceased, even when we came upon him with swords unsheathed. He was reading from the Quran.

We asked him to tell us of the marvels we beheld. He stopped chanting then and told us that the city and all its inhabitants had been fire worshippers. Once, the young man, who was the prince, traveled on a caravan to trade. On that trip he learned of the apostle of God and submitted to Islam. When he returned to the city he beseeched his father and mother to convert the city to the worship of Allah and away from the false idol of the fire. But they refused and Allah sent his wrath upon them turning the city into black stone.

We were amazed, but our eyes beheld the very punishment of which he spoke. We asked him if we could help him. He said he wished naught but to perform the Hajj. Abu Sin gently took the boy and led him into the light. We took him to our camp and fed him for a week or so. For most of that time, he chanted the Quran. I think it was good for the men to hear the words of Allah. When the next caravan came from Damascus towards Mecca, we did not attack it, but instead approached it. We bought that lad a place on the caravan with some of the booty from his city. We all wish him well, he was so innocent.

Dear al-Iskander, I shall write again soon. We have much time between our raids and I use that time to think of home. I miss you especially, and Mommy and Nanny. I am still angry at Daddy, not because I still think him wrong about Ismail, but because he was so mean to me about it. I have not decided yet whether I shall forgive him. As for Ismail: I have forgiven him. And now that I ride with Abu Sin, I also have for the most part forgotten him.

I wish you could see me on horseback, little brother. And I wish I could see you. I wish you a sweet year my brother al-Iskander ben Dunash HaCohen al-Tustari, may God lift His face to you and be gracious to you.

From your sister Karimah, in the land of Moab.

From Nissim in Kairawan
to al-Iskander son of Dunash in Fustat, Fall 1032

To al-Iskander ibn Dunash HaCohen, may his light shine brightly, al-Tustari, in Misr, with wishes for a happy and healthy New Year free of worry or concern.

My dear al-Iskander, how very thoughtful and proper of you to write to me in your father's absence. I very much appreciate your efforts—they were quite mature for a young man your age. Your Arabic and Hebrew grammar and syntax were just fine, but your dependent clauses were too many. Your hand, while inexperienced, was quite readable. I hope you will save this letter for your father so he may read my praises and be doubly proud of you, as I know he will be proud when he reads the letter you undertook to write on his behalf.

I am asking you now to be sure that this letter or an exact copy of it also be read or otherwise transmitted to your father's cousin, your uncle Sahl Abu Saad al-Tustari of the Caliph's court. Abu Saad should know that 1,536 Kutama garments for the Caliph's Berbers are being sent by fast caravan. They are carefully wrapped in leather bundles and placed in wooden chests so that they will need a minimum of pressing upon their arrival. Each bundle holds two dozen garments. There are four bundles per crate. Each camel has two crates, so I employed eight camels to carry the garments to al-Kahira.

I pray that Sahl Abu Saad knows of all the details of the agreement with your father and can forward the garments, if they meet his approval, to the Wazir of the court. I also put my faith in Abu Saad to transfer the remainder of the payment to the families of the academy here in Kairawan either in my care or through one of his bankers in Kairawan.

Remember al-Iskander, not only your father and I, but the students and their families of Kairawan are counting on you to exercise your responsibilities as an adult. Your letter to me gives me faith in your capabilities. I am sending you copies of this letter by both land and by boat, for the matter is important. I have also sent copies to the Tustaris of al-Kahira via the Taherti family's private mail service here in Kairawan.

Young al-Iskander, I would not worry about your father. He is an experienced traveler on the sea and has accompanied many of his shipping ventures for much longer periods. He does not relegate these large consignments to his Muslim partners. Before you were born he often took to the sea. It was only when Karimah, may her memory be for a blessing, was born that he heeded your mother and traveled less. So tell your mother not to fear, for she too came to Fustat once by boat. And you, young man, put your faith in God, that the Almighty will bring your father home safely—if not before the New Year—for time is short —then by Yom Kippur. And if not by the Great Fast Day, then by Sukkot, God willing.

In the meanwhile, I will seek to allay your fears much as I have tried to relieve your father's sorrow about your sister's departure from this world, now almost an entire year ago, peace be upon her.

Do not our sages tell us that there was once an old man with two children, one who did great works of charity while the other did naught? The one who gave much charity sold his entire household and its contents that he might give more to others. One time it was the end of the holiday of Sukkot, on the feast of Hoshanna Rabba, and his wife gave him ten dirhems that he might go buy something in the bazaar for his children to eat. As he was coming towards the market he met the charity collectors. They said, "Here is the champion of charity coming our way!" They asked him to contribute for the purchase of a cloak for an orphan. He gave them the dirhems he had in his hand.

Then he was ashamed to come home empty handed to his wife. What did he do? He went to the synagogue where he saw the used citrons that the small children parade around with on Hoshanna Rabba. He stuffed them into his cloak and fled to the port and took passage on a sea voyage until he came to a great port city.

There, the Caliph was stricken with a stomach ailment. His physician told him that his cure was to drink the juice of citrons picked the week before—and that the citrons which the Jewish children carried on the festival of Hoshanna Rabba

Burton L. Visotzky

were particularly efficacious. Of course, his courtiers could not find any such thing in his city, for there were very few Jews there.

They went to the port and found that poor Jew. Since his cloak was stuffed they suspected him of theft. Yet when they searched him they found old citrons. "Where did you get these?" they asked him. He confessed, "I took them from the floor of the synagogue in my town after the children discarded them." They brought the citrons to the Caliph, who drank of the juice and was healed. He gave that poor man gold equal to the weight of the citrons. He supported his wife and children and his aged father for many years after that in great luxury.

Elsewhere, we are told that the great sage Rabbah bar Bar Hannah said, "Once I was traveling on a ship and we lowered anchor near a small island of sand and reeds. We stepped out on that island for relief from the rolling of our ship and from the waves. Yet when we went to light a fire to cook our meal there, it turned out that the island was actually the back of an enormous fish. That fish felt the flames and rolled over in the water, capsizing all of us. Were our boat not anchored nearby, we would have perished."

Rav Safra said that once he was traveling on a ship and a fish raised its head out of the sea. It was so huge, it blotted out the sky. And that fish said, "I am a lesser creature of the sea, only three hundred miles long. Today it is my turn to be swallowed whole by the Leviathan."

This reminds me of the midrash about the prophet Jonah, who when he was swallowed by the large fish was told, "I will show you the depths of the ocean and all therein. But know you, that today it is my turn to be eaten by Leviathan."

Jonah said to his fish, "Bring me to Leviathan." Now the fish had transparent eyes, as large as the windows of the great synagogue of Alexandria, and Jonah saw all the marvels of the deep.

When he came to the Leviathan he said, "O Leviathan, I have come to see your abode, for in the world to come, I shall put a hook in your tongue and haul you onto land so that you may serve as the meal at the banquet for the righteous in the Garden of Eden!"

At that, the Leviathan opened his mighty maw to swallow them whole. But Jonah showed the Leviathan the sign of Abraham our father. "Behold the covenant!" he proclaimed. At that the Leviathan turned and fled.

Al-Iskander, since you have written to me that my stories bring you pleasure, let me close this epistle with one more tale, from our own time. Although it too involves pirates and taking captives on the sea, you will see that it has an end that benefited all the Jews, from Spain to the very Holy Land itself. Once it happened that the Caliph of Spain sent his naval commander to harass and capture ships of the Rum in the Great Sea. They sailed as far as the coast of the Holy Land and to the Islands of the Greek Sea. There they encountered a ship from the town of Bari, in Italy, which had upon it four great rabbinical sages from the Rum who were traveling to meet with the rabbis of Iraq.

This naval commander captured the boat and sold off his captives at various ports. These great sages of Torah kept their identities secret from him, lest he ask a higher price for their redemption. They were so successful at keeping their identities secret that to this very day we only know the names of three of the four of these rabbis. The first was sold at Cordoba, he was Rabbenu Moshe. The second was sold on the coast of Afrikiya, and he made his way to our city of Kairawan. He was my teacher, may he rest in Eden, Rabbenu Hushiel, father of my colleague and the Head here in Kairawan, Rabbenu Hananel. Finally, the last Rabbi was sold in Alexandria of Misr, and he made his way to your city of Fustat. He was your great teacher Rabbenu Shemariah ben Rabbenu Elhanan. So you see al-Iskander that God protects and supports his beloved even if it seems there is cause for fear. So do not fear nor worry; God will care for your father and your family; for surely your father is among God's beloved.

Be sure to read my letter regarding the garments to your uncle Sahl, Abu Saad al-Tustari. Send him my wishes for a prosperous New Year, along with my felicitations to your household.

From Nissim in Kairawan
to al-Iskander son of Dunash in Fustat, Fall 1032

To al-Iskander ben Dunash al-Tustari, I add this sheet to my previous epistle. I recall now that you mention the names of many of your revered Karaite elders in your letter to me. My dear boy, it is right and proper that you should respect your elders and your teachers. But you should know that your al-Kirkisani and Salmon ben Yeruham argue against the rabbinic masters of the earlier generations.

I will send you under separate cover a copy of the letter which the late revered Rav Sherira Gaon of Pumbedita, in Baghdad, sent to my own late father, peace be upon him. In that letter Rabbenu Sherira, may he rest in Eden, answers my father's question regarding the composition of the Mishnah, and in so answering he delineates the entire chain of rabbinic tradition from its beginnings at the time of Moses and the Bible until our very day. That is a history worth reading, and I hope you shall profit by it.

You said you were not sure of the meaning of the various titles which Rabbenu Sherira Gaon explicates. What does it mean to be called sage or rabbi or Rabbenu or Rabban? Allow me to explain to you briefly, son. My summary shall have to suffice until you read Rav Sherira Gaon's epistle:

Those who came first had no title, so Isaiah, Ezekiel, and even up to Haggai, Zechariah and Malachi are simply called by their names. Even Hillel and Shammai are called by name only, and not by title.

We call Moses by the name Moshe Rabbenu to give glory to the title Rabbenu, our master. We do not so give glory to Moses, for he who saw God face to face needs no further glory. Besides, if we wished the title to glorify Moses, we would say Rabbenu Moshe and not the other way.

The title Rabbenu is used by the Jewish community for the leaders of the courts and the academy. We use the title Rabban to indicate the patriarch of the land of Israel in Talmudic times, such as Rabban Gamaliel or Rabban Shimeon. These great men can trace their lineage back to King David, peace be upon him.

Everyone called Rav is from Babylonia and everyone called Rabbi is from the Land of Israel. Just as one honors a father, so too, one honors a teacher. You, dear boy al-Iskander, bring honor to your father Dunash, may God cause his light to shine ever brighter, and to your teachers of the community of Scripture. May students like you flourish among the Jews.

Do not forget the letter to Sahl Abu Saad al-Tustari.

From Karimah
to al-Iskander, Fall 1032

Dear Brother, I must tell you of our recent adventures and of a place we beheld upon a small mountain. Do you remember at the end of the Torah when God tells Moses that he is to die and sends him up a mountain? Al-Iskander, I have walked upon Mount Nebo in the land of Moab! It is some distance from the tomb of Aaron, much to the north.

Upon the mountain are old buildings. I think they once were churches. There are pictures and words on the floors which are made from small tiles. Abu Sin says these tiles are called mosaics. There is Greek writing in the mosaics on the floors, but of course I cannot decipher it. At least I know now that the language is Greek. There is one beautiful hunting scene. The men wear odd caps upon their heads. Some hold animals by reins and among the animals are camels, striped horses, and a large bird called an ostrich. I have actually seen such birds running wild in the wilderness here, they look as though you could ride them like they were horses. There are also pictures of lions and oxen and ducks. There is one mosaic of men fishing on what looked to me to be the River Nile.

Some of the people in the mosaic pictures have little circles behind their heads. In many of the pictures are the fruits which can be found here in abundance. There are also grapes in the pictures, but we have not seen any here in the wilderness. I would guess that these are the fruits of the Holy Land mentioned in the Bible. From atop the mountain looking west you can actually see the Land of Israel. I was actually teary eyed when I realized what my eyes beheld. There before me was the River Jordan and the land promised to our ancestors. Is it really possible that I stood in the spot that Moses had?

As I write this I realize how closely God has guided me along Moses' own path. For I have left the land of Egypt, gone through the Sinai, and stood upon that mountain. And I have come to the land of Moab, been to the place where Aaron died and now have visited the place where Moses breathed his last. O al-Iskander, what does this year's journey mean? I did not think I was fleeing home or my ancestors when I left with Ismail. I have spent a year away from our customs and observances. I do not know when it is the Sabbath, I certainly have eaten unclean foods, and I do not even know when Yom Kippur fell this year. But I do know it has likely fallen. So I ask your forgiveness, brother, as we are supposed to do at this time of year. I have deprived you of the guidance that only a big sister can give. I have missed laughing with you.

I have learned so much and there is yet more for me to learn. I must continue my journey and see now where God leads me. Perhaps I shall be more fortunate than Moses and someday come into the Holy Land. I would love to see Jerusalem and sit at the feet of our Karaite elders there. To do so, I first would have to make a great atonement and mighty repentance. But not yet. There is too much life to live here under the stars, riding with Abu Sin.

Near Mount Nebo there is a much smaller mountain where there is a grave site of the Shaykh Hatim of the Tayy Badawi. On either side of the grave there are columns, and each column has carved upon it the image of a woman. Each woman has her hair disheveled and appears to be weeping. No doubt, these columns were meant as a memorial to Hatim of Tayy. But the Badawi of these parts swear that if you camp on the mount at night, you can hear the women wailing.

Of course, all the men of Abu Sin scoffed at this legend. We made our camp not upon the mount, but not too far from it. Sure enough that very night we were awakened by the sound of weeping and wailing. Abu Sin explained that the rock on the tomb was carved in such a way that the wind would whistle through it and make that sound. We all went back to sleep. But we were awakened just before dawn by the shouting of one of our stoutest men. He was frantically running around our camp, looking for his camel.

We found the camel some ways off, on its knees with blood pouring from its throat. The man was distraught, but slit the remainder of the animal's throat and put it from its misery. That morning we feasted on camel flesh while he told us his story.

The night before he had a dream in which Hatim al-Tayy came to him and said, "Do you dare visit my shrine and bring me no offering? I shall take your camel as my gift." Then, in the dream, Hatim al-Tayy took his *jambiyya* and slit the camel's throat. It was this that woke our man and set him looking for his camel.

We suspected the camel driver of some chicanery, but were hard pressed to believe that any Bedu would slay his own camel unless he had to. As we were murmuring about it over the last of our unexpected breakfast feast, a strange man leading a she-camel came upon our camp. He said to us, "I am Adi ibn Hatim al-Tayy, and my father has sent me with this camel, begging your forgiveness. For he was angered by your presence last night; but it does not behoove him to take as a gift that which was not willingly offered. Please take this camel in exchange for the one which he slew."

Of course we were astounded, for we sat at the foot of the mount upon which Hatim al-Tayy was buried. We asked his son how his father had communicated his desires. Adi ibn Hatim explained that his father had come to him in a dream and said that Tayy hospitality demanded that he should be offering a camel to these strangers rather than taking one from them. We all marveled at the hospitality of Hatim al-Tayy, whether alive or dead. His son Adi now rides with us.

Brother, I hope to write more to you soon, there is so very much to tell and your willing ear is so very far away. I wish that you now were riding with us too.

To al-Iskander ben Dunash, from his sister who has seen the Promised Land.

From Sahl Abu Saad al-Tustari in al-Kahira to Nissim in Kairawan, Fall 1032

To the distinguished rabbi, light of the exile, leader of the academy in Kairawan and master of the Maghreb, Rabbenu Nissim, peace be upon you, and may God bring you an abundance of blessings. I was deeply honored to receive an epistle from you, esteemed rabbi, and especially so as it was transmitted to me by my dear younger cousin, the boy al-Iskander ibn Dunash. His father is a cousin to me and dear to me as my own brother, Abu Nasr; so I am honored to look after his business in his absence, especially as it concerns the doings of the Caliphal court in which I have an interest, praise be to God.

I have received the 1,536 Kutama garments, which I have examined, found adequate, and forwarded 1,508 of them in the name of Dunash to the bursar of the Berbers in the court of the Caliph, may his reign shine bright upon Fustat and all of Afrikiya. Payment has already come to the house of al-Tustari and will be forwarded to you and the households of the Kairawan academy via the Taherti family there in due time.

I am also sending you a new consignment on behalf of Dunash and the al-Tustari interests. This time we are sending, by caravan, marked for you, care of the Souk al-Yahud, 79 bolts of linen. We have examined the workmanship of the garments you sent here and determined that your seamstresses should be able to cut 19 garments per bolt, one more than you did in the last batch, thus increasing the yield per bolt, decreasing waste, and producing higher profits for you and for us. We would like the 1,500 new garments by your Hannukah. Send them by fast caravan if need be, as you did with the last batch. The terms of the last consignment remain in force for this batch as well, but you will pay for the caravan charges and any spoilage.

Please note that in appreciation for the stories you have sent to my cousin Dunash for circulation among us here, I am depositing with the Tahertis in Kairawan a gift to your academy of 54 dinars. This amount is the rent revenues from certain properties we hold in Kairawan, and so we wish to donate the proceeds back to the community from whence it came. The Tahertis will determine with you how the moneys should be spent. If we are satisfied with their report, we will consider the possibility of making this an annual donation.

Abu Saad al-Tustari, advisor to the Caliphal court in al-Kahira. To Rabbenu Nissim, Father of the Court in Kairawan, with the help of the Almighty, may His name be praised. Via the mail service of the Commander of the Faithful.

From Nissim in Kairawan
to Sahl, Abu Saad al-Tustari in al-Kahira
with a copy to al-Iskander in Fustat, Fall, 1032

To Abu Saad, Sahl al-Tustari, advisor to the Caliph and to the Wazir in al-Kahira, may God keep you and protect you and the kingdom.

And copy to al-Iskander ibn Dunash HaCohen al-Tustari in Fustat, Misr, by caravan.

To the great leader of the al-Tustari family, may God protect you and expand your influence, and to the young scion of the family, may God raise you to the good deeds of your illustrious forbears.

I am delighted to report to you, Sahl Abu Saad, and to your cousin Dunash, through his son, al-Iskander, may his light shine forth, that I am in receipt of three precious gifts which you have sent to me and to the community of the Jews in Kairawan. Did not the Almighty Himself give three precious gifts to the world, when He created it with wisdom, discernment, and understanding, as it is written in the Book of Proverbs, "In wisdom God established the earth, He created the heavens with discernment, and with His understanding divided the depths." And with these three gifts God built the Tabernacle in the wilderness, and the Temple in Jerusalem. And with God's wisdom, discernment, and understanding, may it be rebuilt in the future. And may these three precious gifts bring the king messiah, of whom it is written in Isaiah, that "the spirit of the Lord shall rest upon him, and it shall be the spirit of wisdom, discernment and understanding."

Abu Saad al-Tustari, it was with wisdom, discernment, and understanding that you bestowed upon us here in Kairawan three precious gifts immediately following the end of the Sukkot festival. On that holiday we prayed to God for rain, and you poured forth gifts upon us. We received the generous profits from the first batch of Kutama garments. And we received with joy your very generous donation of 54 dinars. Finally, we received the shipment of the seventy-nine bolts of linen and a new order for garments. No doubt, we, too, will be required to use our wisdom, discernment, and understanding in the sewing of the garments, for there is virtually no margin for error and the women who will sew these are still so very young. We put our faith in the Lord.

I infer from your letter that our friend and benefactor Dunash has not yet returned to Fustat from his business travels. I urge you who also read this, al-Iskander, not to fear, for your father is experienced in the ways of the sea. Indeed, I myself am stopping my prayers that he may voyage home to you speedily, for the shipping lanes grow more risky at this time of the year. Our sages tell a tale which will illustrate my reluctance to pray on his behalf:

Rabbi Yonatan said, "Three great gifts God gave to the world, they were: Torah, and the heavenly luminaries, and rain."

Others add, "Peace, too, was a gift from God."

Still others say, "The Land of Israel was a gift of God."

And our sages taught, "God's mercy is a gift as well."

Rabbi Isaac bar Maryon said, "Even the ability to take passage on the sea is a gift from God, as it is written in Isaiah, 'Thus says the Lord, Who gives a path through the sea'—this refers to passage in the Sea from the feast of Pentecost up until Sukkot; 'and a route through mighty waters'—this refers to the period from Sukkot until Hannukah.

Once a merchant sailed on the sea and asked his brother, "Pray for me." But the brother said, "How shall I pray for you? Is it not said, 'when you bind your palm fronds for the holiday of Sukkot, then it is time to bind your legs to dry land, as well.' If I go up to the synagogue, all the congregation will be praying for rain for their crops. So do not depend on me to pray that no rain may fall."

Once a rabbi was in Asia Minor and wished to journey home to the Holy Land by boat, for it was just before Hannukah. A certain matron said to him, "In this season you would travel by sea?!" Then his father came to him in a dream and moaned, "Woe that my son might not have a grave!" Yet he listened to neither of them, and what they feared came to pass.

My dear Sahl Abu Saad and al-Iskander ibn Dunash, have no fear, for I have faith in God that no harm shall come to Dunash HaCohen. He knows not to risk his life, for he is responsible to his household and to his community. If he is not home soon, he, too, will winter in Asia Minor—if, indeed, he made it to Antalya. So I shall not pray that he make a safe voyage soon, but pray instead that he bind his feet on dry land.

My sincerest thanks to both of you—to you Abu Saad for your legendary generosity, for the opportunity to do business with you on behalf of my academy, and for your continued ministrations on behalf of the Jewish community within the Caliphal court.

And to you al-Iskander, for standing in your father's stead. Although you are yet a boy, as the sages say, "When there is no man present, then strive to be a man."

From Karimah in Trans-Jordan to her Nanny in Fustat, late Fall, 1032

Dear sweet Nanny, I am eager for your ears and eyes. So read this slowly to yourself when you are sure there is no other listening nearby, for as they say, the walls have ears. Something happened and I must tell you, even if you are unable to reply to me. I know I can trust you to tell you the truth and that you will love me always, even if you judge me harshly. I beg your forgiveness in advance, Nanny dear, for I did not have Yom Kippur in a synagogue this year and confession is necessary for my soul. As difficult as this may be for you to read, it is much more difficult for me to tell it. But I cannot keep this inside me anymore, for it shall consume me from within.

I expect that al-Iskander has read to you my letters of how I have been riding with the band of Abu Sin, how we raid caravans and take either protection money or booty. I think I have written how I do not speak during these skirmishes nor allow anyone to know that I am a woman. I may have even remarked that we come away with a great deal of money. The wealth of the Damascus caravans is astounding—and we have had more than our share of plunder. We take the caravans after they have traded the goods from Mecca and al-Medina in the cities of Wadi al-Qura. This means, among other things, that the caravans are well provisioned, so at the very least we eat well.

I do not even have to cook, for there is a cook—although not nearly as good as you, dear Nanny—from the nearby Badawi who serves us hot foods daily. It is almost as though we were in al-Kahira and able to go out to the street corner and order hot delicacies to bring home for our supper. For these services we pay the local Badawi, and since we also provide them protection, everybody benefits.

Our material wealth is hidden away in a series of caves. We actually have a quartermaster who separates the booty into categories. There is a cave of jewels, pearls, and gold. There is a cave of clothing—this cave is high up off the ground, cold and dry so that the clothing does not molder. You would be pleased at how tidily the clothing is kept, even in a cave. There is, of course, a cave of weapons—both our own and those that we have captured. Along with the weapons there is armor. These, too, must be kept very dry. We even have a cave of tapestries and embroidery, taken from the caravans. All of this wealth, plundered from the Muslim Hajj.

Our life is simple. We ride, we practice sword technique, we feast and drink, we sing long into the nights. When our spies inform us that it is worth our time and trouble, we swoop down upon a caravan. Abu Sin is a good leader to the men and a gentle teacher and companion for me. He knows so many things that I have come to believe they call him the Philosopher because of his wisdom.

Last week, we rode on a raid of a mid-sized caravan. There were some forty of us attacking a caravan of about fifty camels with riders and hangers on. They were Hajj, mostly unarmed, intent on getting home safely. It should have been an easy raid. They should have paid us protection money with little demurral. They should not have put up any fight at all. If they fought, it should have been an easy victory. It was none of those things.

I believe what happened is my fault, for our custom is to ride around the caravan first to intimidate them. I was riding with Adi ibn Hatim al-Tayy, to keep an eye on him because it was his first raid. I rode close to him and he called out to me. I did not answer him as it was my custom never to speak on a raid. He did not know this and thought I could not hear him. He rode up just behind me, for he was an excellent rider, and pulled at my robes. As they gathered close around my body, my horse stumbled for a moment. I feared I would go down, but then righted myself immediately. By then it was too late, for I had cried out and when the robes were tight against my body, the caravan guards saw I was a woman.

One of them rode out to attack me. Adi foolishly rode up to defend me, but was unschooled in the way of the sword. The caravan guard cut him down with one sweep of his scimitar. When I saw Adi fallen, I rode to avenge Adi's senseless death. I heard Abu Sin shouting at me and it took me a moment to hear him, for I had already engaged the man who had killed ibn Hatim. Finally, I understood that Abu Sin was shouting, "The Wadjaina, the Wadjaina!" I realized that I had not unsheathed my sword.

I ride well now, even without holding the reins, so I stuffed them beneath my thigh. I urged my horse into battle by directions from my thighs and calves. I held my Wadjaina in my left hand and my sword in my right hand. I parried a blow of the scimitar with my scabbard, and the sheath flew out of my hand. My entire left arm felt numb from the blow. Now that my left side was exposed, I wheeled my horse to face my attacker. Since he had a scimitar and I a straight sword, I had advantage of striking from a greater distance.

Nanny, I plunged my sword into that caravaneer's horse's breast. The horse dropped to its knees, freeing my sword. The man who killed Adi jumped from his mount. I swung a backhand blow at him, for he was to the left of my horse. I realized that if I turned my wrist a bit I could simply stun him with the flat of my sword. But he still had his scimitar in hand, red with Adi ibn Hatim's blood. I did not stay my hand nor turn my wrist. My blow met him clean with the blade of my sword. A line of blood sprang across his neck and shoulder and he fell to his knees.

The heat of battle was upon me and I was like a madwoman. I kept my horse turning, now holding the reins in my left hand, and galloped back to our camp. When I dismounted, I, too, fell to my knees. I vomited for what seemed to be like hours. I was fevered and delirious, wailing and hysterical.

Finally, Abu Sin and the men returned. Adi was the only casualty, and since our men drove off the caravan, we recovered his body. There was no booty, only the lost life of Adi ibn Hatim al-Tayy.

There was no need for us to have attacked that caravan. We had plenty of gold and jewels and other booty. Life was good. Yet we attacked and took young Adi with us. I feel that with the loss of Adi's life, my own life has ended, too. I am responsible for his death. Worse, Nanny, I feel I have killed Karimah bint Du-nash HaCohen al-Tustari. How can there be forgiveness for this egregious sin?

Burton L. Visotzky

Abu Sin held me and tried to comfort me. He and the men said I was brave to ride to Adi's defense and to avenge his death. Blood vengeance is the way of the Badawi. Abu Sin told me that it was also so with the Muslim tribes and even so in our own Bible. I recall something about cities of refuge, where murderers flee from the family of the one whom they killed. But where can you flee if the avenger is your very soul? I cannot sleep at night, for when I do I see that blood upon the caravaneer's neck. I awake weeping and nauseous every morning. I cannot keep food down until mid-day and yet I do not grow thin.

Dear Nanny, I feel as though some evil spirit inhabits my belly. My mind whirls and my body rebels. I cannot stay with Abu Sin any longer. I am dangerous to the group and dangerous to myself. If my head could only clear, I could think what to do.

O Nanny, can you forgive your Karimah? May God forgive me, too. I will write when I know what I am to do, and when Abu Sin can no longer read my mail. Destroy this letter, it is from a Karimah you should not know. I want no one in the family to read of my horror. Is it any wonder that Father considers me dead?

Chapter Seven
Fall, 1032

From Dunash in Constantinople,
to his son and wife in Fustat, mid-Fall, 1032

To al-Iskander ibn Dunash, light of my eyes and offspring of my loins, who grows to manhood quickly in my absence. And to my household, the wife of my youth, with whom I hope to grow old in years, in Fustat, with the help of God Almighty.

From Dunash, in Constantinople, in the name of the Merciful.

Blessed be the Lord who resurrects the dead. The Lord is just in all His ways. Find comfort, true comfort, my folk. To my son al-Iskander, to be read aloud, every word, to my household. My son, do not despair nor be ashamed, but read what your father writes to the household at this troubled time and understand what it means to be a man.

It had been my intention to take a barge down to Damietta and outfit a boat for a sea voyage in hopes of trading with the Rum at Antalya. Instead, upon leaving Damietta we were overtaken by a storm which pushed us away from the shore route and out to the high sea where we remained for days, giving up hope of survival. The winds were such that the masts of the ship broke and we were without sails. The oars were useless and the rudder for naught. The waves flowed freely into the ship and the bales became waterlogged. We had to throw a great deal of the cargo overboard. Many passengers were lost to the storm.

The winds drove us to Caesarea in Palestine. I had little but soaked bundles and the clothes on my back. I took refuge in the synagogue there for five days until my goods dried out. Then I set about assessing the damage and determining the best way to restore the losses. I put my trust in God. I found a ship that was to sail along the coast and boarded it with the goods that remained. We made our way up to the Greek Islands, navigating the coast and shoals with great difficulty. But with every stop our profits grew. We ascended the Aegean through the Hellespont, into the Sea of Mamara, and landed in Constantinople.

There, on the side of the city closer to the lands of Ashkenaz, I traded goods in the Covered Bazaar. There is also an immense church there which has a dome in the middle, and many smaller domes surrounding it on the lower portions of

Burton L. Visotzky

the building. But the central dome is a marvel, for it is very high up in the air and has no visible support. There are windows all about this dome, so it seems to float up in the air of the church. In the dome and on all the walls art works are painted onto the plaster. There are depictions of the Christians' Isa, his mother, and many of the Imams and Qadis of the church. They call this massive church by a name in Greek that sounds like Aya Sufia.

My trading in the Grand Bazaar was successful and I took a boat from the port there called the Golden Horn, which is a small tributary to the Bosphorus. We crossed the Bosphorus, an easy voyage, and landed on the other side in Little Asia. There we traded more goods. The people there were amazed to meet a Jew from Misr. They said, "We have our own Jews in Little Asia and Byzantium, but we did not know that the Muslims of Africa and Egypt still had them, too." I reassured them it was so, and we went about our business. The Bosphorus leads north to a much larger body of water called the Black Sea.

There I was able to make fabulous trades of the silks, even though they were water damaged and salt stained. The people of these regions are so barbaric as not to know the quality or cost of any goods. I traded with them my silks and linens for their furs. Upon my return to Constantinople I traded the furs for gold, but learned that these furs were not worth as much as the barbarians had told me. It just goes to show how ill educated traders in the north can be.

I confess to you that I was unable to write either from Caesarea or Constantinople from depression. I was so upset at the loss of goods, the waste of time, and the enormous effort that it would take, God willing, to break even, that I drank excessively. I could not write. I beg your forgiveness. I am certain that you worried about me, as I spent most of my time fretting about you.

Dear Wife, I know that we had quarreled far too much before my journey. We both know that part of the reason I undertook this journey was for some respite from the constant recriminations about Karimah. I have missed you every day that I am gone. I pray to be home within the month. But I also know that we parted on bad terms and I have abandoned you these many months. I worry for your health and state of mind. I feel sure, God willing, that the al-Tustaris will look after the financial state of the family in my absence. I am pleased that my trading not only recouped my earlier losses, but that I will come home with a small profit.

Wife of my youth, I pray that you will have me back as your husband upon my return. Yet I should understand if you were through with me. Therefore I have issued a writ which sets you free. The matter is in your hands. If you wish to be separate from me, accept the bill of divorce, according to the laws of the Torah and our community. But if this is not your decision and not your desire, do not lose these long months of waiting, perhaps relief is at hand. I believe that with the help of Heaven I can be home in one month's time, surely before the rabbis' Hannukah, God willing. I pray that you wait for me.

I still believe that I did the proper thing in regard to our daughter. How could I face the community when my daughter ran off with the son of my Muslim partner? There is no greater shame. She is a stubborn and rebellious child. I cannot resurrect her from the dead, even though God in His grace has resurrected me from the heart of the seas. If you have me back, and I pray to God that you will, it must be on these terms. I am your loving husband, Dunash.

Al-Iskander, my son in whom I put my faith—I know this is a difficult letter with hard truth in it. I also know that none of what I have written here is new to you, even though we have never spoken of it. Some things are best not spoken of. Yet there are times when one must speak from the heart. I have done so and now if you have read this letter to your mother, you know how things are. I pray that you encourage your mother to find it in her heart to have me back in the household when I return to Fustat, please God. I am your loving father.

From Karimah
to al-Iskander, late Fall, 1032

To al-Iskander ibn Dunash HaCohen al-Tustari...From Karimah, a pilgrim to Jerusalem, in the name of the Merciful.

My dear brother, so much has befallen me in the month or so since the last letter I wrote to you. I still have it with me; I have read it and shall continue where I left off. Reading it now, after the events have reached their end, the stories seem like fantasies. By God I wish that it were so that life was only stories. But things happen to us that we do not wish and those things change us. We make mistakes which force us to grow, not always in ways we could predict.

I am a pilgrim to Jerusalem now, a wish I have long harbored. But never did I dream that the one making the ascent would be the empty shell I find myself. I had been unwell for a month and more after the senseless death of Adi ibn Hatim. Every night I had nightmares. Every morning I was sick. My body rebelled against me in other ways. It is as though the blood that flowed on the day of Hatim's death now sought retribution by refusing to flow any longer. Abu Sin was very gentle with me during this period and often had to soothe away my evil dreams. My hair was growing thinner from the demon which possessed me.

In the end, Abu Sin had one of the Badawi women prepare a potion for me, some folk-medicine which was supposed to bring me relief. Instead, no sooner had I drunk it than the most violent cramps came upon me. I thought my insides would explode until the pains abated. This took almost an entire day. It took another two or three days after that until I was able to walk normally.

When that happened Abu Sin insisted that I ride again and return to sword practice. I was loathe to touch the sword, but Abu Sin had the men convince me that I must have my sword skills, for they could save my very life. Although by then I was determined to leave the band of Abu Sin, there was wisdom in the suggestion. When I drew my sword from the sheath, I found it had been cleaned and sharpened. It gleamed in the sunlight. One might never know that it had been bloodied. But I knew, and Abu Sin understood my feelings of guilt and revulsion. Nanny will explain.

He said to me, "Wuhshah, it is time to cease being Kamar al-Zaman and return to being the Karimah that you are." He insisted that I take my share of booty. I did not wish to take it as I knew now, by my own hand, that it was blood money. But Abu Sin said that if I were to travel, it would buy my safety. And if I arrived safely in Jerusalem, perhaps there I could make restitution for my sins. Does not the Bible say somewhere, "Charity saves from death?"

Abu Sin would not say goodbye, although the others made a feast in my honor the night before I left. It was almost like old times, feasting and drinking and singing late into the night. In the morning Abu Sin told me that if ever I was in trouble, the sword would save me. I scorned him then, but he was insistent.

"Karimah, little sister," he said, "I do not only mean that your skill with the weapon will defend you. To anyone who makes his life on the roads, it will be clear that this is a sword of the Banu Hilal. They will understand when they see it that you either rode with us or took it from us by force. No one has a Banu Hilal sword, but that they have earned it. It will protect you and serve as identification should you ever need it. I gave it to you when you saved my life. May this sword someday return the favor."

When he finished his speech, I mounted my horse and turned to ride away from my life with Abu Sin. Just before I spurred my mount, I stopped and looked down at him. I held the sword aloft and said to Abu Sin, "Some stick!" At that I galloped off, with the sound of his laughter in my ears.

I rode for two days, camping alone under the night stars. On the third morning I crossed the Jordan River. I did not even have to dismount to cross, despite the rains which have fallen. From the rains and the shortness of the days I can tell that soon it will be winter. I shall try to spend it in the Holy City among the community of Scripture there, God willing. Perhaps I will visit the rabbinic community to see them light the oil lamps for Hannukah. May my days there be an atonement for me. From your loving sister Karimah, a contrite pilgrim. To her brother al-Iskander, whom she misses and loves.

From Nissim in Kairawan
to al-Jskander and Abu Saad al-Tustari
in Fustat and al-Kahira, Winter, 1032

To Abu Saad, patron of the academies of Jerusalem and Babylonia, and philanthropist to the communities of Scripture in Jerusalem, Fustat, and all the Diaspora, Sahl al-Tustari, in the court of the Commander of the Faithful, al-Kahira.

And to al-Iskander ibn Dunash HaCohen, in Misr, with the help of God.

Dear Sahl and, if I may, to your esteemed brother Abu Nasr, as well. And to Dunash, may he return to us soon with God's support, care of his faithful son al-Iskander, and their household. I will begin with an expression of sympathy to you and to all Jews, as I am sure you have heard about the horrible massacre in Fez. Our reports here in Kairawan indicate that 6,000 Jews were killed by the rampaging Berbers there and many women were taken captive. The Lord is our Rock. Blessed be the True Judge. My heart is broken with this news of the slaughter of our brothers in the Maghreb. If members of your family were among them, my deepest condolences to you. It is most unfortunate that the Jews of Fez do not have the protection of our Caliph, whom you so ably serve.

This letter announces the shipment of one thousand four hundred and ninety seven first quality Kutama garments for the Berbers of the Caliph's court. May they never know such deeds as those of their accursed western tribesmen. In the course of the work for you, the girls who are of the households of our academy stitched speedily and efficiently with almost no margin for error. As you requested, Abu Saad, they each cut an extra garment from every bolt of cloth which you bestowed upon us. This made it difficult, for the seams of this batch of garments were much narrower than in the previous batch. As a result the girls tell me that for many of the garments they had to double stitch, but that they did so on the inner seam where it is not visible. "Your servant was careful with them, for in watching over them there is much reward. Who understands errors? Forgive me for hidden flaws. Protect your servant from evil men, let them not have power over me."

Al-Iskander, I wish you to read the following stories, first to your entire household and then to your father upon his return to you, God willing. For both he and your uncle Abu Saad are exemplars of philanthropy, giving generously to the community of Israel and loaning, as it were, to God Himself.

Our sages tell the story of the great rabbis who once went up to Daphne of Antioch to collect charity on behalf of their students. There was a man there titled Abba Yudan who had given charity with great generosity, but he had fallen on hard times having suffered some business reversals. When he heard that the sages were in town, he entered his home looking pale. His wife asked, "What is wrong that you look so ill?"

He explained to her the circumstances, "Our rabbis are here and I do not know what I can do for them."

Now his wife who was very righteous said to him, "Do we not still have one field remaining? Go now and sell half of it and give them the proceeds."

When he had done so, the sages blessed him saying, "May the Omnipresent fill your needs."

When our rabbis left he went out to plow. While he was plowing that half field God enlightened his eyes, for the ground split open before him and his ox fell into the fissure. When he went to help it out, he found there a buried treasure. He said, "My ox was injured to my benefit!"

When the sages next returned to Daphne of Antioch they asked after him, "How is that Abba Yudan doing?"

They were told, "Who can even get in to see Abba Yudan? Abba Yudan the goat trader, Abba Yudan the donkey dealer, Abba Yudan the camel merchant!"

When they came to him he said to them, "Your prayer for me bore fruit, and then even the fruit bore fruit."

They in turn told him, "Even though there were others who gave more than you, we put your name at the very top of the honor-roll of donors." Then they placed him next to them at the banquet quoting from Proverbs, "A man's gift makes a place for him, ahead of the other leaders."

Once Resh Laqish went to Bosra, where the community leader was called the Father of Deception. God forbid he was really a deceiver, but he was crafty in donating to charity. For when there was a public charity drive he refrained from giving his pledge, and this made all the others give a bit more to make up for him. When all the pledges had finally been collected, he gave a matching-grant. Resh Laqish placed him next to himself at the banquet, quoting from Proverbs, "A man's gift makes a place for him, ahead of the other leaders."

We must carefully consider what each soul needs to flourish in this world. The daily conversation of the Jews teaches us this Torah, for do not the beggars beseech us with the cry, *zikhi bi*? Now in Aramaic it means, "gain merit through me" and, indeed, we do gain merit by giving to the beggars. But when they say it over and over it sounds as though they are saying, *sikhi bi*, which means "look at me."

They cry to us, "Look at me, see me! See who I am. See who I was and what I have become." We must learn to look carefully at each person around us and see that even the poorest among us was created in the image and likeness of the One Who Spoke and Created the World. When we truly see one another it is then that we gain merit for ourselves.

Of course, Abu Saad, you are experienced in the ways of the world, and have learned to look carefully at each and every petitioner. Such is the lesson you learn early when serving in the court of the Caliph. Your discernment of people and their needs is legendary. It is because you truly see what each person desires and what they have to offer that you have risen so high in the palace. You will appreciate the following drama:

It is said that Rabbi Yohanan and his brother-in-law, Resh Laqish, went to the public baths of Caesarea. Just as they were about to enter, they were accosted by a beggar who said to them, "*zikhi bi.*"

They put him off, saying, "When we come out we will attend to you."

When they emerged from the bath house, they found him dead. They said, "Since we neglected him alive, let us at least care for him in death."

Thus they took his corpse to prepare it for a proper burial. As they washed his body they found a purse strapped around his neck. There were 500 dinars hidden inside.

They said, "Did Rabbi Abbahu not teach that we must be grateful for those beggars who deceive us? Were it not for those who pretend to beg, anytime we were to refuse a beggar we might deserve the death sentence for our refusal."

I am sure, Abu Saad, that you understand the true meaning of this story. You and your family are generous philanthropists, yet you do not give over your moneys to every demand. You know that there are those who would try to take your funds for no good cause. But you have learned to look carefully, truly see them and determine their needs. Thus do you earn merit in this world and in the world to come.

I will finish for now with one last story, one of my favorite legends in all of the works of our sages of blessed memory.

Rabbi Tarphon was a wealthy man and a colleague of Rabbi Aqiba. Once he gave Rabbi Aqiba six bars of silver. He said, "Buy with this some substantial property so that we both might be sustained by the rents and be able to study Torah free of care."

Rabbi Aqiba took the silver and distributed it among the teachers of reading, the scribes, and the teachers of Mishnah, and those who study Torah in the

Burton L. Visotzky

academy. After some time Rabbi Tarphon asked, "Did you acquire the property that I spoke of?"

Aqiba said, "Yes."

Tarphon asked, "Is it worth anything?"

Aqiba said, "Yes."

Tarphon then said, "Will you not show it to me?"

So Aqiba took him and showed him the teachers of reading, the scribes, and the teachers of Mishnah, and those who study Torah in the academy. And he showed him all of the Torah which they had stored up.

Tarphon asked, "Is there anyone who labors for free? Where is the receipt for my investment?!"

Aqiba replied, "It is with King David, who wrote in his Psalms, "He who gives freely to the poor, is he whose righteousness lasts forever."

Thus did Isaiah teach, "From among you shall be one who shall rebuild ancient ruins, you shall restore foundations laid generations ago, that you may be called 'the one who repairs the breach, who restores the paths for habitation.'"

This was written of you, Sahl Abu Saad, and of your brother, Abu Nasr, and your cousin Dunash. You rebuild the ancient ruins and restore the foundations laid generations ago, for these are the academies of the rabbis and of your community of Karaites. And you assure that there is no breach between them, but that we remain one united community thanks to your generosity. Of you and your family it surely can be said, your "righteousness lasts forever."

We pray for the safe and speedy return of our friend Dunash to the bosom of his family, may it be God's will, quickly and soon at hand. From Nissim in Kairawan.

From Karimah in Jerusalem
to her brother in Fustat, Winter 1032/33

Dear Skandi, I have arrived at the Holy City, "Jerusalem, with mountains about her, like the Lord surrounds His people." It is an incredible place al-Iskander, with people of every race and color, Jews and Muslims, and even Christians. Despite all of the tensions between the Rum and the Caliphate, there are Christian traders from Amalfi who have been given permission to trade here. They bring much needed supplies to the city from the Rum, so they are tolerated. The Muslim authorities here treat them as they treat us Jews, as Dhimmi; protected people of the Book. Although we have some rights to be in al-Quds, the Muslims do not give us the same rights to Jerusalem as they take for themselves.

Their presence looms large over the city, in the most literal sense. Just like Mecca has a Haram al-Sharif, the Muslims also have a Haram here in Jerusalem. Would you not guess, but that it is upon the mountain of Moriah, the place where Abraham bound Isaac. It was this place, brother, that King Solomon built the Temple. When it was destroyed, it was rebuilt and we Jews served God there for hundreds of years, until the Rum destroyed it many years ago.

It is for this reason that our Karaite fathers have made their homes here near the Temple Mount, where the Muslims now have their Haram al-Sharif. Of course we Jews are not able to ascend there, nor would we, for it is the spot where the Holy Temple stood and so it is forbidden for us to walk there in our unclean state. The Muslims do not let us go up to their Haram al-Sharif, for they have built two enormous mosques there and many smaller ones. The two large mosques are quite old, they go back to the days of the prophet's companions.

There is a very large dome on one mosque; it is called the Dome of the Rock. I confess, Brother, that I disguised myself as a man so that I could go up to that mount to look there. Within the dome is this enormous rock. I have heard it told that this is the rock where the Temple stood and the high priest, our ancestor of old, offered sacrifices on Yom Kippur. I have also heard it told that this is the very rock where Isaac was bound. Still others say that this rock is the very foundation stone of the universe, for it is well known that Jerusalem is the navel of the world. They say that beneath the rock lies the very abyss and that should the rock be lifted, the waters of chaos will rise up to engulf the world.

The Muslims say that Muhammad, peace be upon him, rode his horse Buraq there and from that rock they rode up into heaven. There is a place on the rock that has the handprint of the prophet. I tell you Skander, it is the same hand which I saw pressed upon that letter in the monastery at Jebel Mousa. The Muslims press their own hand onto the handprint and then kiss their hands, as though they were kissing the prophet himself. Of course I tried it, brother and do you know what? My hand smelled like the sweetest perfume for hours afterward.

That Dome of the Rock is sometimes called the Mosque of Omar, but that name makes the Shia very unhappy. Unless you want to start a fight among the Shia and the Sunni, one simply calls it the Dome. There is another mosque next to it, further along the Haram al-Sharif. This is called the al-Aqsa mosque. Some say it is as old as the Dome. Others say that the son of the Caliph who built the Dome built al-Aqsa. But it is hard to say, because it has collapsed and been rebuilt more than once. I would guess the current building is over two hundred years old. The Aqsa has a silver dome and is built to hold thousands of the faithful at Friday services—the Muslims come to pray daily, but more come to pray and hear the sermon on Friday, like we do on Shabbat.

As rich as the Muslims are in this city, the Jews are poor. Both the community of Scripture and even the synagogues of the rabbis depend entirely on contributions from outside the land. Since the Iraqi Jews got into a fight with the rabbis of Israel some years ago, the Jews here have grown ever poorer. I do not understand why our teacher Daniel al-Qumisi was so insistent that we come to live in Jerusalem. If I did not have my own private source of money, I should starve here. There is no work to be had, not teaching nor copying. On top of that, they are zealous here about the need for women to be invisible. I do not wish to become Kamar al-Zaman once more, so I do not have much to do with the Jewish community here, Karaite or rabbanite. They depend entirely on what moneys come to them from Fustat and the Maghreb.

Just after I arrived here I went to see the master, Yusuf al-Basir. Here he is known in Hebrew as Yosef HaRoeh. Although the Karaites here speak Arabic, they prefer to talk with one another in Hebrew. Talking with them is like entering the pages of a book. I think it is unnatural to speak Hebrew like that. It is one thing to read and understand it; it is another thing entirely to speak it. In any case, when I went to see master Yusuf I was sure to call him Yosef, as though we were in the Bible.

All he wanted to know was who my father was and who my husband was. I would not tell him either. I do not know if he was interested in these facts because he wished to ask for charity and could not imagine that a woman might control her own funds. Had he asked me, I would have given him money, surely more than he deserved. But he did not ask.

It is also possible that he asked about my family because he is engaged in an argument about who can marry one another within the Karaite community. It is clear that if they remain so strict about who may marry whom, soon there will be no Karaites left. In any case, people from our community are marrying rabbinic Jews. This is as true in Jerusalem as it was in Fustat. Many of the girls I know would have no qualms about marrying a rabbanite boy.

What about you, Skandi, when are you getting married? Has Daddy picked a girl for you? You are already 14, or maybe even 15, by now. It is almost time for you, little brother.

Here in the Holy Land the real center of the Jewish community is between Jerusalem and Jaffa, in the town of Ramleh. There the rabbinical academy holds its sessions and the Gaon of Jerusalem lives there. The Karaites have some followers there, too.

Let me finish this letter by telling you what happened at the end of my visit to Yosef HaRoeh. As you might know from his name, which means the Seer, our master is blind. And yet, he sees.

During my visit with him we were in a dark room. Even so, I could see his eyes, which were white and milky. He turned his head this way and that, as though better to hear me. After quizzing me about my family and my not answering him he said to me suddenly, "You will heal, Daughter."

"What makes you say that, Father?" I answered. I called him father simply because he called me daughter; it took no thought at all.

But he said, "Why do you call me 'father?' Am I your father?"

I was upset by his question and said, "Is not the one who teaches Torah a father to all whom he teaches?" I was proud of this answer, for it gave him honor while allowing me to not reveal any more.

But Yosef said, "I see you are injured, Daughter, and by your true father. I may teach you, but only the one who brought you to this world can heal you. I may bring you to the next world, but only he can help you in this world. Who, then, is your father, Daughter?"

I was upset by this and wanted to leave. I told him, "I have no father. I stand before you an orphan." Before he could say any more, I turned and left. I know I was rude, but I do not intend to go back there to be subjected to his sermons. Do you suppose that Daddy might have alerted him to what happened?

I will see if I can find copy work among the Muslims. They pay well for a good hand, and even more for illumination of manuscripts. I have not painted in a long while. I do not need the money; thank God I have lots of money safely put away. But I long to work. I am bored here and know that writing and painting will calm my anxieties.

The rabbis have finished with their Hannukah. It is rainy, dark, and cold. I will stay here for a while, maybe until Passover, maybe longer. I feel that if I am in Jerusalem, the least I can do is remain here for a pilgrimage festival and celebrate as our ancestors did. Maybe it will help soothe my soul.

I wish you could be here with me, brother. We would go exploring together, as of old. From your sister who loves you and misses our household.

From Sahl Abu Saad al-Tustari in al-Kahira to Nissim in Kairawan, Winter, 1033

Esteemed Rabbenu Nissim, I have received the garments you sent to me. This matter is really between you and Dunash, but I am able to act on his behalf. I found four hundred eighty two and one thousand acceptable garments for transmission to the court. The rest were of a condition which I could not expect even the Berbers to wear. As for those Berbers of the Far Maghreb and their reprehensible actions in Fez, please know that I am privately seeing if there is any way we can offer assistance, particularly in the matter of redeeming Jewish captives. Rest assured that whatever I can do in the Caliphal court will be done. As for our business, you will have payment of your profit transmitted through my banking house to the house of the Tahertis in Kairawan, as was done last time.

Thank you also for the stories about charity. As you realize, I and my family are frequently put upon for donations. Your stories gave me reassurance, for my refusals are not infrequent. I also appreciated your subtlety in reminding me of my offer to consider designating certain rents to your academy. Consider it done. It shall be an annual donation.

Pray for my family and for the continued strength of our Caliph al-Zahir. There is much intrigue in the court. The Berbers do battle with the Turks. The Turks seek to displace the black Africans. The mamelukes have as much power as the eunuchs. The Wazir is constantly on guard that the Emirs and local Qadis do not replace him. I seek only the welfare of our Caliph and his son, may Allah protect him. I have no ambition or any desire for this constant political infighting. You know this to be true as I eschew the same in the Jewish community. I wish only unity and service to God and the Caliph.

My brother Abu Nasr and I send you our warm greetings. In the future you may write to Dunash, who has recently returned and is regaining his feet on land with our help. Or you may write to his son, al-Iskander, who is a good boy with a bright future, please God.

Sahl al-Tustari in the court of the glorious Caliph al-Zahir, may his kingdom grow and his dynasty reign forever, Protector of the Faithful and the Dhimmi, with the help of Almighty God, praised be His name.

From Dunash in Fustat
to Nissim in Kairawan, Late Winter, 1033

To Rabbenu Nissim ibn Shaheen, Second in Kairawan, Father of the Court, God willing.

From Dunash HaCohen al-Tustari, secure in the fortress of Fustat, Misr, in the name of the Merciful.

Blessed is He Who graciously bestows His goodness on the guilty, for He has given me everything good.
"In my straits I called unto the Lord and He answered me,
You sent me to the depths, in the heart of the seas,
The waters surrounded me, Your breakers and your waves passed over me.
The depths surrounded me, seaweed wrapped around my head.

O Lord, my God, You raised me up from the grave."
Blessed is He Who resurrects the dead.

My dear friend and partner Rabbenu Nissim ben Yakov, how much time has passed since I was last able to write to you. I am grateful that you kept faith with me during the period of my unfortunate absence and that you not only wrote to my son and household to encourage them and keep them from despair, but you also kept our business afloat at a time when it was most important to me. I am glad that you took it upon yourself to write to both my darling boy al-Iskander and to my cousin Abu Saad. Both of these stout souls kept my family together. Sahl Abu Saad helped out financially and saw to it that my business interests were not unduly harmed in my absence. My son al-Iskander rose to the occasion and acted like a man. He helped with the business and encouraged my wife.

Nissim, I must be frank with you, it has not been an easy time or good year for me. I have not been myself since Karimah left us. Since her departure from our lives, not all has been well with my household, I cannot say more than that. I had hoped that my business journey would bring back the sense of adventure we used to share. It brought disaster. The ship I set forth in from Damietta was dashed by the waves and much of the cargo was lost. I had a brief time in the Holy Land and then went on to Byzantium to trade in Constantinople and the North. I did well, but knew not what I would find when I returned to my household.

I have managed to salvage the voyage. I ultimately made a small profit, but not enough to account for my long absence. My Muslim partner in the caravan trade, Bahram ibn Abdallah, preserved my share in our business, Allah bless him. Yet he, too, has his sorrows. His son returned bearded from the Hajj and will not do business with him because he partners with me. Although the Qadi here in Fustat explained that such partnerships are permitted to the faithful, Ismail ibn Bahram wishes only to copy Muslim texts. I was able to help him by having Sahl Abu Saad open a door for him without his knowledge. He is working now at the Mosque of al-Hakim in al-Kahira. It is the least I can do for my faithful partner of so many years. But I know that it hurts Abu 'Smail that his son will not take over his business.

I am blessed in that my son al-Iskander is both ready and willing to help in my business. When the day comes, he will be an able successor; I put my trust in God. Since Karimah is no more, I pin all my hopes on the boy. I mourn her loss even after all the troubles I have seen.

As for my wife, I have returned to her. I had followed the custom of the India traders and offered her a divorce document should she grow impatient awaiting my return. Thank God, day by day, she did not exercise it. Nor, however, has she destroyed it. I wish to see it torn in two, but I dare not ask her for it. She

Burton L. Visotzky

must have her desire in this matter. But I pray to God for the stability of our household in these times.

During my terrible voyage I often found solace in wine. But never, Rabbi, never even once did I console myself with a slave girl or, God forbid, a prostitute. I remained pure to my household and my family. I wish only to resume relations once again, but will not demand my rights as a husband. If you have advice, pray tell me. Forgive me for burdening you with such an inappropriate personal matter, but I cannot approach the teachers here. I am too well known and I do not wish tongues to wag. I know that I can trust you and count on your discretion, please God.

I spend long hours walking Fustat now, noticing the joys of being on solid ground for the first time. I am determined to rebuild the business without the help of Sahl Abu Saad; we already owe him in so many ways. So I walk and I think. One of the things I have been grateful to the Almighty for is my relationship with you, dear teacher. On my return your letters and stories were there to console me. Thank you, friend, for you bring relief to the heart.

Once when I walked to the south edge of the city, I found I had come to the Muslim cemetery there, which they call the City of the Dead. We certainly would never use such a name for our burial places. We call ours a resting place or a good inn; in faith that we will but rest there a short while before the resurrection in the time to come.

The Muslims have feasts at the graves of their relatives, as do the Copts. There is a constant hubbub in the City of the Dead, unlike the calm and quiet which marks our own eternal homes. I was startled to see that entire families actually live in the City of the Dead. They look to be the dregs of the poor of our city. I suppose the memorial monuments at least provide them a roof over their heads. The poor will always be with us.

As I peeked between the walls—I did not wish to be seen lest I be surrounded by beggars, nor would I enter for I am a priest and so am not allowed to be defiled by the presence of the dead—I saw that one poor family had strung a line from one grave stone to another. Their laundry was hanging out to dry on that line. Rabbenu, I know what I saw was a desecration, but it struck me as poignant that the living and the dead could have such a thin line between them.

I spend a lot of time thinking about death since the shipwreck. I know that Karimah's parting has also made me wonder what life really means. What ultimately are our values? What separates us from the gentiles? When do we give in and when should we fight? Rabbenu Nissim, I am but a businessman, a man who sews rags for the mighty. God has been good to me, blessed be His name, and I try to do right. I wish my family were whole again, as before. Forgive me, dear friend, I will write again when I am feeling better. From Dunash who has seen the City of the Dead and those who live there.

From Nissim in Kairawan
to Dunash in Fustat, late Winter or early Spring, 1033

To Dunash, "vomited unto dry land," Dunash HaCohen al-Tustari, firm in the fortress of Fustat, Misr.

Dear Dunash it is a joy to hold your letter in my hands, your words have been absent from my life for a long time. I truly missed you brother and worried for your safety. "Deliverance is the Lord's." Indeed my friend, your letter to me reminded me too much of the prophet Jonah, for was he not depressed after his fateful voyage? Did he not say, "My death is better than my life?"

Dunash friend, forgive me for being stern with you, but we have known one another a long time. You have suffered a great deal this past year. First you lost your darling daughter. Then you lost your ship and possessions. Although you are too modest to even mention it in your letters, I have little doubt but that your own life was endangered in the wreck. Now you come home after a long absence and find your household distant. It is only natural that this should depress you and make you wonder about your life.

You must not despair. God put each of us on this earth for a purpose. You have worked hard and given greatly to charity, earning much merit. That merit has stood you in good stead, for you have held fast throughout this difficult year. Remember, you are created in God's image. That means you must have faith in yourself as well. As our fathers of old have taught us, "It was a great act of love that God created humanity in God's image and likeness. It was an even greater act of love that God made it known to us that we were created in God's image and likeness."

Allow me, Dunash, to correct some misapprehensions you have. First, regarding gentile cemeteries; I do not know the way of the Karaites, but according to rabbinic law, gentile cemeteries do not impart unfitness. Only Jewish corpses can render a Cohen unfit for Temple service, so you need not fear ritual unfitness from the so-called City of the Dead, unless there are Jews buried there.

Second, you congratulate yourself on not having taken recourse with a slave girl or a prostitute. This, too, is not actually prohibited by the Torah. But common decency and custom demand that you remain pure to your wife. Do not expect me to congratulate you for resisting your evil impulse. It is what one would expect from any decent man. I am glad that you have done so, but you cannot expect merit for it.

Of course, you cannot force your wife. Yet it is taught in the Talmud that once a woman went to our Holy Rabbi and complained to him, "Rabbi, I have set for him a table and he overturned it."

And Rabbi replied to her, "My daughter, what can I do, for the Torah permits you to him," meaning that she is his wife and he her master. The Talmud says there that "it is like one who brings home meat from the butcher. If he wishes he can eat it salted, or roasted, or baked or boiled." Nevertheless, the law is eminently clear that men cannot force their wives—but if the women consent then the men determine how to have relations. Still, I adjure you Dunash to remember, it must be she who initiates.

Old friend, I recommend patience. Attend carefully to your household; she has waited a long time for your return. Listen to her and keep her confidences. When you are with her try to be of cheerful countenance, like Hillel the elder. I will write to you about him at another time.

For your own maladies, I tell you this: study Torah, for it is the cure for the entire body. We know from Scripture that it cures each part of the body: for the head, it is written, "Place a garland upon your head." For the heart, it is written, "Write them upon your heart." For your throat, it is written, "They are a necklace for your throat." For your hands, it is written, "they shall be a sign upon your hands." For all your bones, it is written, "A balm for your bones."

When God gave the Torah at Mount Sinai, the Jews who had come out of Egypt were broken from slavery. So the Blessed Holy One directed His ministering angels to heal them, that they may receive the Torah as whole human beings, in joy and love. God's Holy Spirit comes to rest upon a man not in sloth, nor in sadness, nor in levity, nor frivolous behavior, nor in meaningless gestures. The Holy Spirit rests upon a man in joy and love.

So embrace the joy in your life Dunash. It comes to you through the study of Torah. With Torah in your life you shall have joy and love. God's presence in your life shall bless your marriage once again, so that the spirit of love and joy might rest there, too. May it be God's will.

From Karimah in Jerusalem to al-Iskander in Fustat, Spring, 1033

Al-Iskander, my dear brother. I do not know if you will have already heard about the disaster. I am well, thank God, and will have left the Land of Israel by the time you receive this letter. I am making arrangements to send it to you by boat from the port of Yaffo.

I had planned to bide my time in Jerusalem in the hopes of spending a pilgrimage festival there. Since Passover was soon to come, I spent my days wandering the streets within the city. I sometimes went out, but if I did so I always carried my *jambiyya* or if it was dark, even my sword. I was not alone in going armed on the outskirts of the city.

I found many bookstalls in the bazaar—even some of Hebrew and Jewish books—which I happily bought since I was flush with dinars and dirhems. I spent many a happy day curled up with a book—sometimes a history, sometimes a sacred text, mostly poetry, and this always in Arabic. Often children gathered nearby me to listen to my reading. I tried to find a place where I could espy the Haram al-Sharif and the mosques upon it, for the sight was uplifting.

Although I would not go back to see Yosef HaRoeh, I associated with the community which has formed around him. It was reassuring to me to hear the Arabic of our Jews, and the concerns of the community of Scripture. Oddly enough, I was also drawn to seek out the Christian merchants from Amalfi, hoping to hear in their voices some echo of Mommy's accent. They did speak Arabic, but not the same Jewish dialect as we speak, nor did they sound much like our mother. They took me to see some of the old churches in the city, especially those on the Mount of Olives where their Isa died. Like Muhammad, peace be upon him, Isa apparently also went up to heaven. Only Isa did not have a horse to guide him as did the prophet, or Elijah of old, who had an entire chariot.

There were some haunting pictures on the walls of the churches there and they reminded me of the monastery at Jebel Mousa. As it happened, I was to be reminded of Mount Sinai again on Passover. Now I know that you are thinking I am confused, Skandi, between Passover and the Pentecost. But I have not been away for that long. I know that Passover marks the Exodus and Pentecost the first fruits of summer and the giving of the Torah at Sinai. But this year, Mt. Sinai came to the mountains of Jerusalem.

Preparations for Passover were interesting. The rabbinic Jews burn their leaven in bonfires throughout their quarter of the city on the morning before Passover begins. They have an evening supper where they claim to recount the Exodus from Egypt, but they do not even mention Moses. Instead they tell stories about the rabbis of olden times and try to explain that four different types of children are referred to in the Bible. The only part of their Passover feast familiar to me was when they chanted from the book of Psalms. I was happy for the holiday hospitality, even from the rabbanites.

On the day of Passover itself, when the rabbinic Jews were in their synagogues and we in our congregation of Scripture, a rumbling sound began throughout the city. It reminded me of the flood which overtook us that day at the wadi near Mount Sinai and I said so aloud. I was hushed and rebuked, for there are no wadis near Jerusalem nor any bodies of water to serve the city's needs. But the rumble persisted and soon we felt it beneath our feet.

It was an earthquake! Apparently these happen in the Holy Land from time to time. I know that al-Aqsa has been leveled by an earthquake in times past and had to be rebuilt. This earthquake seemed as if it was centered in the Jewish quarter. The very ground split open before me, as it did for Korah and his band when they challenged Moses. We did not know whether to hide within the buildings or seek safety in the streets. Someone said to stand in the doorway, but I watched an entire door frame collapse and the lintel atop it crashed to the floor.

Brother, the synagogue of the rabbinic Jews was totally destroyed in the quake. Worse—and I watched it happen with my own eyes—the outer walls of al-Aqsa simply crumbled. I do not think any of the faithful were at prayer at the time, but the mosque is now a ruin. The silver dome has vanished! The devastation is awesome. Even a part of the Western Wall came down in the quake. What have the people of Jerusalem done to deserve God's wrath? I cannot believe such a terrible event could be punishment for sin, even my sins.

Following the earthquake two things happened. The first was looting and the second, a plague. I was determined to be harmed by neither. I recovered my treasure and took as much gold as I could carry on my person. The rest of the gold, and it was much gold, brother, I took with me to Yosef HaRoeh. He knew who I was before I even spoke.

"Is it time to seek your father?" he asked me.

Again, his question upset me. But I responded, "No, but it is time to do right by my Father in Heaven." I gave his attendant the gold purses. He whispered something to Yosef, no doubt about the large amount of money I was giving him.

Before he could speak I told him, "This is to help the Jews of Jerusalem recover from the earthquake. I must leave the Holy City now, but I wish to help. I pray this gold can be of assistance. I only ask that you give to the thorns and to the roses equally."

Yosef said that he would use the money for all the Jews of Jerusalem, rabbanites and Karaites alike, as I requested. As he said, "The roses would not survive without the thorns to protect them. I shall see to it that your money helps the poor of both communities. If there are funds remaining I shall donate them for the rebuilding of the rabbis' synagogue."

I thanked him and left Jerusalem. I could not even bear to look upon it from a distance, for the city was covered with smoke. I went down to Yaffo to seek a ship to flee. The city is built around the port and is very seedy, much worse than Damietta or Alexandria. The sailors there are unsavory and I carried my *jambiyya* or sword with me out in the open, as a warning to keep people away. I had donned my Kamar al-Zaman costume once again, for it was clear that I would be better off traveling as a man than as a woman.

As I made my way to the docks to try and book a passage, I was accosted by a man with a long, straight, two-pointed sword. He said not a word, but unsheathed his sword and thrust it at me. I parried with my sheath and then drew my sword as well. He was a good fighter, sure on his feet. All the while we battled he kept saying that I was desirable. I found this disgusting and was determined not to let him subdue me in battle for fear of what he might do to me. I was clearly in men's clothing, so his desire could only have been of the most unnatural kind. I thought to myself that it is true what they say about sailors.

We were fencing all this while. I had not had such a work out with the sword in some time. It dawned on me that his mode of fighting was exactly like my own. I wondered if he, too, had been trained with the Badawi—for his sword indicated this as well. Again, he said that I was desirable, but finally I realized that he was calling me by name as Wuhshah. I had been hearing it as a compliment, but he knew who I was! I did not let down my guard as I asked, "How do you know my name?"

"Abu Sin told me to look out for you," he replied and lowered his sword. At that I sheathed my sword as well. We were both winded by then, but he smiled at me and we began to laugh. "Mustafa the sailor at your service," he introduced himself to me. "By what name do you wish to be known?"

"I am Karimah bint Dunash the Jew," I said. "I am seeking a boat away from here."

"Where do you wish to go?" he asked.

I had not thought ahead that far, so when the answer came unbidden to my mouth, I was as surprised as he, "Amalfi," I told him.

"Amalfi is held by the Rum," he replied. "Getting there is no easy matter. It may take us some time and perhaps a detour for a bit, but we shall make our way. I shall deliver you to your destination, sooner or later."

I was grateful, for now I had a way out of the Holy Land at a time when it was unsafe to be there. And, I had a destination, even though I still do not know what I shall find there. I have learned to trust these instincts, in-sh-Allah. If something tells me Amalfi, then I shall go there and see what is to be learned there.

I am posting this with a boat in the port of Yaffo that is heading to the Nile delta. I feel secure that this letter will get to you. I do not know when I will be able to send you a letter next, as I am about to embark on a sea voyage. Send my love to Mommy and tell her I am well. If she has heard about the earthquake, be sure to tell her I have written and am fine. Do not tell her I am voyaging to Amalfi, for I know she worries unduly about sea travel. I will write to you when I can, dear brother. I kiss your hands.

From your sister embarking on a journey to the heart of the seas. To her brother, al-Iskander ibn Dunash HaCohen al-Tustari, at the Sugar Factory and Sweet Shop in the Small Bazaar of Fustat, Misr, with the help of God.

Chapter Eight
Late Spring, 1033

From Karimah on the Mediterranean, to al-Jskander in Fustat, Late Spring, 1033

Little brother, your big sister is now a sailor. We rode the coast from the Land of Israel north around the basin of the Great Sea. We tried to stay close to land as our ship was small and we did not trust open waters. It was safer to ride close to shore, even with the danger of shoals. The captain of our ship was a Turk by the name of Kemal. My new friend Mustafa had told him of my skill with the sword, but all that Kemal wished to know was whether I had skill with a needle. "I am a woman," I told him, "of course I can mend straight."

At that, Kemal set me to work pushing needle through canvas to mend the lateen sails. Brother, I do not understand the differences among all the variety of the sails, but I do understand that they all share in common the need to be mended. Thus far, there is little glory to being a sailor. I sit in the belly of the ship, sometimes with the water sloshing around me, and sew. The ship itself is actually also sewn. I only pray that when we get to dry land I am not required to sew the wooden planks together. Despite my sword training, I cannot imagine that such stitchery would be good for my hands. As it is, my hands are cut up from the sewing and the sea salt.

We are using a type of chariot-boat here that is common in the Red Sea. The boat rides high on the water and so is not very good for the heart of the seas. But, if we remain close to the shore we can skirt over many of the shoals; and with oars we have great speed. I wondered why it was that this ship was stitched instead of nailed, as I have seen in ships of Misr and those from the Rum and the Maghreb. I thought that the Turkish sailors might be fearful of the holes which the iron nails put into the planks and so, preferred stitchery.

They gave their reason with solemn faces, so I do not think that they were joking with me. They explained that there are mountains which have very strong magnetism in the waters of the Red Sea, and some believe in the Great Sea, as well. The sailors told me that they had seen with their own eyes ships whose nails flew out of the boat to hew to the mountains. These ships simply broke apart in the waters; and the sea near those mountains was littered with the remains of boats that have been torn asunder. Because of these magnetic mountains, they prefer to stitch their boats' planks together and ride the waves securely.

After two weeks on the water, and take it as a sign of my regained health that I have not been sick from the rocking of the boat, we came to the city of the Rum called Antalya. It is a large city with a good harbor. It is situated on a part of Little Asia where the shoreline turns from running due west towards the south. It is secure from the currents and strong waves which are found elsewhere on the Great Sea. We skirted Antalya and sailed further south, to a small site called Phaselis. Here Mustafa and Kemal and the rest have their camp. Do not be surprised, for these men are friends of Abu Sin and so, the camp is a camp of pirates. All told, they have three fast boats, each of the other two very much like the one we took from the land of Israel.

I was recruited to their band for they were one sailor shy; they usually have 13 on a boat. Six oars are arrayed on either side and there is a captain at the rudder. All three boats work together on the raids of ships from the Rum. Now we are a gang of Muslims preying upon Christians, rather than on other Muslims who had made the Hajj. We operate with the knowledge of the Caliph, who is quite content to have us disrupt trade among the Rum. They say it is for the glory of al-Islam.

One of the men on one of the boats had drowned in a recent skirmish, so they were happy to have me round out their number, especially since I had proven my skills with a sword. I have been assured that their raids are not all that different than those of Abu Sin—they much prefer to intimidate rather than actually to do battle. Their biggest threat is burning the enemy ship, for then all goods and lives are lost. The Rum sailors would rather pay a ransom than have us throw fire at them.

I was very surprised to learn that many of the sailors cannot swim. They claim this is common. I was amazed since Daddy had taught us to swim when we yet were youngsters. Maybe growing up on the Nile made him cautious for our lives. He used to say that the Torah commanded that he teach us swimming, just as he was commanded to teach us Torah. It is true that these sailors are under no such commandment. I have offered to teach others to swim, but it is very awkward as when we swim my garments cling and they all can plainly see that I am a woman.

Yet none of them will approach me and I feel entirely safe. I do not know whether this is because Mustafa told them how good I am with the sword or whether it has been given out that I am under Abu Sin's protection. There is one other woman with our band, her name is Guziella. I very much enjoy having her company, although I do not see very much of her. Although she cooks for us and organizes our raids, she never actually goes out on the boats. She brings the number of our band to forty.

Phaselis is very primitive, but very secure. There must once have been a city here long ago. There is a broad but broken stone avenue which runs from one set of harbors to the other. Actually, there are three harbors. Two are next to each other and give out onto the sea. The third is further along, around a bend in the waters, out of sight. This hidden harbor gives us our real security; for if we are pursued we can always row fast enough to disappear into our hidden harbor. But we camp near the twin harbors. We fish here and enjoy the shallows. It is here we also swim and bathe.

There is an old stone road leading from the twin harbors to the hidden harbor. Along the road are the remains of ancient buildings with beautiful carvings of leaves and grapes on some of the stones. Some of the buildings even have parts of mosaic floors. There is a broken aqueduct at the edge of the town where our lookouts are posted at night, lest anyone try to come at us from the land.

Once or even twice in a week we ride north near Antalya. There one of the boats harasses a promising looking ship. Often that ship, which is always larger than ours and better manned, gives chase south. This is what we wish to happen. If the wind is with us we sail just out of bow shot. If need be, we pull oar. My hands are entirely callused now from the oars, the sword, and the constant sewing. We do our best to lure that ship out of sight of Antalya. If we can, we lure them all the way south to Phaselis. If not, there are inlets and rocks further north that can also serve our purpose.

As I write this to you I realize that our boats know where to meet for the ambush we set up. This must be is what Guziella does with her days. Sometimes we drop her off of the side of our boat onto a fast moving single-sailed boat called a gulet which can tack among the anchored ships. She must spy at the port of Antalya to learn which boat will be our next prey. She probably flirts with the sailors and they tell her everything she needs for us to know. Brother, I have new respect for her, for though she appears weak and womanly, she has learned to contribute as a woman, while I ape the ways of the men.

When we have lured a ship far enough south, our lead boat reverses course, so that it now confronts the ship it had first harassed and then fled from. By then we have another boat behind the enemy ship and yet a third at its side, ready to board up the rigging if need be. Most of the captains of these boats know the rules of piracy and will pay us protection money. Sometimes it is necessary to board them and threaten to take captives. If they do battle, we try not to throw fire, for then the ship and its cargo are lost to us as well. They, of course, know this, and sometimes are emboldened to resistance.

Burton L. Visotzky

Al-Iskander, I am tired, for the sun and water bleach the energy from me. I will write you again and tell you more. In-sh-Allah, I will find a way to send you these letters before too long.

From Nissim in Kairawan, to Dunash in Fustat, Late Spring, 1033

To Dunash HaCohen al-Tustari, in Misr, with the help of God. From Nissim ibn Yakov ibn Shaheen, Second in Kairawan, after the Festival of Passover and the disaster in the Holy City, in the name of the Merciful.

Dear Dunash, I pray this letter finds you and your household well, having celebrated the festival of unleavened bread with much joy. By now all in Fustat must have heard of the tragedy which befell the Holy City during Passover. It is a tragedy of unimaginable proportion, for the great synagogue of the rabbinic community there was utterly destroyed. Portions of the Western Wall—the only remnant of our Holy Temple which the ancient Romans, may their bones be ground to dust, left standing—tumbled to the ground. These giant stones damaged the buildings which abut the wall and filled the alleyway before the Wall where the pious go to wail.

I have heard tell that for a change the Karaites in Jerusalem have funds to distribute to those in need from the emergency; but we here in the Maghreb are nevertheless organizing our own fund to help the Jews of Jerusalem. It is true that this fund will be administered by the Jerusalem rabbinate, but I am certain that all Jews, rabbanite and Karaite alike, will benefit from the fund. Was it not the case that before the tragedy the rabbanite charity apparatus cared for the destitute of the Karaites, as well as for their own? I hope that I can count on you to subscribe, Dunash, even if you must give less than you have in the past. I know that you would not wish to absent yourself at this hour of need.

Indeed, it befits you to greet all people with cheerful countenance, as did our elder Hillel; who was famous for always being of good cheer and never succumbing to sadness or to anger. Know dear Dunash, that once two men even made a wager that whoever of them might lead Hillel to lose his temper would win 400 dirhems. One Friday afternoon when it was known that Hillel was bathing in preparation for Shabbat, this man went and called out to him. Hillel came from the bath, dried himself and dressed in a gown, and asked him what he wished.

"Are you Hillel?" the man asked.

"Yes," said Hillel, "how can I help you?"

"Can I ask you a question then?"

"Please," said Hillel, "ask what you wish."

"Why then are the heads of the Baghdadis long and not round?"

Now Hillel had originally come from Iraq, yet he was not insulted by this question. Instead he told that man, "My son, you have asked a difficult and important question. The answer is that the midwives of the Land of Israel are not skilled enough to tie up the heads of the infants when they are born, so they come out round, and not long like this," at which Hillel pointed to his own long head.

The man went away and Hillel resumed his bathing. Just as Hillel reentered the water, that man returned and shouted, "Is Hillel within?"

Again, Hillel dried himself and came out to greet him. He asked that man, "My son, did you perchance forget something?"

That man said, "Yes, I wanted to ask why the eyes of people from Damietta are bleary and small?"

Hillel patiently replied, "You have asked another good question. In Damietta there is sand on the shore and wind from the water. People there shut their eyes to keep the wind and sand out, and so their eyes come to appear small and bleary."

The man went away and Hillel resumed his bathing. Just as Hillel reentered the water, that man returned and shouted, "Is Hillel within?"

Again, Hillel dried himself and came out to greet him. He asked that man, "My son, did you perchance forget something again?"

The man asked Hillel another ridiculous question and then another. Finally, the man himself grew disgusted with all the coming and going, while Hillel remained perfectly calm. That man said, "Are you really Hillel the Elder who is the leader of the people Israel?"

Hillel calmly replied, "Yes."

At that the man shouted, "May there be no more like you among the Jews! You have caused me to lose a wager of 400 dirhems."

Hillel replied, "You should learn to master your disposition and put anger from your heart. Of this Solomon said, 'Remove vexation from your heart and evil from your flesh.'"

Our sages also tell the story of a certain gentile who went to Hillel and his colleague Shammai and asked, "How many Torahs do the Jews have?"

Shammai drove that man away with a builder's cubit. But when he asked Hillel he replied, "Two."

The man said, "Two?"

"Yes," said Hillel, "the written Torah and the Oral Torah."

Burton L. Visotzky

"I believe you regarding the written Torah, but I cannot believe there is such a thing as the Oral Torah," the gentile said.

"Well then," said Hillel, "let us begin with the written Torah."

"But I cannot read it," the man protested.

"I shall teach you," said Hillel and had him repeat, "Alif, Ba, Jimm, Dal."

The next day the man returned and recited the first four letters of the alphabet. But Hillel said, "No sir, but it is Dal, Jimm, Ba, Alif."

"Yesterday you said the other way," that man sputtered.

"Since you are so willing to depend upon me to read from the written Torah, now depend upon me for the Oral Torah as well."

Dunash, I know that you will understand the deeper meaning of this story and will explain to al-Iskander why this story is a favorite of the rabbanite community. It is also taught there that once a man came to Shammai and asked of him, "Will you convert me on the condition that I learn the entire Torah while standing upon one foot?"

Shammai drove that man off. Yet when he came to Hillel he asked the same, "Will you convert me on the condition that I learn the entire Torah while standing upon one foot?"

Hillel converted that man and taught him, "That which is hateful to you, do not to your fellow. This is the entire Torah. Everything else is commentary. He then told him in Aramaic, 'zil gmor,' Go now, study."

Dear Dunash, be strong and of good courage. I look forward to hearing from you soon. Please send my very best to al-Iskander. I pray that he continues to help you with your work and that his reward here be these stories which he wrote to me that he enjoys. Peace upon you and upon your household.

From al-Iskander in Fustat, to Nissim in Kairawan, Late Spring, 1033

To Rabbenu Nissim, Second and Father of the Court in Kairawan, may his Torah enlighten the entire Diaspora, God willing.

From Dunash HaCohen al-Tustari, may his light shine forth; at the hand of his son, scribe and apprentice, al-Iskander ibn Dunash, in Misr, in the name of the Merciful.

Esteemed teacher and master Nissim ibn Yakov ibn Shaheen, Second, may God bless you and keep you. May your Torah go forth from Kairawan and the word of the Lord from Afrikiya. I am writing to you on behalf of my esteemed father, Dunash, who sends you his greetings. We all have received and enjoyed your stories and letters. My father is working very hard these days to try to make up for the losses he sustained in his sea journey. We are, of course, grateful to God for his safe return. We put our trust in God that our profits will be regained and that we can return to prosperity, in-sh-Allah.

My father has enclosed 6 dinars for your appeal for the Jews of the Land of Israel. He is sending you the funds and asks that you oversee their proper distribution in the Holy Land through your trustworthy contacts there. This is his entire contribution to the disaster fund. I know you will understand that he cannot give you more at this time. But my father has asked—for although he will not ask on his own behalf, he will ask on behalf of others—he has asked the al-Tustari uncles, Sahl Abu Saad and Abu Nasr, and they are sending to you 66 2/3 dinars—the sum of two ransomed captives—for your efforts on behalf of Jerusalem. I, al-Iskander, add my own contribution of 27 dirhems. It is all that I have saved. But if you say it will go to the needy, then I trust you to gain merit on our behalf.

My father sends you his warmest wishes for peace to you and to all your disciples in Kairawan and elsewhere. He says he will write to you in his own hand when he is feeling better.

Thank you, master, for your letters and your time. They seem to be the one thing that we can count on to make father smile. He works constantly, much more than before his voyage. He does not look so well either. I do not know if this is because of the boat or just the long winter. Perhaps now that spring is here he will perk up.

For his father Dunash HaCohen al-Tustari, from al-Iskander ibn Dunash, your devoted student and learner of your Torah, in Misr. To Rabbenu Nissim, in Kairawan, please God.

From Karimah at Phaselis, to al-Iskander in Fustat, Early Summer, 1033

Dear Skandi, I want to tell you more of my adventures on the high seas. We have been most successful lately, as the ships of the Rum are taking advantage of the season and running the seas. So we are taking advantage of them. We have rarely had to board a ship, but by isolating and surrounding each ship, Mustafa is able simply to call up to its captain and demand tribute. We usually get one sea-chest or more from these ships—which we always check before we allow them to escape.

Last week, one of the ships sought to resist us by throwing Greek fire down upon one of our boats. Since our boats are much smaller than theirs, it is an easy matter to carry with us a barrel of water to flood the boat. The Greek fire actually floats atop the water and continues to burn. I was terrified and ready to jump into the ocean, but the other sailors in my boat merely took their oars and splashed the burning *neft* into the water. Then they rowed close to the fire and pushed it beneath the ship that had thrown it down upon us.

The sailors of that ship, which was quite large, had no way to put out the fire without coming down the rigging into the water next to us. We harassed them until the ship's hull began to smolder. The captain of that ship then surrendered to us and as punishment for their initial resistance we demanded not only their gold and jewels, but their casks of *neft*, which they called naphtha. Now we have plenty of Greek fire to throw for ourselves.

The insects are quite bothersome in Phaselis and we all have been getting eaten alive. One of the sailors finally took a group out to one of the islands on the coast. We brought empty barrels with us. This island, I am sorry to say, was mostly inhabited by snakes. The sailors all donned the boots they had brought along—there was a pair for me as well which were far too big, but I was not going to go barefoot on that island. The snakes struck at us but could not penetrate the leather of the boots. Up till now I had only thought of boots as something to wear when riding a horse.

We came to a stand of strange looking trees. The man who had led us to the island took his sword and struck the tree with his blade, making a gash running on an angle down the side of the tree. At the bottom of the gash he attached a small tube by hammering it into the tree. We did this with seven or eight trees and by the time we returned to the first tree, sap was dripping from that tube. We placed a barrel beneath each tube and then rowed back to our ship. Three days later we returned and found each barrel was about one-third full of gooey sap. We took the barrels back to our boat.

The sailors rub their bodies with this sticky sap and when they do the bugs will no longer come near. At nighttime, when the bugs are at their worst, we light the wood of one of those dead trees and the smoke keeps the bugs away. Later this summer we will return to the trees we tapped for the sap. The gashing and tapping kills them, so we can use that wood for the smoke it produces. Our sailors are careful not to cut more than ten trees in any year, so that there might always be a supply of "camphor" for them. That is what the tree sap is called: camphor.

Brother, even though it is just the beginning of summer we have amassed fabulous wealth, more than we ever had when I rode with Abu Sin. We store the treasure in caves, just like we did with the band of Abu Sin. Our group of forty, however, uses caves that open into the water. In order to get into the caves one must be able to swim under water for a short distance. The mouth of these caves is otherwise invisible. They were discovered by a sailor named Ali many years ago. Now, we refer to the hidden mouth of the caves as the "Bab-Ali."

I had a great deal of difficulty being able to hold my breath long enough to swim under the water, through the mouth of the cave, and up the channel, until I was again above the water inside the cave. It was not that the distance was so long or that the cave mouth was so deep beneath the surface, but that I was afraid. I kept opening my mouth under the water and the air would escape. I had to come up to breathe before I even reached the cave mouth. I had resigned myself to never seeing the treasures all collected in their hiding place.

Finally, a sailor named Kasim taught me a trick for keeping my mouth firmly shut. Many of the sailors love to suck on sweets. I am not like you, Skandi, so I do not always have a candy in my mouth. It is hard for us to find sugar sweets out here and the water would likely melt them in any case. But the sailors love to make a candy of bees' honey and sesame seeds. They pour the honey over a pile of the seeds. If there are enough seeds mixed in, the candy can harden into a small log. Then the sailors break off a piece and suck the sweetness out and chew up the seeds. I think that you would love this candy, Skandi!

The only trouble with the candy is that it sticks to your teeth. The sailors are always poking their fingers or a stick or even a knife between their teeth to dislodge a sticky sesame seed. Everybody always jokes when they see someone doing that and we all cry, "Open, sesame!" In any case, Kasim showed me that if I chewed a sesame candy when I dived under the water, my mouth would certainly remain closed long enough for me to reach the cave. I am glad I tried it. Not only did I have the satisfaction of actually succeeding at the dive, but when I came up it was amazing.

There must be a fissure high above within the cave. Light streams in and shines upon the upper floor of the cave where the water cannot reach and so it remains dry. The sailors have taken care to put the chests of gold on this spot so that the light makes the gold glitter. It seems as if the gold and jewels themselves are lighting up the cave.

There was so much wealth there that I could not believe my eyes. I asked how the wealth was meant to be divided. The sailors explained that many of them have families in the Turkish territories and they go home to them in the winter months. When they disband for the winter, each person in the band gets one share. The three leaders each get an extra share. That makes 43 shares, so they divide the gold and jewels into 43 piles. Then each sailor has a turn being blindfolded. After they are spun around, the sailor reaches out and picks a pile. That pile is his to keep. Everyone agrees that this is a fair method of dividing the wealth. Because no one knows which pile they will get, everyone makes sure that we divide the piles as evenly as possible. And there is more than enough wealth. Everyone agrees that the three each deserve their double share: Kemal for planning the raids, Guziella for her spying, and finally, Mustafa for recruiting members. He has never recruited a member who did not work out well for the gang.

I confess, al-Iskander, that although I had determined to repent and give up the raiding life, I quite enjoy this. It is not so much the wealth, as the sea and the sun and the sand and the comrades. We live a fairly carefree life. We are not always worrying about business or keeping accounts as we do in Fustat.

Of course, so far there has been no real violence. Perhaps if it were more like the experiences I had with Abu Sin I would be less at ease about my life as a brigand. What would Daddy think if he could see me now?

Your sister, Karimah, a member of the Band of the Forty at Bab-Ali.

From Nissim in Kairawan, to Dunash and al-Iskander in Fustat, Early Summer, 1033

To Abi 'Skander, friend and benefactor, Dunash HaCohen al-Tustari, and to his son, the dependable al-Iskander ibn Dunash, in Fustat, Misr.

I am writing to both of you, Dunash and your son, because I know that the boy will read to you in any case. Enjoy the stories and enjoy copying them for others. I am keeping my own collection of the stories I am sending you so that I may, God willing, edit them some day for a final time before sending them to copyists here for circulation in the Maghreb and to the far West, as well as in Fustat. Perhaps God willing, after I have awarded my *ijaza* to certify the correctness of the text, the work might be enjoyed even in Jerusalem—where they could certainly use some consolation. Although it is not a text of the law, our rabbis long ago reckoned that stories draw the hearts of men.

I wrote to you of the patience of Hillel and how he was tested with all sorts of questions. This is, you may know, a common motif in our Talmud. It is told that there were sixty philosophers of a certain school who vexed the Caliph. They were constantly challenging his orthodoxy and his authority. One day he asked of his advisors, "Is there no one who can silence these philosophers?"

They told the Caliph that among the Jews there was a Rabbi named Joshua ben Hananiah, who was known for his wisdom and his repartee. So the Caliph called for Rabbi Joshua and bid him to engage these vexatious philosophers in debate and vanquish them once and for all. Rabbi Joshua replied, "Mine is to hear and to obey, O Commander of the faithful."

When he got to the city of those philosophers, no one would tell him where their school was to be found. He went to the maker of the local delicacy, which was roasted sheep's head. Rabbi Joshua asked him, "How much for a head?"

The man replied, "Forty dirhems."

Rabbi Joshua said, "I want you to sell me the first head that comes out of your oven."

The baker agreed and leaned into the oven to find a sheep's head that was well cooked. As he straightened up, Rabbi Joshua grabbed him by the hair. "I now own your head, by your own agreement!"

"What do you wish from me?" the man pleaded.

"I wish for you to take me to the Madressa of the 60 philosophers."

The man agreed and led Rabbi Joshua to their door. He entered there and saw them seated in three rows. Rabbi Joshua greeted them, "Peace unto you of the first row, of the second row and of the third row." Then he continued, "Peace unto you of the third row, of the first row and of the second row." Finally he concluded, "Peace unto you of the second row, of the third row and of the first row."

Having greeted them thus, he insulted none of them, for they were all given equal status in his greetings. They were impressed with his wisdom and asked him what he wished of them. He asked them, "Will you honor me by attending a circumcision?"

They said, "Yes, but not before you answer seven questions which we ask of you."

Rabbi Joshua agreed to these terms so they asked him, "What is the highest point of the universe?"

He replied, "The Temple Mount in Jerusalem."

They asked him, "What is your proof?"

He replied, "It was not covered by the waters of Noah's flood."

Then they asked him a second question, "Where is the center of the universe?"

Again he answered, "The Temple Mount in Jerusalem."

When they asked him his proof he said, "Let us measure the universe together."

At that they asked him their third question, "Which distance is longer, from heaven to earth or from east to west?"

He replied, "From the highest of the seven heavens to the earth is longer."

They then asked, "If a chick dies in the egg, from where does its soul go out?"

Rabbi Joshua replied, "From the same place whence it entered."

For their fifth question, they gave him a crate of sand. "Weave a shirt for us from this."

"Fine," he replied, "if you will but spin thread from this for me to sew it with."

Their sixth request was that he build a house for them in the air.

Rabbi Joshua replied, "I shall be glad to but I need tools. Please leave them at that spot in the air where you would have me build."

Finally they showed him a well. They said, "Would you move this well into the house for us?"

Rabbi Joshua said, "Yes, if you will take this pile of bran and weave a rope for me to pull the well inside."

At that they submitted to Rabbi Joshua saying, "Once Allah's judgment is decreed, eyesight is struck blind."

This story of Rabbi Joshua pleases me for it shows us the cleverness of the sages and their usefulness to the Caliph. Often it is the case that a wise man from one place goes to another place and there displays his wisdom. Is it not told that a man of Jerusalem once went to Athens and when he was there grew near to death? He summoned the master of the inn and entrusted his wealth to him. He told him, "Send for my son in Jerusalem to come and receive his inheritance. You will know it is my son if he does three clever things." With that, the man died.

They sent for his son and told him to come to Athens, but did not tell him the location of the inn. When the son arrived he saw a poor man carrying a bundle of kindling. "Will you sell me that bundle of kindling?" the son asked him. When he had bought the wood he told the poor man that he would double the price if he would take it to such and such an inn. Thus he followed him to the inn where his father had died. When the poor man arrived he knocked on the door. The innkeeper said, "I did not order any wood."

"No," said the poor man, "but it belongs to this man behind me." The son entered the inn, already having done the first clever thing.

When he revealed to the innkeeper who he was, the man invited him for a meal. That man had two sons and two daughters. When they sat down to eat, he set before them five chickens. He asked the dead man's son, "Will you divide the portions for the meal?"

The son said, "It is not mine to serve, but yours."

But the innkeeper insisted so the man's son put one chicken between the innkeeper and his wife. A second chicken went between the two sons. The third chicken went to the two daughters. And the dead man's son took two chickens for himself. They ate without any further comment.

On the next night, the innkeeper served a fat capon. Again he asked that the dead man's son divide it. The son carved the bird and served the head to the innkeeper, the entrails to his wife. To the daughters he gave the two wings and he gave to the sons the capon's legs. The plump body of the bird he took for himself.

Finally the innkeeper said, "Is this how your father taught you? You do not deserve his fortune!"

But the son replied, "Last night I gave you and your wife one bird. You, your wife, one bird, makes three. The same for your two daughters plus one bird makes three. And your two sons plus one bird makes three. I took two birds for myself, also totaling three. So you see, we each shared the same portion."

"And what of tonight's meal?" asked the innkeeper.

"I gave you the head, for you are the head of the family. I gave your wife the entrails, for children came forth from her womb. I gave your sons the legs, for the family stands on their strength. And I gave your daughters the wings, for they shall fly from the family when they marry and move to their husband's family. As for me, I took the part shaped like a boat, the body of the bird, for I came by boat and will leave by boat."

And that is what he did; for having done three clever things he left with his father's fortune in hand.

There are many other stories like this showing the wisdom of Jerusalem over all the nations and the wisdom of our sages over the philosophers. But I suppose there are such stories among every nation. And I have already gone on for too long. I will write more stories later. But if I may, Dunash, I should point out that you, too, have a very clever boy for a son. And, I am pleased to boast, I have a clever daughter. The daughters of Hananel tell me that she sits outside the door of the academy and listens as the boys recite their lessons. Later, they tell me, Ghazal can recite by heart whatever was the lesson of the day. She may not be much to look at, my Ghazal, but as it says at the end of Proverbs, "Charm is false and beauty is fleeting, a woman who fears the Lord is to be praised."

Speaking of children, the girl who used to care for Ghazal, Mulaah and her husband Abu'l Maali, who is my student, are expecting a child. She has just completed her first trimester, praise be to God, and is healthy thus far. We are praying that she have a healthy baby. It would be best if it were a boy, God willing. Now that the trimester is over we cannot pray for the sex of the child since that would be a prayer in vain; but there are those who say one can pray for the child's gender even until the mother is upon the birth-stool. I suppose that a girl would be all right as well. We put our trust in God.

From Karimah in Phaselis, to her Nanny in Fustat, Summer, 1033

Dearest Nanny, I had planned to write you to tell you not to be dismayed at the letters I have sent al-Iskander which I know he must read with you. I had intended to write to you, my dear teacher, of my decision to leave the boats behind and to press Mustafa on his promise to get me to Amalfi. For in truth I read my last letters to al-Iskander in horror at the ease with which I write about robbery, extortion, and theft. I had promised myself when still with Abu Sin that I must repent, and yet I wrote that I was enjoying the life of the brigand. My dear Nanny, I am now one and twenty years, is this what has become of me? Other girls my age are marrying and bearing children while I ride the waves as on a chariot, throwing threats and fire into the very heavens.

I learned to throw Greek fire after that incident when it was thrown down into our boat. The *neft* is easily lit aflame, and once lit, burns steadily. We cut small blocks of it, so that it may fit into our hands, and can toss these upwards into the ships we threaten. I have learned how to use a sling to throw fire. The sling, usually an oil soaked rag, also does its incendiary duty. If I crush or break apart the *neft* once it is in the sling, it scatters when it falls upon the enemy decks and is very hard for them to extinguish.

Two days ago we stopped a small trading boat and demanded a ransom. Too long an argument ensued between Kemal and their captain. I feared they were up to no good, but finally they agreed to give over a percentage of their cargo. They carefully lowered to us 12 large jars of oil—for they were carrying virgin olive oil from the coast to cities further west where olive trees and oil are less plentiful.

As was our custom, Mustafa checked the first of the jars they lowered and found it full of good oil. The other jars were lowered to us with seals intact. We wished to have them that way to preserve their freshness. We stored the jars out of the way and let that boat go free. It was dusk by then and we did not wish to pick our way among the shoals back to Phaselis with such a heavy load on board. So we weighed anchor near the Three Islands, leeward of the big rocks where we would find safe harbor for the night.

It bothered me that our negotiations had taken so long with that enemy boat and I was up pacing our deck when I saw against the light of the moon that another boat was anchored nearby us. I realized then what had been bothering me. During the negotiations the waters around us were glittery. It struck me that perhaps they had poured their oil overboard. I wondered if somehow they had fooled us by giving us empty oil jars. But this made little sense to me, for putting their oil overboard meant that they still would have endured financial loss.

And I had helped move the oil jars into safe position in our boat; they certainly were not empty.

In a flash, I realized that they had, in fact, dumped their oil and it was they anchored nearby, awaiting some signal to row towards us to do battle. I then also understood that the jars did not contain oil, but had enemy sailors inside them, now aboard our boat! I did not wish to sound the alarm, lest I either look the fool if I were wrong or alert our enemy if I were correct.

Instead I quietly gathered three of our strongest sailors and we lifted one of those oil jars and threw it over the side of our boat. We heard the faint cry of the sailor inside as he hit the water. Since all of those jars were oily on the outside, we set them alight with a piece of *neft* and threw each overboard. Soon there were 12 jars hotly burning in the water. The shrieks of the sailors who were inside those jars tore through the night. We manned our boat in silence and rowed to throw fire upon the treacherous ship that had betrayed us with its false tribute. By the end of the night that ship and all its contents were at the bottom of the sea. There was no salvage in the morning, everything had burned.

Oh Nanny, I am grateful to God I did not have to see those burned sailors in the daylight. As it is I have had nightmares just from seeing the jars alight and floating in the sea, accompanied by heart rending screams. Yet I feel little pity, for those sailors would have killed each and every one of us. I thank God for saving guilty me, He has rendered only good unto me. But today I write you that I have arranged with Kemal and Mustafa to keep our original bargain. The next boat we find that is heading west toward the Rum we will not attack, but rather will negotiate a passage with them to take me to Amalfi.

I pray that once I get there I can find news of Mommy's relatives. It is time for me to return to family. I will send these letters along either by land with Guziella, who can arrange their safe passage, or by boat when I board for Amalfi. God willing I can be there by the New Year's holidays and atone among Jews for Yom Kippur. May God forgive me. Your loving Karimah, bound for Amalfi, with the help of God.

p.s. Nanny, please do not tell anyone about what is in these letters. Especially do not tell Mommy about my trip to Amalfi. I do not wish her to worry about my being in the Rum or about my traveling on the Sea. And if I find her family, I wish to surprise her. I think she will like it, but only if you are silent. I adjure you—swear you will not show these or any of my letters to anyone, not even al-Iskander; and do not annul the vow now or on Yom Kippur. From Karimah, with the assistance of Heaven.

Dear Rabbi Nissim, my father has given me permission to tell you I am writing this for him and that he is dictating to me. God and father willing, I may add my further greetings at the end of this letter—in peace, al-Iskander.

And now I, Abu Iskander HaCohen, am sending you this letter of thanks. Business is proceeding but I regret that I am not yet in a position to resume our partnerships with you and your academy. In-sh-Allah next season we will be able to renew our regular trade and perhaps even another contract for the sewing of clothing. I am not yet financially viable enough to make the outlay for the cloth and will not ask Sahl Abu Saad for advance funds. I fear that such a loan would inevitably imply some form of interest which the Torah forbids, even if it is but the "dust" of interest paid in my excessive deference to Abu Saad. I am grateful enough for his introduction to the court of Caliph al-Zahir, may his reign prosper.

Your story of the rabbi who encountered the troublesome philosophers who were a vexation to the Caliph made me think of a recent visit we had in the eastern district of al-Kahira. There, within the very city of Cairo, is the mosque called al-Azhar. It is a great mosque and the Imams who support the Fatimid Caliphate hold forth there. We were invited to attend the dual celebration on the festival of Ghadir Khumm, at which the Shia also commemorate the martyrdom of Husayn. I know that in Kairawan you also have both Sunni and Shia Muslims, but I confess to having been perplexed about the differences between them until I went to the events at al-Azhar. I suppose the Muslims can no more distinguish among the rabbanites loyal to Jerusalem or the rabbanites who attend the Gaonim of Iraq, or even us Karaites. Our divisions are as plentiful and as arcane as those of our Muslim brothers.

Indeed, we share some of their very issues. Am I not a cohen of a long and distinguished priestly line? Therefore, it is manifest that we Jews do believe in the value of family lineage and that leadership should be handed down dynastically. I could also offer as an example the leadership of your rabbis in Babylonia, for they trace their lineage to the dynasty of King David. Yet on the other hand, we Karaites choose our leaders by their knowledge of our traditions, much as you rabbis pick your Heads and Seconds by their abilities to interpret your Talmudic tradition. If you have followed my poor ramblings thus far, I will offer, in the poverty of my knowledge, my impressions of the Muslim community in which we live.

At al-Azhar, indeed throughout the city of al-Kahira, the loyalty of the Imams is to the Fatimid Caliphate and the Shiat Ali. That is why the Festival of Ghadir Khumm is so important to them, for it was at that place that the Prophet, peace be upon him, made as his successor his cousin Ali, who was married to Muhammad's favorite daughter, Fatima. The party of Ali are called Fatimids, but in general the Shiat Ali are simply called the Shia.

Yet early on in Islam there was another group who did not believe in family succession. They appointed an elected leader who represented the way of the people. They call themselves Sunni, for following "the way" or Sunna. Those leaders were deemed to be experts in the traditions of the Muslims, in the Quran and the Hadith.

The Sunni and the Shia actually have battled one another many times. There were even, if I recall, riots between Shia and Sunni in Kairawan, were there not, dear Nissim? But one of the most important battles took place a long time ago in Iraq, at Karbala. There Muhammad's grandson, Ali's son Husayn, peace be upon them all, was martyred. The companions of the prophet who killed Husayn are reviled by Shia to this very day.

Al-Kahira, which was built by the Fatimid Caliphs, is quite naturally the stronghold of the Shia. Not only is the al-Azhar mosque a venerable site for them, but the more recent mosque of al-Hakim is there as well. Our neighborhood, Fustat, is the older of the two cities. I have written to you about our mosque of Amr, which is very old. It and all the mosques of our vicinity are Sunni. In the past there has been trouble on the festival of Ghadir Khumm between the Sunni of Fustat and the partisans of Ali in al-Kahira.

Our Caliph al-Zahir, in his wisdom, has called for an end to the cursing of the prophet's companions, peace be upon him. Since the Sunni are not being cursed or spat upon, they are more inclined to join in the festivities. There is food and music, parades and, dare I tell you, much giving of costly garments from the Fatimids to their supporters. Someone has to manufacture all these garments, dear friend. Just speaking about it rekindles my strength. We will yet recover our fortunes, me for my household and you for your academy. I must rest now, Dunash.

Dear Rabbi Nissim, my father is truly grateful for your attentions. I can tell you that he has not been himself at all. He is sickly and tires very easily. I am happy to report that he had good color and even light in his eyes as he dictated this letter to you. Nothing makes him enthusiastic except the garment trade and the arguments among the factions in the Jewish or Muslim communities. I am sometimes, I am ashamed to admit, grateful for some new dispute, for it brings some life to my father's day. I am not certain but I think that what he said is accurate, that our fortunes are improving and his trading is restoring our family's wealth. If only father's health could be restored as readily. I put my trust in God, Who heals all flesh and does wonders.

To Rabbenu Nissim ibn Yakov ibn Shaheen, Second in Kairawan. From Dunash HaCohen al-Tustari and his son in Fustat, with the help of God.

From Nissim
to various communities in the Maghreb, late Summer, 1033

To our brethren the whole house of Israel who reside in the Diaspora, especially the communities of the Maghreb and Spain; in Sijilmasa and Tlemcen, in Granada and Cordoba, and of Afrikiya: al-Mahdiya, Sousse, Sfax and Qabes, peace to you all and an abundance of blessings.

From Nissim, Father of the Court and Second in Kairawan, Nissim ibn Yakov ibn Shaheen, in the Name of the Merciful.

To all of you, the leaders of the communities of the Diaspora in the West, I write to appeal on behalf of the synagogue of Jerusalem. You know I have close ties to the schools of Baghdad and have represented the academies of Sura and especially Pumbedita to you in the past when appealing for support. Yet today I write to you on behalf of the congregation of Jerusalem.

I do not need to recount for you the stunning tragedy of this past Passover when God's wrath, may it be averted from us, shook the earth and brought down parts of the Western Wall of the Holy City and destroyed the synagogue there. Our sins are many and our guilt is great, but we have the means for atonement. We can and must rebuild the Holy City, for it is our inheritance and our obligation.

Jews of the Diaspora, we must not forget Jerusalem, but place her chief among our joy. All who lament Jerusalem now will be privileged to see her rebuilt, may it be speedily in our day. We pray to God daily that Jerusalem, His Holy City, be restored in mercy, and be permanently rebuilt. It is in our power to hasten the advent of the messianic kingdom and bring an end to the kingdoms of oppression.

In each of your congregations it is your custom to hold an appeal for funds on the Great Fast of Yom Kippur. I know that many of your congregations depend upon these funds for your subsistence, and that the poor of your cities eat their daily bread through the pledges made in this appeal. Brothers, great charity brings great atonement! How great must our sins be that Jerusalem our Holy City has been thus afflicted. How great then must be our atonement.

I call upon each congregation which receives this epistle to raise the sum of 40 gold dinars on behalf of the synagogue of Holy Congregation of Jerusalem as part of this year's Yom Kippur appeal. Do not give less. I undertake to ensure that the funds are honestly distributed and spent. The moneys will not go to foster contention, but to build God's small sanctuary.

We cannot afford to wait—make your appeal this Yom Kippur and forward the funds to me in Kairawan while shipping is still open. I would like to begin our relief efforts there soon after Sukkot and before the winter rains set in.

"Let us comfort them and their mourners. Peace, peace to those near and to those far away, says the Lord. I will heal them.... What shall you call fasting, a day acceptable to God? ...do not turn away from your own flesh."

God is crying out to you. Reply, Here I am. "Then you shall be like a watered garden, a never failing spring. You shall rebuild ancient ruins and restore foundations generations old. You shall be called the mender of broken fences, the restorer of paths for inhabitation."

From Nissim, Second in Kairawan and Father of the Court, Nissim ibn Yakov ibn Shaheen, may their memory be for blessing, with the help of God.

Chapter Nine
Summer, 1033

From Nissim in Kairawan, to Dunash in Fustat, Summer, 1033

My dear Dunash how good it was to hear from you and to share your enthusiasm for financial recovery, God willing. I was also grateful for your account of the divisions in al-Islam and your thoughtful comparison to our own Jewish groupings. You point to the division between those who favor dynasty and those who favor intellectual qualification, which is a division going back to Temple times, when the rabbis replaced the priesthood after the destruction.

But you must know that even your Karaites were founded by one who had dynastic as well as intellectual qualifications. For it says in the works of our teacher Rav Saadya Gaon al-Fayyumi, peace be upon him, that your founder Anan was a learned scholar as well as being a scion of the Davidic family. Indeed, he was in line to become the next head of the rabbinic community in Iraq. But for reasons not vouchsafed to us he did not receive his appointment as Head nor did he become political leader of Babylonia's Jews. And so, he revolted and set out to seduce Jews away from the teachings of the sages.

It was not my intention to write to you of Anan's heresy nor to inflame you, for I know you to be a man of good faith and that you have raised a son of good faith, loyal to the whole house of Israel. And you know that there are serious divisions in our own rabbinic community between Iraq and the Land of Israel. Yet here in Kairawan, Rabbenu Hananel ben Hushiel and I, Nissim, teach our students the Babylonian Talmud and we also teach them the traditions of the Talmud of the West, by which I mean the Holy Land.

Dunash, your ruminations about the Shia and the Sunni Muslims made me wish to write to you of a scholar who became a heretic many long years ago, in the time of our early rabbinic sages:

There was a boy who was scrupulous in performance of the commandments and when Rabbi Elisha ben Abuya came to visit, that boy's father told him, "Go, my son, and climb up to the nest to bring down eggs for our good rabbi to dine upon. Be sure to shoo away the mother bird."

Rabbi Elisha reasoned that it says in the Torah, "Honor thy father... that you might have length of days and great reward." And it also says there, "Do not take the mother bird along with her young... that you have great reward and length of days." Now this boy was performing both commandments at the same time. But when that child climbed the ladder, he waved his arms to shoo away the mother bird, lost his balance, fell and broke his neck, and died.

At that moment Elisha said, "Where is his length of days and where is his reward? There is neither Judge nor judgment!" From that time onward the sages referred to Elisha as the Other, for he revolted and sought to seduce young students away from Torah and towards heresy.

Nevertheless, his disciple Rabbi Meir continued to study with him. Meir reasoned, "It is like a man who eats a pomegranate. He throws away the peel and the rind, yet eats of the sweet fruit." Once when Rabbi Meir was studying with the Other, he was riding upon a horse on the Sabbath, while Rabbi Meir was, of course, walking. Suddenly the Other stopped and said, "No further Meir, you have reached the limit for Sabbath walking!"

Rabbi Meir asked him, "How do you know this, master?"

He said, "I have been counting the footfalls of my horse. I may not believe, but I do not wish you to violate your law because of me."

At the time, they were studying a verse from Proverbs, "A married woman will snare a precious person."

Meir asked, "Rabbi, how can one atone for the sin of adultery?"

The Other said to him, "Just as one fathered a child not his own and departed from Torah, so one must atone measure for measure."

Meir was perplexed and said, "How so?"

The Other explained, "Such a man as he who sleeps with another man's wife must take an orphan into his home and raise him in the way of Torah. Then he will have atonement."

Rabbi Meir said, "Will you not repent then, master?"

But the Other said, "The decree has been sealed against me from on High."

Meir persisted, "Nevertheless, if you will repent in this world, I will stand up to your executioner in the world to come!"

Despite his disciple's promise, the Other died unrepentant. When he was buried, they came and told Rabbi Meir, "Come see, there is smoke rising from your master's grave!"

Meir went to the grave and adjured the flames by quoting the book of Ruth, "Lay down for the night. Then in the morning if he will act as redeemer, good. If not, I will redeem you, as God lives!"

"Lay down for the night" - he told the flames, for this world is like the night.

"Then in the morning" - which is the World to Come.

Burton L. Visotzky

"If He will act as Redeemer, Good," - for God, Who is Good, is the Redeemer; but not for the Other who denied Him.

"If not, I will redeem you," said Meir to his dead teacher. And when Meir invoked God's name by reciting the last words of the verse, "as God lives," the flames died down and Elisha rested in peace. Therefore our sages say, "Blessed is he who raises up faithful disciples who will stand up for their masters."

I also wish to tell you how the great sage Rabbi Eliezer came to the study of Torah and, alas, how he too came to fall from greatness and be banned by his colleagues. But perhaps enough is enough for now, for I wish you to have great reward and length of days, my friend and patron. I promise I shall continue this epistle soon, before the summer is out, so that we can tell our stories and have an end of heresy.

I pray for your continuing strength. May the Lord bring a complete healing to all of your troubles, for God is a faithful Healer and merciful to us.

From Karimah in Amalfi, to al-Iskander in Fustat, late Summer, 1033

Dear little brother, by now not so little, but still my brother. I have arrived in the kingdom of Amalfi without incident, thank God. I was given a wonderful send off by my Turkish ship mates. When the word spread among them that I had decided to leave, they determined to make a division of our treasures so that I might have a share of our booty for the time I was with them. I was entitled to one forty-third of the treasure.

Of course, I had never actually seen how it was done. The first thing that happened was that Kasim and two of the other sailors made an enormous roll of sesame candy on the deck of one of our ships. They left it in the sun and it dried quickly. We each cut long strips with our *jambiyyas*, careful not to cut into the surface of the planking of the ship. Then we peeled and rolled up the candy. It is not only sweet and chewy, but ever so slightly salty from drying on the ship deck in the sea air.

All 40 of us dove into the water with mouths full of candy and entered our treasury through the Bab-Ali. Once inside, in addition to the light that came in through the fissures above, we lit oil lamps and torches. The glitter of the jewels and the gold was quite dazzling. Then Mustafa, Guziella, and Kemal drew a huge circle and marked off 43 paces around it. Each of us went to each of the piles and chose a gem or gold piece to leave by our place. Then we each moved to the next place, and repeated the procedure over again. Soon we got into a rhythm and by the time we had gone once around the entire circle, each place had a fabulous pile of glowing gold and precious stones. It took us the better part of the morning and well into the afternoon. By the end, we were just taking handfuls of treasure and heaping them into each pile. Finally, all of the stacks of treasure from our various raids were distributed into the 43 points of the large circle.

Everybody cheered when Mustafa took me and put me into the center of the large circle. He tied a turban tightly around my eyes so that I could not see and spun me two or three times around. "Now, walk until your feet greet treasure!"

I walked in my bare feet slowly until I approached one of the piles. As soon as my toes touched something, I stopped. At that moment, everybody yelled, "Open, sesame!"

I removed my blindfold to see the results of our day's labor. There before me was a pile of gold and treasure, huge enough to fill three or four camel loads. The fact was, there were piles like this throughout the cave, but no one else will claim theirs until some months from now when they will be even larger. But what was before me was mine, brother, much more than I had ever beheld when riding with Abu Sin. Your sister Karimah is a very wealthy woman, thanks be to God Most High.

The men packed the treasure into seven crates which could be maneuvered through the neck of the entranceway and carried in the water. Each of these was hauled upon the boat and let to drain and dry. They insisted that I inspect each of the crates and mark it with my sign. I chose to draw a sword hilt-basket, so it looks like the Hebrew letter Kaf, for Karimah. Now I have my own mark, it is very smart. We sealed each of the crates with rope tar, so I will immediately know if they have been opened. I reserved some bags of dinars for my use on the voyage and said my farewells.

Brother, I was surprised to find that it was very hard for me to bid farewell to Guziella. I did not realize how much the friendship of another woman could mean to me. It was a good thing having a friend here. I miss Nanny and Mommy, and I miss you, 'Skander.

It was an easy thing to stop a ship from the Rum headed west along the coast and negotiate a passage. I was at first not sure what Kemal and Mustafa said to them, but they assured me that I would be safe. They explained to me that I needed to bring my own food aboard for the month or so of passage and that Guziella had already packed it in a crate for me. As for bedding, I would just sleep on the bales of other cargo. When I asked whether the owners of those bales would not mind, they laughed. It seems, brother, that for the price of 27 dinars, an amount I most easily can afford, I am now a part-owner of the vessel and its contents!

This was something I did not at first appreciate for I had thought to simply pay my fare for passage. But Kemal explained that I would be much safer this way. They also made it clear to the captain that if they got word that I had not received my share of the profits upon arrival in Amalfi, they would find him and sink him with his boat. The syndicate guarantees me the return of my 27 dinars upon safe arrival and a minimum of 40 1/2 more dinars, possibly more, depending upon port taxes and market prices by the journey's end.

The captain showed me every courtesy and became especially solicitous of me after an amusing incident. We sailed west and stopped briefly at Samos and then at Rhodes. In the seas between Rhodes and the Greek mainland, we were met by a pirate ship. I was privileged to meet the famous pirate Jabbara, who this season is raiding ships of the Rum. He sails against Byzantium with the complicity of the Caliph. Our captain was, of course, eager to protect the passengers and cargo, as well as his own life. So he was already shouting across to Jabbara before the pirate boat even had a boarding party formed. I came behind our captain and told him quietly that as an owner, I would negotiate on our behalf.

The captain was fearful, for although he knew that I had been brought on board by a Turkish raiding vessel, he still assumed I was but a rich investor, and a woman at that. I waited, as I knew was right, until Jabbara's boat sent a skiff alongside with their boarding party. I leapt over the side of our ship, for I had knotted a rope around my hand to the out rigging. With one hand on that knot and with my Badawi sword in my other hand, I slid down the side of our ship into their small craft.

"Take me to Jabbara now, or we all will die here," I bravely shouted. When one of those sailors dared to laugh, I took my sword and stabbed it into the boat at his bare feet. I did but nick him, he surely was not hurt. Still, I had the satisfaction of watching his laugh turn to horror as he watched his blood mix with the sea water now rushing into the floor of the small boat. I was prepared for this. I took a small tin cup I had tied around my belt and handed it to him.

"Here," I said, "If you bail fast enough we can return to see Jabbara before your skiff sinks."

Brother, they turned their boat and rowed me to their master. I explained to Jabbara that I had sailed with Kemal and Mustafa and was now on my way to trade my profits in Amalfi. I did not reveal that I owned part of the boat on which I was a passenger. Jabbara was quite gallant. He said, "It is not right that pirates should steal from one another. Be on your way and put your trust in God."

And so, dear 'Skandi, we sailed on unscathed to Messina in Sikilia, but we did not stop there, for it is in Muslim hands and I am sailing now in a ship of the Rum. We none the less benefited from its lighthouse. It reminded me of the Pharos at Alexandria. We used that marker to navigate our way through the narrows between Italy and Sikilia and then sailed up the coast of Italy to stop briefly at Salerno. From there, the captain asked permission to delay our arrival at Amalfi by one half day. He said he wished to give the sailors some relief before they arrived on shore. He said he found that the opportunity for bathing and frolic before they arrived at port made his crew less likely to cause trouble when they put in. Since as an owner I would be responsible for their behavior in port, I readily agreed.

We sailed a bit further west on the Amalfi coast to a stand of three huge rocks in the water, almost small islands, named the Sirenuse. They say that long ago beautiful women inhabited these isles and that their singing was irresistible. Many a sailor dashed his boat upon the rocks because of their song. Once a sailor tied himself to the mast of his ship while the rest of his crew stuffed their ears. He alone has heard the song of these women and survived. Our sailors swam from the side of our ship and rollicked in the waves. We were ready to put to port in the kingdom of Amalfi.

We arrived without any incident, praise God day by day. The captain negotiated the port taxes which were very steep, much like the rocky cliffs upon which the town is built. I must go now to attend to the cargo to see that we get a fair price. At port I can post this letter. I will write to you again soon and tell you what I have found in Amalfi. Remember, do not tell anyone that I am here. It is a secret.

From Nissim
to Dunash, late Summer, 1033

My dear Dunash, please consider this a continuation of the letter I wrote to you some weeks ago. I have been busy here with the appeal on behalf of our unfortunate brethren in the Holy Land, as well as with my usual teaching duties. I share teaching and management of the academy with Hananel. Each of us works to his own strengths and I believe our boys are the better for it. Of course, we both teach Babylonian Talmud. Hananel also teaches the companion material found in the Talmud of the Land of Israel. I am aware that this is the regular practice in Fustat, but you are much closer to the Holy Land. Here our loyalties have always been chiefly to the academies of Iraq, so use of this Talmud from Israel is new to us. I am becoming more familiar with its brief style, which suits Hananel very well.

Of course, we are also called on to serve as judges in the rabbinic court and we reply to legal questions which have been written to us from elsewhere. I try to maintain my loyalty to our teacher, Rav Hai Gaon, but his age is showing so

I, here in Kairawan, am shouldering my share of the work load. In the old days I served as a mere conduit transferring his legal responses from Iraq to Granada, Cordoba, and the far Maghreb. Now, I find myself responding in his stead, trying always to use his legal principles.

Because of your request to me for stories, I am able to teach the students of the academy a good deal of rabbinic narrative and lore. We also are learning to study the grammar of the Torah thanks to the work of our colleague Abu al-Walid Merwan ibn Janah, who has undertaken an analysis of the Hebrew of the Torah with a precision learned from the Arab grammarians. The results provide great clarity to our sacred Scripture. I know many Karaites who have used his method of analysis as well. Maybe you have seen his work under his Hebrew name, Rabbi Jonah.

Rabbenu Hananel still uses teaching techniques which his father imported here from the Rum. As a result, among our students there are few who use books. I wish we would read and write more, as I feel this is what causes Torah to flourish and be disseminated. But Hananel uses the old method of memorization. I confess, our disciples certainly are able to keep enormous amounts of text in their heads and have quick recall of parallel passages and appropriate cross references. Hananel says he prefers the oral memorization method because then he can look a student in the eye and know if he understands the text. It also assures that our students do, in fact, learn the text as we wish them to know it. There are many variations among the written versions of our sacred works.

In truth, I have observed that the Muslims rely on both methods. They will not credit a Hadith tradition regarding the Prophet and his circle unless it has been transmitted mouth to ear. On the other hand, they put great stock in the written word and have created reliable copies of their Quran which are also beautiful to behold. Hananel says that in the Rum the rabbis prefer the oral method so as to prevent the Christians from stealing the mysteries of the Oral Torah. He says the day they translated the Torah into Greek was as bad as the day Israel made the Golden Calf. What he means is that the Rum claim the Bible as their own. At least the Muslims have a separate revelation.

I promised you in my last letter to tell you stories of Rabbi Eliezer the Great. I tell you these tales because they are instructive, but also because you raised the issue of dissension in the Muslim world and, by implication, in our own community.

They say that Rabbi Eliezer's father Hyrcanus was a wealthy farmer who could even afford to hire others to plow his fields. To teach his son, he set him plowing the rocky part of the field. Eliezer sat and began to cry. His father asked him,

"Perhaps you weep because you are plowing the difficult terrain? Come now, you may plow the furrowed land."

But when Eliezer came to the furrows, he sat and wept. His father said, "Why do you weep now? Are you troubled that you have to plow the easy ground!?"

Eliezer said, "No."

"Why do you weep then?" asked Hyrcanus.

So Eliezer said to him, "I wish to study Torah."

At that Hyrcanus said to him, "See here, you are twenty-eight years old and now you wish to study? Get married, have a son, take him to study Torah!"

Eliezer fasted for two weeks during which he tasted nothing. Elijah the prophet appeared to him. When he saw Elijah he sat down and wept. Elijah said to him, "Son of Hyrcanus, why do you weep?"

He told Elijah, may he be remembered for good, "Because I wish to study Torah."

Elijah told him, "If so, then go to Jerusalem to Rabban Yohanan ben Zakkai, and there you can study."

So Eliezer ran away from his home and went up to Jerusalem, for this happened before the Romans had destroyed it. He came to the academy of Rabban Yohanan ben Zakkai, where he sat down and wept.

Rabban Yohanan asked him, "Why do you weep?"

He replied, "Because I wish to study Torah."

Rabban Yohanan asked, "Whose son are you?" But he would not tell him.

Yohanan then asked, "Do you mean to say that you have never learned the recitation of the Shma', nor the blessings of thanksgiving after a meal, nor the daily prayers?"

Eliezer shamefully responded, "No."

"Arise, then, that I may teach you."

But Eliezer sat and wept.

Rabban Yohanan said, "My son, why do you weep?"

Eliezer responded, "I wish to learn Torah."

So Rabban Yohanan would recite with him two laws each and every day of the week, and he would review them until they stuck in his memory. During this time, he went eight days without tasting anything, until the scent of his bad breath came to Rabban Yohanan's notice. He began to move further away from him. Eliezer sat and wept. Rabban Yohanan asked him, "Now why do you weep?"

Eliezer said, "Because you have stood away from me as though I were covered in boils!"

Burton L. Visotzky

Yohanan gently replied, "My son, just as your breath has come to my notice, so may your words of Torah come to God's attention." Then he asked him, "My son, whose son are you?"

He replied, "I am Hyrcanus' son."

He said, "Here you are the son of one of the great benefactors in the world and you never told me!? By your life, today you will dine with me!"

But Eliezer said to him, "I have already eaten at the hostel where I am staying."

"And who are your hosts?" asked Rabban Yohanan.

"They are Rabbi Joshua ben Hananiah and Rabbi Yosi HaCohen."

Rabban Yohanan sent a messenger to them who asked, "Has Eliezer eaten with you today?"

They replied, "No, it is eight days now that he has not eaten."

Meanwhile, back at the farm, the other sons of Hyrcanus said to their father, "You should go up to Jerusalem and disinherit Eliezer from your properties."

So he went to Jerusalem to disinherit him and when he arrived there was a banquet for Rabban Yohanan's academy. All the great men of the city were there to support him. They recognized Hyrcanus and said to Rabban Yohanan, "Look, Rabbi Eliezer's father has come!"

Rabban Yohanan said, "Make a place for him," so they seated him next to Rabban Yohanan.

He caught Rabbi Eliezer's attention and said to him, "Would you offer a word of Torah?"

Eliezer replied to his teacher, "Rabbi, I will give you an analogy. What is this like? It is like a cistern. One cannot get more from a cistern than what has been put into it. So too I, Rabbi, cannot say any more Torah than what I have learned from you."

Rabban Yohanan countered, "I will give you an analogy. What is this like? It is like a well-spring, which gives forth ever more fresh and new water. So you can offer words of Torah beyond what you have received from me. But perhaps you are embarrassed to speak in my presence. I will stand away from you so that your words of Torah can come to even God's attention."

At that, Rabban Yohanan stepped out of the room. Rabbi Eliezer sat and expounded and his face glowed like the light of the sun. Beams of light flowed from him, like the rays of light that came from Moses' face when he came down from Sinai. His brilliance was so illuminating that those in the room did not know if it were day or night. Rabban Yohanan tiptoed back into the room and came up behind him so as not to disturb him. In his joy, Yohanan kissed Rabbi Eliezer on his head and said, "Blessed is Abraham, Isaac and Jacob, that one such as this has sprung forth from their loins."

Hyrcanus then asked, "Who did Rabban Yohanan say that about?"

They told him, "It is your son Eliezer!"

He then said, "He should not have said what he did. Rather it is I who am blessed to have such a son!"

Now Rabbi Eliezer had been sitting and expounding, but now he noticed his father was there. He said, "Father, please take a seat, for I cannot be expounding Torah while you stand!"

But Hyrcanus said, "Son, I did not come here to listen to you expound Torah. I came to disinherit you. Yet now that I have seen all of the praise your teaching garners, I shall disinherit your brothers and give everything to you."

Eliezer demurred and said, "I am not worthy of even one of them. If I were to desire real property, God would provide, as it says in Psalms, 'The earth is the Lord's and all that is in it.' And were I to desire silver and gold, God would provide, as it says in the prophet Haggai, 'Mine is the silver, and mine is the gold, says the Lord of Hosts.' All I wish to have is but Torah, for it also says in Psalms, 'I love Thy commandments, Lord, more than gold and silver.'"

Dear Dunash, I wish to write you more, for although Eliezer had such an auspicious beginning, he came to a bad end because he stubbornly broke from his colleagues. But this letter is long, and paper is short. I will write again and send this letter now by the boat leaving for Fustat. Be strong, be strong, and be strengthened my friend. My greetings to your son and your household, from Nissim in Kairawan.

From Karimah in Amalfi, to her brother in Fustat, late Summer, 1033

To al-Iskander ibn Dunash HaCohen al-Tustari, dear brother I write you this letter to describe Amalfi and what I found here. By the letter's end you may be as bewildered and shocked as I am, but have faith, we have one another. I learned more about myself in the past days than I would have thought possible. Alas, what I have learned has made me less sure than ever of who I am, indeed who we are. It is so painful to share this with you, dear sweet Skandi, so let me begin by describing this quaint city of the Rum.

Read in silence, only by yourself. I again and again adjure you to share this letter with no one, not even Nanny. I originally did not wish Mommy to worry about me. Now I am determined that Mommy never find out I have visited Amalfi for I have found her brother here. Al-Iskander, we have an uncle and cousins who we never knew of before this!

I wrote you about coming into the port. When the captain came to tell me of the punitive taxes and to prepare to unload the ship, I went to see the port master. Our captain is an honest man and naive in the ways of the world, so I had feared he was being taken advantage of, so high were the tariffs on our goods. But the port master said he was required to assess such high duty for two reasons: first to protect the merchants of Amalfi from being undercut by cheaper prices from abroad. Second, to help the kingdom of Amalfi to fight piracy and so to keep trading freely to assure that the citizens of Amalfi enjoyed the best prices.

I actually laughed at the man, for it was obvious to me that the first reason undermined the second. If they wanted cheap prices for the citizens, why were they imposing such high tariffs on cheap goods? It was they who were the real pirates, not only stealing my profits, but stealing from their citizens who would have to pay much more for their goods. The port master admitted that this was the case but asked me, "What am I to do? The king commands me to impose tariffs so that his friends the paper manufacturers can make good profits. The people may pay more, but the rich grow richer."

He was very subtle, this man, but I understood him. I said that not only the rich need to grow richer. And if he accommodated me so that I could assure good prices for the citizens of Amalfi, I would accommodate him. Not just the rich need benefit from a port-tax transaction. After that we quickly settled on a "gift" for him that cut our tax bill in half.

I returned to the boat with our new permits in hand and we marketed our goods most successfully. Most of what we brought to trade was not readily found in Amalfi and those goods that were, we offered at lower prices. Everybody profited, except the king and his friends, but we made sure to send our respects to the court here in the form of gifts to the king and his cronies. Now everyone is happy and our profit is securely counted. My 27 dinars investment has brought me that back, plus a profit of 81 more gold dinars. Brother, that is a three fold return on my investment. I intend to invest in another boat. As you will read, it will be very soon.

Going up from the port is a long flight of steps; I counted some 60 steps, leading to the Duomo di Sant Andrea, which in our language is the church of Andreas. Climbing those steps reminded me, but of course it is different, of climbing up Mount Sinai. I imagine for the Christians of this city, just climbing up the steps to their church is a penance for their sins. The church itself is beautiful; they have attractive bronze doors which they are in the process of installing to replace the old wooden doors. These doors were made in Constantinople and shipped here especially for the church. That should give you an idea of the trading wealth of Amalfi.

Walking up past the church to the left, the hill continues to climb, but there are no longer stairs. There is a stream of water which flows down from the coastal mountains. Even now in late summer it was flowing steadily. Along this stream are many factories which take advantage of the water flow to power their mills with water wheels. In fact, the area is even called the Valle dei Mulini, which means the valley of factories. It sounds so much more romantic in their language.

Much of the area has trees, al-Iskander, huge trees which they cut and then cut again until they can mix a wood pulp with cloth to make paper. I have seen the many paper mills here and bought a great deal of it. It is a beautiful writing surface, don't you think? The paper masters here have shown me many ingenious methods to keep the paper dry once I put it on the boat. Right now I have it wrapped in skins, stored in crates which have been sealed first with bees' wax and then with rope tar to make it water-proof.

Of course, no sooner did I clear the docks than I began to ask about the Jews here in order to find Mommy's family. There is a rabbinic community here. They are small and unhappy to be among the Christian Rum. The oddest thing is that they speak absolutely no Arabic. They speak what they call Latin, which is what the Rum of Italy all know. I was able to communicate with the Jews by speaking Hebrew. There are no Karaites here at all, which I assume will strike you as oddly as it did me.

I had always assumed that Mommy grew up as part of our community of Scripture. We both knew she was from Amalfi and had an accent, but did you ever think she was not raised as a Karaite? I certainly did not. Was it not Mommy who worried about the details of proper food and whether we said our prayers five times daily? Nevertheless, there are no Karaites here, so I began to ask among the rabbinic Jews after Mommy's family. I certainly knew her name and that of her mother and father. I knew the family name she had always told us, and it is a good name of the Rum, Scriabore. We translate it to Hebrew and to Arabic as "scribe," and so I always secretly assumed my abilities at writing came from Mommy's side of the family.

I was unable to make myself clear speaking in Hebrew and I certainly could not speak Latin. But my ship captain could speak Latin quite well, and he has been most considerate of me since the affair with Jabbara and my bribery of the tax man. So I was with my Christian boat-captain translating for me to the Jews of Amalfi, asking whether there were Karaites named Scriabore. He said, it cannot be that name, but must be Scribiore. So I thought, that is well, mother's accent was difficult for the ear and we did not know the name properly.

But then, the Jews said they knew just who I meant, that Scribiore was one of the paper makers of the town, well respected at that. It was Guiseppe Scribiore

Burton L. Visotzky

from whom I bought most of the paper. As we were talking I asked after his family, not revealing that we were related. I judged his age and asked if he had a sister. He said, "I have no sister."

Then I asked him when his family had converted to Christainity. He said, "We are not converts, we have always been Christians!"

I was wholly perplexed but then my captain explained to me in Arabic that converts did not like their Jewish roots exposed and often claimed always to have been Christian. This was a good explanation until I went to another of the paper makers and asked about Scribiore. He said the Scribiore family had been in the business as long as anyone knew. They were always paper makers. I went back to the Jews of Amalfi to make my inquiries about the family. But they, too, said that Scribiore was not a convert. They pointed out that Jews were not allowed into the paper guild in Amalfi. The Scribiore family really was Christian!

I was shaken, but had enough wits about me to ask if Scribiore ever had a sister. They said yes; but it was a great scandal for their family, because she had run off with a Jew from Egypt long ago. I asked whether they knew more, but they told me that this Jew was not from their rabbinic community, he was of the heretical Jews of Fustat and they would have nothing to do with him or his wife. In fact, her running off with a Jew had cost them dearly among the Christians here. Their response was to say, "Good riddance. She certainly never converted to Judaism when she was here and they were most assuredly living together as man and wife." They implied that such promiscuity was all one could expect from Karaites and their gentile concubines. Even though they had no way of knowing it was Mommy they were talking about, I think the Jews here are horribly inconsiderate.

So, al-Iskander, now you know the horrible secret that I know. Mommy might not even be Jewish, which means, I think that we are not Jewish either, except for Daddy. The Bible says we follow the father. The rabbinic Jews say, follow the mother only. The Karaites might be true to Scripture, but they insist on a Jewish mother so as not to completely cut themselves off from the rabbinic Jews. In truth, there is no real conversion any more, especially since Islam and Christianity forbid it. So where does that leave us, brother?

I left home and lost my father. And to think that Daddy was angry with me for running off with Ismail! Even if he was correct that Ismail was the wrong man for me to be with, I think it was terrible of Daddy to condemn me for doing exactly what he himself had done with Mommy!

I came to Amalfi only to lose my mother. All I have left is you, brother, who I love and cherish. But I must leave Amalfi, there is nothing for me here. I do not even speak the language. I am trying to find a share in a ship that is heading to North Africa. I am not ready to come back to Fustat yet, sweet brother, I hope you understand this and forgive me. I will try to find a passage to the Maghreb where I might find a life among the Jews there. If I have learned anything on my voyage it is that I am either a pirate or a Jew, but I cannot be both at once.

I no longer have the stomach to be a pirate, the things I have done make me ashamed of myself. And although the community of raiders is a close one, it is not a place to have a child or even a real home. The Jewish community still draws me near, to find refuge beneath the wings of the Divine Presence. As the Psalmist says, "My father and my mother have abandoned me, may God gather me in. We must put our hope in God, and make our hearts strong and courageous." I kiss your hands and face, my dear brother al-Iskander. I miss you and will write again when I have reached Afrikiya. From your orphan sister Karimah, We put our hope in God.

From Nissim in Kairawan, to Dunash in Fustat, late Summer, 1033

Dear Dunash and al-Iskander, I pray this letter finds you both in good health and that God has prospered your hands in business and restored your former fortunes. We here are doing well, thank God, and although we have less business from you, we are maintained nonetheless through the generosity of Hananel's supporters and my own connection with the farther Maghreb.

Shmuel, the Nagid of Granada, has been very generous to us. We correspond regularly about legal matters. He is a great admirer of the opinions of the Gaonim of Babylonia and an expert in the Talmud. He also serves as Wazir in the court of Granada in addition to his role as Nagid, leading the Jews. I am sure that he is a most pious Jew, even though he is in constant contact with the Muslim court. And yet, he sometimes surprises me—especially with his poetry which sometimes borders on the blasphemous. I suppose he simply writes in the style of the court, but the poetry is jarring to me, especially when compared with his elegant Talmudic reasoning.

Here is a short poem of his to amuse you. It will show you what I mean about the complexity of his mind and his writing.

If you lust, as I lust for the wine poured out at banquet meals,
hear then what my tongue would say:
I shall enlighten you about the path of pleasures,
although you don't believe me,
my brother of groans so fey;

Burton L. Visotzky

Five things fill the heart with joy, and put one's sorrows far away,
these are they:
A graceful girl, a garden, wine, the rush of water in canal, and song,
arouse me to be gay.

I read these poems and understand them all too well, dear Dunash, but they do not enthuse me for the life of the court. I am most content here in the rabbinical academy. Perhaps you in Fustat with the great court at al-Kahira and your contacts there are more sympathetic to such verses. In any case, I write to the Nagid and send him my felicitations because I value the man, his adroitness at the law, and his support of our academy here. At least you must appreciate the rush of water in the canal, given what you have written to me about the rise of the Nile. Perhaps you, too, enjoy the wine of banquet meals. As the Psalmist says, "Wine brings joy to the human heart."

For all of his wine poetry, Shmuel is a great Jewish leader. There is no whiff of heresy about him. He offers his rabbinic opinions within the mainstream of consensus and does not deviate to the right or to the left. As I mentioned, he tends to follow the schools of Sura and Pumbeditha in Baghdad. If I may make a distinction between them, a thousand differences between them, Shmuel is as great in his day as was Rabbi Eliezer ben Hyrcanus in his own. Yet Eliezer, peace be upon him, ended his life alone and in disgrace, for he could not accept the opinions of his colleagues, even when they were in the majority.

It is told of Rabbi Eliezer ben Hyrcanus that he could argue so brilliantly that he could offer 60 reasons to declare a reptile kosher and then argue sixty more reasons to decree the Holy of Holies ritually unfit. Once there was a controversy regarding the ritual fitness of a clay oven. In those days all ovens were made of clay, which as the coals in the oven heated, baked into an ever harder shell. The only problem with these ovens is that if they became unfit in some way—for example a reptile crawling over its surface—there was no way to render it fit once more. For earthenware, according to the rabbis, cannot be made fit because it is porous.

Now bear with me Dunash, for even though these rules may not apply to your community, they are important for you to understand the genius of Eliezer and the man he supported. A clay worker by the name of Ochnai once built an oven of alternating layers of clay and sand. The sand, when heated, would turn to glass. Now glassware does not become ritually unfit, for it is not porous. So Ochnai thought he had solved the problem of the ovens and turned to Rabbi Eliezer to represent him to the rabbis.

Even though Rabbi Eliezer offered them every argument, they did not accept the new oven. When the sages did not accept Rabbi Eliezer's reasoning he said, "If the law is according to my opinion, let this carob tree prove it."

Here the transmitters of the Talmud are in disagreement. Some say that a carob tree uprooted itself and moved one hundred cubits. Others say the carob tree moved 400 cubits. But the rabbis replied to Rabbi Eliezer, "One does not bring a legal proof from a carob tree."

Rabbi Eliezer then said, "If the law is according to my opinion, let this aqueduct prove it."

At that, the water in the aqueduct reversed its flow. But the rabbis replied to Rabbi Eliezer, "One does not bring a legal proof from an aqueduct."

So Rabbi Eliezer said, "If the law is according to my opinion, let the walls of this academy prove it."

At that, the walls began to lean inward. Rabbi Joshua rebuked them, "If the disciples of the sages are arguing about Jewish law, what is it your business?"

Now the walls did not fall out of deference to Rabbi Joshua, but neither did they straighten up, out of deference to Rabbi Eliezer. To this very day, the walls of that academy are off kilter.

Finally, Rabbi Eliezer said, "If the law is according to my opinion, let it be proven from Heaven."

At which a voice came down from heaven saying, "What have you against Rabbi Eliezer? The law is always in accordance with his opinion!"

Rabbi Joshua leapt to his feet and said to God, "The Torah is not in heaven!"

It was explained, "The Torah was already given at Mount Sinai, so we no longer attend to the voice from heaven, for You already wrote in the Torah at Mt. Sinai, "Follow the majority."

Once the prophet Elijah was asked, "What did the Blessed Holy One do when this incident happened?"

Elijah responded that God laughed and said, "My children have outwitted Me, My children have outwitted Me!"

They say that on that very day the rabbis brought all of the objects which Rabbi Eliezer had declared ritually fit and burned them. When he persisted in his opinion, they gathered and voted to excommunicate him. They asked, "Who will go and inform him?"

Rabbi Aqiba said, "I will go, lest someone else goes and unwittingly destroys the whole world."

What did Rabbi Aqiba do? He dressed in black clothing and wrapped himself in a black turban and went to Rabbi Eliezer, but sat at a distance of four cubits from him. Rabbi Eliezer asked him, "Aqiba, what is it with you today?"

He replied, "Rabbi, it seems to me that your colleagues are avoiding you."

Burton L. Visotzky

When he heard this he rent his garments and removed his shoes as a sign of being under a ban. He sat upon the ground and his eyes brimmed with tears. It is said on that day that one-third of the world's olive crop was blighted, as was one-third of the wheat crop and one-third of the barley crop. There are those who say even the dough in a woman's kneading bowl went sour.

So great was the anger that day that everywhere that Rabbi Eliezer looked burst into flames. Rabban Gamaliel, who was the head of the court which excommunicated Eliezer, was traveling on a ship that very day. A huge storm arose and threatened to capsize him. Rabban Gamaliel said, "It seems to me that this storm arose on account of Eliezer ben Hyrcanus."

Gamaliel stood up and prayed, "Master of all worlds, it is known and revealed before You that I did not do this for my own honor, nor for the honor of my father's house. Rather, I did this for Your honor, that there not be dissension among the Jews."

At that the sea grew calm.

Dear Dunash, this is what dissent brings to the Jews. We break into factions and camps, as do the Muslims. It is not good for them or for us. We would be better off if we learned to follow the majority and have unity.

I should tell you that Eliezer came to the end his life still under the ban. As he grew near death, the sages had pity on him and came to visit him. They sat at a distance of four cubits. Rabbi Eliezer snarled at them, "Why do you come to me now?"

They answered, "We have come to learn Torah from you, Master."

He shot back, "And why have you not come before this?"

They replied, "We were otherwise engaged."

Rabbi Eliezer said, "I should be surprised if any of you dies a natural death."

Rabbi Aqiba asked him, "And I, Rabbi, what shall my death be?"

He told him, "Aqiba, yours will be the worst of them all."

Then Rabbi Eliezer placed his two arms crossed upon his chest and said, "Woe unto you, my arms, which are like two Torah scrolls rolled tight. I learned so much Torah and had so much Torah to teach. For I attended my masters and neglected nothing they taught me, until there was nothing left to learn but what little a dog might lick from the sea. Yet I had so much to teach and all my disciples took from me was no more than an eggshell can hold. I could recite three hundred laws regarding a bright skin inflammation, yet no one ever asked me about them. And I could recite 300—and there are those who say 3,000—laws regarding the planting of cucumbers and no one ever asked me about them except for Rabbi Aqiba here."

He continued, "Once we were walking along the road and Aqiba asked me to teach him the laws of planting cucumbers, so I said a word and all the fields around us were filled with cucumbers. Aqiba then asked me, 'Rabbi, you have taught me how to plant them, now teach me how to harvest.' At that I said another word and all of those cucumbers were gathered unto one place."

It was then that the sages asked him all of the arcane questions they had for him during the years of his ban. He replied that this thing was unfit and this thing was fit, this impure and that pure. He did this, going on until his strength failed him. His last word was "pure" and then he died.

Rabbi Joshua leapt to his feet then and said, "The ban is lifted, the ban is lifted!"

At Rabbi Eliezer's funeral they applied to him the verse of Scripture that Elisha cried at the death of the prophet Elijah, his teacher, "Father, Father, horseman and chariot of Israel."

Here I end my tale of the great Rabbi Eliezer. It shows us how correct the rabbinic adage is that they say, "Do not cut yourself off from the community." You, Dunash, have worked tirelessly to unify the Jews, Karaites and rabbanites together. I salute you, as always, and wish you strength and blessing from the Almighty. I look forward to hearing from you soon, dear friend, and to the renewal of our business contacts.

May God bless and keep you and your household. Dunash HaCohen al-Tustari, in the fortress of Fustat, Misr. From me, his friend Nissim, Second in Kairawan, by boat, with the help of God.

From Dunash and al-Iskander
to Nissim in Kairawan, early Fall, 1033

Dear Rabbenu Nissim, I al-Iskander am writing to you on my father's behalf to tell you how much he appreciates your continued letters and attention. He says that these help keep him floating in the sea of life these days as we near Judgment Day. I think he means that the Days of Awe will soon be upon us. I will tell you that my father continues to do business, but that he is leaving more and more of the details to me, al-Iskander, his secretary and apprentice. I am now 15 years old and am happy to be helping my father this way. It is good that I do not yet have a bride, as there is so much work to do to support the business and the household.

Uncle Sahl Abu Saad has been very good about making sure there are shipments we can take part in without too much trouble, so there is a source of income for our home. Father will do business with Uncle Sahl, but would not happily take charity from him. I am also grateful to be able to help my family and learn from my father. I pray for his health every day. Because of his illness we spend almost all of our time together. I feel like Rabbi Aqiba and Rabbi Eliezer, asking my father to teach me all that I can learn from him.

Father is gray and his belly grows large, even though he hardly eats. His cough, which he brought back from the shipwreck, never leaves him. I can even hear him coughing in the night time. Rabbi Nissim, I am afraid for my father. I help carry on the business and I know that Uncle Sahl and Abu Nasr, his brother, would also care for us. But I do not want my father to be ill. I want him to be all better, like before. Are there special prayers that you think I should be saying? Is there any rabbinic text I could study that would help him?

The Muslims here say that the physician ibn Sina is writing a great compendium called the Canon. Do you know if there anything there that could be of help to us? I do not know who else to write since everyone in Fustat considers me a child. You are the only one with the decency to address me as a man.

In truth, I wish to remain my father's child for a great deal longer. Rabbenu Nissim, your stories are a great help. They teach me wisdom and make me forget my troubles. I am grateful to you for your time and attention; along with my father, Dunash HaCohen al-Tustari, may God bless him and keep him strong.

Burton L. Visotzky

Part Two:
Settling

Chapter Ten
Fall, 1033

From Nissim in Kairawan,
to Dunash and al-Iskander in Fustat, Fall, 1033

To my friends in Fustat, I send my very best wishes for the New Year. May you be inscribed in the Book of Life. I was grateful for your letter, Dunash, and that al-Iskander was not only kind enough to write it, but to add his own greetings. I am not familiar with the work by the Muslim sage ibn Sina, but I will ask after his work and see what I can learn from it. We are interested in medicine and philosophy as the Muslims practice it, especially since they transmit the wisdom of the Greeks.

I believe Torah study is the cure for all that ails us in body and in spirit. Indeed, our sages tell the story of a young boy who studied the first book of the Torah and how that brought him and his parents relief. It is said that the lad's father began to teach him to read and recite at age three. The boy was precocious and learned quickly. As a reward his father had a scroll of Genesis made for the boy from which he chanted the sacred text until he knew it by memory. That boy never went anywhere without his book of Genesis tucked under his arm.

Once, an army of the Rum passed through the city taking many captives. They took that boy away from his parents and brought him to a distant city. They put him in a prison and confiscated the scroll from him. The book was placed in the royal library and the boy was left forgotten in the jail. One night the king was unable to sleep and called for unusual books from his library that he might either be entertained by them or put to sleep by them. The court page brought him the scroll of Genesis and as it was in Hebrew, the king was unable to read it. No one in the court could read it to him either.

The king asked how the book came to be in his library and was told of the young boy with the scroll under his arm. He had the boy called up from the prison cell and commanded him to read. That boy read from "In the Beginning," all the way to "And the heaven and the earth were complete." Then the boy translated into the king's language while he and all the courtiers listened in astonishment. When they asked him the meaning of the text, the boy interpreted it for them. When he was finished the king fell to his knees and proclaimed, "Blessed be God Most High, Creator of heaven and earth."

At that the king asked the boy how he came to be imprisoned. The boy related his story and concluded, "And I am sure that my parents are very worried about me."

The king was touched by the story, as much as he had been astonished by the reading of Genesis. So he commanded that the boy be cleaned and dressed in costly garments. Then he was returned to his village and his parents with pomp and ceremony. They were richly rewarded. The parents wept with joy for they had despaired of ever seeing their little boy again. All of this came to pass through the whim of a father who taught his child Genesis. I say whim, for it is our custom, even though Genesis is the first book of the Torah, to begin teaching our children with the book of Leviticus.

When I was but a child, younger than al-Iskander is now, I asked my father, who was then Head, my rabbi and teacher, peace be upon him, why we begin our studies with the book of Leviticus. I said to him, "Father, is it not odd to begin in the middle of a book and then skip backward and forward? Should one not start at the beginning, then read the middle and finally the end?"

My father, may he rest in Eden, said to me, "My son, may God's face shine upon you, you have asked a good question." My father always encouraged me to ask questions so that I might learn. He said to me, "Our sages of blessed memory knew that when the Temple stood in Jerusalem our ancestors could offer sacrifices to God to atone for our sins. And the order of the sacrifices is contained in Leviticus, for it is the Torah of the Priests. Now that the Temple is no more," my father explained, "we begin teaching our children at Leviticus, so that their study itself may serve as atonement for our sins, as in the days of old."

In addition to what my late father, may I be atonement for him, explained to me, I have also seen written, "Why do we begin with Leviticus? For Leviticus teaches of purity. So let our children who are pure come and study of purity, that they may remain pure and bring us to purity as well."

Study and observance of the commandments are the most effective things we can do to influence God's decree, for these bring the greatest rewards. It is said of the great Rabbi Hiyya that once he was a guest at the home of the butcher in Laodicea in Little Asia. A table of gold was brought before him by 13 servants, who carried it suspended from golden chains which were adorned with precious gems. When they set it down before him they recited from Psalm 24, "The earth and all that fills it is the Lord's." When they removed the table they recited from Psalm 115, "The heavens are God's heavens, but the earth has been given to humanity."

Rabbi Hiyya asked his host by what merit he attained such riches. The host said, "I am a butcher. For as long as I have been so it has been my custom to take the best animal in my shop and set it aside to be eaten in honor of the Sabbath. If a better animal comes along, I sell the first and dedicate the latter for the Sabbath. It assures that my table will richly honor God on every Sabbath eve."

So you see that there is great reward for study and for the punctilious observance of the commandments. But do not forget that acts of charity also bring great reward and save one from death. Rav Huna was a great scholar who studied much Torah. Once a fire broke out in his neighborhood, but it did not touch his house or the house of his neighbor. Huna was pleased that this woman had been saved through the merit of his study. But he was told in a dream that he had been saved by her merit! It was this woman's custom every Friday to heat her oven and use up her wood so that the poor might be able to bake their Sabbath bread. And if they were too poor to have dough to bake, she provided them with flour as well. That way they might experience the joy of the Sabbath and the pleasure of the two Sabbath loaves which remind us of God's miracle of the manna.

I hope that these tales bring you cheer and pleasure as we enter the Days of Awe and celebrate the New Year and the Great Fast. I pray that you both be rewarded for your great merits in the coming year. I trust I have replied to al-Iskander's questions. Dunash, I look forward to a year of good health and, God willing, good business. My warmest wishes for the New Year to your entire household.

To Dunash HaCohen and his son, al-Iskander ibn Dunash HaCohen al-Tustari in Fustat. From Nissim, Father of the Court in Kairawan, by boat, in the month when the ram's horn rouses us to repentance.

From Karimah in Kairawan, to al-Iskander in Fustat, Fall, 1033

Dearest Brother al-Iskander, greetings of peace to you and good wishes for the New Year. I write to you from Kairawan in Afrikiya, after a long and fruitful journey from the Rum. It is just after Sukkot and the Jewish community here, which is rabbinic, is taking down the little huts they had built for the holiday throughout the Jewish section of the city. I wish you and our household a blessed New Year. I hope you had an easy fast and are now enjoying the festival.

I want to recount my journey here and God's bountiful blessings. When I left Amalfi it was again upon a boat in which I was a part owner. Like a good al-Tustari, I invested my gold so that it would not sit idle. The boat we bought into was carrying a mixed cargo of goods from the Rum and from trade on the

Great Sea. I had little doubt that the consignments, especially the finished textiles, would draw a fine profit at the ports of North Africa.

What I had not reckoned upon was the difficulty we would have shipping in a boat from the Rum, for there is great hostility now at Sikilia towards the Christians, who have been raiding ships that sail from her ports. We decided to lower our flag and sail as a pirate, with no identification. I was confident that my experiences in Antalya and my success with Jabbara would see us through.

We were unable to put in at any port of Sikilia, however, so suspicious are they. We skipped along the coast from harbor to harbor: Messina to Palermo to Mazara and then across open waters to the port at Sousse. We were received in Afrikiya with no difficulties, even if the Sikilians were suspicious. Once we came to Sousse, which is a very modern city, I was able to engage the merchants and learn what the market would bear. The prices at the port were good, even after the port taxes and the necessary gifts. But they were far from spectacular. After some inquiries, I learned that I would do far better taking the cargo inland to Kairawan. There they have a station on the caravan routes westward, so prices promised to be much higher.

I offered each of my partners in the voyage the opportunity to continue our consortium on to Kairawan. Those who said yes were grateful to me later when we counted our profits. Those who said no were offered three percent above the best market prices in Sousse. Everyone was happy, especially after I promised the partners who stayed with me that I would assume the risk of protecting the caravan.

I did one last thing before we left Sousse. I climbed to the top of the Ribat. The fortress commands a great view of the plains, of the caravan routes out of the city, and of the sea. While I was atop the Ribat I carefully evaluated the port and shore line. I determined a place where I could enter the water in complete seclusion.

That night just after sunset, I went down to the sea. I waded into the water and when it was as high as my neck, I took off my robes. This was difficult as they were heavy with sea water, but I needed to be unencumbered by my garments. I wished nothing to interpose between me and the purifying waters of the sea. I let go of my clothing and immersed completely, my head, my hair, everything. I did this once, and then again, opening my mouth under the water for good measure. When I came up I felt I had been rendered clean, fit to rejoin the Jewish community if God would forgive me for my sins. Since my arrival in Kairawan where I have access to the Jewish calendar, I have counted back the days. The night of my immersion was Yom Kippur.

Here in Kairawan it is very different than in Fustat or al-Kahira. The cara-vanserais dominate the city. Brother, this place has caravans from the east, as we knew from Daddy's business ventures. From here they organize many caravans west to the farther Maghreb. I have seen trains of 50, 60, even 100 camels leaving for Tahert and Tlemcen, for Fez, Sijilmasa and even Marakesh. One caravan promised to go directly to Ceuta and from there to ferry across the straights to Sefarad, taking goods to Malaga, Cordoba, and Granada. I immediately sold our stock of Rum goods to the Sijilmasa and Fez caravans, reasoning that the Sefarad trade could just as easily get goods from the Rum overland.

In any case, we made another fortune. Skander, you simply must have Daddy give up on the craziness of sea journeys and have him concentrate instead on organizing caravans to the West. The Jews here will, I am sure, be helpful. Daddy will continue to garner his profits while halving his risk. I do not know how you can convince him of such a plan, but you really should do so. Make him think that it was his idea. If I can make money as a trader, Daddy can become as rich as Uncle Sahl.

But do not have him send olives or dates here. Everywhere you look there are olive groves. I have never seen so many olive trees, all neatly planted in rows. Between the rows they plant other crops and sometimes other trees as well. There are myriads of date palms here and the dates are deliciously sweet. They make a cookie with date meat in the center which they roll into a cracked-wheat dough. I want to learn how to bake these cookies. They are called makroud. Maybe I can send you some!

The city has an interesting construction, unlike anything we have in Misr, unless you count the fortress inside Fustat. There is an old city here with its own wall. Within the old city is the Great Mosque, the Bir Barouta, some other places I will tell you more about, and the Jewish Bazaar. But there also is an outer city with an outer wall. This wall is bounded by the wadis. The Jewish quarter is within these two sets of walls at the South end of the city. Most of the Jews live there, not like Fustat where we live pell mell with our Coptic and Muslim neighbors.

The Grand Mosque of Kairawan is loyal to the Caliph and follows the Shia order of the Friday prayers. It is big and beautiful, and has a very large, square minaret. Below the minaret is an open courtyard surrounded by a portico. The columns that hold up the roof over the portico are each different. There must be fifty or sixty such pillars, and every one is unlike its neighbor. They say these columns were gathered from the Roman ruins here when the mosque was built—at the time of Sidi Uqba in the very first century of al-Islam.

Nearby is the well that gives Kairawan its special status; it is the Bir Barouta. They say that Sidi Uqba's dog was named Barouta, and that the dog dug here to find water. When the well of Bir Barouta started pumping water, a goblet surfaced in the well. It was a goblet that the Prophet, peace be upon him, had accidentally lost in the well of Zamzam at Mecca. So there is said to be an underground connection between Kairawan and Mecca.

What amazed me about the well were not the legends, but the way in which the water is pumped for the pilgrims to taste. They use a water screw, which brings the water up from the ground by turning the screw. To bring up enough water, those who wish to drink from the well must climb a very narrow staircase to the second floor of the building. There, a blindfolded camel walks round and round, turning the screw and pumping the water. The water is sweet and refreshing. But how did they get that camel up that narrow flight of stairs?

There is another mosque within the old city walls that may be almost as old as the Grand Mosque. It is much, much smaller, but in its own way just as beautiful. It is called the Mosque of the Three Doors. It is named for the three arched stone doorways that lead into the mosque. Although there they pronounce the name of the Fatimid Caliph at the Friday sermon after the reading of the Quran, they pray according to the rites of the Sunna. There is some tension between the Sunni and the Shiat Ali here in Kairawan.

Brother, I kiss your hands and face. I wish you the happiest of New Years. Write to me as I plan to be here in Kairawan for some time, God willing. You can send me a letter at the perfumers in the Souk al-Yahud, inside the Old City walls. I long to hear from you—it is now two years since I have seen you last. Please write; but do not tell Mommy or Daddy where I am or how to find me. I am very angry at both of them, which you will understand if you got my letters. I sent you copies by more than one boat, since I thought what I had learned in Amalfi was very important.

From Karimah in Kairawan, to al-Iskander in Fustat, Fall, 1033

Oh, 'Skander, how complicated life can be. I was ready to come back to the Jewish community here in Kairawan and there are virtually no Karaites in this city. This was something I realized when I was journeying here, but I did not think hard enough about who the rabbis of this place were. Before I tell you about my meeting with them, let me tell you of my welfare here.

As I have written to you, there is a great deal of profit to be made if one has capital and is willing to undertake a certain amount of risk. My own experiences have taught me that there is no more danger of loss to brigands than there is to the ever present tax farmers. If one assumes that raiders must be paid, and if one firmly instructs the caravans to not resist but to be willing to pay any reasonable sum demanded of them, then the risk is minimal. Further, by reckoning this way in advance, I can share those taxes among the other members of the caravan consortium, much as I would for "gifts" to the tax farmers.

Needless to say, nothing compares to accompanying the consignments yourself. But I have reluctantly decided that I do not wish to do so unless absolutely necessary. I am tired of the rigors of the road, of men making unwanted advances, of carrying the sword. I will tell you that the sword presents me with special problems here in Kairawan, where it is considered unseemly for a woman. I do not wish to become soft, so I have bought a small house with a private courtyard. Buying a house was relatively easy, as I had one of the men in my consortium act as *epitropos* for me.

It was hard to find the right house, as the buildings here usually share a courtyard. Finding a private one cost me a bit. Nevertheless, it is worth the price as it allows me to practice with my sword and *jambiyya* daily. Recently, my courtyard has become the home to a group of girls I am teaching to read and write. I will tell you more about that later.

I wished to pay my respects to the rabbinic court here and knew that the best way was to make a contribution to the fund for the poor. To this end I was introduced to a rabbi named Hillel ibn al-Gassus. He was a handsome man, my age, who blushed and stammered when he spoke with me. I had taken care to dress modestly and wore a veil; but Rabbi Hillel was so timid that I began to wonder if he had ever spoken to a woman before.

I told him that I wished to make a contribution to the needs of the poor. I said I would like to give dinars for bread, for oil, and for the orphan students in the school who are learning to write and read. I named what I knew to be a reasonable sum for such a gift. Ibn al-Gassus thanked me effusively in the name of his teachers. The Head is a man called Rabbenu Elhanan. But then he thanked me in the name of the Second, Rabbenu Nissim ibn Shaheen, who I realized with a start was Daddy's Rabbenu Nissim.

Of course I did not wish Rabbenu Nissim to know that I am Karimah bint Dunash, so I told ibn al-Gassus that my name was Martha bat Boethius. He looked at me oddly and laughed nervously. He said, "Miss, your gift is very generous and I am happy to accept it in the name of the academy of Kairawan. We shall see that it is properly distributed to the poor as you request. But surely you cannot be named Martha bat Boethius, can you?"

I had chosen that name because I once read it in a rabbinic text I had copied when I was still in Fustat. How was I to know that very few names of women appeared in that work and that this rabbi would catch me out using a fake name? I said to him, "My father, may he rest in Eden, was a great scholar and a priest. He named me this name in Hebrew after that great woman of Jerusalem."

"Do you have a name in Arabic, then?" asked Hillel ibn al-Gassus, still visibly nervous. "Might it be Sittuna, as would be the translation of Martha?"

Now I thought very quickly and remembered the name of a priest who was not an immediate member of our family. "Yes," I told him, "in Arabic I am called Sittuna bint Haroun."

So now I am known in the Jewish community of Kairawan by the name of Sittuna. I do not wish for Rabbi Nissim to find out that he knows my father. I do not want him writing to Daddy to reveal my whereabouts. I do not wish him to learn that I was raised in a Karaite household. I certainly do not wish him to know that my mother is probably not even Jewish and that our parents are not really married. I had hoped to leave all this deceit behind me and here I am with a new name. When will it ever stop?

Of course the gift I gave led both rabbis to wish to meet me. I was invited for a Sabbath meal at the home of Rabbenu Hananel—apparently that is his name and not Elhanan. It was as though I had entered a pond stocked with fish, so many were his daughters, flipping around this way and that. I had thought they would be secluded, but we all ate together; not only Hananel, but also his wife and his nine girls—imagine that 'Skander, most are close to you in age or somewhat younger.

I was very surprised to see that Rabbi Nissim was invited too, along with his little daughter—a most unusual girl. Rabbi Nissim is widowed. Rabbenu Hananel's girls told me that when the daughter was born his wife died during the delivery. In any case, the girl has a big head and a tiny body. She must be about three years old. She runs around and talks non-stop. Hananel's daughters all hold her and play with her like she was a doll. But she listened to everything that was said and at the end of the meal asked me directly, "Sittuna, will you come to visit us again?"

I had no idea what to answer her, but I looked up and saw a look in Rabbi Nissim's eyes. So I told her, "Yes."

Then I asked her if she would like me to read to her. This caused a huge stir as Hananel has not taught his daughters to read. Obviously, Rabbenu Nissim's daughter, her name is Ghazal, has not learned to read either. As for Rabbi Nissim, he is much younger than I would have thought. He seems to be in his late 30s or early 40s, with no gray in his beard. He wore a beautiful white silk turban, and I wondered if it was one that Daddy had sent him. Of course I did not ask.

Rabbenu Hananel speaks almost no Arabic, so we either spoke Hebrew—again with the Hebrew—or his daughters very rapidly translated. In the course of that meal I invented an entire life for myself, because Hananel's father was from the Rum, so I had to tread with care. He married a girl who speaks beautiful Hebrew, Arabic, and I think Latin. Yet she also cannot read. So now I know Rabbenu

Hananel and his women—although there were so many of them I am still not sure I know their names. Those are so jumbled in my head I cannot even be sure which name belongs to his wife and which to his daughters.

And there is Rabbenu Nissim, and his daughter Ghazal. As odd looking as that girl may be, she is very smart. Poor Rabbenu Nissim has no more idea of how to treat her than Daddy knows how to treat me. Poor thing. Of course the day after that Sabbath luncheon all of Hananel's daughters came to find me at my house. They even had Ghazal in tow. I do not know if they are coming with anyone's permission, but I have begun to teach them to read and write. They know a great deal of the Torah text by memory, which helps with the writing. But unless I pick an unusual text for them to read, I cannot tell if they are reciting from memory. Need I tell you that the one quickest to learn is Ghazal?

Of course, it was also Ghazal who found my sword. Thank God it was in the sheath when she found it. I have forbidden her or any of the girls to touch it. They do not know that I can use it. I told them it belonged to my late father, may he rest in peace. As far as anyone here in Kairawan knows, I am an orphan. It is just how I feel, sweet brother. I have no one in the world but you. Please write to me, I long to see your face and kiss your hands. At least I can read your words and hear you speak to me that way.

Your sister Sittuna bint Haroun, who is Martha bat Boethius in Kairawan. To al-Iskander HaCohen al-Tustari in Fustat, with the help of God.

From Nissim in Kairawan, to Dunash and al-Iskander in Fustat, Fall, 1033

My dear friend Dunash and his son and apprentice al-Iskander, peace and an abundance of blessings. As you may know, Kairawan is not such a big city that we do not almost instantly learn of the arrival of a new member of the Jewish community. People here are especially careful to inform either me or Rabbenu Hananel, may God watch over him and his entire household. We recently learned that someone new had come to our town and was a wealthy ship owner. Further, she is a woman! Before we even had the opportunity to send a messenger with greetings and welcome to her, she sent word that she wished to make a donation on behalf of the poor of Kairawan. Needless to say, we were delighted to have a person of such generous instincts joining our community, for however long she wished to stay.

I sent one of my most trusted pupils, Hillel ibn al-Gassus, to welcome her and receive the gift on our behalf. Rabbi Hillel returned to us smitten like a small school-boy. Although ibn al-Gassus is in his early twenties, he remains as yet unmarried. One would think, however, that he nevertheless had some shred of worldliness. He came back with a generous gift of dinars, for bread and oil, even for the teachers of reading who generally are ignored by the community. Do you know that were it not for them no one could learn Torah? Yet they are ill paid and mistreated by the parents of their students, to say nothing of the tricks the boys play on them in class, God help us.

In any case, this woman was wise enough to donate a small endowment for those teachers as well. I assumed this was a wise woman of middle years, perhaps a widow, who understood the needs of a community. But Rabbi Hillel said that no, she was quite young, maybe even younger than he. Then I understood the cause of his stammering. I am afraid I teased him a bit, for I asked him if she was pretty. Before he could stop himself he said, "Her face shines like the full moon on a cloudless night, master." He blushed so red then that I felt pity for him. He was quick to add, "But she was veiled and modest, a proper daughter of Israel."

I felt it was necessary to learn more and when I asked Rabbi Hillel her name, the fool told me she called herself Martha bat Boethius. I was angry at this and asked him, "Do you not know when you are being played for a fool? Martha bat Boethius is the name of a woman from the Talmud; that cannot be her name. Do we know nothing about her?"

Hillel ibn al-Gassus told me, "She claims to be an orphan. She says her father was a Cohen who named her Martha in admiration for that rich woman of Jerusalem."

I could not press ibn al-Gassus any further. He is useless, stammering and blushing like he was ten years old. I called for Rav Mevorach berav David HaBavli, who carries a bit more gravity. He had also made inquiries after this mystery woman. Mevorach, alas, is also unmarried, so I fear his inquiries about a rich and pretty woman may not have been entirely uninterested. Nevertheless, Mevorach was able to tell me that she has an Arabic name, not that it really tells me any more about her: Sittuna bint Haroun.

I was determined to get to the bottom of this, so I had Hananel's wife issue an invitation for Sabbath lunch. It would have been inappropriate for me to invite her. But Hananel follows the custom of the Rum and does not seclude his women if there is a man visiting who is well known to the family. The Muslims here frown on this, but Hananel ignores it and follows the customs of his father, Rabbenu Hushiel, may he rest in Eden.

It was quite a lunch. I came with Ghazal and of course Hananel had his minyan of women. Counting this Sittuna there were 12 girls and two men. Hananel and I held our own, even though he was stymied, as usual, by his lack of Arabic. His daughters are quick at translating for him and sometimes I believe he understands more than he lets on.

All of the girls, including Hananel's wife, were very taken by our philanthropist. She is small and dark. Beneath her veil, her hair was cut very short. Her eyes, I must admit, are quite captivating. They are the shape of almonds. Throughout the lunch she was reticent about her background. I am convinced she is hiding something of her past. On the other hand, she is here, she is generous, and does not seem to be an ill influence.

Quite the contrary, I was delighted to learn that she not only reads and writes, but was willing to teach Hananel's daughters. I trust this will make him rethink our academy's curriculum. If only our boys would read more fluently, we could teach them so many things beyond the Talmud. On the other hand, they have prodigious memories for Talmud and it is generally acknowledged that our students in Kairawan rank among the best anywhere.

Hananel's girls now have begun visiting her home—which has its own private courtyard—to learn reading and writing. Those girls have returned home bearing tales that I should not be listening to, especially since the stories they tell are so outlandish. They said that they have seen her sword! What, I ask, could any woman be doing with a sword?

In any case, this Sittuna has the boys of my academy all atwitter. If only that might get them to read and practice writing, I would look the other way. She surely is a distraction to their studies. But is that not the way of the world? As the Talmud says, "Shall one study Torah with a millstone around his neck?" Now some say that refers to a wife. But there is a difference in custom between the academies of Babylonia and the Land of Israel. I believe this statement refers to the distraction the unmarried boys have just thinking about women. If one has a wife, then one is less distracted, for there is no longer any mystery regarding what goes on between a man and wife.

This rumor of that woman with her sword reminds me of a story told long ago. Once, a foreign king besieged the Holy City of Jerusalem. Within the city was a pious girl, who when she saw her fellow Jerusalemites in such distress, dedicated herself to God and tried to save them. She went forth until she came to the city gate. There she told the guards, "Let me go forth. Perchance God will be gracious and work a miracle at my hand."

The guards were cautious, for they did not want the Jews within fleeing the city and breaking the siege. Further, they challenged her, "Perchance you lust after one of these infidels?!"

She disdained them and said, "God forbid! I put my faith in God Most High. I pray that he will aid me and enable me to slay the leader of these evil besiegers." She swore a vow to them and they allowed her to leave the city.

So she went and made her way to that king. She said to him, "Master, the rumor in the city is that you shall soon take it. I have come to pray to you that you might spare me and my family."

Now she was a very beautiful woman, small of stature and with beautiful almond shaped eyes. The king was entranced with her but had evil designs. He said to her, "I will save you and your family, but only on the condition that you marry me."

She said, "Sir, I am a pure daughter of Israel. Yet to save my family I would have married one of your soldiers. How much more so, it is my honor to marry the king himself."

This delighted that king and he said, "Then lie with me tonight."

She replied, "Just today I am completing my period of menstrual uncleanness. Allow me to go and immerse myself in flowing water, so that I may return to you tonight clean and pure."

The king was so delighted with his prospects for the evening that he bade her go. He invited his Wazir and his generals to dine with him. They ate together and drank until they were all quite tipsy. When the time came for the girl's return, the Wazir and the generals withdrew, leaving the king to his pleasures. That girl arrived and drank with him until that king, with God's help, fell fast asleep.

Then she took the king's own sword and, dedicating herself to God most High that He strengthen her hand, she raised that sword and cut off the king's head. This she concealed in her robes and she made her way back to the city gates. Once there she revealed her trophy to them. They recognized the head of the evil king who was besieging them. They raised it on a standard over the city's walls.

When the king's troops recognized the head of their master, they went to his tent and found his slain corpse. At that they fled headlong away from Jerusalem. The men of Jerusalem went forth in battle and chased their enemy all the way to Antioch. The people of Jerusalem were freed by the bravery of a girl and the sword she wielded with the help of God, Most High.

Dear Dunash and al-Iskander, since the arrival of this strange woman has led me to write you a story about a sword, let me conclude this letter with another story from the Talmud, about a scribe, as it were, writing the Holy Torah.

When Moses ascended on high to receive the Torah, he found the Blessed Holy One sitting and writing calligraphic adornments on the letters, for it is our scribal custom to put these crowns on seven of the letters of a Torah scroll. Moses, who was a very modest man, was prepared to have the Torah unadorned and so he asked God, "What is staying Your hand from giving me the Torah writ plain?"

God replied, "Moses, many generations from now there will be a man named Rabbi Aqiba ben Yosef. He will infer mound upon mound of laws from these jots and tittles."

Moses was amazed and so asked God, "Can You show him to me?"

God said, "But turn around."

At that Moses found himself seated in the eighth row of Aqiba's classroom. Now I tell you, Dunash and al-Iskander, that even in those days it was like our own academy; there were usually seven rows in the lecture hall and the brightest students sat at the very front. But there was our Master, Moses, sitting in the back row. He was so perplexed by the dialectic, the Talmud says, that he grew dizzy with incomprehension. A point of law arose and the students pressed Rabbi Aqiba. Although he offered them proofs, they refuted each and every one until he finally said, "This is the law given to Moses at Sinai!"

Now in a sense this is true, for according to this Talmudic tale, Moses was atop Mt. Sinai when he heard this exchange. Yet Aqiba was also telling his students to question no more, this is our received tradition. And I need not add that in the story, our master Moses does not understand the argumentation.

But as the Talmud itself continues the tale, when Moses heard his name, he grew stronger and felt consoled. He returned to God and said, "You have such a one as he, and yet You give the Torah to the likes of me?"

But the Blessed Holy One replied, "Silence, this is according to My plan."

So Moses then asked of God, "Master of both worlds, You have shown me his great learning, will You show me Aqiba's reward?"

Again, God told him to turn around at which Moses beheld the Roman torturers weighing out Aqiba's very flesh in the marketplace.

Moses cried, "Thus is his Torah and such is his reward!?"

But the Blessed Holy One replied, "Silence, this is according to My plan."

Dunash, dear friend, this story teaches us that we must put our trust in God, for there is a divine plan, even if we are not privy to it. We must have faith that our suffering has a purpose. And al-Iskander, son, this story also teaches that the sages of blessed memory would grow in Torah, so that as the centuries passed, even Moses, our master, might not understand the complexities of the law. But we must study the rabbis' law, for it has the same authority as that given to Moses at Mt. Sinai.

I have told you a story of a woman with a sword and another of a scribe. In this case, the scribe was the very Blessed Holy One, praised be His name. For all who copy our sacred works imitate the deeds of the Blessed Holy One, Who handed to Moses the Torah written by God's very hand. This is the same hand that brought us forth out of Egypt. May it bring redemption to us and to the whole house of Israel, speedily in our day.

From al-Iskander in Fustat, to Nissim in Kairawan, Late Fall, 1033

Our master, Rabbenu Nissim, may God bless you and keep you. Your letter with the stories of the sword and the scribe brought us great pleasure. I especially thank you for your subtle yet clear replies to my letters and questions to you. I am writing on behalf of my father, but he will trust me now to conduct the business for him simply at his word. He will not read my letters, as it is too difficult for him to do so. Although he still does business, he spends most of his time indoors in a cool dark room, resting upon the diwan. We have recently installed a new sofa for our business associates to use while father stretches out.

I act now as his eyes and ears. I am learning to inspect goods and to be sure that all is packed carefully whether for sea or for caravan travel. Since our disaster at sea, I have been encouraging Father to use the caravan routes more. He says there is less profit, but so be it. Risk is also an expense. We do good business, but Father's health remains poor. May God bring him a complete healing.

I am wondering if you would consent to act as our agent for a caravan shipment—the contents of the consignment are listed below. I know that Daddy has used you for sewing but I regret I have none to send now. But he has also used you to be agent in Kairawan. Daddy also uses the Taherti family there, and we will continue to use them. I do not wish that they should think that I desire to take bread from their mouth. But some of the letters you have written to me have given me an idea that you can be helpful in another way.

I do not wish for you to offer these items in the markets of Kairawan. I have discussed this with Daddy and he agrees that we wish you to act as middleman for us to send these goods to the far Maghreb. I have noticed that you have contact with the rabbis of the cities there such as Tlemcen, Sijilmasa, Marrakesh and Fez. You will notice I do not wish you to represent us in Tahert, which we will, of course, leave to the Tahertis.

It would be good to organize a caravan in Kairawan with the goods we are sending and sell these items in the West. I know this will mean a great deal of letter writing for you and some organizing in Kairawan. But this should be less work than actually bringing the goods to market in Kairawan. I feel certain that you can help us penetrate those cities through your rabbinic contacts in a way we have been unable to up till now.

A Delightful Compendium of Consolation   175

I also wonder what you might think of the advisability of organizing another, much larger caravan to go through Kairawan all the way to Ceuta and then across the straits to Sefarad. I am thinking of your close association with the Nagid Shmuel, Wazir at Granada. I know that Granada has great ability to import over land without recourse to ferrying goods from western Afrikiya. But your established relationship means that you send goods to Rabbi Shmuel, as well as him sending goods to you. This, of course, makes his caravans more efficient.

My father has considered this plan carefully and believes it will be of great benefit to us and to you. It would allow us a trade route independent of our al-Tustari relatives, which is good for our immediate family pride. I write to you as honestly as I know how. Rabbi, I do not have any motive but the honor of my father's house and support for you, my revered teacher.

I should tell you that I am attending the sessions of the rabbis here in Fustat, along with those of our masters of Scripture from the Karaite community. I do not wish to reject my family's traditions, God forbid, but to expand my knowledge so that all Jewish traditions are in my mouth. I have gained so much from the stories that you have sent me that I am now also eager to learn your rabbinic law.

Father says to add what he is sure you need to know in order to undertake this commission on our behalf: for your acting as middleman we will offer you 8 percent of the profit on each caravan of goods. For each new contact you open for us in the market places of the far Maghreb, we offer a 2 percent finder's fee, which means that you will have 10 percent of the profits on this caravan. Daddy estimates your share of the profit in this shipment to be approximately 27 dinars. I do not know how he was able to keep all of the numbers counted without looking at them, but Daddy says he may be tired, but he is not addled. He tells me I do not convert dirhems to dinars quickly enough to keep up with the calculations, and that I should spend more time practicing my multiplying and dividing.

Daddy also wishes that you inform us whether you will contact the Nagid in this matter, then he can determine what might sell well in Sefarad. I am sending a copy of this letter by boat and another with the caravan that is carrying to you the following items, each marked Rabbenu Nissim and sent to you at the Jewish Bazaar in Kairawan.

To Rabbenu Nissim, Second in Kairawan. From Dunash, my father, may he grow in strength and health; and his son, al-Iskander, in Fustat, Misr.

2 large palm-leaf baskets of kohl
18 fine linen gowns
12 short shawls for outdoors
3 medium boxes of coral beads already strung
2 jars of small porcelain beads, not yet pierced for stringing

8   bales of flax
4   bolts of linen cloth, middle grade
41 pounds of Chinese silk thread, first quality
6   bushels of hazel nuts in their shells
16 small silver serving bowls
8   silver anklets
34 pairs of shoes made in Misr, various sizes for men and women
1   silk duvet - this is a gift to your household from my father

Please acknowledge receipt and indicate final point of sale intended. Also, acknowledge plans regarding Granada. From Dunash and son.

From al-Jskander in Fustat, to his sister in Kairawan, late Fall, 1033

To Sittuna bint Haroun who is Martha, at the perfumers of the Souk al-Yahud, in the old city of Kairawan, in-sh Allah.

From al-Iskander ibn Dunash HaCohen al-Tustari in the fortress of Misr, by caravan, in the name of the Merciful.

Dear Sister. I kiss your hands and send my love to you, although I confess to you that I am angry with you, maybe even more angry than Daddy was when you left home two years ago. I do not even know what to call you. You think it is admirable or adventurous that you have had so many names. I think it shows how confused you are about who you want to be, as though being an al-Tustari were somehow not honorable.

You think that it is all right to travel the Great Sea from one end to another and only settle down when you desire to. You disdain what Daddy does by working hard and trading on our behalf. He does it for us, for us. He risks his life on his ship journeys so that we might eat and we might study and learn to write and read. And your response is to leave, to run off, to leave your Jewish life behind while I stay here and do both your work and my own. And then you put into port as the owner of a ship, when you bought your passage with stolen goods.

Karimah, I have waited to have the opportunity to tell you all of this for two years and I am afraid that there is too much to tell you. I am upset with you and upset that you might ignore this letter; like you used to go into your room with your hands over your ears when Daddy or Mommy would yell at you.

You write me stories of your adventures, I suppose to entertain me and have your little brother think you are so very grand. You tell me you are Kamar al-Zaman today and you have found a city of people made of black stone. Did you think that only you could read the *1001 Nights*? When I read your stories from the *Nights* as though they had happened to you, I realized that your fabulous life on the road was all a sham. I do not know anything of what you have done because I cannot know if anything that you have written me is even true.

And if it is true and you are a master of the sword, should I be proud that my sister has slain one man or burnt another with oil and naphtha? Do you think it was good for me to read that my own sister was robbing caravans and pirating ships, perhaps the very ships that Daddy had invested in? And what could you think that I would feel when you wrote to me about your being with this man or that?

Did you not know that Ismail would return to Fustat and that I might have to face him in the street or in the shop? His father is, after all, still Daddy's Muslim partner. Yet because you were angered or interested in someone else, you put Daddy's business at risk. And this is not even to speak of how you hurt Daddy and Mommy and me by leaving home without even a goodbye.

Ismail is a lovely boy, we all like him and always have, dear sister. But does that allow you to throw off the generations during which our family followed the customs of our ancestors? And shall I be happy now that you have returned to Judaism, but not to our community of Scripture? At least on this last point I soften towards you, for I have come to love the stories of the rabbis and am now sitting at lectures in their law. But I have not given up the community of Karaites nor thrown off our customs. I pray that the community in Kairawan brings you back to us, dear Karimah.

You have recently written to me of Mommy's family and that she might not be Jewish. You are right to worry that this might make us neither here nor there. But why do you suddenly worry, when you were so quick to reject it all on your own not months before? You complain again and again that Daddy was unfair to you for mourning over your loss to our family and community. But what he did, he did out of love for you. He was hurt. You abandoned us and all things Jewish, you admitted as much in your letters.

So it was you pushing us away, all the while complaining to me that Daddy was at fault. He is not perfect; I know because I live with him every day. I pray he lives until one hundred and twenty, and Mommy too. But I am here and you are there, yet you tell me whether Mommy and Daddy are kosher enough or whether they are really married. If you are right in your judgments then I am a *mamzer*, and so are you! You condemn yourself, dear Sister.

Finally, and this was the most galling thing you did these past two years, you told me to keep secrets that I did not wish to know in the first place. You made me, your little brother, your confidant, telling me things I never should have to hear. And then you tell ME who I can and cannot talk to about the many, many disturbing things that you wrote to me. And you wrote letters to Nanny about your escapades without even knowing that dear Nanny has been in that Good Resting Place for many months now; that is how self-centered you have become! Do you think it fair that I had to keep it all inside me? That I alone should be the bearer of your secrets? You were totally inconsiderate of me, even as you demanded that I be considerate of you and your adventures and your secrets.

You put a wall between me and Mommy and Daddy that I did not wish to be there. At least Daddy did not demand that Mommy and I join him in his mourning for you. You are as stubborn as he is. But you hurt me, Karimah, almost every time you wrote to me, you hurt me. Each letter was an expression of your love for me and your trust. I know that. But you could not see beyond your own nose to ME and what might be good for ME. I did not need to be adjured to silence and secrecy so that I had no recourse but to swallow your lies whole and let them sour in my belly.

Even so, I did need to hear from you. I miss you terribly. I have been hard pressed to carry the burdens of the household all by myself. To be honest, and this has nothing to do with you, I would not have made it through these past two years were it not for the attention of Rabbenu Nissim of Kairawan.

So now it is my turn to adjure you. I do not wish him to know that we are related. You are there and will have his attention. I do not want the attention he also gives to me to become focused through the lens of Karimah. Please leave me my own lifeline to his wisdom and his Torah. I am not a child any longer, but a man. I consider Rabbenu Nissim my teacher. Do not stain that for me with your stories and your lies. Karimah, if you cannot write the truth to me, then do not write me. I am a separate person and not your mirror.

I wish to hear from you. I could use my sister in my life again. But you do not know anything of my life. And, to be honest, your stories have kept me from knowing your life, I fear. I do not wish to hear from Kamar al-Zaman or Lady Badr or even Wuhshah. I will address my letters to you as Sittuna or even Martha. But when you write me it must be as Karimah. No more stories, Sister, just you.

From your brother al-Iskander, who misses you and wants you in his life. Do not forsake me.

Chapter Eleven
Late Fall, 1033

To Abi-Skander in Fustat, Dunash HaCohen al-Tustari and his son and partner, al-Iskander ibn Dunash HaCohen.

Dear friends and business partners, I am writing to you with joy. I am very
pleased with both of your business propositions and will tell you about the caravan you sent and the disposition of the goods to the Maghreb. Thank you also,
Dunash, for the silk bedding which now graces my diwan; it is beautiful. I also
am pleased to see you opening new trade, Dunash; it is a hopeful sign. I prayed
to God that you might have a speedy recovery.

In any case, your al-Iskander must be commended. You will see by my salutation that I have elevated him from apprentice to partner in your family business.
Forgive my presumption, Dunash, but a father should be made to see the capabilities of his son. Your 'Skander is a very good boy who worries about you and
executes your plans efficiently. Praise God day by day.

Before I proposed our business to my colleagues in the West, I sought the
advice of someone who knew the caravan trade. I did not wish to ask the Tahertis,
lest they think that I was trying to take bread from their mouths. But the people
I know here in Kairawan are disciples of the sages, not businessmen. The person
I would share such plans with is Rabbenu Hananel, who does not understand
the first thing about North African commerce, even though he can explain every
detail of the business transactions in both Talmuds.

I realized that I might seek advice from the woman, Sittuna. I knew she was
wealthy and had some experience in shipping. Further, when she first came to
Kairawan she had a caravan of goods from Sousse. It was to my benefit and yours,
Dunash, that I made inquiry. Sittuna thought your proposition was not only fair,
but wise. She pointed out that the terms for me were very generous, for which
I thank you again.

Then Sittuna said that the caravan of goods you sent was really very small and
that camel trains that small were at higher risk from brigands. I reasoned with her
that a large caravan would make a more tempting target to raiders, but she was
firm, "Large caravans have more protection, small caravans are too vulnerable."

She proposed to buy goods in the marketplace and take goods from her warehouses in both Kairawan and Sousse. Within a week, an enormous caravan was formed. Further, she insisted on offering me the same terms as you had. And then she said I was to write to you and tell you that for organizing and initiating this plan of expansion to the Western markets, she would offer you ten percent of her profits, as well. I could not follow all of the details of the offer so she clarified:

After deducting for expenses and tolls and gift-taxes, profit remains.
10% of total profit goes to me, Rabbenu Nissim, as middle-man.
10% of her profit goes to Dunash and son for their origination fee.
90% of Dunash and son's share of their goods is theirs.
80% of her share of the profits is hers.

This seemed to be such a good prospect for you that I accepted immediately. She said there were two more conditions. The first was that you had to be informed that these terms held for this and any future venture. I told her that I did not understand why she offers each of us such favorable conditions. She said that she had learned when she was yet a child in her father's house that it is better to share good fortune with partners.

I asked her then what her second condition was. She said that she alone must bear the entire risk for the caravan. I said this was not acceptable, that caravans were frequently raided by brigands and that the risk should be spread among all members of a consortium. But she said that she had great expertise in the security of caravans, this was her specialty. If, God forbid, there was a natural disaster like a flood or an earthquake, we would share the loss of goods. But as for brigands, she would be the absolute guarantor.

I was quite uneasy agreeing to this odd stipulation. But again, it was clearly to our mutual benefit. I do not know this woman well at all, yet she was putting up goods and services as a very palpable show of good faith. Ultimately, I agreed and she said, "God willing, none of us will regret it." Then she announced that she herself would accompany the caravan westward for the first three days and would return back to Kairawan thereafter. If the caravan left on a Sunday, she would be back in time for the Sabbath assured that our goods were safe and in capable hands. Again, I had no choice but to agree.

The truly strong objection came from Ghazal. "How can you send her away for a week?" she wailed, "She is teaching us to read!"

I reassured her that Sittuna would return to us soon and return to her tutelage. I must speak with Hananel and see if he is sufficiently accepting of his daughters' learning that we might make this teaching a formal arrangement with Sittuna.

In any case, I worried lest Sittuna return before the Sabbath without ample time to make her preparations for Sabbath meals. I also wished to show my gratitude to her for her participation in our consortium at such favorable terms, and her willingness to oversee the security of our caravan. Finally, I felt I owed a meal to Hananel and his family who have been very gracious about hosting me and caring for Ghazal. So before Sittuna left with the caravan I took the step of inviting her and Hananel's family for a Sabbath meal upon her return to Kairawan.

Truly, Dunash and al-Iskander, I was not thinking clearly. How would I be able to feed all these people? Kairawan may have a great academy, but it is not Fustat. We cannot simply go out to the street and buy prepared foods to bring home. If I were to serve a Sabbath meal for 14 people, I must have help. I went begging to Mulaah and Abu al-Maali to ask for their assistance. Mulaah knew her way around my household when she cared for Ghazal and al-Maali is my student. I was forthright with Abu al-Maali and told him that while I wished them to join us for this Sabbath banquet, there would be 16 of us including them. I needed help.

Abu al-Maali reminded me that Mulaah was now in her eighth month of pregnancy. I had forgotten. I told him then that I would find other help, but of course, they were still invited to the Sabbath luncheon. He said, "Nonsense, Rabbi, I will ask my wife. You buy the food, we will make it."

Bless that boy; I pray his wife gives him a beautiful and healthy son, God willing. That Friday morning Mulaah came to my home with Hananel's four eldest daughters. She gave me a list and sent me with the girls to the market. By the time we came home with the food, Mulaah and al-Maali had taken carpets from the academy and put them in my courtyard. The places were set and Mulaah was seated upon my sofa giving orders to al-Maali. I apologized for taking him away from his studies. He replied, "This too is Torah, Rabbi, and I must learn it."

I laughed at his clever remark, for it is from the Talmud and was said by one of Rabbi Yehuda's students when that saint found the boy hiding one night beneath his marriage bed! Mulaah immediately got Hananel's girls cooking. Even Ghazal ran back and forth carrying vegetables, helping set out the food. They were all so excited to be making lunch for Sittuna. As for me, I was moved by all the bustle and happiness of the girls. I long for this domestic bliss, which I have not had since my wife's death. At least Ghazal seems happy these days and is making progress. But she is still so small of stature and her head remains too big.

I have come to the end of my paper. I will send this letter with the caravan that leaves today for Fustat, God willing. I promise to tell you of the Sabbath lunch I gave in my next letter and to add some stories which that lunch brought forth in my memory. Perhaps by then I will know the results of our new caravan venture. In any case, rest assured. I have written the Nagid Rabbenu Shmuel and expect he will send me a favorable reply soon.

Until then I am your most grateful and devoted partner, Nissim *berav* Yakov, may his memory be for blessing.

From Nissim in Kairawan, to Dunash and al-Iskander in Fustat, Late Fall, 1033

To my dear friends and business partners, may God continue to shine His face upon us, Dunash HaCohen al-Tustari and his son al-Iskander, in Fustat, in the rainy season.

Friends and colleagues, I have waited some weeks to tell you of the Sabbath luncheon that I gave upon Sittuna's return to Kairawan, for I awaited word from our caravan and from the Nagid Shmuel, Wazir of Granada. As I predicted, Rabbenu Shmuel is willing to have our goods come to the court there and proposes favorable terms of sale. He says we may sell at whatever the market will bear. So long as we dedicate one percent of the profits to his disposal for gifts at the court of Granada, he will ensure there are neither tolls nor port taxes. I know that these often amount to a large part of the expenses charged against profit. Yet, I do not know whether those expenses in fact add up to a full percentage of the final profits. In any case, I do not feel we can turn down this entree into the Andalusian market, so I told him that we would begin to prepare a large consignment for the Spring, when shipping from the West reopens. Dunash, I seek your keen and quick calculations whether the Nagid's proposal is to our favor or to his.

The caravan we shared with Sittuna was to have stopped at Tlemcen, Sijilmasa and then on to Marrakesh, returning northeastwards via Fez, if there were yet goods to sell. As it turned out, the caravan was finished by Sijilmasa and returned laden with dried fruits and woods which we will be forwarding to you for sale in Fustat or points east. Sittuna assured herself that the caravan was in good hands. She oversaw hiring the caravan master who sold the goods, as well as the guards who protected it. There were no raids and no protection money was paid. That added to our profits. The demand for our goods in Tlemcen and Sijilmasa was such that our profits were excellent there, far better than I have ever secured in Kairawan.

Your goods drew 112 dinars profit, while Sittuna who had half again as much as you, drew 168 dinars. Of hers she gets 134 1/3 dinars, and we share 33 2/3 dinars, or 16 5/6 dinars each. You also get 101 dinars from your goods, while I get 11 dinars. The total profits then are: Sittuna: 134 2/6 dinars; I, Nissim: 27 5/6 dinars; you both: 117 5/6 dinars.

I commend you for a fine idea. I wish to send you the money quickly, so that the dinars do not sit idle. But I did not wish to drag the Tahertis into our private business and so have sent the coins in sealed bags as part of the caravan, rather than through inter-bank accounting. I pray for the safety of the profits as well as our new caravan of goods, now on its way to Fustat, God willing.

Our Sabbath lunch upon Sittuna's return was quite wonderful. We ate birds with bread and currant stuffing. For a final course the girls had baked makroud cookies, using the sweet dates of Kairawan. After we ate, in place of a word of Torah, Sittuna put the girls through their lessons. They read to us what they said was their weekly Torah reading. Each girl stood and read to us from a book, not a scroll. I think they did not wish to offend the men by reading from the scroll as we do in the synagogue. But Sittuna showed us the book they were reading from and it had two columns to a page and the calligraphy was exactly the same as in a Torah scroll. We were all most impressed.

Each of Hananel's daughters, as well as my Ghazal, read from three to six verses. Sittuna said this added up to a weekly reading according to the rabbis of the Land of Israel. Hananel agreed. I was perplexed, for we who follow Babylonian custom read a much longer section from the Torah each week. Hananel explained that in the Land of Israel it took three and sometimes three and a half years to complete the entire Torah from Genesis through Deuteronomy. We here read the cycle in the course of one year and then start all over again on the final day of Sukkot. According to the rite of the Land of Israel, readings are only one-third as long. I wonder if they leave the synagogue any earlier or if the rabbis there just preach for a longer time. In any case, I could see Hananel was deeply impressed with his daughters' newfound skill.

Sittuna actually had the girls chant from the Torah. She signaled them when to end a verse, when to pause and the like, by making motions with her hands and fingers. She says she learned this from a cantor in the Hijaz at Wadi al-Qura. It reminded me of a story from the Talmud that I have written commentary upon. It shows how through mere gestures and allusions people who know one another well can understand each other. I told these stories at lunch that Sabbath and I will tell you now:

Once our Holy Rabbi, Yehuda the Patriarch of the Land of Israel, had guests for lunch at his Sabbath table. During the meal, his pious and learned maidservant came to him and said, "Rabbi, the ladle knocks against the jug. Will the eagles fly to their nests or shall I remove its companion's crown?"

Rabbi replied to her, "Remove the crown, by all means."

This is what that clever woman meant: "the ladle knocks" meant that the ladle she used to draw the wine from the barrel was knocking against the wooden bottom for the barrel was empty. The "eagles" were the guests at table. She wished to know if they would be going home soon or whether she should open another barrel of wine—that is what she meant by "removing the crown." When Rabbi Yehuda told her to remove the crown, he signaled that she should pour more wine from the second cask, and that is exactly what I did for the guests at my Sabbath meal!

This allowed me time to tell the tale of Rabbi Yehuda the Patriarch and his friendship with the Emperor Antoninus. The emperor sought our rabbi's advice, but Rabbi Yehuda was always very careful to signal it to him through gestures so that the courtiers of the Rum, who were enemies of the Jews, could not say that the emperor was depending upon a Jew to run the empire. Perhaps you should tell this story to your cousin Sahl Abu Saad, so he can continue without difficulty to advise al-Zahir, may his reign prosper.

At one time Antoninus said to Rabbi, "I wish to make my son the next emperor. I also wish to remit taxes one-third for the city of Tiberius. But you know that it is not our custom to proclaim two enactments at the same time."

Now Rabbi was eager for the tax abatement to come to Tiberius, which was a home to many rabbis. So he had his disciples act out the following before the emperor. One climbed upon the shoulders of another. The one on top was holding a pigeon, which he released when he was firmly seated on his colleague. With this, the Emperor Antoninus understood that he was to appoint his son as emperor, and then the new emperor could remit the taxes as his first act.

Another time, Antoninus complained that his advisors had turned against him. He wished to dismiss them all but feared for the stability of the empire. Rabbi walked with him to his garden. There he reached down and plucked a radish. He walked a bit more and plucked another radish. Then he walked even more and picked a third radish. Thus, the Emperor Antoninus understood that he should dismiss his bad advisors one at a time rather than all at once.

The Talmud of our rabbis is full of good advice, both political and practical. It says there, a man should be sure to marry his daughter to a scholar. And the Talmud also says a man should sell everything he has in order to marry a daughter of scholars. If he cannot find a daughter of scholars, he should find the daughter of a leader of the generation. If he cannot find such a one, let him marry his daughter to the head of a synagogue. If he cannot find such a one, let him marry his daughter to a collector of charity. If he cannot find such a one, let him marry his daughter to a teacher of reading.

Dunash, I tell you, the same is true for sons. You should marry your al-Iskander to the daughter of a scholar, as our sages have taught. And I, what shall I do with my poor Ghazal? Dear Dunash and al-Iskander, May God bless you both for your willingness to have me as a business partner. As it says at the end of the prophet Zephaniah, "Thus says the Lord: I will make you famous and praised among all the nations of the land, when I restore your fortunes before their very eyes." May it be God's will.

Write to me of your plans for the large caravan to Shmuel the Nagid and Wazir in Granada. From Nissim *berav* Yakov, Second in Kairawan. To Dunash HaCohen al-Tustari and son, in Fustat, God willing.

From al-Iskander in Fustat, to Nissim in Kairawan, Winter, 1033

Dear teacher and master, Rabbenu Nissim, may your light shine forth. I enjoyed your stories of the gestures very much. Do you really think our sages of blessed memory were able to converse with the emperors of the Rum in the same way that Uncle Sahl can speak with the Caliph al-Zahir? Or do the rabbis, may they rest in Eden, sometimes just tell stories for the sake of the point they wish their students to learn? If so, I imagine that stories of the emperor would best hold their attention. How can we know what is just a story and what really happened?

I received the caravan of dried fruits and wood, we have stored it in our warehouse here. I reason we should sell the dried fruit near the end of the rainy season when householders long for the taste of fruit and are yearning for summer. I also will sell the wood just at the beginning of the Spring, when the shipping lanes have not yet opened, but people wish to begin building and making repairs from the damage of winter winds and rain. Please send me your permission to keep the goods in storage for so long and the dinars, therefore, out of circulation.

I have also received the dinars of profit that we made in our consortium of goods to the West. According to my calculations we owe you 1/6 dinar, which I will credit to you for our next transaction. I am grateful for your ensuring the safety of our goods by joining them to a larger caravan. Please convey my father's thanks to your Kairawan partner there for her generous terms.

I tell you, master, that the profits are a great help to us, as Father is doing poorly. God help me, I am doing my best to manage the business on my own and trying to disturb father as little as possible. The dinars you sent me have enabled me to invest with Uncle Sahl, and with Bahram ibn Abdallah in a Hajj caravan. We feel the caravan will yield good return, as my father's old partner Bahram sent his son Ismail to accompany the caravan. The son has been to Mecca and al-Medinah before and knows his way around the markets.

Now if I may, dear rabbi, I would like to ask you a personal question on behalf of a friend, unrelated to our business. This is not something I have discussed with anyone here, as I promised my friend discretion. This friend from our community of Scripture told me that his mother had come from the Rum and that he is not sure that she was a Jew before she married his father. I know that according to the Torah, the identity of a child follows the father. But I have heard that the rabbis are punctilious about insisting that it is the mother who determines whether or not her son is Jewish.

This friend turned to me because he knows that I am interested in your rabbinic law. This is one of those areas in which your rabbinic community is more stringent than we Karaites are. I could not answer my friend because I do not know rabbinic law and it is not my place to speak about such grave matters. I also do not know the attitudes of the Muslim authorities toward women from outside the community becoming Jews. Nor, of course, do I know anything about how the Christians think about these matters. Teach us, Rabbenu, what is the law in this case?

I would be grateful if you sent me the reply to this question to a private place, where no one in my household might receive it. I would not want to compromise my friend, who is relying on me. I can be reached care of the Sugar Factory and Sweet Shop of the small bazaar in the fortress of Fustat.

Rabbenu Nissim, I thank you for all you have done for me and my entire household. Thank you for answering this question, too. I await your reply.

From al-Iskander ibn Dunash HaCohen al-Tustari, in Misr. To Rabbenu Nissim, may his light shine forth throughout the Diaspora, in Kairawan, with the assistance of Heaven. God willing.

From Karimah in Kairawan, to al-Iskander in Fustat, Winter, 1033-34

To my only brother, al-Iskander ibn Dunash HaCohen al-Tustari, may he grow to Torah, marriage, and good deeds, in Fustat, Misr.

From his loving sister who misses him, in the name of the Merciful.

My dear brother, I kiss your hands and your eyes and beg your forgiveness. It was never my intention to hurt you, for you mean so much to me and I need you as an anchor in my life. I am sorry if you thought that some of the things I have told you were inappropriate to your ears. I wrote to you as I would have to my very best friend, speaking from my heart about the things which most concern me. It crushed me to think that I had angered you, much as it crushed me to learn that Nanny had died, peace be upon her. She was like a second mother to us both. Blessed is the True Judge.

I admit that I did not see people turned into black stone, but otherwise all that I have written to you is true. Perhaps I used the language of the Nights to convey some of the adventure, but that does not make what took place any less correct. I do not live a lie, only a lonely life. I think you are right, dear sweet Skandi, when you say I am confused about whom I wish to be. I think I am finding out who I am here in Kairawan.

I waited to write to you until I knew that Rabbenu Nissim explained the results of the caravan venture we jointly undertook. I do not wish Nissim to know that I am the daughter of Dunash, but that does not stop me from accepting responsibility towards my family. You are correct about that, too. I have learned a great deal on the road and on the seas in these past two years, and I shall use it to help our branch of the al-Tustari clan. We, too, shall have greatness.

I feel certain that the caravan to Granada is a good idea, but only because of the special circumstances of Shmuel the Nagid also being Wazir there. He will open the court to us the same way Uncle Sahl has opened the court in al-Kahira. I expect we should do very well and that the one percent he asks is a reasonable price to pay for the accommodation he is offering. We must be ready to have our caravan at Ceuta cross the straits before mid-summer. Although we will not know what the market bears in Granada, we can rely on the Nagid for those numbers.

I am also confident of our security on the caravans and I will tell you why. You will not be happy to hear it as it has to do with my personal life these last two years, but it affects our business together and I want to be completely honest with you. You are my only brother and I must be able to tell you everything and not hide things from you. There is too much hidden in my life. Please be the one person now who will hear and know who I really am. I can endure harsh judgment if only you will hear me, dearest al-Iskander.

I accompanied the caravan from Fustat to be sure it mustered properly. I chose the caravan Shaykh and the guards, but I needed to inspect them first hand. I rode on horseback, which impressed them. More so, I carried my Badawi sword and let them see me do my exercises so that they would know it was not merely for show.

On the second day of the journey, after we were beyond Kairawan too far a distance to expect help, a group of Badawi raiders came down upon us. I took my

Burton L. Visotzky

sword still in its scabbard and rode out to meet them, prepared to pay if need be, but also prepared to fight, if God willed it. At first, they asked a very high price for protection. I think the raiders assumed that a woman would succumb easily. I refused and said I must consult my caravan. As I rode back I made a point of drawing my sword, for I wanted them to clearly see its Badawi origins.

At that moment a rider darted forth from the Badawi ranks and pulled alongside me. He gestured to my sword and said, "Some stick!"

I looked up in astonishment into the eyes of Abu Sin. "What are you doing here?" I stammered.

He said, "I could ask you the same question. But I will tell you that it was decided in Baghdad that my protection was no longer needed for the Hajj on the road to Mecca. I was informed that my activities there would not be tolerated any more. What was I to do? I came to Afrikiya, where my Berbers have long lived. They were happy to come home. I and the Badawi who ride with me are happy to have new hunting grounds. I fear we could grow fat here with the caravan trade."

"Perhaps," I replied, "but not with my caravans!"

We laughed and Abu Sin gave me a guarantee that we would never be raided by his men, nor would we ever be approached by other brigands, for he would let it be known that we were under his protection. I thanked him; we dismounted and shared a meal and tea. After we dined, he asked if I still exercised with the sword. We spent the afternoon together thrusting and parrying. Brother, I am no longer as good as I once was, I must practice more.

Abu Sin told me that he had returned to his life as a philosopher since I had left him. He asked, "Wuhshah, would you not consider returning to our life together?"

Brother, I longed for him at that moment, but God enlightened my eyes. I told Abu Sin that I must think before I replied to him. He agreed to meet me again on my return. Our caravan moved on and our men held me in the highest esteem. I believe they know that we are no longer vulnerable to an attack, and this makes them relax and enjoy the riding. They sang as the camels moved across the sands.

I left them on the fourth morning and turned back for Kairawan. I was half a day's journey from them when Abu Sin joined me. He was alone. We rode in silence most of the day and camped together that night. It was almost like old times, but there also was sadness. We rode together on the next day as well, talking about my time on the waters of the Great Sea and his long trek from the Hijaz across upper Egypt to the Maghreb. On the sixth day, which was Friday, I bid him farewell. I told him my place was with the Jews of Kairawan. It was time I returned to my ancestors.

Abu Sin joked that long ago, when the Jews left Egypt, we, too, were Badawi. But he understood and said, "I will always watch over you, Karimah. Go now. Live your life."

When I returned to Kairawan, Nissim had arranged a Sabbath feast. Hananel and his women were there, and at the luncheon I had all of the girls show off their new reading skills. They chanted the Torah portion of the week. Rabbi Nissim was incredibly gracious. He has no idea what to do with his daughter. Do you think all fathers suffer from this malady, Skandi?

He really is quite charming, this Rabbenu Nissim. He had invited one of his disciples and the boy's wife. Her name is Mulaah. She is very pregnant and very sweet. It turns out it was she who had supervised the preparations of the meal. The food was delicious and I was impressed that a woman that pregnant could be that commanding. Nissim's daughter Ghazal was very comfortable with Mulaah. I really like the woman and feel sure I have made a friend. It is good for me to have a girlfriend. Aside from Guziella in Phaselis, I have not had a girlfriend to talk to since I left Fustat. I hope Mulaah's baby does not keep her from our new friendship. I will make time to help her when the baby comes. We have already met for tea and gossip. Mulaah is teaching me the ways of Kairawan. Her family originally came from Fustat. I still have to decide how much I can tell her.

In the meanwhile, I continue teaching Hananel's girls and Ghazal. They are reading rather fluently. Now that we can read Scripture, I wish to teach them rabbinic lore. There are books of that here. Most of the other books which we read and copied in Fustat, the rabbis and students here simply know by memory. Some of the boys of the academy have asked if I would tutor them in reading. Of course, this is wholly inappropriate behavior. I can see that it is just a form of flirting, but I must be concerned for my reputation.

Hillel ibn al-Gassus and his colleague Mevorach, who comes from an Iraqi family, make it a point to see me somewhere almost every day. They are both unmarried. I wonder if Rabbi Nissim already has in mind a match for me? If so, he will be disappointed. His boys are exactly that, mere boys. After my travels, they are of no interest to me. The only unmarried man I have met in Kairawan who seems to me truly to be a man is Rabbenu Nissim. But he is Second and Father of the Court, an important senior rabbi. Al-Iskander, you wrote to me that you know him. Write again and tell me more about him. Will you do that for me?

Dear al-Iskander, little brother. I pour out my heart to you like water. Please write me a letter with news of Fustat. I am happy we can do business as partners. I wish to help the family, but it is not as though Daddy actually needs my help. Please do not betray me to him. I am not ready to deal with his anger or with what I learned about Mommy and Daddy when I was in Amalfi.

Burton L. Visotzky

I am becoming sure of myself here in Kairawan, but I still am not sure how to think about Mommy and Daddy. In most things I am a woman, but thinking about them makes me feel like I am still a girl. I will stop this now, Skandi, since you wrote that you do not like it. Please do not be mad at me. I am your sister and I need you.

From Sittuna in Kairawan, with the grace of God. To al-Iskander al-Tustari, in the Sugar Factory and Sweet Shop in the fortress of Fustat, Misr, by caravan, In-sh-Allah.

Excerpts from Nissim's "Scroll of Secrets," his personal diary. Late Winter, 1034

— *Rabbenu Shmuel ben Hofni has died. "If fire consumes the mighty cedars, what shall we do, we who are moss upon the wall?" With the death of Rabbenu Shmuel the academy of Sura comes to an end. There is no longer a Gaon to rule there, and since the Muslims took over, the Sura academy is in Baghdad.*

All that remains is the academy of his son-in-law, Rabbenu Hai Gaon, son of Rav Sherira. Rav Sherira wrote to my sainted father Rabbenu Yakov ibn Shaheen, peace be upon him. And the academy of Rabbenu Hai berav Sherira, the great academy of Pumbeditha, it too is now in Baghdad.

Our master Rabbenu Hai Gaon is no longer young. What will become of Torah when the academies that produced the Babylonian Talmud cease to be? Shall Hananel and I, here in Kairawan, carry on the traditions of Iraq? Even Hananel uses the traditions of the rabbis of the West, the Talmud of Jerusalem.

Woe unto us at the death of Rabbenu Shmuel ben Hofni. I must teach my students from his Introduction to the Talmud. It really is a very good work and neither Hananel nor I have anything like it. Now that reading has returned to our academy I can also ask our students to read from his commentary to the Torah. I will never forget the first time I heard his question about the story of Adam, Eve, and the snake, "If serpents spoke at the time of Adam and Eve, why do they no longer speak in our day?"

Even my father, peace be upon him, had no answer to that far reaching question about the nature of the stories of the Torah. Can it be that the stories of the Torah are like the stories that we rabbis tell; fictions to teach a higher truth? Could this, God forbid, be true of the historic accounts of the Bible as well? Enough! What I am writing borders on heresy. Did Rabbenu Shmuel ben Hofni come to such questions from his well known reading of the books of the gentiles? Or did he have so many questions that the Torah and the rabbis did not address, that he turned to those outside works for enlightenment? Now I will never be able to ask him about the works of the physician ibn Sina.

Of course, Rabbenu Shmuel had his harsh side. He wrote against the rabbis of Jerusalem and Ramle, and he wrote ferociously against the Karaites of the Land of Israel. I believe his work on the forbidden marriages of relatives was a direct attack on Yosef HaRoeh of the Holy City. Still, I will miss reading his work and especially his letters. He was a good teacher to me. Peace be upon him, may his memory be for blessing.

If I were to eulogize Rabbenu Shmuel ben Hofni what could I say? He reminds me of that story in the Talmud where a scholar asks his colleague to bless him at his departure. That scholar said, "Rabbi, may I give you an analogy to what this resembles? It is like a man who is on a journey. It is hot and he is hungry and thirsty, and he finds a fruit tree with a stream flowing by it. He eats of the fruit and drinks from the stream and relaxes in the shade of the tree. And when he goes to leave, what does he say? Tree, how shall I bless you? If I were to wish sweet fruit for you, behold you already have sweet fruit. If I were to wish abundant shade for you, behold you already have abundant shade. And if I were to wish a stream to pass nearby, behold here is that stream. This, then, is my wish for you: that all that sprouts forth from you may be just like you.

So, you, master, what shall I wish for you? Shall I wish you Torah? Behold you have much Torah. Shall I wish for you wealth? You are rich already. Shall I wish sons? Behold, you have fine sons. This then is my wish for you: that all your offspring be just like you."

—Hillel ibn al-Gassus and Mevorach beRav David HaBavli were arguing again in the academy. I worry about those two, for they are study partners who are used to dialectic. But this argument between them seems personal. I should have patience, for the Talmud teaches us by quoting Proverbs, "As iron sharpens iron, so one sharpens his colleague." Thus two disciples of the sages will sharpen one another in their knowledge of the Torah's law.

I would not wish to separate them from one another, for the Talmud quotes the prophet Jeremiah at that place, "Is not My word like fire? says the Lord." Just as fire cannot come into being except by striking two things together, so Torah grows when disciples study together. And yet, I fear that they may be arguing over that woman Sittuna. This would not be good were she to come between them. The fact seems to be that she has noticed neither one nor the other, even though they throw themselves before her almost daily. It is unseemly and perhaps I should put a stop to it.

I do not wish to alienate those boys, they are my best students. I am constantly challenged by them. Does not the Talmud quote Solomon's Proverbs? "She is a tree of life to those who hold her tightly." Why is the Torah likened to a tree? Just as a small tree ignites a larger tree with fire, so a student of Torah can ignite the mind of his master.

I will keep them studying together. The Talmud is quite explicit when it says, 'Either companionship or death.' This statement was not explicitly said about study, even though it is quoted in the context of that great sage Honi and his alienation from the academy. Nevertheless, I always quote it to my students when I encourage them to find a study partner.

I think the deepest meaning of "companionship or death" is its most surface meaning. Loneliness is deadly. Did not Honi ask to die when he realized that no one of his generation was yet alive? Did he not simply pine away for lack of a partner? Now this may have been a study partner, but the Talmud also teaches that his son had died. So we may reason that if his son is dead, how much more so is it likely that his household was gone as well. I believe Honi missed his wife and the close companionship she brought to him. That was the loneliness which made him pray for his own death. The Talmud refers to that as "requesting mercy."

— The woman Sittuna has been very generous. It is as Hillel ibn al-Gassus first described her, she is as beautiful as the full moon. She is so young and vibrant, she twinkles like the stars. And when she smiles her teeth are like precious pearls. But the very end of Proverbs teaches us, "grace is falsehood and beauty is a lie, it is a woman who fears God who should be praised."

I wish I knew more about her. Who is her family? What is her lineage? She calls herself Sittuna, but the name means nothing more than Miss. It is the same with her name in Hebrew, actually Aramaic, for Martha only means Miss. Now she is quite the Miss, I do admit, but who is she? Could my suspicion be even possible?

Still, I trust her with business. She has given good advice and brought us a fine profit. She is generous to Dunash and his son, and yet she claims not to know them. She says it is sufficient that they were my partners in a venture. Does that mean she wishes to benefit my academy? Or might it mean that she has some personal regard for me?

Now in the matter of Hananel and his daughters I have made Sittuna a conspirator with me. Her teaching them reading will cause other girls in our community to learn to read, too. This means, of course, that their husbands will practice reading day and night, lest their women shame them. I truly believe that reading is the future of the rabbinic academy, even if Hananel still holds fast to the power of memory. In this he is closer to the Babylonians than I am. Reading holds the key.

Perhaps I could set this Sittuna to copying more works for me. If there were multiple copies of the works for the academy, the boys would read them. And it would give me more opportunity to have contact with her. I sound like Hillel and Mevorach now. But so be it, either companionship or death.

From Nissim in Kairawan,
to al-Iskander in Fustat, Winter/Spring, 1034

My dear boy al-Iskander, I write a response to your legal question. This answer is to you alone and is not to be considered a ruling of rabbinic law. Rather, I write this to you for the sake of your education. You may transmit it to your friend as good advice; you may even quote the response by the name of the authority. You are in no way authorized to offer this as a ruling in your friend's case, as I do not know all the particulars and would only rule if I were able to conduct a full examination of your friend as to the relevant details.

Nevertheless, I am impressed, for you have asked a very complex question of rabbinic law. As it happens, a similar, but even more complicated question was asked of my father, peace be upon him, shortly before he died. I was at the time just about your age, al-Iskander, and it still stands out to me because my father took the trouble to explain it in detail. It was a very unusual circumstance.

A member of your Karaite community had asked this question to the rabbis of Fustat and they, in turn, appealed to the rabbis of the Land of Israel. The question was: a Jewish man married a woman from the Rum. She was a Christian and did not convert; but he nevertheless lived with her as a husband lives with a wife. Further, in every way she lived as a true daughter of Israel, observing all the laws of family purity, the food laws, the Sabbath laws and so forth. What was the status of the marriage and what was the status of their child?

The rabbis of Israel decreed that no conversion had taken place and that the couple could not remain married, as the marriage was forbidden by the Torah. They further opined that the offspring of the marriage were not members of the Jewish community. Thus far, it was a straightforward matter, although it was made more complicated than usual because the husband in question was a Cohen, and the rabbis of the Talmud already forbade a member of the priestly clan to marry a convert. But the rabbis of Fustat were upset by the rigidity of the rabbis of the Land of Israel, particularly as the couple involved was not of the Palestinian community. Because my father had close contacts with Fustat, as well as with the academies of Babylonia, he was sent the same question. They did not bother to inform him that the rabbis of the Land of Israel had already ruled on it, otherwise he would not have replied. Once he replied, it was too late. He earned the ire of his Jerusalemite colleagues.

My father's response, in summary, was this: First, with regard to the conversion which had not taken place; he reasoned that a female convert must immerse in either flowing water or a ritual immersion bath. Since this woman had immersed regularly as part of her observance of Jewish family purity and since, at those times, she recited the same benediction which would be recited to affect a

Burton L. Visotzky

proper conversion, then one should deem her earliest immersion as effective for conversion, since she clearly had both chosen to live as a Jew and knew the laws of Israel and observed them.

Thus far the conversion issue, which answers part of your friend's question. According to my father's ruling, if your friend's mother truly lives as a Jew and immerses in accordance with Jewish law, then she is to be considered Jewish, as are her offspring.

But the case my father replied to had a second part which made it much more difficult, for the man was a Cohen, who is forbidden to marry a convert. Under normal circumstances, Talmudic law requires that the couple divorce but that the children, nevertheless, are admitted to the Jewish community. It was here that the rabbis of the Land of Israel had been unduly harsh, for they forbade the children as well, reasoning there had been no proper conversion.

My father determined that the conversion should hold and the marriage as well. Here was the problem he sought to overcome. Ezekiel the prophet, who you know was himself a priest, says that a priest should marry a virgin from the seed of Israel. This would clearly preclude a convert and it has been our custom to interpret thus. However, we nevertheless allow priests to marry widows, who are not virgins. We have always ruled that only the High Priest is required to marry a virgin. Further, in Leviticus it is commanded that a priest not marry a loose woman, which our sages take to include any women who had been a gentile. Hence their prohibition against priests marrying converts.

My father reasoned as follows: first, the Temple is not standing, so there is cause to be lenient. Second: only the High Priest must marry a virgin, so there could be room for the marriage of a convert. Third: the Torah explicitly demands that a priest not marry a loose woman. By annulling the marriage, it would retroactively make the relationship of the couple to be promiscuous. Elsewhere, the Talmud says, One must not make intercourse promiscuous, and the meaning there is clearly to prefer upholding marriage over annulling it. So, my father upheld the marriage as valid.

On these grounds my father ruled retroactively that the conversion was a valid conversion. Since the marriage stood and this priest was not likely to serve in the Temple, he would not force the marriage to dissolve. Finally, and most emphatically, he pointed out that the offspring are not tainted and are to be considered true offspring of the house of Israel. This is in accordance with the majority rulings on this issue throughout the ages.

Alas, the child of that couple died at an early age. Those with evil tongues said it was God's punishment for that couple having married in the first place. Others said it was God's way of punishing them for ignoring the wisdom of the sages of the Land of Israel. Most of the community, I am happy to say, offered their condolences to the couple at their loss of a first-born son. Since that time, al-Iskander, the couple has had two other children, a daughter and a son. They are leaders not only in the Karaite community of Scripture, but are held in high esteem by the rabbinic community, which they, in turn, support.

I thought all of this would be of great interest to you, complicated though it may be, since you are such a clever boy and are so interested in the details of rabbinic law. In fact, this question was raised in the year your mother came to Fustat as your father's bride, may they live and be well, please God. As we say, the one with understanding will understand. Or as it says in the Midrash to Proverbs, "A word to the wise is sufficient."

From Nissim ibn Rabbenu Yakov ibn Shaheen, Second and Father of the court in Kairawan. To al-Iskander, curious for the Torah of the Living God; by caravan.

Chapter Twelve
Spring, 1034

From Karimah in Kairawan, to al-Iskander in Fustat, Spring, 1034

To al-Iskander ibn Dunash HaCohen al-Tustari, in Misr, at the Festival of Passover, may God redeem us speedily in our day.

From his only sister in Kairawan, in the name of the Merciful.

My dear brother, half a year has passed and I have not heard from you. I wrote you some months ago regarding the caravan west and write to you now about the caravan to Granada. I know I too have not written for a while. I am busy here in Kairawan, thank God. I continue to teach the girls how to read. I now am teaching not only Ghazal and the daughters of Rabbenu Hananel, but also Mulaah and many of the wives of the boys in the academy. Some of the young boys and girls are also students, so my courtyard is filled all morning. I barely have time in the afternoon for my sword practice.

Mulaah and some of the others come with their babies to the classes. We practice reading and writing, we gossip about the men and care for the children. It is wonderful to have this constant companionship. I was not wrong to hope that Mulaah would be a good friend. She was raised on stories of her grandfather in Fustat. When she tells them, it is almost like being home.

I pray that this letter finds you well, and that you and our family are having a joyous Passover. I want to tell you how we celebrated Passover here. Before I do, however, let me tell you that we are ready to send our goods to Shmuel the Nagid in Granada. I can join my goods to a caravan in the weeks following Passover. If you send whatever goods you have with a complete reckoning of contents, I will add my thirty-four camel loads—that is my current estimate of my share—and we will do business with Sefarad.

It should take your caravan two or three weeks to come here, so send me an inventory by boat when it sets out so I can make all of the security arrangements. We will follow the same procedures as last time for the finances. That way you and Daddy will receive part of my share of the profits, and Rabbenu Nissim and his academy will also benefit from the business. May we both gain merit through this act of charity to the rabbis.

Rabbenu Nissim held a large Passover Seder in his home on the first and second evenings of the Festival. You know that the rabbinic Jews of the Diaspora have a second night of the holiday, something the Torah, of course, does not mention and our Karaite community certainly has no interest in. I admit I thought the second night was wholly unnecessary, although I was grateful for the festive meal, the chance to be out for an evening with friends, and the opportunity to sit in Nissim's home.

He follows the Seder of Rav Amram, may he rest in Eden. Rav Amram was the Gaon of the Sura academy almost one hundred fifty years ago. Nissim prefers his order for the Passover ceremony to that of Rav Saadya Gaon, who came from the Fayyum. The rabbinic Jews in Fustat follow the order of the Fayyumi, while here in Kairawan they follow custom of the Sura academy.

In any case, Nissim says that according to Rav Amram, women are obligated to drink all four cups of wine, which made the Passover Seder much more fun. Most of the women are not used to drinking, even when we mix the wine with water. To be honest, the men of the academy are not much for drinking either. It is not like when I was among the raiders of caravans or on the sea. Those men knew how to drink. So here at the Passover Seder almost everyone got tipsy, except for Hananel and his wife. They said that it was the custom in the Rum to drink wine with every big meal, so they had the stomachs for it.

The other interesting thing is that we recline at the Passover banquet. All of the elder men recline, and their wives kneel behind them. But Nissim insisted that I recline, leaning on my left arm, as the men do. I asked whether it was because I did not have a husband behind whom to sit. Nissim hesitated before he answered and then he told me that Rav Amram says that important women are obligated to recline, just like the men. Hananel's wife was the only other woman reclining. She acted as the hostess for the evening.

Rabbenu Hananel and Nissim's students did not recline, but kneeled along with their wives. It seems that disciples do not recline when their master is present. I felt odd reclining when so many of the married boys were sitting upright. But their wives said I was their teacher, so it was proper for me to recline, no matter what their husbands did.

They did not serve the usual mutton, out of respect for the Paschal lamb, which can no longer be offered since the Jerusalem Temple was destroyed. So we had stuffed chicken, much like we did that first Sabbath luncheon I ate at Nissim's. Except then the chicken was stuffed with bread and now we had matzah in its place. They eat Haroset here for the Passover Seder. It is a mixture of dates and hazelnuts, wine and cinnamon.

There was a great deal of washing of hands at this banquet. Nissim told stories of the Exodus, and the ancient rabbis, and the four sons. I could see Hananel reciting silently from memory. Even though Hananel is First and Nissim only Second, Nissim got to do the telling because it was his home. This custom goes back to when Nissim's father was the Head and Hananel's father was Second. Since that time, the first Passover Seder is held in the home of ibn Shaheen. Rabbenu Nissim actually used a book with the words of Rav Amram written out. We all joined together for the singing of Psalms both before and after the meal.

Hananel's girls sang their hearts out. It made for a beautiful chorus. I am sad to tell you that Ghazal refused to open her mouth. I know that she can recite virtually the entire Order of Passover. Perhaps she was shy in front of all those guests. But I fear she resents the attention that her father pays me. He had me sitting on one side of him and Ghazal was on the other. She was constantly leaning back upon him until she was practically in his lap. She is so starved for his attention, he finally had to take her into his lap and read that way. I could see her following the text with her eyes. But no matter what I said or what Nissim said, she would not sing. She can be quite single-minded that Ghazal. She is so tiny and odd looking.

The exact same performance took place on the second night. The only difference was that Rabbenu Hananel and his family were at their own home. Mulaah and Abu al-Maali came to Nissim's. That was very nice for me. Between us, Mulaah and I acted as hostess. I think this made Nissim very happy. But poor Ghazal was positively sullen.

Brother, I hope you had a joyous Passover with Mommy and Daddy. I wish all of you the true joy of the festival. I miss all of you, especially on Passover. Is it not odd that I wish to be in Egypt on the holiday of our exodus from there? But being with Nissim makes me long for the joys of home, before there was all the trouble between me and Daddy, and before I knew what I now know from Amalfi.

Oh al-Iskander, will you not write to tell me what is new at home? I long to hear from you, my brother. Send me news of the caravan to Granada and news of the household. From your sister with joy on the holiday of our freedom.

From al-Iskander in Fustat, to his sister in Kairawan, Spring, 1034

Dear Sittuna, who remains my sister. Thank you for the joint caravan venture already undertaken. The financial arrangements are most satisfactory and a help to the household here. We agree to continue the same arrangements for our extension of trade to Granada through the good offices of Shmuel the Nagid, who is Wazir there. I know that Rabbenu Nissim has been instrumental in opening this door for us, so I am pleased he will be garnering profit from the venture. I do not consider his share of the profits an act of charity, rather it is the share due to him for his part in the business. We must be prepared to pay when one contributes to the business, even if it is not material goods. I do not consider your share of profits to our family to be charity either, but your obligation to us. I am pleased we are doing this business together, for it takes some of the burden off of me.

I will be sending eight camel loads of goods for the Granada caravan. The details of the goods in the consignment will be invoiced by boat and copied with the overland shipment. I regret that we cannot contribute more to the larger caravan at this point. As it is, not only do you own the 34 camel loads that you have mentioned in your letter to me, but you also have a share of the eight camel loads we are sending. You own this share not only by virtue of being family, but also because we have taken profits from the wood and dried fruit shipments that returned here from the last caravan and used them to buy this consignment.

I am sending Rabbenu Nissim his share of those profits under separate cover, as I did not feel I had the liberty of reinvesting his profits. I trust from all I hear from you and from my master Rabbenu Nissim, Second of Kairawan, that you can afford to keep your dinars invested and need not take your own profit out of the joint venture at this time. I detail what I believe to be fair percentages in the invoice that follows separately.

You asked that I write to you even if I judge you. Sister, I am offended, even to the point of disgust, at the personal price you pay for our security arrangements. I do not wish to know about such matters and would prefer if your lack of morals did not directly affect our joint business ventures. I would have rather heard that you used your sword to gain us security or had paid a protection price to the brigands than what you did do to assure free passage of our goods. Please, please do not write to me about such matters ever again.

I was no happier at reading how you have insinuated yourself into the circle of my master, Rabbenu Nissim. I have been his disciple for some time now, reading his work and deeply valuing the honor he bestows upon our family through his correspondence with us. And you recline as hostess at his Passover Seder. You must work hard at the study of Torah, it does not simply come to you by charm or beauty or even by virtue of birth. At least you are serving as a teacher of reading and writing. If you are also copying the works of the rabbis, I am eager to have such copies. This, I would value from you above all other things. Then I would be more forgiving of your access to my teacher and master.

Since you are so very close to the master, I assume that Rabbenu Nissim has already told you what he has written me. But perhaps not, as he does not really know who you are yet. So I will tell you that in the time of Rabbenu Nissim's sainted father, Rabbenu Yakov ibn Shaheen, may he rest in Eden, it was determined that our parents are married according to Jewish law and that we are fit offspring. You are not a *mamzer*, then, in any legal sense of the term.

Rabbenu Nissim also mentioned that we had an older brother. Did you know that? I am certain if you reveal to him your dark secret that you are of the family of Dunash HaCohen al-Tustari, he will explain this to you. Sister, it is time to claim your family. If this costs you the attention of Rabbenu Nissim, I cannot blame him; you brought this on yourself with your stories and disguises. You should not be ashamed of us, nor of who you really are. We are both getting too old for such behavior, and the family can no longer afford it.

From al-Iskander, still your brother. Now you have heard from me.

From al-Iskander in Fustat, to Nissim in Kairawan, late Spring, 1034

To my revered teacher, Rabbenu Nissim, abundant peace to you. I am attending the lectures and the court sessions of Rabbenu Ephraim ben Shemariah here in the Jerusalemite community of Fustat. I find his teachings complement well your own work which emphasizes the traditions of the rabbinic masters of Babylonia, may they grow in strength. Your stories, as you know, brought to me a love of rabbinic traditions. It seems appropriate for me now to learn the laws of the rabbis, as well. In any case, I continue to practice the customs of my community of Scripture, for I do not wish to depart from the path of my fathers. But your Oral Torah has proven a worthy challenge for me in these troubling days.

I thank you also for explicating the response of your revered father, Rabbenu Yakov ibn Shaheen, peace be upon him, regarding the case of the convert from the Rum who married a Cohen of our Karaite community. As you can imagine, your father's ruling brought me great solace. I deeply appreciate your tact and discretion in the answer you sent me. I beg you to forgive me for having been less than forward in my original question to you. I feared for your response. Now, I have comfort from you and consolation, as always.

The dried fruits and precious hardwoods which you sent in the winter caravan have been sold at market. We again, praise God, have done very well. I am sending with this letter your 17 dinars profit, which is your share of the al-Tustari's part of the transaction. I also add the 1/6 dinar we still have of yours in our hands from the last caravan, so the total is 17 1/6 dinars. Our own principal and the share of Sittuna bint Haroun have been reinvested into the goods for the Granada caravan. We are able to send eight camel loads.

The buying and investment for this shipment has been entirely up to me. I do not feel that there are sufficient funds to invest more, even for so promising an opportunity. Much of our profit from the last caravan went to the physicians who have been treating father. In any case, our eight camel-loads will bring the total caravan to 42 camels from our consortium. I do not know more than that, but I am certain you will verify everything with Sittuna before sending the goods on to Rabbi Shmuel, Nagid of Granada. Please copy for me the manifest of goods in the consignment when it is sent. I put my trust in God.

I wish I could be writing to you at Father's dictation. The physicians have given up bleeding him and he no longer eats solid foods. I fear he will not live to see the holiday of Pentecost, and that is but three weeks away. If you could send more stories to console him, that would be very good. He still replies to me when I speak to him, so I am sure that he would appreciate it. Of course, it would be a help to me, as well. I thank you, master, in advance.

Revered Rabbenu Nissim, I wrote to you last time with a very personal request which you graciously honored. I make bold to do so again, for the days of mourning my father draw near, and we will need the entire family to be as one. Would you please, master, tell Sittuna bint Haroun of the gravity of her father's illness. Rabbenu Nissim, you need to know that Sittuna is my sister, Karimah bint Dunash, away from home two years and more. I have honored her desire to be in Kairawan without lineage until this point. I can no longer honor that request; our father is dying.

Does not the prophet Malachi teach us the following?: "Behold, I shall send unto you the prophet Elijah, before that awesome and terrible Day of God is come. He shall reconcile the hearts of fathers to their children and the hearts of children to their fathers." We need for you to be our prophet Elijah, Rabbenu. Please help us in our need. I put my trust in God.

From your devoted disciple al-Iskander ibn Dunash HaCohen, may his light shine, al-Tustari. To Rabbenu Nissim ibn Shaheen, Second in Kairawan, please God.

Excerpts from Rabbenu Nissim's diary, "The Scroll of Secrets." Late Spring, 1034

—*I was not entirely surprised when al-Iskander ibn Dunash wrote to me that his sister Karimah is our Sittuna. I was nevertheless confused at first and initially thought the boy had erred, that he was so upset about his father's impending death that he had resurrected his sister in his imagination and somehow confused her with Sittuna bint Haroun. Our Sittuna has been generous to al-Iskander and to Dunash, so it would only be natural that he might imagine that lovely woman to be his dead sister. I myself,*

I confess, have given reign to my desires and imagined her to be the daughter of my dear friend.

Something in the boy's seriousness and the anguish of the letter made me recognize that he was telling the truth about Karimah and that my own suspicions had not been the mere hopes of a smitten old fool. Yet, if Sittuna is Karimah, then she most assuredly is not dead. Quite the contrary, there is none so vibrant as Sittuna, she breathes life into every room she enters. And if Sittuna were Karimah, it would explain why she was so generous with her terms for the caravan we undertook with Dunash and his son.

It must be admitted that her very name has always caused me discomfort. It was so obvious that she took the name Martha bat Boethius directly from the Talmud. But it is an apt name for the daughter of a wealthy and prominent cohen, for Boethius himself was one of the 24 leaders of the Temple priesthood. Her Arabic equivalent, Sittuna, fits the name Martha perfectly, and is Haroun not father of the tribe of priests, brother of Moses, the priest Aaron of the Torah? If she be in truth Karimah, she is well named, for she is truly dear.

But if Sittuna is Karimah I have been deceived for two years and more. First, I have been cruelly deceived by Dunash himself. I do not yet understand the circumstances, but if she left home it is hardly cause for Dunash to have told his friends that she was dead. God forbid! His tale was unscrupulous, for I wrote to him and spent hours of my time gathering the stories of our sages to console him on his loss. Yet he knew perfectly well that his daughter was still alive. It is a theft he has committed, as our sages say, a theft of the mind.

However generous Dunash has been to me, however many business proceedings we have engaged in together, can I now trust him? Of course, if what al-Iskander says is true, Dunash is breathing his last. He will not have to answer to me for his deceptions, but to the Blessed Holy One. How can a father turn his own child away? How could he reject her so completely as to mourn for her as though she had died? What could she have done?

—What could she have done, indeed? Did not Karimah herself deceive me? She did not tell me who her father was. I understand now the conversation that I most recently had with her, for al-Iskander must have written to her of my father's response, peace be upon him, regarding her parents' peculiar marriage. Surely, she understands that I would never repudiate my father's legal decision and that I view her as a Jew in every sense. But she did not know this when she first came to Kairawan. So perhaps her caution was understandable, even if not commendable. Would I wish to enter a town and inform the Jewish community that I might be a mamzer? It could only bring disaster. I sympathize with her desire to hide her lineage.

But what do I know then of this woman I have come to admire? I know now that she comes of a fine and pious and generous Karaite family from Fustat. I know that somehow she has her own fortune. Perhaps I should be suspicious of how she amassed these funds during her years away. And where was she during those many months that she gained such expertise in caravan security?

Why would Sittuna lie to me? Why could she not tell me that she was Karimah bint Dunash? I recall that when Rabbi Eliezer went to Rabban Yohanan ben Zakkai's academy he was reluctant to tell him that he was the son of Hyrcanus. Is this what motivated Karimah? I cannot even determine what I should call her, let alone how I should think of her. I know now that my instincts and suspicions about her identity were correct. I am by nature and by training in Talmudic dialectic quite suspicious. Perhaps I need to learn to trust my feelings more, instead.

Our sages teach that there are situations where for the peace of the household, one may not be required to tell the entire truth. They tell us that Sarah our mother laughed when the angels announced to her that she would have a son. She said, "After I am worn out shall I know pleasure? Is not my husband too old?" And yet when the Lord reported to Father Abraham what it was that she had said to Him, He told Abraham that Sarah had said, "Shall I truly give birth when I am so old?" Now this clearly does not report all that Sarah had said to God. Yet the Blessed Holy One spared Abraham's feelings and made it possible for him to be with Sarah and for her to bear Isaac. Whereas if God had told Abraham all that Sarah had said, Father Abraham would have been hurt by his wife's scorn of his old age.

There is no peace in the al-Tustari household. Quite the contrary, Karimah fled and dissembled, and Dunash disowned her and, in his own turn, lied. And through all of this, each put young al-Iskander in the middle. It is truly he who kept peace between the factions around him and did not tell everything for fear of destroying the family. Now that his father is about to die, young al-Iskander has taken upon himself the awesome burden of betraying both his father and his sister's wishes in order to reconcile them to one another. Surely this is in the cause of household peace.

The boy is to be admired, that is certain. Yet I wonder if in the end he told Karimah all of the truth, for when she came to ask me about her parents' marriage she was under the impression that she still had an older brother. Could al-Iskander have told her about the brother yet have hidden from her that the brother, peace be upon him, is long dead these many years? I clearly wrote to him that he long ago had an older brother, and that the poor child was long dead. What could he have told Karimah? To tell her she has an older brother yet not to say that he now is dead is an act of malice. She was beside herself with grief when I explained that all of this happened almost thirty years ago, well before she or al-Iskander were born. I consoled her for the loss of a brother she never knew. I could not bring myself to tell her of her father's illness, I was deeply remiss. But my God, Dunash, Karimah, and al-Iskander are guilty of hurting one another, perhaps beyond repair.

Burton L. Visotzky

And what shall I, Nissim berav *Yakov, peace be upon him, what shall I do? Obviously, it is proper for me to reconcile daughter to father and father to daughter. It is my role to reconcile sister to brother and brother to sister. But who will console me? Where is my comfort? How shall I trust the man who was my patron and partner, even as he lies dying? How shall I trust his young son whom I thought to be my disciple and now I learn has a streak of malice for his only sister at their time of mutual grief? God forgive me, how can I continue to contemplate what I have been thinking about these past weeks without pause? I have been considering contracting marriage with a woman I did not really know at all. Had I written Sittuna's name into a marriage document, it would have been fraudulent. Praised be to God that I have not exposed myself to such humiliation, nor caused Sittuna to bear witness in vain.*

I am no Elijah. I am not a prophet, nor am I the son of a prophet. But I must try to reconcile them to one another. I can worry about myself afterward. Time is short. Dunash is dying. It is a commandment to fulfill the stipulations of the dying.

From Nissim in Kairawan, to Dunash and al-Iskander in Fustat, early Summer, 1034

To Dunash, may God restore you to complete health. And to al-Iskander, I received your letter, son, regarding the caravans, and the goods arrived almost immediately afterward. The entire caravan is now on its way to Shmuel the Nagid of Granada. God willing, we will all profit handsomely from the consignment.

I was very sorry to read, dear Dunash, of your ill health. I have prayed to God to give you strength and healing in the days ahead. We must put our trust in God. I will also convey the news of your illness to your daughter Karimah. Al-Iskander was kind enough to inform me that she was living here in Kairawan. Indeed, she has been our business partner under the name of Sittuna. I tell you this so that you know that your daughter is looking out for your welfare, as is your son. Just as al-Iskander cares for you in Fustat, so Karimah cares for you here in Kairawan.

You need to know that she has been here for some time and is a pillar of our community. She teaches reading to the women and the children of the academy. Her works of charity are manifold. She supports the academy with the same generous business contracts with which she shares her wealth with your family. She is careful in her observance of the rabbinic laws, and I am sure that on her own she does honor to the traditions of her ancestors, the community of Scripture. I tell you also, my dear Dunash, that you have raised a charming and attractive daughter. I enjoy her company, as do the households of my academy. She copies the works of the sages for us and will not accept payment for this pious—and onerous—task.

Since al-Iskander wrote to her about another matter which she then brought to my attention, I have known that she is your daughter. Needless to say, she was ashamed not to have informed me of her esteemed lineage before this time. Almost immediately after our conversation, she left to oversee firsthand the security of our joint caravan to Granada. I expect that she will return by the Sabbath, God willing, and that she will use the time away to reflect. I regret that she left before hearing of al-Iskander's letter regarding your health. I am sure that if she knew you were not well, she would be on her way to Fustat rather than heading west.

As for your own conscience, old friend, I leave that between you and your Creator. I regard it as though you had stolen something from me, though the theft was from my thoughts. If nothing else, your own story to me about Karimah led me to write to you the stories of our sages.

For did it not happen once that Rabbi Meir, Rabbi Yehudah, and Rabbi Yosi went on a journey from the Land of Israel? They approached a certain town on Friday eve before the Sabbath and sought hospitality. Rabbi Yosi and Rabbi Yehudah deposited their purses of dinars with their host for the Sabbath, but Rabbi Meir did not. Instead, he went off and buried his purse in the cemetery. When the Sabbath ended Meir retrieved his purse, while they asked their host for their money. He denied that they had ever given him anything. They implored him and offered to share their funds, if only he would return them. But he denied everything and they could not make him relent The other rabbis asked Rabbi Meir why he declined to leave his money with that man and he said, "I was disturbed by him, I do not know why. But I had no confidence."

They then asked why he did not warn them. He said, "What could I have warned you about? I was uncertain and merely had my doubts. This was not cause to slander a stranger to you."

They all leased a house in the town and invited that man to be their guest, in hopes of persuading him to have pity and restore their funds. It happened that the man had eaten lentils at home that evening for his dinner and some of those lentils stuck to his hands and the hem of his clothing.

When Rabbi Meir saw the lentils sticking to that man's hands, he left his companions to their hosting. He went to that man's house and said to his household, "Your husband has asked that you give to me the purses that those men left with him on Friday afternoon. He said you would know that he sent me by this sign: I am to tell you that he ate lentils for dinner."

Later that evening, after that man had gone home, Rabbi Meir restored the purses of dinars to his companions. When that man asked his wife for the dinars the next morning she proclaimed, "Did you not send for them last night by the sign of the lentils we had eaten?"

The man was so infuriated that he took out his sword and chopped off that poor woman's head.

I hope that this story strikes your heart Dunash, and brings you to appreciate people's follies. Thoughtfulness cures the heart, as does the study of Torah. And contrition and penitence avert the evil decree, dear friend.

Was this not so in the case of Elazar ben Durdaya who wandered from the way of the sages for 12 years? During those years there was not an idol he did not worship, nor a harlot he did not visit. Yet when he reflected upon his life and the pleasures he had experienced, he felt that they were nothing but sins against God and he regretted his actions. He put his head between his knees and wept. When he died, a voice came forth from heaven proclaiming, "Elazar ben Durdaya has been accepted as a true penitent and has attained the world to come."

Our sages also taught a parable which I think you would like to hear, Dunash, and you, too, al-Iskander. They speak of a farmer who had two calves. He fed and watered them well, so that they grew fat. One day, one of the calves ran away to the wilderness and remained there a long time. She finally returned, after her owner had despaired of ever seeing her again. He rejoiced greatly over that calf, feeding her and giving her drink and grooming her. She achieved even greater favor than the calf that had remained, for she returned after he had given up on her. Thus is the status of the penitent in God's eyes.

Our sages teach us, Great is penitence, for it brings healing to the world, as it is written, "Return you backsliding children, I will heal your backsliding." Elsewhere it is taught that once a person has repented, it is as though he had died to his life of sin. We must not remind him of his former ways. Thus, those who heed the advice of our sages spend their days in penitence and devotion to God and to one another.

Dear friend Dunash, I pray you soon know God's healing. May al-Iskander, your devoted son, read these words to your ears, and may they enter both your hearts. Thus ends my Compendium of Consolation. May God bring you comfort, now and always.

From al-Iskander in Fustat,
to Nissim in Kairawan, Summer, 1034

To Rabbenu Nissim, Second and Father of the Court in Kairawan, with the help of God.

From al-Iskander ibn Dunash HaCohen al-Tustari, may I be atonement for him in his eternal rest, in the name of the Merciful.

Blessed be the True Judge. My master and my teacher, Daddy, has departed. He passed quietly in his sleep last night. I thank God he did not seem to be in too much pain and now, in any case, he is at rest. Although he ate little these past weeks, his belly was swollen. The physicians said that what was in his belly was eating him from within. Now he is gone. This morning we buried him in the Jewish cemetery south of the city. I am at home where we are observing the days of mourning. Mommy is with the women who are still wailing and ululating and beating their breasts. They should stop soon; we have only paid for the professional wailers to lament until mid-day. After that we will begin receiving the community to offer us their condolences.

I have eaten the meal which the boys of the rabbinic synagogues have brought for us. The funeral had representatives from the Jerusalemite synagogue where I study on occasion, as well as from the synagogue of the Iraqis. I suppose they are here because Daddy supported them when he could. Perhaps they are here out of respect for Uncle Sahl and Abu Nasr. Of course, our Karaite community of Scripture has come to console us. They are in the courtyard singing Psalms and dirges. I am hiding out from all of the ruckus to write to you, dear teacher, for you are like a second father to me.

Daddy was just 56 years old. I overheard someone at the cemetery say that dying in your fifties meant that God was angry with you. Does this mean that Daddy was "cut off" from life and the community? I know that they did not mean for me to hear them, but it was hurtful to think that Daddy died when he did because he had made God angry. I cannot imagine anything my father could have done to make God angry and the eulogizers at the cemetery certainly had only good things to say about him.

Rabbenu Nissim, what is to become of us? I can continue working in Daddy's business, as I have learned it well these last two years. But I am only 16 and do not have sufficient money to make the kind of profit that Daddy used to. I hope that Karimah might help us, but we are not on the best of terms since she left home. I am angry she was not here these past two years and more. I am especially angry that she did not come when I wrote that Daddy was dying. Maybe she might not have gotten here to see him when he was still conscious, but maybe at least she would have been here for the days of mourning.

Your own letter with your final stories came to us just before Daddy stopped talking. He smiled at what he called your sermon to him on his death bed. Then he asked me to write to Karimah and tell her to come. I did not tell him that I had already written her to come as I did not wish him to be upset with me or disappointed again with Karimah. That is why I am angry she is not here.

Dear teacher, you have been so kind of late. I am ashamed that I have burdened you with my personal troubles and our family's difficulties. But I look to you for guidance, as I consider you my rabbi. Although you are far away in Kairawan, the stories that you have sent make you seem to be very near.

Please make my sister come to us or at least write. Mommy needs to hear from her. As do I, al-Iskander ibn Dunash HaCohen al-Tustari, may I be atonement for him in his eternal rest.

From al-Iskander in Fustat, to Karimah in Kairawan, Summer, 1034

To Karimah, still hiding in Kairawan, in the name of the Merciful.

Daddy was buried this morning while you were off somewhere sleeping with your Arab. It seems you prefer sleeping with Muslims to being home where you belong. Now Daddy is dead and Mommy is alone and you are not here.

I wrote to you that Daddy was sick and you did not even have the decency to reply by letter, let alone come on a fast boat to Fustat. You who claim to have traveled all over from the Hijaz to the Maghreb, could you not find your way home? Maybe it is true, you have no home.

Your Nissim, as you call him, wrote that after you were forced to reveal that you were of this lowly family, you fled to the desert, I assume to your Badawi lover there. You gave Rabbenu Nissim the excuse of checking on the security of our Granada caravan. It was a convenient excuse for you, big sister. Under the guise of dutiful attention to your family, you again flee your obligations to us.

I will never forgive you that you could not be here for Daddy when he was dying. You could not write him a word of apology for all the pain you caused him. You could not even be here for his burial or mourning days.

We cannot survive without your money, otherwise I would tell you to go to hell. The least you can do is help me support Mommy. I pray that she will not also die an early death from anguish over you. How could you do this to us?

From al-Iskander ibn Dunash HaCohen al-Tustari, may I be atonement for him in his eternal rest. To Sittuna bint Haroun at the perfumer's in the Souk al-Yahud of Kairawan, with the help of God, by boat.

From Nissim in Kairawan, to al-Iskander and his mother in Fustat, Summer, 1034

To the honored household of the late revered Dunash HaCohen al-Tustari, may he rest in Eden, in the fortress of Fustat, Misr, with the support of Heaven.

From Nissim ibn Yakov, peace be upon him, Nissim ibn Shaheen, Second and Father of the Court in Kairawan, in the name of the Merciful.

Blessed be the True Judge. I received with great sorrow the sad news that my friend and patron, Dunash HaCohen al-Tustari has passed to his eternal reward. Your husband and father was a great man. He was true to his community of Scripture and supported them with all his heart. He assiduously followed their customs and raised his family in the Karaite traditions of his fathers. Yet he never lost sight of the unity of all Israel. He supported the academies of the rabbis in Fustat and in Kairawan, in Baghdad and Ramle. He used his family connections for the betterment of Jews everywhere in the empire. And he never hesitated to share his wealth or his business, so that others might prosper. It may truly be said that Dunash was one of the great men of the generation.

Although we will mourn him and we will miss him, we will find solace and consolation from the memories we all share of him. The book of Solomon's Proverbs teaches us that "the memory of the righteous is a blessing." Our Dunash died at an early age, taken by God to his bosom while still in his fifties, much as God took the prophet Samuel of Ramah. There are times that God takes those whom He loves sooner than we wish. But the wisdom of God cannot be questioned, for He is the True Judge.

Rather than seek to measure out blame for your father's untimely death, it is better to seek comfort from the Almighty. There is no blame, only righteousness. Dunash, peace be upon him, departed from this world without sin. He left a son who knows the traditions of his elders and those of the rabbis. He left a daughter who teaches reading and writing so that children may study Torah. He left a household devoted to acts of charity and righteousness. We shall miss Dunash in this world, but with the confidence that he is in that good resting place until he rises to receive his eternal reward in the time to come.

Burton L. Visotzky

Al-Iskander, please send your mother my deepest condolences for our loss. Tell her that Karimah left to care for the caravan before she heard that your father was ailing, and that she still has not returned. Do not alarm your mother or upset her further with reports of Karimah's continued absence. I do not know where she is, nor have I heard from her. By now, God willing, the caravan should have reached Ceuta. Perhaps she had to accompany it all the way to port.

I know that when she returns she will be devastated with the news of your father's death. She was angry with your father and he with her. That only makes it harder to hear the news that a person has died. She was confused about what she learned in Amalfi, and only beginning to understand that what you both thought was a problem has not been one for the span of an entire generation. She will need to mourn upon her return to Kairawan. She will need the support of her family, most especially her brother whom she loves dearly. Al-Iskander, you must be a man now, for as our sages teach, where there is no man, strive to be the man. I will do everything I can to help you through this difficult time. Write to me whenever you need, about whatever matters you wish. Do not forget that your uncle Sahl Abu Saad and Abu Nasr have deep resources to help you and your mother. Most important, son, study Torah. It is the best consolation. I will not write more now, for you have what I have already sent. I hope that you will reread it in the months ahead and that it will bring you solace.

May God comfort you and your entire household among the mourners of Zion and Jerusalem. With the blessings of God upon mourners, from Nissim ibn Yakov ibn Shaheen, in Kairawan. To al-Iskander and to the household of Dunash HaCohen al-Tustari, may he be remembered for blessing, in Fustat, I put my trust in God.

Excerpt from Rabbenu Hananel's Commentary

Our masters have taught:
In the case where one hears of a death immediately
One observes the mourning periods of seven days and thirty days.
In the case where one hears of a death at some distance of time,
One observes only one day of mourning.
What constitutes immediately and what at some distance?
Immediately means that one has heard within thirty days of burial.
At some distance means after thirty days following burial;
This is the opinion of Rabbi Aqiba.
But the sages say: it is one and the same,
They both observe the seven and the thirty.

Said Rabbah bar Bar Hannah quoting Rabbi Yohanan,
Anytime you find an individual who is lenient
And the majority who are stringent,
The law follows the stringent ones;
Except for this case, for although Rabbi Aqiba is lenient
And the sages are stringent, the law follows Rabbi Aqiba.
For Shmuel taught, the law is always lenient in cases of mourning.
Indeed, Rabbi Hiyya observed but one day of mourning
For his father and his mother,
Because it was a case of hearing the news at a distance,
And we learned three things from him:
The mourner is forbidden to wear leather sandals;
In the case where one hears of death at some distance of time,
One observes only one day of mourning;
And any part of that day counts as though it were the entire day.
Further, if one does not observe seven days of mourning
One should not rend his garments,
Yet one should nonetheless rend his garments
If he is mourning for his father or mother.

From Karimah in Kairawan, to her brother and mother, Late Summer, 1034

To al-Iskander ibn Dunash HaCohen, may his memory be for blessing, al-Tustari, and the household in Fustat, Misr, with God's comfort.

From Karimah bint Dunash, may I be atonement for him in his eternal rest, HaCohen al-Tustari, here again in Kairawan, in the name of the Merciful.

Blessed be the True Judge. Woe to those who are gone and will not return. Dearest brother, I have read your angry letters and I beg you to hear me out and to read to Mommy this letter of my sorrow and condolence to you both. I am today finally returned to Kairawan after twenty-four days with the caravan to Ceuta and another three weeks on board ship returning to Kairawan via al-Mahdia.

Skandi, you must decide what to read to Mommy, poor thing, and what is just for your own eyes. Despite your very angry letter to me, I was not with Abu Sin, nor is it my intention to ever be with him again. Al-Iskander, although I have written you for almost three years now, you have not attended to anything I have told you. Instead, you want to be a self-righteous little prig. I cannot and will not abide that from you. I wrote that I understood that you might judge me. I did not invite you to freely condemn me in every letter you wrote. Nor did I expect that you would write me half truths about our family that left me reeling in shock.

Were it not for Rabbenu Nissim, I would not know what to believe from you. I wrote you in all honesty what I learned in Amalfi. You wrote back that we had a brother, and left me to infer that we had that brother still. With that unsettling news in my heart, I then learned that he died long before we were ever born. You also wrote that I am not legally a *mamzer*, implying that morally or otherwise you consider me so. Then you wrote me that Daddy was dead and condemned me for being off with Abu Sin, when I had done no such thing.

I forgive you, for I know now that you were tending to Mommy and to the family business and to Daddy dying. That was too much for any person, and I know that you feel I have abandoned you. Nissim says that the sages teach that love and grief destroy the normal order of things. I took that into account when I read the anger in your letters. I am so sorry, I still never wish to hurt you. Because you are my brother who I love, I will explain to you why the cruel thing you wrote is very, very wrong. I did not buy protection for our caravans with the price of my body.

You may not approve, but I had a true relationship with Abu Sin. That relationship ended on the last caravan when I told Abu Sin that my place was with the Jews of Kairawan. I did not know it then, but he left Afrikiya shortly after that and went back to his Banu Hilal in the Hijaz. I have not seen him since I said farewell. I wrote to you that I had repented of that life. Nissim says that the sages teach that you should not rebuke a penitent for her former errors. Once she has repented, that life is dead to her. Rabbenu Nissim refuses to ask me anything about those days and will not let me tell him. He says that if my repentance is true, all that I did then is now dead and buried. Brother, that life truly is dead to me; it is as though it had happened to a different person. Indeed, I was a different person then.

I was upset to learn about our dead brother and even more upset that you forced me to reveal to Nissim who my family was. I did not think that I was ready to do so yet, but so be it. Now I have no choice, for you not only forced my hand, but Rabbenu Nissim's, as well. I think you were wrong to do that. And I think you were wrong to condemn me. Let it end with this: if you ever write me a letter like that again, I shall have Rabbenu Nissim read it. Then he will know truly who his devoted disciple really is. The one who understands will understand.

Because Abu Sin has left Afrikiya, our caravan was constantly under threat from Berber raiders. I had to accompany it the entire land portion of the journey to assure that our goods would arrive unscathed. I feel a strong obligation to you and to Mommy to look after our financial interests. Nissim understands that we act now as a family, not a consortium. We shall still give Rabbenu Nissim his ten percent. I have enough to live on here. I will send you all of the proceeds of this and future caravans. That way you and Mommy will not have to depend unduly on Uncle Sahl and Abu Nasr. Depend on me, Brother, I am your sister and I will not abandon you.

Mommy, I am so sorry I was not there to say goodbye to Daddy. I wish I could have made up with him for the last years of separation. I see now that I was foolish to run off with Ismail, but Daddy made it almost impossible for me to come home again. I love Daddy and I will miss him always. I love you and miss you and Skandi, too. I will come home when the Granada caravan returns here with goods. I myself can bring them on to Fustat and see you both. We can cry together then.

When I came home today, Rabbenu Nissim and Rabbenu Hananel greeted me with the news of Daddy's departure to his eternal rest. Nissim consoled me and Rabbenu Hananel instructed me how to have my day of mourning. I tore my garment and removed my shoes. Hananel's women and Mulaah have brought me mourner's food and are staying with me. Ghazal, for her part, threw a tantrum at my return. Despite that, I am well cared for here. But I long to be with you in Fustat.

Mommy, I kiss your hands and eyes. I want you to kiss al-Iskander for me. He is my brother and I love him no matter what. Mommy, do not let him squirm away or refuse. He must have a kiss from his sister Karimah. And al-Iskander, kiss Mommy for me, too.

From Karimah, a mourner for her lamented father, may the memory of the righteous be for blessing, in Kairawan, I put my trust in God.

To al-Iskander ibn Dunash HaCohen al-Tustari, whose father would be proud of him; and to my mother, light of my life, may she live until one hundred and twenty. May the good Lord comfort you among the mourners of Zion and Jerusalem. At the home of Dunash HaCohen al-Tustari, may I be atonement for him, in Misr, by fast boat, with the help of God.

Chapter Thirteen
Fall, 1034

From Nissim and Karimah in Kairawan,
to al-Iskander and mother in Fustat, early Fall, 1034

Dear Mommy and al-Iskander, I am writing this letter at Nissim's request. He is talking through me; but I am writing in my own words, from my own heart. The month of Elul has come and I awaken every morning to the sound of the ram's horn being blown in the rabbis' synagogues. We prepare for the New Year and the Great Fast with sadness in our hearts over Daddy's absence from our lives. We put our trust in God.

The Granada caravan was a great success, thank God. Nissim's contacts with Shmuel the Nagid, who is Wazir at the court of Granada, opened every door for us. Our goods were sold at the highest prices. We have been offered very attractive terms to sell goods from Sefarad to the markets here and in Fustat. If we could interest Uncle Sahl Abu Saad in representing us to Caliph al-Zahir in al-Kahira, we would be in an excellent position, quite literally as middlemen between the two kingdoms.

I, Karimah, will accompany the caravan to Fustat. By the time of our arrival it will be the end of the shipping season. If we warehouse the goods for a month or two we should get excellent prices. I expect to leave for Sousse immediately following Sukkot, God willing. I will be at Fustat two or three weeks later. Can you contact Uncle Sahl, Brother, and determine his interest in joining this business venture?

Nissim and I have been discussing your role in the family business, al-Iskander. I know that you are now expert and can carry on Daddy's ventures in a way that brings us all pride and profit. But Nissim informs me that you have a strong desire to increase your knowledge of Torah and study with a Rabbi Ephraim, who is master of the Jerusalemites among Fustat. I believe that the profits from our joint Granada venture, along with the caravan I will be bringing, should allow you leisure to study full-time with him if you wish. Of course, we are delighted to have your help and wisdom in the family's business; but I was away for almost three years. During that time you learned the business and kept it viable, denying yourself the education and pleasures a man your age should have.

I will be coming to Fustat and can oversee the sale of goods and such. I want you to take this time to study if you have the desire. This does not mean that you will abandon us, as you still will be home, and you can discuss each decision with me. But you know how highly Nissim values Torah study. He tells me you share this value. So, as the sage Hillel once said—or at least as I once copied what he said—"All the rest is commentary, go now, study."

Mommy, do not despair. Although I am sending al-Iskander away during the day, you and I will have much to do. I am not, God forbid, asking that you become involved in trading and caravans. But you are an expert at stitchery and the making of a trousseau. Would you help me gather all the items that I need if I am to marry when the eleven months of mourning for father come to an end just after Pentecost next summer? I am not sure that this news will surprise you, but I hope that you are pleased. Nissim and I have agreed to become husband and wife, God willing. Because of his responsibilities to the court and the academy of Kairawan, we will be living here. But I want my preparations and our home linens to be from Fustat, with you.

Skander, my little brother, you are to become a disciple of the sages and the brother-in-law of Rabbenu Nissim. And I, praise be to God for His mysteries, am to become the wife of a sage! I wish Daddy were alive to see this, but I honestly do not know how he would feel seeing his children so involved in the world of the rabbis. Our community of Scripture was his life, and I shall always honor our Karaite teachers and precepts.

Nissim and I are working out our own rules for Sabbath observance and for permissible foods. He is very stringent about the rabbinic laws, but as you know, the rabbis are more lenient than us Karaites about both Sabbath observance and food. I think there shall be no more chicken, only pigeons to be eaten as fowl. For my part, I will have Sabbath lamps lit on Friday night and eat warmed food on Saturdays. Nissim gets to be more stringent, while I am more lenient.

Al-Iskander—do not read the next few lines to Mommy, they are just for you. I am not letting Nissim see them either—just us, Brother. In truth, I am not put out at having to be more lenient. You know how lenient I have been in my travels, so to me rabbanite law is just enough. But I am also distressed and want to share with you my consternation about Ghazal. When I first met her she was a lovely girl. It is true she had a big head and a tiny body, but she was bright and funny. This was only so long as she was the center of everyone's world. When Nissim began to attend to me she became sullen. Now that she knows we are to be married, she has reverted to tantrums and bed-wetting. I do not know if this is because of me or because of her deformity. The physicians here, who see her regularly, say that it will pass. She is a midget, true, but in all other respects normal. She is so bright and yet so difficult.

Dear Brother, I pray to God that you are pleased with my news and are pleased to be able to study. I feel you deserve at least this from me and hope that you can accept it as my obligation to you. With love from your sister, Karimah.

From Nissim ibn Yakov ibn Shaheen, in his own hand. To al-Iskander and his mother, of the house of Dunash HaCohen al-Tustari, may his memory be for blessing. I write to you both as a supplicant, for you are Karimah's family, and in lieu of her late father, peace be upon him, I wish your permission to take Karimah, also called here Sittuna bint Haroun, as my wife. You know, as do I, that Karimah will only do what she wishes of her own volition. I have told her, however, that I am a traditionalist and she has given me leave to write this request.

I wish to establish with Karimah a faithful household in Israel. I wish her to be mother to my child Ghazal and wife to me according to the laws of Moses and Israel. I do not wish to live my life alone any longer. Nor is it fit that Karimah, now fatherless, should be alone. As the rabbis of the Talmud teach us, it is better to dwell as a couple than to sit alone. Karimah has written to you that I am prepared to respect the laws of her ancestors, the community of Scripture, even as our household will be of the congregation of Jewry here in Kairawan, which is rabbinic.

I am honored to be joining the esteemed family of al-Tustaris. I was partner and friend to Dunash, may he rest in peace, and only had the highest regard for him. I have equal regard for his offspring, al-Iskander ibn Dunash HaCohen, who brings honor to his father's name. And for his mother, wife of the late revered Dunash, I pray for an abundance of God's blessings. May this news serve as a comfort and consolation to you in this most difficult year of loss.

From me, Nissim ibn Yakov, may he rest in Eden, ibn Shaheen, Second and Father of the Court in Kairawan, and from Karimah, with the help of God. To the household of Dunash HaCohen, peace be upon him, and his son al-Iskander ben Dunash HaCohen al-Tustari, in Fustat, God willing.

From Nissim in Kairawan, to Karimah in Fustat, Late Fall, 1034

To the daughter of my esteemed friend and patron Dunash HaCohen, may he rest in Eden, abundant peace and blessing. I was so pleased to receive your letter by boat and learn that you have been welcomed into your home again after three years' absence. I know that you were apprehensive about your mother's health, may God grant her length of days, and how you would be greeted by your brother, al-Iskander. Know that he is a very good boy, but was heavily pressured by the burdens of the household without you. It was only natural that his resentments would focus on your absence and that your father's death would bring forth frustrations that al-Iskander was far too respectful to pour forth upon your revered parents.

I am reminded of the Midrash about the prophet Jonah, where the prophet worries that God's anger at the Ninevites might be deflected on to the Jews, should those gentiles repent. When Jonah fulfilled his mission, God in the fullness of His mercy did not harm either the Ninevites or the Israelites; but the idea is there nonetheless. Anger exists; and if it cannot be directed at the cause, it gets displaced elsewhere.

I have often seen this when the parents of my students die. My students are actually very angry at their parents for abandoning them, but they dare not express that anger. First, they understand all too well that their parents do not wish to so abandon them. Secondly, they do not wish to transgress the commandment to honor one's parents. So they are angry at their households, or at their study partners, sometimes even at me, their teacher. So al-Iskander spewed forth his anger at you. In truth you had abandoned him, but not with the final abandonment which he experienced in caring for your father as he was dying.

Now you have returned to Fustat. I am pleased that your mother, may God bless and keep her, is recovering from the heavy blow of your father's death. I am very pleased that al-Iskander accepted your offer to take time for his studies. You know that his hours of Torah study will strengthen his heart and tighten the bond between you once more.

I am especially pleased that you and your mother are preparing your trousseau for our wedding. As you are named, thus you are, truly a dear one. Would it be out of place if I wrote that I miss having al-Iskander's sister nearby me?

You did not write to me whether Sahl Abu Saad was willing to extend his influence in the court to promote trade between Granada and al-Kahira. I do not know whether this is because you have not had an audience with him yet, or because he refused and you are too discreet to send me bad news in a letter. In any case, Karimah, our own transactions with the Maghreb and Sefarad continue to bring us sustenance, as does our small share of Hananel's dealings with the Rum. If the Fustat trade continues, we will have enough for ourselves and be able to continue to support your mother and brother without involving your uncle Sahl.

You may know that traders away from home send letters to their households. Often in our community, faithful husbands send their wives divorce papers, lest the women cannot bear the waiting or fear their husbands to be lost at sea, God forbid. Yet here I sit in Kairawan sending a letter to the one I would have be my own wife, who is far away acting as the trader. And instead of writing her about divorce documents, I write to her of my expectations for our marriage, God be praised.

I have been contemplating the nature of the document that will bind us, as we not only must make the usual stipulations regarding your dowry and my marriage gifts to you, but we must also consider the stipulations regarding the mixture of Karaite and Rabbanite customs in our home. Despite my loyalties to the Babylonian academies and their traditions, the Palestinian formularies of marriage documents have more flexibility to include the various stipulations we require. Can you either purchase or yourself make a copy of the prayer book that is found in the Jerusalemite synagogue there, for it has an example of this document type? Otherwise I shall have to rely upon the "Formulary of Rav Hai Gaon," which follows our Iraqi custom.

I am well, thank God, and Mulaah comes almost every day with her baby to spend some time with Ghazal. On the days that Mulaah cannot come, one or more of Hananel's lovely daughters comes to mind Ghazal. If it is not too much gossip, I should report to you that Hillel ibn al-Gassus has his eye on Hananel's eldest. In any case, the girls all read aloud together, virtually anything they can find in Hebrew script. In addition to the texts of the Torah and the prophets, the girls love to read the fox fables that you copied for them. They especially like the fables of the two jackals, Kalilah and Dimnah.

It is a joy to hear Ghazal laughing again. She says to tell you that she misses you, but she wants you to enjoy your time with your mother and brother for as long as you desire. I suppose Ghazal wishes she herself had a mother or brother, but soon we shall give her the first. God willing, she shall have the second in good time, as well.

I will end my letter to you with a word of Torah, if I may. It is from the Talmud of the Babylonians, "Come and see just how good a good woman is, for of the good woman it is written in Proverbs, 'A man who has found the right woman has found goodness, indeed, he has secured God's favor.'"

From me, Nissim ibn Yakov, may he rest in Eden, in Kairawan. To Karimah bint Dunash HaCohen al-Tustari, peace be upon him, in Fustat, with the help of God.

Marriage contract of Rabbenu Nissim and Karimah, in Kairawan, Summer, 1035

We put Jerusalem above our greatest joy.

My beloved is mine and I am his.

I found the one I love; I will not let him go.

You have captured my heart, my sister, my bride.

This is the one, she is bone of my bones, flesh of my flesh.

In the name of our God, the Merciful, may we prosper and succeed.

In an auspicious sign on this 30th day of Sivan, which is the first day of the new moon of Tammuz, in the year 4795 since the creation of the world, which we count as the year 1346 according to contracts, 965 years since the destruction of our Holy Temple, may it be rebuilt speedily in our day, this contract of marriage is being written in Kairawan, which is at the well called Barouta in Afrikiya of the Maghreb, to testify that the groom Rabbenu Nissim ibn Yakov ibn Nissim ibn Yoshiahu ibn Shaheen, Second of the academy and Father of the Court of Kairawan, said to the virgin bride Karimah bint Dunash HaCohen, may his memory be a blessing, al-Tustari, also known here as Sittuna bint Haroun: "Be thou my wife according to the prophet Moses and Israel the chosen, and I shall work to feed, sustain, support, maintain, earn for, and honor you, according to the custom of Jewish men who feed, clothe, and honor their wives faithfully, according to my ability and the best that I can afford. I will conduct myself toward her with truthfulness and sincerity, I will not grieve or oppress her, I will not take a co-wife nor purchase any slave or maidservant without my wife's approval, I will ransom her with my own funds if need be, and I will give her marital relations to the extent habitual among Jewish men. I give over to you 50 dirhems in honor of your virginity, as is the custom in the community of Scripture, as your marriage price, and as is appropriate for you in accordance with rabbinic law.

"I, the groom Rabbi Nissim ibn Yakov ibn Shaheen, Second of the academy and Father of the Court of Kairawan, also give to the bride, Karimah bint Dunash HaCohen al-Tustari, an additional gift of 150 gold dinars of which 50 are paid now and the remaining 100 dinars are the delayed gift, according to custom."

Throughout this marriage contract a dinar is a dinar.

Then the virgin bride Karimah bint Dunash HaCohen al-Tustari, also known here as Sittuna bint Haroun, replied to him and accepted that she would work and serve and honor the groom Rabbenu Nissim ibn Yakov ibn Shaheen, Second of the academy and Father of the Court of Kairawan, in purity, holiness, and fear of God, to honor him and hold him dear, to be his helpmate and do in the household what a Jewish woman is accustomed to do, and her desire will be toward him. She consented to become his wife and the mother of his child and any children that they may have in the future, God willing.

She also agreed to follow the Sabbath laws of the community of the people of Kairawan, which are of the traditions of the sages and rabbis, may their memory be for blessing. In turn, the groom has agreed to follow the restrictions of the community of Scripture as regards the eating of birds. Any meats which shall be eaten shall be slaughtered and prepared in accordance with the rabbinic custom, and so, fish. The bride retains the right to teach writing and reading to the girls and children of the community of Kairawan, whether in her courtyard or outside her home. She can transact business on her own behalf with her own property without permission of her husband and without recourse to an *epitropos*, where it is the custom, provided that she guarantees any loss of usufruct to her husband.

The bride brought with her to the marriage, a trousseau from the woman's quarters, the following:

422 dinars gold, in purses of al-Kahira
1 two-pointed Badawi sword with hilt, worth 42 dinars
1 jewelled scabbard, worth 37 dinars
1 *jambiyya* dagger, worth 3 dinars
the goods in the warehouse near the perfumer's in the Jewish
market in Kairawan, worth 380 dinars
her share of the goods in the Warehouse of the Three Mice
in the fortress of Fustat, Misr, worth 78 dinars
her goods in the warehouse of Sousse, Afrikiya, worth 216 dinars
2 gold necklaces
8 sets of earrings with precious stones
6 silver bracelets
4 silver anklets
2 worked gold bracelets
1 tiara of silver and gold appliqué
98 strung pearls
3 gold and jeweled dressing pins
1 silver jewel box with gems
1 silver mirror
and other various jewelry, worth 61 dinars
silverware for serving including:
1 tea pot
2 large serving platters
3 small serving platters
16 various serving pieces
1 large platter with tripod - the latter is carved wood
8 large chests of carved hardwood
copperware for service including:
7 large cooking pots
4 small cooking pots
2 pans for cooking

4 ladles
2 soup pots
4 heating surfaces
4 copper ovens,
1 large candelabrum,
various clothing, worth 371 dinars
in addition:
1 full set of Kairawanese robes, undergarments and veiling
3 robes of Kutama style for women
6 embroidered robes shot with gold
8 silk robes
18 various silk head coverings with veiling
4 Chinese silk shawls
3 linen shawls
1 woolen shawl for winter
6 white outer garments for winter
1 winter mantle lined with fur,
2 kerchiefs from Amalfi,
bedding including:
3 large goose-down quilts
2 silk duvets
4 embroidered duvets
8 Tabari sofa cushions with embroidery
19 reclining pillows with colored covers
4 mattresses with covers
6 woolen blankets
8 embroidered large silk wall hangings
6 small wall hangings in frames
7 large carpets in the oriental fashion
8 floor coverings of wool
16 small rugs of Egyptian cotton
54 books and scrolls
3 illuminated scrolls
4 writing sets with reeds
2 silver writing sets
a bride's trunk with private wear, valued at 26 dinars
1 pair of leather riding boots
the house and courtyard in Kairawan wholly owned by her
her one-third share of the house, courtyard, apartments, and warehouses in
Fustat, a gift-inheritance from her late father, may he rest in Eden

Burton L. Visotzky

The bride will not leave Kairawan without permission of the groom.

We undersigned below testify that the groom, Rabbenu Nissim ibn Yakov ibn Shaheen, Second of the academy and Father of the Court of Kairawan, handed her the edge of this marriage contract, then he took from the cup and gave her to drink from the cup, and said, "behold you are sanctified to me with this ring, in accordance with the custom of the prophet Moses and the chosen people Israel. This marriage contract may be collected from me and from my heirs after me, from all properties which I possess or will acquire, from the choicest property, and even from the shirt off my back, from this day henceforth."

May they build and prosper! This contract was willingly concluded without force or constraint, with acceptance of all the stipulations of the contract, not like mere promises or mere formula, but according to the stringencies of documents.

All is strong and binding
as written and sealed before us who are the witnesses:
Shmuel HaLevi ibn Yusuf ibn Nagrila, Nagid of Granada, Witness;
Hananel ben Hushiel, Head of the academy and the court
of Kairawan, Witness;
Jacob ben Amram, Nagid of Kairawan, Witness;
Ephraim ben Shemariah of Gaza, the perfumer, colleague of the
Great Sanhedrin and Head of the Court in Fustat, Misr, Witness.

From Karimah and Nissim in Kairawan, to al-Iskander in Fustat, Fall, 1035

Dear al-Iskander and Mommy, I am so happy that you made the journey to Afrikiya to be here for our wedding. How good it was for me to have my family together at our time of joy. You know how I valued the time we spent together in Fustat last year while preparing for the wedding, when al-Iskander began his studies with Rabbenu Ephraim ben Shemariah. I was pleased that Rabbenu Ephraim came to Kairawan and participated in our ceremony. I am sorry if he was a bit put out at signing at the end of our marriage contract, but there can be no question that Shmuel the Nagid and Rabbenu Hananel ben Hushiel are greater sages than Rabbenu Ephraim ben Shemariah. I suppose he had a right to sign ahead of Jacob ben Amram, who is only a political figure, but it was precisely political considerations that dictated Jacob ben Amram have precedence. Please tell your teacher how thrilled we were that he graced us with his august presence, al-Iskander—and make it sound like we actually mean it.

I personally found your rabbi to be a bit stuffy. He was that way when I was in Fustat, but he was the master there so I did not mind paying him the homage he seemed to expect. But here, among the great men of the generation, he still was haughty. Only Nissim seemed able to make him smile and enjoy the festivities. Every time Shmuel the Nagid or Rabbenu Hananel came near him he looked as though he was engaged in some strenuous competition. I know he is a great man and your teacher, Skandi, but you have to admit he thinks very highly of himself.

In truth, I was happy that you studied with Rabbenu Ephraim last year, and we are thrilled that you will continue your studies. Nissim says that on the days you were in attendance in the Madressa here, everyone thought a little clearer and sharper. He says that even though you are trained in the texts of the Land of Israel, you jumped right into the dialectic of the Babylonians and made a very strong showing. I am proud of you, brother, for honoring the family name among the rabbis of Kairawan. I am proud of you for representing the Jews of Fustat among the great men of the generation who were here for the wedding week. I am proud of you for showing the rabbis that a member of the community of Scripture can master their Torah as well as that of the Karaites. Mostly, I am proud that you are my brother. Thank you, al-Iskander, for being at my wedding.

I want you to read all of this to Mommy, because I want her to know how much I appreciate you and that I am grateful for everything she did for me. I was so delighted to be with her in Fustat preparing the trousseau. I was very happy to look through my teary eyes at the henna ceremony here and see her smiling at me. I think I understand Mommy much better now than I used to. She is an amazing woman to have journeyed away from her home and to have adopted a different culture in order to be with her husband. I honor her and kiss her hands and eyes. May her light shine forth now and always.

Please let Uncle Sahl and Abu Nasr know that our last shipment is on its way by sea. We now have a regular interchange between the Caliph's court in Fustat and the court in Granada. Tell Sahl Abu Saad that Shmuel the Nagid said the exact same thing that Uncle Sahl himself said, "Without the Jews in court, trade between the two kingdoms could not be so smooth." I pray that we can continue this very profitable business of serving as middlemen.

As for our own business, I am grateful that you are supervising the Misr end. It is all I can do to keep track of the caravans criss-crossing through Kairawan and Sousse, from East to West and back again. I feel that I no longer have even to buy any goods, but merely to organize the caravans or shipping and provide protection and warehouse space here in Afrikiya. Thank God that we are in the middle. Thank God for Uncle Sahl Abu Saad and Abu Nasr. Thank God for Caliph al-Zahir in Misr and Habus in Granada. Thank God for you and for Mommy. And thank God for Nissim, day by day.

I only wish I knew what to do with Ghazal. Now that you have seen with your own eyes what an odd little creature she is, you may better understand my frustrations with her. I thought that you were very patient with her, al-Iskander, particularly when she interfered with your time in the academy here. And Mommy, I just know that she loved the things that you brought her from Fustat, and I am so sorry that she could not be coaxed into saying thank-you. She can be such a little beast and tyrant. Thank God, I suppose, that she did not disrupt the wedding. I am going to have Nissim write on a separate sheet so he cannot read the things I have written about that girl. He keeps saying she's just going through a phase, she will get better. I say that she needs to know that her acts have consequences and if she does not behave then she will be given no privileges at all.

I do not want to end this letter complaining to you both. So let me repeat how grateful I am that you were here in Kairawan. I know that for Mommy especially it must have been hard to get aboard a boat and sail to Sousse. I do hope that al-Iskander thought it a great adventure and that he enjoyed meeting all of the rabbinic masters here. I pray that al-Iskander is happy minding the business in Misr and studying with Rabbenu Ephraim again. I am happy with my family in Fustat and happy with my life in Kairawan. I suppose I should sing the last Psalm aloud, Halleluyah!

I kiss your eyes and your hands, from Karimah bint Dunash HaCohen, wife of Rabbenu Nissim, to the household of Dunash HaCohen al-Tustari, peace be upon him, in Fustat, God willing. God's blessings and my prayers that you be inscribed for a good New Year. There is more from Rabbenu Nissim.

To Umm Karimah and al-Iskander, peace and an abundance of blessing. From Nissim ibn Yakov, in his own hand.

Karimah has not let me read what she has written to you, so forgive me if I repeat her expressions of our joy that you both were here in Kairawan for our wedding. I know that her own journey to Fustat before the wedding was very important to her. I know that she needed to feel that she was no longer cut off from Fustat. Your journey here wholly healed that wound for her. As for me, I thank God for the privilege of being part of your family.

You both know of my own history and how my first wife, peace be upon her, departed when giving birth to my Ghazal, may she be distinguished for long life. You know that Ghazal is an unusual daughter and that she requires special attention. I praise God daily that Karimah is so patient with her. Were it not for Karimah, my daughter would not have learned to read. It was Karimah who brought Ghazal to study and to reveal her excellent memory for text. Al-Iskander, I apologize if in her enthusiasm my daughter answered the questions which were posed to you in the academy here. I know that you needed time to recall and cannot be expected to have memorized the Babylonian traditions. She is impetuous and likes to call out and be first with an answer. I am certain she did not mean to embarrass you before the assembled colleagues. In any case, my dear boy, seeing your face was like beholding the face of God, you have brought me favor.

Indeed, al-Iskander, I hope you appreciate that your Rabbi Ephraim ben Shemariah did not journey to Kairawan out of deference to me or to meet Rabbenu Hananel or even the Nagid Shmuel ibn Nagrela. Nor did Rabbi Ephraim grace our academy because of the years of support that the al-Tustari family has given to him and his students. Nor did he do so out of respect to your late father, may his memory be for blessing, although I am sure that all of these played some part in his coming. No, al-Iskander, your sister and I had the honor of having Rabbenu Ephraim ben Shemariah sign our marriage contract because you are his chief disciple.

I know there are many students who study along with you, but I could see how pleased he was to watch you as his representative here in Kairawan. I appreciated his restraint when he refrained from speaking or offering any opinion in order to allow you the opportunity to speak. He was not silent from fear of error or, God forbid, from fear of being contradicted by colleagues far more knowledgeable than he, but for you, dear boy. I could see the pride lighting his eyes as he looked urgently around the room when called upon to speak, in order to find you that you might have your opportunity to shine. I know, for I am experienced in these matters, that you will soon have your own disciples. May God grant Rabbenu Ephraim what every master wishes: that you, his disciple, overtake him in wisdom and stature, speedily and in our day, amen.

And to Karimah's mother, my thanks that she brought her grace upon us. Her presence illuminated all of Kairawan and the west. I felt as though the good Lord had resurrected my own sainted mother, peace be upon her, to rejoice with us. Before I met your daughter I was lonely and depressed. Now I am a man again. As the Psalmist said, "God took poor me from the dust, He raised me from the refuse heap, to seat me with the mighty, with the great men of His people, He sat me with the joyous mother of her children, Halleluyah!"

From Nissim ibn Yakov, peace be upon him, ibn Shaheen, with blessings of peace and health for the coming year. To Umm Karimah and al-Iskander ibn Dunash, may he rest in Eden, Dunash HaCohen al-Tustari, in Fustat, with the help of God. By boat.

To Abu Kathir Ephraim ibn Shemariah Mahfouz, of Gaza, member of the Great Sanhedrin and master of the Jerusalemites in Fustat, Misr, at the square of the perfumers, God willing.

From Nissim ibn Yakov, peace be upon him, Second and Father of the Court in Kairawan, Rabbenu Nissim ibn Shaheen. By the hand of his personal scribe, in the name of the Merciful.

To my esteemed colleague Rabbenu Ephraim, may God bring peace and quietude upon you and the members of your honorable court in Fustat. I am writing to you about the matter which you so delicately raised during your stay here in Kairawan for my wedding festivities. First, allow me to express my gratitude, as well as that of my entire household for your extreme graciousness in honoring us with your presence. I could not have been more honored than by your insisting to sign our marriage contract, which is now a valued part of Jewish heritage by your having put your illustrious name upon it. I know that my colleagues Jacob ben Amram, the Nagid here in Kairawan; and my friend and Head of the Academy of Kairawan, Rabbenu Hananel ben Hushiel shared my excitement at your signing your name along with theirs. Needless to say, we who are humble would not have dreamed to ask you on our own to put yourself out in such a fashion, so we are all grateful.

As to your accusation that Rabbenu Hananel is responsible to the academy of the Land of Israel for 60 dinars in contributions, allow me to clarify the case as you raised it to me in such explicit and repeated detail during the wedding festivities. You say that a gift in kind worth 60 dinars was given through your good offices in Fustat for the academy in the Land of Israel. You point out, and there is no one to dispute it, that you had converted this into goods from your own perfumery for sale in Kairawan and the Maghreb. You had them sent via boat to al-Mahdia and then by caravan to the perfumers' market here in Kairawan. This sale of your goods was to have been jointly effected by our own Rabbenu Hananel and by Jacob ben Amram. Following the realization of the 60 dinars price you expected, they were to transfer the funds via the Taherti's banking interests back to Fustat for your distribution in the Holy Land.

Thus far, these are the facts of the case which you laid out to me. You will forgive me for having allowed my wedding week to pass before examining the details of this case on your behalf. I did so thereafter with alacrity for although you were, of course, too delicate and considerate to say such, there was implicit in your query an accusation against my cherished colleagues Rabbenu Hananel ben Hushiel and our Nagid, Jacob ben Amram. God forbid that anyone might think that they had diverted your goods for themselves, when those goods, minus refund to you for your expenses and profit, were in fact to be traded in the perfume market. Heaven forefend, lest anyone hearing your story conclude that it was your intention to besmirch the reputations of these two giants of the community, one a great master of Torah, the other a great man of the generation. For by your description, one could only conclude that you thought that they had diverted these funds for their own use.

Now let me rehearse for you and for everyone to whom you show this epistle, that Rabbenu Hananel ben Hushiel is a champion of the academies of Jerusalem. It is he, and he alone, who introduced the study of the traditions of the West into the academy here. It was he who first suggested a synthesis of the Babylonian traditions with those of the Land of Israel. Indeed, it is Rabbenu Hananel who insists that we defer to the authority of your court and academy as the true representatives of the Land of Israel here in the Maghreb. Were it not for all of this, you would not have entrusted us with the perfume goods in the first place.

Further, you were here in Kairawan for the wedding this summer. Perhaps you felt slighted by the colleagues of the academy. Perhaps you felt that Rabbenu Shmuel, Nagid and Wazir of Granada, did not pay you sufficient deference. God forbid, I pray that I was not at fault for offending you. But whatever your reasons, you have now accused the greatest of our generation, Rabbenu Hananel, who is my colleague and teacher, of diverting the funds of the academy of the Land of Israel.

One might wonder why you did not sell those goods directly in Fustat yourself or send them on to the Holy Land. One might wonder why your own personal goods became mixed up in the transmission of charitable funds at all, dear and esteemed Rabbi and Master of Fustat. But we would never, God forbid, raise even the dust of a suspicion that your motives were ever anything less than pure, such is your regard among us. But you should not, in turn, play the prosecutor against our master Rabbenu Hananel. As our sages say, "Woe to the poor city whose doctor suffers gout."

I only wish that I could have taken you by the hand on my very wedding day to show you what I have now seen. Your cases of perfume sit in the warehouse in the perfumers' marketplace here, with all the others. Each is clearly marked in your name as having been sent to the care of Rabbenu Hananel and our Nagid, Jacob ben Amram. Your consignment sits in that corner of the warehouse of goods designated for sale after the close of shipping. It cannot be otherwise in Fustat than it is here in Kairawan, that you will get much higher prices for the perfume in the winter months when women long for a scent of Spring than you could selling your volatile goods in the hot summer.

If Rabbenu Hananel was guilty of anything it was the desire to maximize your profits for your own benefit and that of the academies in the Holy Land. I know, since he has kept a copy of his reply to you in the Nagid's archives that he has indicated that neither the Nagid Jacob ben Amram nor Rabbenu Hananel himself will accept any commission for handling the transaction. It is, and I quote, their "contribution to this esteemed project of benefiting our colleagues in the academies of Jerusalem and Ramle." I will also note, for I asked the warehouse master, that Rabbenu Hananel and Jacob the Nagid are personally sharing the warehouse expenses from their own funds.

Here then is my finding in the matter of the accusation regarding the esteemed Rabbenu Hananel ben Hushiel, First, and the esteemed Jacob ben Amram, Nagid of Kairawan, in the matter of the sale of perfumes of Rabbenu Ephraim ben Shemariah of Fustat on behalf of the Academies of the Holy Land. The accused are innocent and blameless. There is no guilt whatsoever on their side. They have acted in good faith and with the best of business acumen in carrying out their charge.

As it is the month of Elul and we are in the period of penitence before the New Year and the Great Fast, it behooves you to seek their forgiveness in this matter. I will not command it as you are my eminent colleague and Rabbenu Hananel ben Hushiel deems your court to be superior in matters of the provenance of the Holy Land.

Again, let me express my humble delight that you honored us with your treasured presence this past summer at my wedding festivities. Although you raised the unfortunate charges at that time, I trust that my careful investigation has allayed your suspicions and laid these accusations to rest. I know that these accusations must have lain heavily with you or you would not have been so intemperate as to raise them in my wedding week. I pray that you benefited from the time you spent with us in the academy here. I know we all were deeply impressed with your profound erudition. We all agreed that never was there a better embodiment of the teaching of your venerable predecessor Rabban Shimon ben Gamaliel who said, "All my life I was raised among the sages, and never have I found a better tonic than silence."

In closing, I pray that you continue to find my new brother-in-law al-Iskander ibn Dunash HaCohen al-Tustari to be a growing light in your community. I know that you recall how his father Dunash, may he rest in peace, continually supported your disciples. I do not have to tell you how invaluable for you is this connection to the brothers al-Tustari and the court at al-Kahira. But I wish to emphasize the good nature of the boy, his desire to learn Torah, and to sit at your notable feet. I know that you would never allow anything to get in the way of your guidance of your disciples, precious master.

With every wish for a happy, healthy, and prosperous New Year. I am Nissim ibn Yakov ibn Shaheen, Second and Father of the Court in Kairawan. To Rabbenu Ephraim ben Shemariah, may he live forever, of Gaza, in the Court of Fustat, God help us all.

From al-Iskander in Fustat, to Nissim and Karimah in Kairawan, Winter 1035-36

To my dear master and teacher Rabbenu Nissim, and to his wife, my sister, my greetings to you in this season of Hannukah. My studies are progressing well. The last of the overland caravans have arrived and I have stored our goods for sale in the Warehouse of the Three Mice in the fortress of Fustat. I will sell those crates of perishables and spices as soon as possible. As for the remainder, mostly dried fruits, I will wait until winter progresses and peoples' tastes long for flavor, so they will be willing to pay a greater price. The items of stitchery I have stored in our own warehouses in the hopes that there will be a call for them from the Caliph's court, God willing.

We now are studying the Talmudic tractate Mo'ed Qatan. In the final chapter are the laws of excommunication and lesser bans. I write to you about this so that Karimah will understand why it is so apposite to what has happened here in Fustat. You should also know, dear brother-in-law and teacher, that Rabbenu Ephraim has now made mention of the commentaries of the Babylonian Gaonim, and he has referred to your *Key to the Closed Passages of the Talmud* more than once. What is more amazing, considering his fury just a few months ago, Rabbenu Ephraim is consulting Rabbenu Hananel ben Hushiel's commentary on Mo'ed Qatan and using it for his teaching. He also consults a scroll of the Iraqi Talmud and a book of the Talmud of the Land of Israel.

In the meanwhile, the gossip here simply must be repeated, God forgive me! There was a Jew here named Abraham ibn Daud ibn Sighmar who was accused of visiting a Muslim prostitute and paying her more than 100 dinars as her price! Actually, the total amount was 112 dinars. That alone is cause for scandal. She could feed a family for years or ransom three captives with such a fortune. Perhaps we should inquire whether she wishes to invest with us—forgive this poor student for his bawdy sense of humor. I am reminded, Rabbenu Nissim, of a story you sent once to me and to father, peace be upon him, about a prostitute and a student from the academy of Rabbi Hiyya. But that is neither here nor there.

In any case, Rabbenu Ephraim put this Abraham ibn Daud under a ban and then, my master being who he is, threatened to ban anyone who would speak out on his behalf as well. When ibn Sighmar after six weeks still refused to apologize,

Burton L. Visotzky

Rabbenu Ephraim moved to confiscate his property and declare it ownerless and available to all. At this, the fellow publicly cursed Rabbenu Ephraim ben Shemariah and his entire court. He denied all the charges he was accused of and refused to obey the court. He threatened to take the case to the Caliph and invited one of the Muslim Qadis to represent him.

Thank God, the Qadi had the good sense not to intervene in an internal Jewish matter, although there are those who say that Uncle Sahl had to pressure him. I do not know the attitude of the Muslims in this case. They asked Rabbenu Ephraim whether he would revoke the ban. He adamantly refused. Then they tried to go over his head and appealed to the Gaon in Ramle to have the court of the Holy Land revoke the ban.

Here is where the law comes in, for the Gaon's court in Ramle replied, exactly as Rabbenu Ephraim had been teaching us, "The toot (of the shofar) that binds is the toot that releases," which is the rabbis' way of saying that only the court who put one under a ban can release that person. This being the case, Rabbenu Ephraim has the upper hand. Our master Ephraim ben Shemariah taught us the following story from the Babylonian Talmud on this subject:

Once there was a disciple of the rabbis who had a reputation of being promiscuous. One rabbi asked, "How shall we proceed? We could ban him, but the rabbis need him. But if we do not ban him, will that not profane God's heavenly name?"

Another rabbi asked, "Has anyone heard any traditions that have bearing on a case like this?"

They said to him, "What is the meaning of the verse in Malachi, 'The lips of the priest are guardians of wisdom, seek Torah from his mouth for he is an angel of the Lord of Hosts'?" What this means is: if he resembles an angel of God, then seek Torah from his mouth. But if he does not resemble an angel, do not seek Torah from him."

So Rav Yehuda banned that student. Much later, when Rav Yehuda had grown feeble, the rabbis came to visit him. That disciple also came with them. When Rav Yehuda saw that student, he began to laugh. The student was offended and said, "Is it not enough that you have banned me? Now you laugh at me as well!?"

Rav Yehuda said, "It is not that I laugh at you, but that I am delighted to be headed toward the next world without having pandered to the likes of you." At that, Rav Yehuda's soul came to its rest.

The student went to the Madressa and asked to be released from Rav Yehuda's ban. They told him, "When a teacher was as important as Rav Yehuda, there is nothing we here can do for you. Perhaps you could go to the Nagid and he will release you."

So the student went to the Nagid who told his disciple, "Go look into this matter. If he deserves release, then release him."

So that disciple looked into the matter and was inclined to release the banned student. But the old man Rabbi Shmuel bar Nahmani stood up on his feet and said, "If the sages did not take the ban of Rabbi's maidservant lightly, but upheld her ban for three years, then for our colleague Rav Yehuda, how much more so!"

As it happens, that aged sage had not come to the Madressa for many years. The fact that he came there on that very day was deemed not as mere coincidence, but to teach the rabbis not to release that student! And so they did not release him from the ban. He left the academy in tears and while he was walking away from there a wasp came and stung him on his "cubit" and he died.

I think, Rabbenu Nissim, that the Talmud is trying to teach us that he was punished measure for measure; for he was punished upon the very place he sinned! I dare say, my dear teacher and sister, all of my fellow students enjoyed this story immensely. But we were disturbed by what followed it, for the Talmud there teaches that if one cannot fight his evil impulses then he should go to a place where no one knows him, and he should wear black garments and a black turban and do what his heart desires, so long as he does not profane God's heavenly name brazenly in public.

Now was it not the case with Abraham ibn Daud ibn Sighmar that he went in private and did what he could not resist? It was not his intention for the matter to be known. He certainly did not wish to defame the Jews, but merely to be with that woman. And yet the rumors caused the matter to be known and then Rabbenu Ephraim publicly rebuked him. Ibn Sighmar argued that it was Rabbenu Ephraim who caused God's Holy name to be defamed in public. I am certain that our master is correct in this matter, but I cannot think how to refute this Abraham ibn Daud's outrageous argument. He actually wishes to put Rabbenu Ephraim under a ban. I do not have to tell you that our master Ephraim almost burst from anger when he heard this.

Enough of this terrible gossip. It is dark and cold here and no one has anything to warm their hearts except this scurrilous prattle. I will try to keep my mind on our business enterprises and my studies from now on, and not pass along these scandals.

From al-Iskander ibn Dunash HaCohen al-Tustari, with wishes that light ever increase for you both. With the help of God.

Chapter Fourteen
Spring, 1036

From al-Iskander in Cairo,
to Nissim and Karimah in Kairawan, Spring, 1036

Dear teacher and brother Rabbenu Nissim and to my sister, abundant peace and blessings at this most auspicious time. I have no doubt that you have heard the news of the death of the late Caliph al-Zahir, peace be upon him. You know that al-Zahir was an influence for good and tolerance; none of the excesses committed by the previous Caliph, his name need not be mentioned, were committed against the Jews or the Copts in Fustat. There was little rioting or tension between the Sunni and the Shiat Ali during the reign of al-Zahir. His 15 years of rule, the years of my growth and attainment of manhood, were years of peace and prosperity for all the Fatimid empire.

You also recall that al-Zahir's wife, may she be distinguished for long life, had been one of the household slaves of Uncle Sahl before her marriage to the Caliph. That beautiful and wise woman not only gave al-Zahir an heir, but brought Sahl Abu Saad and his brother Abu Nasr closer to the court of al-Kahira. It was through them that Daddy was able to gain contracts with the court for garments. I recall that your girls in Kairawan sewed some of the clothing we used to send to the court.

When the commander of the faithful al-Zahir, peace be upon him, was taken by Allah; his son al-Mustansir became our Imam and Caliph. The new Commander of the Faithful is yet very young, but he is pious and shrewd. He listens to his mother very carefully, for she is schooled in the intrigues of the court. If Sahl Abu Saad had power in the reign of al-Zahir, how much the more so in the reign of his son. Our Uncle Sahl is now the undisputed Wazir to the Caliph, the Commander of the Faithful, the sultan of Egypt and the Maghreb, al-Mustansir!

Abu Saad—for that is what he said that I should call him—he said that my saying Uncle Sahl in public was demeaning for me as it implied that I relied only on my family ties and not on my wits—Abu Saad invited me to the inaugural ceremonies for our new Caliph. It was my first time inside the Eastern Palace of al-Kahira and a grand place it is. The hall of women, which is where the mixed audiences take place, is overlaid with gold. It is almost impossible to look up there; it is so bright from the sun reflecting off the golden walls.

But we were not supposed to look up, but keep our eyes to the ground. Abu Saad took me from there into the Iwan, where only the men are allowed. We also went to pay our respects at the monument to Husayn, for al-Mustansir, as was his father al-Zahir and his father before him, is a direct descendent of the great martyr of the Shia. Then we went back through the Iwan to the plaza before the festival gate. From there a great procession formed. It was to pass north, go round the mosque of al-Mustansir's grandfather al-Hakim, and then return back south down the great parade ground Bayn al-Qasrayn, through the gates of al-Kahira, stopping at the ibn Tulun mosque and finally ending with festivities at the mosque of 'Amr ibn al-As. There, on the broad space before the Nile they set up many tents for food and music.

Abu Saad had me riding just behind him and Abu Nasr. It was very awkward as I had never been on a horse before and we were expected at certain points to leap off and bow to the ground. I was uncomfortable enough getting on and off the horse and taking care at not getting my feet caught in the stirrups. But dear teacher, Rabbenu Nissim, I do not know if I did right or wrong with the bowing, as I feel we Jews are not allowed to bow to any but to our Almighty God, may His name be praised. But I did what Abu Saad and Abu Nasr did. It is not as though we bowed to idols, or even to Allah. To be honest, I do not see any difference between the oneness of Allah and the oneness of God, may His name be praised for ever and ever. If there is but one God, then the Muslims and the Jews must worship one and the same God.

Daddy, peace be upon him, would have loved the parade and the festivities. I know because Mommy cried when I told her all about it. She remembered the first time Uncle Sahl invited Daddy to the court, and how he used to go out and watch the Muslims and the Copts at the Nile celebrations. And now we were actually riding in the procession.

The Commander of the Faithful had his hair cut very short. He rode a mule that had no ornament at all as a sign of his humility before Allah. The Caliph was wearing all white. He had a beautiful white robe made of Dabiqi linen, with very wide sleeves. Abu Saad said it cost ten thousand dinars! His turban was also white, no jewels or ornaments, but positively gleaming. All the Commander of the Faithful carried was a whip in his hand. The simplicity of al-Mustansir was very affecting.

The courtiers all wore fabulous robes of Rumi brocade, shot with gold. Even I got to wear one, although I had to give it back at the end of the day while Abu Saad and Abu Nasr and the real courtiers got to keep theirs. There were ten thousand horses in the procession; it seemed to go on forever. The lead horses all had golden saddles and jewels on the bridles and collars they wore. All the

Burton L. Visotzky

rest, had buqalamun cloth draped over them. As if the shimmering cloth were not impressive enough, al-Mustansir's name was woven into the fabric.

This interests me, for you and I know that ten thousand garments of that nature take time to make. How did they know in advance when to make the garments for the new Caliph? Do you think they had them made long ago and kept them in storage against the day that al-Zahir might die? Did al-Zahir order them made so that he could assure his son would become the new Caliph and look splendid? The amounts of money spent on clothing and gold saddles must be incalculable.

These horses were followed by thousands more horses covered in chain mail, as were their riders. Then there were the army officers, the Amiri and Hafizi regiments, the commander of the army and the chamberlain, the director of the treasury and the keeper of appointments, the Emirs of the collar and the courtiers. I was among the latter for this part, which put me near the end of the procession, yet not immediately with the Wazir and the Caliph.

Following all of us were all of the Imams and the Qadis and, chief among them, Uncle Sahl Abu Saad. He looked very grand in his brocade. But when the Caliph came through the gates, all of the courtiers leapt from their saddles and bowed to the ground, kissing with their finger tips at the hooves of the Caliph's mule. Our Commander of the Faithful, Caliph al-Mustansir, was entirely surrounded by the Juyushiyya and the Rayhaniyya regiments made up of fearsome black Africans. Abu Saad explained that these are the only troops that al-Mustansir's mother really trusts, for they are the only ones as dark as she is. She has pushed aside many of the Turk and Berber regiments, which worries Abu Saad. He does not want to spur rebellion against a young Caliph.

When the procession came to the mosque of 'Amr, it was a great gesture to the Sunni Muslims here in Fustat. Earlier in the day, during the Khutba at the mosque of al-Hakim, in addition to the usual reading of the Quran, they read out a prayer for the Shia of the Fatimid empire and their new Caliph. So when they came to the Sunni mosque, no one expected that the Caliph would bow there. Yet he did. He, who could have served as Imam and taken that mosque as his own, instead dismounted, bowed to Allah, and listened as the Imam there read the Quran and then blessed the new Caliph by name.

I believe that one gesture assured that al-Mustansir will reign for 50 years or more. The entire city was united when the Caliph said that we all worship the same God. He said that he was commander of all the faithful and would do his best to respect all of the various parts of the empire. Of course, it was actually Abu Saad who had written the speech on behalf of the new Caliph.

When the speech was over, Abu Saad bowed and kissed the hem of al-Mustansir's robe. Even the Jews and the Copts were weeping and cheering and shouting, "Long live the Caliph!" by that point. Then the courtiers were taken to begin the banqueting at the banks of the Nile. We were not far from where they do the Nile celebrations when they cut the canal each year. The Caliph had an entire tent of gold brocade from the Rum. It shimmered in the sunlight. For everyone else there were tents, food, and music. Even the Jews partook of the fruits that were set out. There was great hope for the empire, in-sh-Allah.

I mentioned earlier how people were affected by al-Mustansir. I just wrote to you about the cheering. But I think the most impressive thing on a day of horns and cymbals and shouting was the silence that respectfully settled on the crowd at his first appearance. It reminded me of something we had studied in the Talmud.

Our rabbis taught: if one sees the kings of the gentiles, one should say, Praised are you God, Our Lord, King of the Universe, Who has given of His honor to His creatures. Rav Sheshet was blind. Once all of the population was going out to greet the king, so Rav Sheshet went along with them. A certain heretic said to him, "The fit buckets are used to draw water from the stream, but what business do the broken buckets have at the river?"

Rav Sheshet replied, "Let us see if I cannot see more than you."

When the first regiment passed by, a huge shout greeted them. That heretic, who was back in the crowd said, "The Caliph has come!"

But Rav Sheshet said, "Not yet."

Then the second regiment passed and another huge cry went up from the crowd. That heretic said, "Now, the Caliph has come!"

Rav Sheshet replied, "The Caliph has not come yet."

A third regiment passed, and was greeted in utter silence. Then Rav Sheshet said, "Now, the Caliph is come!"

That heretic asked him, "How did you know?"

Rav Sheshet explained, "Kings on earth are like the King in heaven, of Whom it is written in the Book of Kings, 'Go forth and stand upon the mountain before God and behold God pass before you. And a great and powerful wind arose, pounding the mountains and smashing boulders, but God was not in the wind. And after the wind an earthquake, and after the earthquake fire, but God was not in the earthquake nor in the fire. And after the fire, the thin sound of silence.'" When the Caliph came, Rav Sheshet pronounced the blessing for seeing a king of the gentiles.

Dear Sister, it was exactly this way when the Caliph appeared before the throng in Fustat. There was ear splitting noise: shouting, drumming, horses and mules braying, music blaring and then, suddenly, no sound but silence. That is what we heard, or did not hear, when al-Mustansir had his advent as Caliph. And after that, again the noise, like the wind and earthquake and fire of Elijah.

The celebrations went on for three whole days. It was almost as exciting as your wedding in Kairawan, with all the dignitaries and important people. Abu Saad was exceptionally gracious. He is so very good to me, and to Mommy, too. I feel we shall soon have as many clothing contracts as we wish, so see if the households in your academy are ready for work and profit!

I end now so that I have time to review my studies. We read and write everything, but Rabbenu Ephraim makes us memorize texts also. I have to review and review and review until they stick in my head.

From al-Iskander in al-Kahir and Fustat. To Rabbenu Nissim and his household, my sister in Kairawan, at this most auspicious time, may God protect all of us.

From al-Iskander in Fustat, to Karimah and Nissim in Kairawan, Fall, 1037

To my dear sister Karimah bint Dunash, may he rest in Eden, HaCohen al-Tustari, and to her noble husband Rabbenu Nissim, Second and Father of the Court of Kairawan, may his light shine forth.

Rabbenu Nissim, my master and teacher, you will forgive me please for putting my sister's name ahead of your own in my greetings, but I am filled with family pride at the continued ascent of the al-Tustaris. Uncle Sahl Abu Saad has become Wazir to the Caliph, the Commander of the Faithful, al-Mustansir. You know that the Caliph was son to our late Caliph al-Zahir and his wife, Umm Malik. She had been in service to Uncle Sahl before she married al-Zahir, peace be upon him. It is only natural that Abu Saad should have continued influence then over Umm Malik and her son, the youthful Caliph.

Since the Commander of the Faithful is really still a boy, he relies on Uncle Sahl Abu Saad for almost everything. In only one area does his mother hold sway, and that is in regard to the protection of the Caliph himself. Umm Malik, as we now call his mother, is ferocious about protecting her son and personally oversees his body guard. Each of these she hand-picked from among the black African troops here. All of this may be very fine for her peace of mind, but it causes political conflicts for Abu Saad to mediate.

In order to have the palace turn black, as it were, many of the Turkish troops were either dismissed or demoted. Of course, the Turks do not wish to lose their jobs and influence. So Uncle Sahl Abu Saad is trying to placate them by finding them work on his own staff and that of other courtiers. While that is good for the Turks, it pits the Wazir's staff, who work under Abu Saad, against the courtiers of the Caliph. This could be an untenable and dangerous situation. I think Abu Saad spends as much time worrying about this conflict as he does all the other affairs of state combined.

Abu Saad has elevated his brother Abu Nasr to a position of power in the court. This way, as Abu Saad explained it, there is a second set of eyes to keep watch over the affairs of the Caliph. Abu Nasr was very forthcoming about the palace intrigues. He said, "Ever since Sahl and I were children, we've watched each other's backs."

There might also be some tension because Abu Saad is Jewish. But al-Mustansir has many Jews and Coptic Christians in his government. That leads me to the other factor that contributes to our feelings of safety. Because of al-Mustansir's modesty and genuine openness, relations between the Sunni and the Ismaili Shia are very good right now. There is a feeling of religious tolerance. Everyone proclaims that we all worship one and the same Allah, each community in our own way.

But for all of that, I still worry. I heard a ditty circulating on the lips of the Muslim worshippers at their Friday prayers. It was said in good humor, but still makes me nervous. It went,

> The Jews these days have gained the right to rule
> They hold the honors and the gold and jewel.
> The Wazir to the king comes from their pool.
> Folks of Egypt, do not be a fool,
> Since even Heaven has become their tool,
> Become a Jew and follow them to school!

There are elders in the rabbinic academy who can remember when the Caliph's grandfather, may his name be erased, ruled over al-Kahira. They recall that he destroyed synagogues and churches. They explained that al-Hakim was a madman who turned on the Jewish community after having been very good to them at first. His madness extended to requiring our Jewish fathers to wear badges indicating their religion. The Dhimmi, among them people of the book like Copts and Jews, should have had protected rights under Islam. But under the Caliph's grandfather it was not so. Only now are the synagogues being restored and funds raised to repair the damage of twenty-five years ago.

So there are members of the Jewish community who are very nervous. They wish that Abu Saad and Abu Nasr were not so very visible. They say that it is inevitable that palace intrigue will bring down a Wazir. They feel the Jewish

Burton L. Visotzky

community will suffer when this happens. I find this discussion hypocritical, for while these Jews complain about the dangers of having uncle Sahl hold power, they benefit from his court status daily. Even Jews from the Maghreb are writing Abu Saad asking for favors. They wish to hold the rope at both ends—to complain that power is dangerous, but to take as much advantage of it as they can.

When I told Abu Saad that I found this kind of behavior mystifying, he commended me to read the works of Husayn ibn Sina, a great courtier. He served as court physician, but was also a famous astronomer and philosopher. He wrote a Canon of Medicine that all the court physicians rely upon. But Abu Saad says he wrote even greater works of politics and philosophy. I have heard it said that ibn Sina wrote more than two hundred books! I read parts of his teachings about an earlier philosopher named Aristo. It explained much about the human condition.

In the work which I read, ibn Sina refers to the mind, the soul, and the body. He says that Aristo teaches that the soul is divine and immortal, part of what he calls the active intellect. What captured my attention was that ibn Sina wrote that the Greeks teach that the body and soul are like the blind and the lame. The blind beggar supports the lame beggar and thus two incomplete beings fit with one another to form a complete being, each supplying what the other lacks.

This reminded me of a story about the Emperor Antoninus and our Holy Rabbi Yehuda the Patriarch. Do you remember, Rabbenu Nissim, that some years ago it was you who introduced me to these stories? In the one I am thinking of, Antoninus asks Rabbi Yehuda about the relationship of the mind and the body at the time of resurrection of the dead. Our Holy Rabbi tells him exactly the same as ibn Sina says that the Greeks teach. He tells of a king who had an orchard which had beautiful ripe figs. The king wished to set watchmen over the orchard so that no one would steal the fruit. He assigned a lame man and a blind man for the job. The lame man told the blind man that there were tasty figs nearby. The blind man said, "I cannot see them. You get them."

The lame man said, "But I cannot walk."

What did they do? The lame man rode on the blind man's back and together they stole the figs. Later, when the king returned, he asked what became of his figs. The lame man said, "I did not take them; I cannot walk!"

The blind man said, "I did not take them; I cannot even see them!"

Now the king was no fool, so he commanded the lame man to ride on the blind man's back, and tortured them together.

"So," Rabbi Yehuda told the Emperor Antoninus, "in the world to come the soul will claim to God, 'I did not sin. Since I have left the body, am I not pure?' And then the body will say, 'I did not sin. Since the soul has left me, have I not been like a broken vessel tossed on the trash heap?' And what will the Blessed Holy One do? God will reunite the body and the soul and punish them as one."

I tell you this story now, for it reminds me of the Jews of Fustat who wish that Abu Saad be powerful enough to be able to help them, but not be too powerful. If he helps them he is like the pure soul. If he is too powerful, then he will remind them of the lowly body. According to these nay-sayers, either way God will punish us. I pray that they are wrong.

My uncle tells me that ibn Sina recently died in the East. I know he was born in Bukhara, and lived at Isfahan and Samarkand. I do not even know whether these cities are loyal to Baghdad or to the Turks. Abu Saad says that the politics of the East are ever changing, and al-Islam is a complex world. I, for my part, learn my lessons and see to our business interests here in Fustat. I put my trust in God.

From Nissim and Karimah in Kairawan, to al-Iskander in Fustat and Cairo, March, 1038

My dear al-Iskander, warmest greetings from me and from your sister Karimah.

I was most interested in your report of the philosopher ibn Sina, as was your sister, who recalled hearing of him long ago. You have inspired me to learn his writings. I have not yet studied his works, I confess, primarily because my teachers did not particularly value philosophy. They felt it was not an essentially Jewish endeavor and concentrated, instead, upon study of the Talmud. Chief among these great Talmudic scholars was Rabbenu Hai Gaon. I lament telling you of his recent passing, may I be atonement for his precious soul. Rabbenu Hai disliked what he called speculations. He preferred the law, instead. I myself have seen and copied dozens, if not hundreds, of his responses to legal questions. He adjudicated the law for rabbinic Jews throughout the entire Diaspora, from Baghdad in the East, to Granada in the West.

He much preferred to write on Jewish law, what he called the need to restrain human behavior, rather than engage in theological speculation. He would not have liked your ibn Sina's musings on body and soul, despite the fact that you have found a similar tradition among our rabbinic texts. He absolutely despised the rabbis' works of Shiur Qoma that purport to measure God's body. In this he was in rare agreement with the Karaites who disdain any activity as foolish as trying to measure the Blessed Holy One. Rabbenu Hai would hiss that only an idiot could imagine God to be reducible to human measurements. No, Rabbenu Hai did not care for anything so abstract as speculation. He only wished to inhabit the four ells of the law.

His work without a doubt will be continued. Rabbenu Hananel and I will write legal responsa, as we have been doing so for some time. That young scholar in Fez, Rabbi Isaac ibn Yakov, who is only five years older than you, continues to make his way through the Talmud, epitomizing the law and omitting the lore and stories. I am glad for my Compendium when I see how that one from Fez is so narrowly limiting his focus of study.

Rabbenu Hai's death truly marks the end of an era. First the light dimmed from Sura and now from Pumbeditha. With Hai gone to his reward, neither of the two great Talmudic academies will shine forth any longer. Why al-Iskander, those two schools taught the Torah of Babylonia for almost eight hundred years! It was to Iraq that we Jews were first exiled, twice that number of years ago. The towns and academies of Babylonia were The Exile. Now we have become a Diaspora, scattered across God's world like the peoples of the Tower of Babel. From Babylonia we go forth to Fustat and Kairawan, to Provence and Mainz, to Granada and Narbonne. Afrikiya and Franj—or Ashkenaz as it is called in the Bible. Sefarad and Amalfi, these are the new world of Jews outside of the Holy Land. Al-Iskander, the world changes. They even study Talmud now among the vineyards in Troyes. God only knows what may come of that!

Forgive the ramblings of an old man, al-Iskander. I am nearing 50 years of age, one-half the years of my late teacher Rabbenu Hai. He was a giant, and I am so small. I know that I am living in the best of times. The academy here flourishes. The Empire is strong and your Uncle Sahl Abu Saad has great influence over our glorious Fatimid Caliph. Our colleague Shmuel the Nagid is the Wazir in Granada, praised be the Name. I thank God for your sister, who is my scribe and my household. I could not do without her attention to Ghazal's many needs, the work of the academy and, to say the least, our still flourishing business, thank God day by day. She copies my writings and provides texts for Rabbenu Hananel and his students to memorize. She still teaches reading and writing to the women and children.

But I feel that the work is great, my time is short, and the Master is insistent. I do not know why in this golden time that I feel such a sense of foreboding. Yet I do, al-Iskander; I am afraid of what the future might bring us. I am laboring hard to write and teach, so that my work might find fulfillment. I think that Rabbenu Hai, may he rest in Eden, was more of a father-figure to me than I realized. That old man, who lived so far away, has gone and left me feeling bereft and lost. Blessed is the True Judge.

I wish to end this letter of lament and death with a cause for joy. So I tell you that your sister Karimah is with child. God willing, she will bear a son to

Rabbenu Nissim this coming winter. If the evil eye does not befall her, God may grace us with a new soul sometime between Sukkot and Hannukah, we pray. With blessings of peace, Nissim ben Yakov ibn Shaheen.

Karimah to al-Iskander, by her own hand: Brother dear, I read what Nissim has written you of our good news. I am feeling well, thank God. I have none of the sickness that the other girls often experience early in pregnancy. I continue to teach, to copy, to do our business, and to exercise. So far there is no visible sign of my child, but by the hidden signs, the news is certain. Tell Mommy of our joy and let her find solace that soon, please God, there will be a namesake for Daddy, peace be upon him.

Nissim and I told the good news to Ghazal to prepare her for becoming a big sister. She is now eight years old and I have been her step-mother for almost three years. Skander, she greeted the news with a tantrum rather than with any joy. Nissim says it is likely part of her medical condition that she has these fits of anger. I do not see what being dwarfish and having a big head has to do with her kicking and screaming the moment she stops being the center of everyone's attention. When she wishes, Ghazal can be perfectly charming. But I am certain she sees me as a threat to her having exclusive rights to her father.

I suspect that she has been this difficult in the hopes of driving me away and having our master all to herself once more. Now that there will be a child of our own, Ghazal certainly must give up that fantasy. I pray that when the baby actually comes she will have a change of heart. Most eight-year-old girls here are already happy to be little mother's helpers—at least if Rabbenu Hananel's girls are any example. Whether I like it or not, I have Ghazal to care for. I yearn for my own child, may he come in good time and be healthy, God willing.

If the baby is, in fact, a boy, I will explain to Ghazal how wonderful it is to have a little brother to command. I kiss your hands and eyes. Do the same for me to Mommy.

From al-Iskander in Fustat, to Karimah and Nissim in Kairawan, Summer, 1038

My dear sister and brother-in-law who is my teacher and my master of Torah, Mazal Tov and Mabruk! May the joyous event come with success at an auspicious hour and under a good constellation, God willing. I am so pleased to read your wonderful news. Mommy was truly happy. I have not seen her smile like this since Daddy took ill, except for the week of your wedding. She sends her prayers and good wishes. Mommy says to tell you, "May the evil eye ne'er befall you!" I am to be an uncle! I would pray that you have a daughter whom I myself could someday wed, as did our sages of old, but for the fact that I have just turned 20 years of age.

This is not to say that a 20-year difference between bride and groom is untenable, God forbid. Indeed, between you, dear sister, and you, my master, there is a difference of 23 years. But just as the rabbinic sages decreed 13 years is the age of majority, so too, some among the rabbis, as well as all of our Karaite community of Scripture count 20 years of age as the time for adulthood. What I am trying to say is that the joy of my birthday has been attenuated by the desire of the community in Fustat to start thinking about a bride for me.

I resent this for it will interfere with my studies and our ability to do business, since everything takes time. You are right to quote the Chapters of the Fathers, Rabbenu Nissim, the time is short, the work is much, and the Master is insistent. I confess I also worry that I am not considered such a good match by my own merits, but rather through those of my uncle Sahl and even your merits, Rabbenu. I have lineage now, good family, connections. People seem to ignore me and the fact that I have worked hard to master the traditions of the community of Scripture as well as those of the rabbinic sages.

You know how few can make a claim to being knowledgeable in the two Jewish communities' traditions. You know that our family has constantly sought to unite the Jewish community and supported all of the various factions and denominations. You know that I have been a loyal Karaite, as well as a student of the rabbis' texts and traditions. But when anyone speaks of my attributes as a groom, all I hear is how wonderful my relatives are. I know it is wrong and immodest, but I would like to think that it is I who am getting married to a bride, not you or Abu Saad. I wish for a bride of good family, but I wish to have a bride for her own good merits, first and foremost.

The Mishnah Taanit teaches us that on the 15th day of the month of Av, the girls of Jerusalem used to dress in white and dance in the vineyards. What did they say? "O boys, take a good look at what you are choosing. Do not pay attention to beauty, but look to good family, for the Book of Proverbs teaches that, 'Beauty is false and prettiness is vain. A woman who fears the Lord is to be praised.'"

I suppose this means that if you come from a good family you will turn out to be God fearing. But I cannot help recall that the Talmud there teaches the tradition a bit differently, and says that the pretty girls used to say, "Look for beauty, for don't you want a beautiful wife?" While those girls of good family used to say, "Look to family, for wives will bring you good offspring." The Talmud ends on a realistic note, for it comments that the ugly girls used to say, "Take what you can get, for God's sake! Just be sure to treat us well and adorn us in gold."

Rabbenu Nissim, is it wrong for me to hope that I might find a wife who is pretty and comes from a good family? Is it too much to hope for a wife who I actually enjoy being with and who truly is a helpmate to me? I would hope to be as satisfied with my household as you are with my sister or as Daddy was with Mommy. I put my trust in God.

Our business continues to flourish, God be praised. Our contacts in the Maghreb have been especially fruitful. Between Shmuel the Nagid and Uncle Sahl, we have become the middlemen of first resort. Karimah can attest to the fact that our ships and caravans grow mighty in number and are virtually invulnerable thanks to being under the joint protection of al-Kahira and Granada. You must see this even more in Kairawan than I do here; but by land and by sea we grow daily in wealth. We have restored Daddy's losses, praise be to God, and now are again most comfortable.

God willing, we will give much charity this year, even more than last. It is satisfying to me to know that I can support the scholars here as well as the academies in the Holy Land. I continue our custom of sending funds to Iraq, although things are strained between the Fatimids and Baghdad. The Babylonian academies seem to be on the wane. I look for your advice, Rabbenu Nissim, on how or if to continue support of Sura and Pumbeditha now that Rabbenu Hai, peace be upon him, has passed unto that better world. It might be more politic to leave off our support of Iraq at this juncture, but I do not wish to harm the Jewish communities of the rabbis or the Karaites there.

For all of our immediate success, nothing we have compares with the wealth of our al-Tustari uncles. I have seen with my own eyes that in Abu Saad's pavilion there are 300 enormous vases each made of silver. The mamelukes polish this silver daily and in each vase a tree is planted. One would not be surprised to see the very leaves of those trees sprout gold. As it is, they bear rich and delicious fruits. Recently, as a gift to celebrate the birthday of the Commander of the Faithful, Uncle Saad and Abu Nasr gave 200,000 gold dinars to the treasury, so that al-Mustansir and his mother could buy clothing for their personal body-guards to honor the day. Need I point out that the clothing was purchased through an al-Tustari trading consortium and manufactured under contract to the al-Tustaris?

I will send an accounting of the caravan profits from this season, as well as the shipping news later in the year when Sukkot has passed and it is time to count our harvest, as it were. I enclose with this letter an account I have copied of a recent court proceeding. It shows our Jewish communities that we have true friends among al-Islam. That community is even more divided into factions than our own. For now, our Jewish congregations in Fustat are working well together. As you will read, we feel confident of rebuilding the sacred structures which were damaged or demolished back when Karimah was a baby, before I was born.

Let me close my letter of congratulations, good news, and prosperity with mention of the other sacred structure which is now gone. I refer to the death of our teacher, Rabbenu Hai, Gaon of Pumbeditha, peace be upon him. I know that he was your special teacher, Rabbenu, particularly since the death of your sainted father, may he rest in Eden. But all Israel feels the loss of our master Rabbenu Hai Gaon. Our rabbis teach that when a sage dies, his academy suspends its studies. And when the Head of the Court dies, all the academies in the city should suspend their studies. What shall we do for Rabbenu Hai Gaon, then, who was First to all of us in the Diaspora? We all mourn and lament his passing. As the Talmud says,

> An ancient scion came from Babylonia, who carried the Book of
> Battles...
> God was angry at the world and snatched a mighty soul,
> Yet the heavens rejoiced at her arrival,
> As though a new bride had arrived
> For the One-Who-Rides-the-Clouds,
> Rejoicing at the arrival of a pure and righteous soul.

It is as though the Talmud had those words waiting as an advanced eulogy for our late lamented master, Rabbenu Hai Gaon. How shall we count our loss?

Did not our ancient master Rabban Shimon ben Gamaliel teach that since the Holy Temple was destroyed, there is no day that does not bring a fresh loss? When Rabbi Eliezar died, the honor of Torah ceased. When Rabbi Joshua died, there were no longer men of sound advice. When Rabbi Aqiba died, those who sow Torah ceased. When Elazar ben Azariah died, the crown of the sages ceased to be. When Ben Azzai died, the diligent students ceased. When Ben Zoma died, the great preachers ceased. When Shimon ben Gamaliel died, the locusts came and our troubles increased. When Rabbi Yehuda the Partiarch died, our troubles trebled.

If all of this was true in the day of our ancient sages, how much the more so do we have to fear now that our master Rabbenu Hai Gaon has died. We could add to this rabbinic text and declare, When Rabbenu Hai died, the Babylonian Diaspora scattered. Woe unto all of us for this most grievous loss.

Is it any wonder that you feel uncertain, dear Rabbenu Nissim? Your personal loss was also a loss to the entire Jewish people. Please accept my sincere condolences on the death of our teacher Hai Gaon. May the Lord comfort you among the mourners of Zion and Jerusalem.

From al-Iskander ibn Dunash, peace be upon him, HaCohen of the great house of al-Tustari in Fustat and the court at al-Kahira.

To Rabbenu Nissim, Second and Father of the Court of Kairawan, with blessing for mourners, and to my sister Karimah bint Dunash, with the support of heaven and with success at her coming hour. By the Caliph's fleet.

Transcript of the findings of the Qadi's court, from Spring, 1038

I attach the copy of the findings of the Caliphal court. It refers to the Babylonians' synagogue in Fustat, which last year finally was rebuilt after it had been razed in the time of al-Hakim, may his memory be forgotten. The rabbis collected funds from our communities and throughout the Jewish world. Uncle Sahl and Abu Nasr contributed generously. You know how much the communities of Kairawan and the Maghreb gave, as I have heard that you helped organize the appeal for funds on the synagogue's behalf.

You may not know that there are certain extremist Muslims who believe that al-Kahira, and Fustat as well, should be for Muslims only, in the manner of Mecca or al-Medina. They heartily approved of what the late Caliph al-Hakim had done in his madness and they vehemently opposed the rebuilding of the synagogue. When all else failed, they appealed to the Muslim Qadi's court, protesting that the Sunna of al-Islam forbids the building of new synagogues in Islamic cities.

Of course, the Jews argued that the synagogue was not new, even though every bit of it had been built just this year. But the essence of the argument was that there had been a synagogue where this one now stood. Therefore this synagogue is not new, but should be considered merely a remodeling of the old structure. This ruling is extremely important to us, for it will deter those Muslims who wish to drive the Jews from Egypt. No longer can they destroy synagogues with the smug hope that they will never be rebuilt. So long as they know that we will rebuild, and that the Muslim courts permit it, they must stay their hand.

Here is the document I copied:

Praise to Allah, Lord of All Worlds.

In the name of Allah, the Merciful and Beneficent.

Here are the findings of a case for which the truth has been determined. We put our trust in God.

The one who petitioned Allah was Ibrahim al-Ansari, who came and kissed the ground before the glorious Imam, may Allah make his rule eternal and strengthen the Faith. Ibrahim al-Ansari claimed that the synagogue of the Zuwayla quarter, a synagogue of Rabbinic Jews, is new, having been recently built. He requested that his complaint be brought to the attention of our tribunal, that we might learn who has jurisdiction in this case, hear the complaint, and order the demolition of said synagogue under the Sunna of al-Islam, so that the triumph of right might prevail.

The Qadi heard the matter and ordered that the head of the aforementioned synagogue be brought to testify. A subpoena was issued and the Jewish elder, Abu Imran Moshe ben Yakov ben Yitzhak al-Israeli, physician to the Caliph and Head of the United Jewish Communities of Rabbanites, Karaites and Samaritans, appeared before the seat of judgment of our lord the chief Qadi, may Allah extend his shadow over him. The plaintiff was the above mentioned Ibrahim al-Ansari, who charged that the synagogue was unlawful and should be removed from control of Abu Imran Moshe al-Israeli and the Jewish community, and remanded to the court of al-Islam for destruction.

In response to the Qadi's examination of him as witness, Abu Imran Moshe replied that the synagogue was ancient and that the Jewish community had exercised rightful authority over it in accordance with Islamic law for a period of more than forty years. Abu Imran Moshe further entered affidavits of proof to this evidence.

Our lord the Qadi asked Ibrahim al-Ansari whether he, in his turn, had any proof to offer that the synagogue was, in fact, illegal. He replied that he had neither document nor any testimony to prove his accusation. Then the Qadi ordered the Jew, Abu Imran Moshe, to produce his evidence to substantiate his response to the charges. He produced the following Muslim witnesses: Bahram ibn Abdallah, courtier and tradesman to the Caliph; his son Hajj Ismail ibn Bahram, scribe to the Imam of the Mosque of al-Hakim; Qasim ibn Fahkr al-Din of the Wazir's staff; Ali ibn Hamid, the perfumer; the honorable Hajj Khattab ibn Nasr Mujahid, caravaneer; Hajj Mansur ibn Badr, trader in silk and fabric; Suleiman ibn Ayub of the wheat market; and the Hajj Ramadan ibn Ali al-Sandabisi, India trader.

They testified before our lord the judge that they knew the Synagogue of the Rabbanite Jews which stands at the head of the Zuwayla Quarter on the street called Darb al-Nabbadhin...they were completely familiar with this structure, its boundaries and its rights, with an awareness of the law which precludes ignorance or error. They testified that the synagogue mentioned was an ancient structure and not recently built. In addition they unanimously testified that the synagogue in question was, in fact, a *Waqf*. It was considered a *Waqf* for many years, authorized and verified as under the supervision of the Rabbanite Jews for worship according to their custom and it is under the supervision of whomever is the Head of the United Jewish Communities of Fustat and al-Kahira. They further testified that the aforementioned Elder Abu Imran Moshe has exercised control for more than forty years.

This was made known by the witnesses under the questioning of the chief judge, our lord the Qadi. It was affirmed by the Chief Qadi as a valid substantiation of fact: decisive, credible and sufficient. He gave judgment in accordance with the facts and findings, and his decision is binding and compulsory. This document has been read out and verified before him in the presence of witnesses on this, the 9th day of Sha'ban in the year 429.

From al-Iskander in Fustat to Karimah in Kairawan, late Summer, 1038

My dear sister, I am writing you a letter in private as I used to, which you can read with your own eyes. I wanted to write to you in a matter that concerns us both without the possibility of offending our master, your husband. I write this letter in sympathy to you, dear sister, as you are now in a household that endures an angry young girl. I know how disconcerting that can be to the peace and well-being of any home.

I confess that I also write in my own self-interest. I had not thought as I wrote my last letter to you and our master Nissim, how my letter might be read. Only after I had sent it off did it occur to me, with dismay, that Rabbenu Nissim might read what I had written and draw the wrong conclusions regarding the intentions of my letter. I only wished to congratulate you and offer my prayers that your child may come in due time and be healthy. I know that Nissim must wish for a boy, and I wanted to show both him and you that there could be joy in bearing a daughter as well as a son. I want for you to be safe and happy, Karimah.

Only some days later, after I had reread my own copy of the letter I had sent, did I realize that Rabbenu Nissim might take my talk of marriage as an indication that I would consider Ghazal as a possible bride. There is, after all, only a 12-year difference between us. Further, I had written about marrying a niece. Ghazal is almost that to me, if there is such a thing as a step-niece. It would establish Rabbenu Nissim as doubly related to the al-Tustaris. That would be good for him. It would certainly do me no harm to be Rabbenu Nissim's son-in-law, even as he now is my brother-in-law. He commands universal respect in the rabbanite community among both the Babylonians and the Palestinians.

So, dear Karimah, you can understand why it might be natural for Rabbenu Nissim to think such a match to our mutual advantage. But the thought of marrying Ghazal strikes me with horror. If half of what you write about her is true, she will never be fit to be a wife to any man. I have absolutely no reason to doubt your descriptions of her as a self-centered harpy. God forbid I might be burdened with a wife such as her. I trust in you to be sure to dissuade Rabbenu Nissim from any thought of proposing a match between me and Ghazal. I know that no matter what has passed between us over the years you could not wish me such ill.

I do not wish to insult our master. I pray that Rabbenu Nissim did not take umbrage at my letter to him, nor construe that when I wrote that I wished a wife who could be a help-mate and whom I might enjoy, that I was implying that Ghazal would never do for me. It may be true, but that does not mean that Nissim need know how strongly I feel. I simply could not abide that girl when we were at your wedding week. She trampled over everyone who let her. I love and revere Rabbenu Nissim, as my teacher and as your husband, but that does not require me to wish for his unattractive daughter as my wife.

I know that everyone will take this rejection as a sign that I, and no doubt others, simply could not bear her dwarfish stature and her huge head. In Ghazal's case, however, the body houses a similarly deformed soul. I do not know if she has become that way because she fears that people will reject her in any case. It does not matter. I could not live with her. Please help me be sure that this may not come to pass.

I realize that you do, however, still have to endure her mean spirit day by day. I thought perhaps that if I shared some texts with you that we are studying, it might help you get some control over her outbursts. I know if you tell her that these are traditions I am struggling to master, Ghazal will learn them by memory straight off. I pray that she might actually absorb the content and abide by the Torah lessons that are taught here. What follows is from the Babylonian Talmud at the end of the first chapter of tractate Kiddushin. It concerns honoring one's mother. Surely, even Ghazal will realize that this applies to her behavior toward you.

Our rabbis taught that there are three partners in every person: his mother, his father, and the Blessed Holy One. So when a person honors his father or his mother, the Blessed Holy One says, "It is as though I were dwelling among you and you had honored Me." Yet when a child troubles his father or his mother, the Blessed Holy One says, "It is a good thing I am not dwelling with them, else that child should be troubling Me, too."

The rabbis asked their colleague Ulla, "How far does honoring of parents go?"

He told them the story of a certain gentile named Dama ben Netina who had the opportunity to do business which would profit him 600,000 gold dinars. But the key to the business ledgers was beneath his sleeping father's pillow, and Dama refused to disturb him. In the very next year God rewarded that gentile by giving him a Red Heifer in his flock. The sages of Israel approached him to buy that red cow and he said to them, "I know that I could name any price at all and you would pay it to me for this Red Heifer. But all I ask is the 600,000 dinars that I declined last year in favor of honoring my father."

They also tell the story that when a certain rabbi came from Iraq to the Land of Israel he reported that once he was wearing a golden cloak and was seated among the great men of Baghdad. His mother came and tore that cloak off of him, then hit him in the head and spat in his face. Yet he would not shame her.

So my dear sister Karimah, you see that these traditions should encourage Ghazal to show respect. She must learn that we are commanded not to shame our parents, or those who act as our parents. God will judge us by our behavior towards our elders, this is certain. I put my trust in God.

Before I close this letter, a word of business if I may. I am certain you know of the attacks by the Rum navy against Sikilia. The courtiers of al-Kahira believe that the Byzantines are not simply engaged in piracy, but that this is a war of the Christians against al-Islam. The Rum realize that if they can blockade Sikilia and her ports, it will cripple Fatimid shipping in the Great Sea. I am sorry to tell you that our family consortium lost a ship this summer.

Our losses in the ship are serious, but not unbearable. We had spread the risk among a very large number of traders shipping with us. The intelligence we had received from the court made it clear that even though the waters would be calm, the risks of enemy action would be high. To that end, I made sure to warn everyone in advance of such risks and to undertake no promises of repayment in case of attack. Each merchant accepted our terms in exchange for a lower tariff on goods and a higher share of profits to them if the voyage reached successful conclusion.

Nevertheless, it is we who bear the costs of the ship herself. The Rum navy threw Greek fire and burnt her as she tried to flee by rowing. Thank God our crew was saved by a barque of the Caliphate that was sent to guard the ship. In truth, there was little they could do to prevent the attack and I am grateful they at least served as a life boat for our sailors. I have provided for our men.

I realize that this puts an extra burden upon you, dear sister, in the latter months of your pregnancy. But the opportunities for caravan trade are excellent when there is no alternative by sea. I have already outfitted three long caravan trains to head west. I trust that you will receive those goods soon and direct them to the appropriate ports, whether in Kairawan, Sousse, al-Mahdia, or points west. If the straits remain open, we certainly should continue our trade with Granada and al-Andalus. If my calculations are accurate, we should recoup the loss of our ship with the profits from the three caravans now heading to you, God willing.

Burton L. Visotzky

I put my trust in you, and, of course, in God Almighty, may His great name be praised.

From al-Iskander ibn Dunash HaCohen al-Tustari, trader in Fustat. To his sister Karimah bint Dunash HaCohen, wife to Rabbenu Nissim, may she give birth before she travails, and may she bear a son before her labors start. In care of the Perfumer's at the Souk al-Yahud, in Kairawan, with the help of God.

Part Three:

Exile

Chapter Fifteen
Winter 1038 – Summer 1049

From Karimah in Kairawan
to al-Iskander in Fustat, Winter 1038-39

My dear brother, Blessed be the True Judge. Our son is dead. He died after living only a week, may God have mercy on his precious soul. It was clear from the moment that he was born that he would not live very long. I was not well in my final two months of pregnancy. Once I entered the eighth month, Nissim became very concerned. He said that the rabbis teach that seventh month babies live, but eighth month babies do not. Nissim also had me make out a will lest I die in childbirth. I am sure that his terrible experiences with the loss of his first wife at the birth of Ghazal made him so concerned.

Once I entered the ninth month, Nissim grew less worried. I, however, felt more and more alarmed. The movements of the child in my stomach seemed unusual. But I had never borne a child, so I still do not know whether my premonitions were correct or not. I wonder now if my time in the wilderness of Moab and what happened there might have damaged our boy somehow. May I be atonement for his soul.

The labor was horrifying to me, more painful than anything I could have imagined. As the rabbis have taught, this is the ten-fold curse of our mother Eve that women suffer: we bleed when we lose our virginity, and bleed again every month. Childbirth is so painful, and yet we yearn for our husbands. Our men rule over us, for they speak their needs, while we only think of them. We sit veiled, and locked in the house as though in a prison, banned from society. For all these curses, I would endure childbirth again this very moment if only I could have our baby back.

He died after having tasted only one Sabbath in his short life. Rabbenu Hananel was very thoughtful and solicitous of Nissim and me. He decreed that there should be a funeral on the afternoon of the eighth day. Normally they do not have funerals for babies unless they have lived a month. But Rabbenu Hananel said that one must be lenient where it comes to grief, and that it would be better to have a funeral so all of the community of Kairawan could express their sorrow with us.

Burton L. Visotzky

Our baby was buried on the same day that he should have been circumcised. We would have named the boy Dunash Yakov ibn Nissim ibn Shaheen. That way, both Daddy and Nissim's father would have had namesakes in the boy. As it is, the students in the academy started calling Rabbenu Nissim by the *kunya* Abu Yakov, almost before the baby was born. That way, Nissim got to have a nickname to go along with his many titles, and his father Yakov, peace be upon him, might once again be mentioned in the academy. Even though our boy was never formally named, everyone now calls Rabbenu Nissim by Abu Yakov. That is, everyone who knows and loves him. So many of his students and the community are in such awe of him that they call him just Rabbenu, or simply, the Gaon. Nissim always fusses when he hears that latter title, insisting that only the heads of the Babylonian and Jerusalem academies can have such a sobriquet. The boys, though, merely wish to show their respect.

Nissim was deeply shaken by the baby's death. I fear he blames himself. He said to me that first he killed his wife and maimed his daughter. Now he has killed his son. It is so painful to me, Skandi, that I cannot tell him it is I who am at fault here. No matter, very little will dissuade our Nissim from his grief.

On the day of the burial Nissim went to the synagogue to the corner where the circumcisions are performed. They have a custom in Kairawan to set a special chair for the prophet Elijah, who they say attends every circumcision. They say that the prophet Malachi commands this when God says through him, "The messenger of circumcision who you desire is coming, says the Lord of Hosts... Behold I send you Elijah the prophet, before that great and awesome day of the Lord comes upon you."

Nissim held the baby on his lap, as though he had taken him to the synagogue to be circumcised. He sat on that chair for an hour, Skandi, until I thought he had lost his mind with grief. But then Nissim rose from the chair and took that little body to be purified and wrapped in its tiny shroud. Later, some of the old timers recalled that when Nissim was a baby his father Rabbenu Yakov, peace be upon him, sat in that chair for an hour holding baby Nissim the very same way. I realized then just how much Nissim had been looking forward to the boy. "The Lord gives and the Lord takes away, blessed be the name of the Lord."

Now all we have is Ghazal as our dubious future. She was subdued when the baby was born, all the more so when he died. Yet in her quietude I detect a small relief that she remains our only child. I say "our" but in truth; she is not nor ever will be my daughter. If I dare to ask something of her or rebuke her in any way, she snaps at me that I am not her mother. I told her that, nevertheless, as an adult in the household, it is required that she show me some respect. Her response was to suggest that perhaps I might wish to find a different household. I have not told this to Nissim, for he is so frail now. All he has is Ghazal.

You were quite correct about her desire to learn those texts once I suggested you were struggling with them. She learned them very quickly. Although she can recite them by heart, she still does not understand their import. It is clear that this is a girl who can spend her entire life learning Torah and miss the whole point. She judges people by their ritual pieties and is unable to see to their common human goodness. I wish I could feel more generosity towards her, but she shows not a drop of sympathy for me. It is as though Nissim lost the baby and I had nothing to do with it.

The only consolation I have is that it is no longer so very hot during the day. In the last months of my pregnancy I found the heat absolutely unbearable. I was huge in the final month of pregnancy. It was as though I was the full moon. As the rabbis say, my belly was between my teeth. Now I am, of course, much thinner. I have begun to regain the strength in my arms and my legs. Still, it is impossible to imagine ever climbing onto the back of a horse again. There are times that I just ache for my life on the road with the Badawi or long for my time on the sea. Mostly now, I just ache. It is as though those days were stories I had heard once very long ago and almost have forgotten.

Cool weather or hot, the flies of Kairawan are thick in the air. They settle on the manuscripts I copy, on the food I prepare, on any part of my body that might be exposed. It makes me grateful for the veil. Their buzz is constant; I rise to it and fall asleep to it at night. It sounds like the murmur of the old men, praying in the synagogue. The flies wear me down, Brother, my life here seems measured out in the buzzing of the flies. They ruined a tray of makroud cookies I had baked, for they settled on the pastry just after I had brushed on the honey glaze. Will I never know sweetness again here in Kairawan?

Al-Iskander, forgive me. I have my work, my teaching and my copying. I have a husband who is good to me, who is renowned and respected, and whom I love. I have my family, that is you, little brother, and we do not worry about money, thank God. I must remind myself what the rabbis teach: give thanks for what is past, and cry out for the future. I put my trust in God.

From al-Iskander in Fustat,
to Nissim and Karimah in Kairawan, Late Summer, 1041

Dear Abu Yakov, my master and brother-in-law, with greetings to my dear sister.

I write a letter of good tidings about the good fortune of the Jews of Fustat. May God, Who neither sleeps nor slumbers, watch over and protect us. Last summer our Jerusalemite Synagogue here in Fustat was rededicated after many years of collecting funds from the Jewish community and with the help of our Uncle Sahl. The building had been in disrepair for too long because of the havoc wreaked in the time of al-Hakim, may his name be erased. As if it were not bad enough that the Jerusalmite synagogue was unusable these past 25 years, the synagogue of the Babylonians was fully rebuilt three years ago and withstood a court challenge two years ago. I wrote to you about it then.

Our community of Jerusalemite rabbanites under the leadership of my teacher Rabbenu Ephraim ben Shemariah has long desired that our synagogue also be restored. It shamed us that the Iraqi Jews had raised the funds to open their structure while ours remained in ruins. I must admit that were it not for their having completed their own restoration and withstood that court challenge, I am not sure we could have completed the fund raising necessary for our own restoration. Once their building stood, people were more able to believe that our synagogue could also be restored. Uncle Sahl and his brother were most generous. They must receive credit now for having restored two rabbanite synagogues, even though they and their families remain loyal to the Karaite community of Scripture here.

The leadership of Rabbenu Ephraim has been inspiring. His right hand, our cantor Abu'l Ali Yefet ibn Daud ben Shekhaniah, did everything necessary for the beautiful building and the wonderful rededication ceremony. Yefet serves as our cantor. Indeed he even composes his own liturgical poetry for the congregation. He sang a very beautiful poem he composed for the rededication ceremony. Yefet ibn Daud is the third generation cantor in his family. His grandfather, may he rest in peace, was a cantor in Tyre who came down to Egypt some years ago. Yefet not only sings for us but also acts as the kosher butcher for the Palestinian rabbinic community in Fustat, as did his father.

Yefet also serves as our communal scribe. He makes a good living from the three jobs combined. He was most assuredly a leader, having given from his own purse as well as collecting from everyone else. He kept very careful records which he posted prominently in the community, written large in his beautiful Hebrew handwriting and then copied in Arabic, as well. He listed the items donated by each contributor and their value. The Tome of Contributors is an old rabbinic tradition. The largest donors were written at the head of the List of Honor. Our cantor Yefet followed a similar custom, grouping the donors by those items they have given. People love to see their names published in this way.

You will be proud to know that our family features prominently in the List of Honor for the Palestinian synagogue. Not only are Abu Saad and Abu Nasr there, of course, but we are, too. I gave a contribution in my own name, as I had a very particular wish to please Yefet. I also made a contribution in memory of Daddy and Mommy, may I be atonement for their souls. Finally, I was very proud to give of my own funds to honor my master Rabbenu Nissim and his esteemed household, my sister, who is, after all, a daughter of Fustat. May you both be distinguished for long life.

It is a privilege to have helped rebuild this old and famous synagogue. They said at the rededication ceremony that it was on this very spot that Moses brought the plague of hail down upon the evil Egyptians. Other speakers claimed that the small stream outside the synagogue—where we wash our hands before entering the sanctuary—is the very place where the prophet Maryam, peace be upon her, placed her brother Moses in the bulrushes. The elders of the Jerusalemite synagogue also tell us that the prophet Jeremiah made his Lamentations here. It is our custom to sit on the floor on the ninth day of Av and sing Jeremiah's dirges commemorating the destruction of the Temple. We did so recently in the new building.

You may know that our synagogue has restored the old book depository, our Geniza. We store all of our worn-out Hebrew and Aramaic texts there. Many of the pious ones in the community even deposit Arabic texts there. In the restorations to the building, we kept the depository intact and enlarged it by extending it upward to the second floor of the building. I imagine it will hold quite a few more books yet. They say at the bottom of the pile of old books in that room is a Torah scroll written by Ezra the Scribe. This seems unlikely to me, but one never can know the age of some of the old books in there. No one has ever opened up the room to inspect it for there are rumors it is protected by Jinn!

I wish you could see the new building; it is very beautiful. The doors are carved lattice-work. Abu'l Ali Yefet, the cantor, dedicated them in honor of my betrothal to his daughter. Yefet is a wonderful father-in-law. He himself wrote and illuminated the marriage contract for my marriage to his daughter, God preserve her for good, prolong her life, and fulfill her desires. I know you had hoped to write the contract in your own hand, but I could not deny my father-in-law this gift to his own daughter.

My new brother-in-law Shelomo sings beautifully, like all the men of his family. I have no doubt that he will take his place as cantor and ritual slaughterer after his father. He is already learning the trade. All that remains for Shelomo is validation of the family succession by the Gaon in the Land of Israel.

As for me, I am now three and twenty years of age. I am glad to have waited as long as I did for the right mate. She comes from good family lineage, has wealth in her own right, is not unpleasant to look at—may the evil eye ne'er befall her—and she reads and writes both Hebrew and Arabic. She is only eight years younger than I, so we will not wait very long to have children. I count myself blessed that another man did not preempt me. God must have been watching over this poor soul. He is my help and my protector.

God willing, the resumption of shipping to Sikilia will persist throughout the autumn months and there will be freedom of travel on the Great Sea next summer season. We have prospered mightily from the caravan trades, as you more than anyone know. Yet I feel that the burden should not be entirely upon you in Kairawan. It is true you are the fulcrum in the balance between East and West. But even so, it would be better if we could spread our risk by shipping sea cargo once more. The profit margins are so much higher, it is worth the risk. If we ship from ports of Misr, I can make the arrangements and take some of the burdens of business from your shoulders. I am certain that we can have access to as many Caliphal contracts as we are able to carry. But we cannot venture upon the seas without some peace between the Rum and al-Islam.

May God grant peace to us and to our kingdom. May God shine upon the Caliph al-Mustansir, Commander of the Faithful and leader of Misr and the Maghreb. May God keep all of us, our families, and our community, safe from harm, now and forever more.

From al-Iskander ibn Dunash, pbu'h, HaCohen al-Tustari, and his household, in Fustat, Misr, with the help of God.

From al-Iskander in Fustat to Nissim and Karimah in Kairawan, Fall, 1044

To Abu Yakov, Rabbenu Nissim ibn Shaheen and my dear sister Karimah, peace and an abundance of blessings.

I write about a matter that is between Muslims, but surely will touch upon every one of us. What has come to pass already affects our ability to correspond with one another, to say the least of our ability to continue our trading. I fear that your Kairawan Imam al-Mu'izz has irrevocably sinned against the Caliph, our Commander of the Faithful, the benevolent al-Mustansir, may God's blessings be upon him.

Long the courtiers here have been saying that the Malikite school in Kairawan was a pernicious influence on your ruler al-Mu'izz. Did he think that those in al-Kahira have not read their treacherous expositions or not realized what a danger these interpretations posed to the Fatimids? Did al-Mu'izz imagine that allowing the Malikites to circulate such writings there would be perceived as innocuous? Surely a man who has ruled for so long as a client of the Fatimids could not be so naïve as to promote the interests of the Sunni against the Caliph's Shiite principles. Distance from the Caliph's court does not confer invisibility.

Your Imam of the Great Mosque in Kairawan has stopped including the Commander of the Faithful al-Mustansir's name in the Quranic readings during the

Friday worship. No longer is there any blessing offered for the Fatimid rulers of al-Kahira and Misr during the Khutba lecture. I have heard it reported—and write to you to please confirm this—that al-Mu'izz openly proclaims his loyalty to the Sunni Caliph of Baghdad! If this is true you must realize, Rabbenu Nissim, that you, too, will be suspect, due to your ties to the rabbinic academies of Baghdad. You must somehow make it known that you have no part of the schism of the house of al-Mu'izz and his Banu Ziri kinfolk against al-Mustansir, may Allah protect him.

Uncle Sahl has asked me to inform you that he understands you are in a difficult position, for you cannot openly repudiate your local ruler without bringing reprisals upon yourself or your academy. On the other hand, if we are to have any chance to be able to continue our business enterprises, you must find some way of showing your loyalty to your kin here and to the Fatimid Caliph who has sent all of us so much opportunity. Abu Saad is especially anxious that the Jewish community not find itself in between two warring parties—for this act of disloyalty by the Kairawan Banu Ziri undoubtedly will be punished by the Caliph. It is certainly in the interests of all of the Jewish community to remain as far from this battle as we may.

Sahl Abu Saad has felt it proper to demonstrate his unquestioned loyalty to the Caliph at this time of strife. He offered his intelligence network to the Caliph's service. Abu Saad is shrewd and has developed a series of contacts throughout the East over many years now. He uses Jews from Babylonia, of course. He has contacts among the Iraqi Karaites as well as the Rabbanites in Baghdad. All his years of generously supporting the academies have given him reliable trading partners who now are as eager to trade information as they once traded silks.

But Abu Saad tells me that he has not relied on the Jews alone. He says that if the Jews were the sole source of his information, both they and he would be suspect. It is not his desire, he says, to put us all in danger. Further, Uncle Sahl always wants a second source of information, whether it is for business prices or political gossip or military intelligence. He says that having that second source helps him verify the first source and assures him of the quality of what he knows.

Interestingly, he has far less information about the Maghreb and the further west countries of Sefarad. It was only through our contacts with Shmuel the Nagid in Granada that those trade routes opened. But the caravan routes to the east, to Baghdad and down to al-Medinah and Mecca, he has always kept a close watch over those. They were the chief source of Abu Saad's fortune in both dinars and in political power. He told me things that surprised and amazed me, for he has had his contacts among the Badawi there for many, many years.

No sooner did his former maidservant marry the last Caliph al-Zahir, then Uncle Sahl realized his stars were in the proper conjunction. His moment for greatness had come. Through his caravans he personally cultivated relations with two of the Badawi tribes that roamed upper Egypt and the Hijaz: the Banu Hilal and the Banu Sulaim. Those Badawi long ago learned how valuable it was for them to sell the information they gathered to various masters. Uncle Sahl has now schemed with Caliph al-Mustansir and found a way to make those fickle Badawi loyal to their Fatimid masters.

In essence, what Uncle Sahl proposed is as simple as it is nefarious. He wishes to punish al-Mu'izz and his Banu Ziri for rebelling against us. So he has given the Badawi tribes of the Banu Hilal and the Banu Sulaim free rein to ride against the towns and cities under Zirid rule. This does not bode well for you. Al-Mu'izz and the Zirids may have built fortresses in Kairawan, Sousse, and al-Mahdia, but they cannot protect caravan trade against the Badawi raiders. So long as shipping remains difficult due to the Rum, those cities will be strangled. Even with shipping open, there is no way to transport goods from the ports to cities of the interior like Kairawan.

Of course, the booty is irresistible for the Banu Hilal Badawi. Those brigands will grow old and fat on the spoils they are about to capture. Uncle Saad says he expects this action of the Badawi to go unchecked for years, until al-Mu'izz and his Banu Ziri vanish from the earth. The only worry we might have is who, then, will stay the Badawi's hand? Sahl Abu Saad says that ultimately the Kutama Berbers will oppose the Badawi. It will not pay to be a Jew in Afrikiya during the coming years. It will seem like the days of Gog and Magog finally have come upon you.

If you glean anything from the thicket of politics I have just written to you let it be this—times are dangerous. The future is not bright for Kairawan. Your best hope lies in the Caliphate of the Fatimids and not with the rebels of al-Mu'izz and his house of Banu Ziri. You must discretely have the boys of your academy find their way east here, or west to Granada, or even north into the Rum.

Take heed, this is not idle chatter. Abu Saad not only is certain of what he hears in the court of al-Kahira, but he is equally certain of what he knows from the Banu Hilal and Banu Sulaim. He told me that many years ago he made use of their information when Daddy begged him to keep an eye on you during your travels in the Hijaz and the wilderness of Moab. Uncle Sahl says that back then one of the Banu Hilal kept watch over you and sent constant assurances to Daddy that you were alive and well.

I told Uncle Sahl that I never heard a breath of this in my father's house and that I was sure that you knew nothing of this. Uncle Sahl Abu Saad just laughed and said that we still thought of our father as a simple man. Abu Saad said Daddy was a true trader of the noble house of al-Tustari. When I asked him what that meant he said that one needed to know how to mourn with one face, while the other face looked far and wide to see to one's best interests. He told me that you, Karimah, must know this lesson, having learned it when you traveled in the wilderness. He asked me, "Is that not why she has taken Rabbenu Nissim's family name of ibn Shaheen?"

When I looked puzzled he reminded me that in Arabic the Shaheena is a bird of prey that can see its meal, even if it be but a finger's breadth, from miles high on the wing. Abu Saad says it is time for you to be of the ibn Shaheen and keep a lookout, far and wide. But you must also be like Daddy and keep a face of mourning for the public. God willing, you will survive the coming onslaught of the Badawi. It would be best if you, Rabbenu Nissim, and my esteemed sister could make your way east to al-Kahira. There will be no lack of students or business opportunities here in Fustat in the coming times. Soldiers need uniforms and rations. These we can provide.

It would also be nice for you to be here when my household brings forth a child. God willing, we will have a healthy boy just around Passover. A first-born will come into Misr at the time of the Exodus. I pray to God it will be a good omen. Thus far, all is well. We put our trust in God. Let me close this letter of disturbing tidings with this news of our family's joy. By caravan with the help of God.

From Karimah in Kairawan
to al-Iskander in Fustat, Winter 1045/46

To my dear brother Abu Husayn, al-Iskander ibn Dunash al-Tustari, may God shine his light upon you and your family. There, I have given you a *kunya* of your very own. I pray that your wife and the baby are well. I would love to see baby Yefet, whom I call by his Arabic name, Husayn. I will do this to distinguish baby Yefet from your father-in-law. I am saddened that you did not name him for Daddy, peace be upon him, that he might have a living namesake. Still, I am happy for you and your household. May the evil eye ne'er befall you.

I wish that we could travel to see you, but the country-side between Afrikiya and Fustat is most dangerous. The Banu Hilal and Banu Sulaim have begun their marauding against Cyrenaica and Tripolitania, and have had the effrontery to lay siege to Tobruk. The inhabitants of Gabbes are terrified that these Badawi will come into Afrikiya from the south and that their fair city will find itself surrounded. For the moment we are safe here in Kairawan, but there have been riots of the Shiat Ali—who remain loyal to al-Mustansir and the Fatimids—against the Banu Ziri who are now aligned with Sunni Baghdad.

The mood of Kairawan is not good. The common folk, Jew and Muslim alike, fear the day when the Badawi finally fall upon us. Most of the folk here relied on the caravan trade. Needless to say, the Banu Hilal have seen to it that there is almost no caravan trade any longer. Only large and heavily armed convoys can make it from one city to another, which means that only the richest traders can afford such an undertaking. Thanks to our wealth and to the power of Uncle Sahl Abu Saad, we are among those who still can move our goods. But I have had to take precautions so that our wealth does not attract the eyes of rioters or looters.

Rabbenu Nissim continues to teach the boys of the academy and few have actually left here yet. He says that we will know when the time comes to leave, but until then he is determined to maintain the holy site where his revered father taught Torah. This stubborn piety has infected Rabbenu Hananel as well. He also refuses to send the boys away, clinging to his memory of his own father. I just hope they have made plans to evacuate the students when the time finally does come upon us.

Hananel had the good sense to send the youngest of his girls to the Rum to be safe with his wife's family there. Nissim, for his part, has begun thinking about seeing to Ghazal's safety. For me, the sooner he sends her off the better. I wish her well; I wish her happiness; I wish for her safety; but elsewhere. She remains so very difficult to live with, and now that she is 15 she is more cantankerous than ever. Nissim is so lax with her; I wish he could exercise some discipline. Nothing she does seems to have any consequences. My dear master either says that it is the age she is going through or that her unfortunate deformity is the cause of her misbehavior. Any meal she deigns to attend is like torture to me.

Enough complaining, it does me no benefit nor is it attractive. I pray that your baby Husayn brings you nothing but joy. At least Nissim is clever enough to realize that it will not be easy finding a match for Ghazal. Who would want such a dour woman with that giant head and child's body? Our master feels that he can find someone who appreciates the quickness of her mind and her mastery of rabbinic traditions. I must tell you brother, I have never found men of the rabbinic academies to appreciate a woman who is smarter than they are. How much more will they disdain one who is ugly of form and ugly of soul?

But still, Nissim makes inquiries. He does so because he wants to see her settled. He does so because he wants her in a safe place. He does so because he believes that she will bring him a grandchild. Mostly, I believe he does so because Ghazal is so shrill in her demands that he find her a husband. But if you confront Nissim and ask him why he does so, he will look you right in the eye and say, "Because she is my daughter."

I believe that Rabbenu Nissim secretly hopes to convince Shmuel the Nagid in Granada to help him find a husband for Ghazal. This would be a perfect solution for Nissim, for it would place Ghazal out of harm's way in al-Andalus. If the Nagid were to have a hand in the match-making, one could rest assured that he also would see to Ghazal's financial future. This is an issue for Rabbenu Nissim once again. He was not very well off before he married me. Once we wed and praise be to God, our fortunes grew, our master felt sure that a sufficiently high dowry would be fair compensation to whomever married Ghazal. But now, with the caravan trade strangled and the shipping so insecure, there are no guarantees that we can provide a sufficiently rich dowry to make Ghazal appear attractive.

I know that he has been in correspondence with Shmuel the Nagid. Since Rabbenu Shmuel is not only Nagid, but also Wazir to the court at Granada, he has endless funds. Even so, it will take some time for such a delicate favor to come to pass. As far as I am concerned, sooner is better. As Hillel said, "If not now, when?" Shmuel the Nagid writes us witty and delightful letters. He is always enclosing an irreverent poem or a keen observation about court life. For all of that, he has a prodigious memory for rabbinic law. He is "like a plastered cistern that does not lose one drop." I would say that he embodies both sets of praises set forth in the Chapters of the Fathers, for in matters of the law he is the cistern, while in his poetry he is "an overflowing fountain." And yet with all of his own talents, Shmuel ibn Naghrela also is a great patron to other scholars and poets. He says that God has blessed him with the means to support Torah in all its forms in Sefarad.

One of Shmuel the Nagid's proteges is a young fellow from Malaga, named Solomon ibn Gabirol. This ibn Gabirol is two or three years younger than you are, my dear Abu Husayn, and already has achieved high repute as a philosopher and poet. He circulated his first poem almost ten years ago, when he was but the age Ghazal is now. He writes poetry for the synagogue, but also writes secular poetry, deftly capturing the mood of the day. I want to share some of ibn Gabirol's poems with you, brother, for they speak the voice of my heart.

The heart's confused, and wisdom's shut away;
Although the body's seen, the soul's at bay.
As those who roam the earth find only ill,
The man upon the land has neither joy nor thrill.
The slave might kill his master yet today;
The serving wench abuse her queen as play.
The son does rise against his parents dear;
The daughter will no more her parents fear.
My friend, I've looked around this lonely world;

The very best I've seen is: life unfurled!
The days of a man's life are filled with toil;
His end is but to molder in the soil.
Till finally the dust returns to dust,
Then mortal soul ascends to Soul; it must.

Ibn Gabirol has written many poems that are much more cheery than this
one I have copied out for you. Still, it captures not only my attitude, but that of
many of Kairawan just now. I am going to copy out two more of ibn Gabirol's
poems for you dear brother. These were read in the synagogue in Granada on Yom
Kippur, and Shmuel the Nagid sent them to us shortly afterward. They reflect on
the somber mood of Yom Kippur day, and so, appeal to me now. The first poem
is clever for each stanza begins with a letter of ibn Gabirol's name. Do not worry
Skandi, I will not tax you with all of the verses.

Lord, what is man, if not the merest flesh and blood?
His days like shadows pass, like water in a flood.
Until his time is up, and he returns to mud.

A carcass on the refuse heap
Full of guile, in sin doth creep,
A bud that fades, which scythe does reap;
Were You to judge him in his keep,
Your wrathful Face would make him leap.
Have mercy then, Your love is deep.

In dirt and filth does he e'er roll,
False praise and fakery his goal.
The pure and precious does he foul,
So if You make him pay the toll,
He'll wither like dry grass on coal.
Have mercy then, love his poor soul.

This poem has three more stanzas, each with six rhyming verses. Shmuel
the Nagid wrote that the people of his congregation wept at the pathos of this
poetry. The Nagid is enough of a man to admit that he was jealous of the power
of ibn Gabirol's cleverly wrought verses. The last poem of ibn Gabirol I copy for
you is also very long, it has 17 stanzas and spells out his entire name in Hebrew:
Solomon the young, son of the House of Judah. I will write some of the verses
for you, but not all of them. I do not have the letter of Shmuel the Nagid in front

of me, and I cannot remember all of ibn Gabirol's lines, even with the help of the lettered verses as a reminder.

> A lowly man can look and see,
> From whence he came, to where he'll flee.
> Better for man to not be born,
> Than all his works from him be shorn.
> How can a man aspire? Be great?
> When closing snare shall be his fate?
> So let the bad man change his way;
> Repent before his King and pray,
> Perhaps he can with God abide,
> The Rock Who will his future hide.
> O Lord, have grace upon Your flock,
> Who, sinners, on Your door do knock.
> To You we lift our tearful eyes;
> Our prayers, please God, do not despise.

From his sister Karimah, wife of Rabbenu Nissim, Second and Father of the Court, in Kairawan. By caravan, with the assistance of Heaven.

From al-Iskander in Fustat to Karimah and Nissim in Kairawan, Winter, 1048/49

May God have mercy upon us. I put my trust in God. I write to you, my master, and to my esteemed sister with news that is difficult to report and frightening for our family. God is the True Judge, the Rock in Whom there is no flaw.

The Turkish troops in al-Kahira have killed our uncle Sahl Abu Saad al-Tustari, pbu'h. They said they held him responsible for their continued disfavor in the Caliph's court. Our Caliph, Commander of the Faithful, may Allah give him favor, was rightfully wary of giving too much power to the Turks who are Sunni and who might show loyalty to the Seljuks, who are our enemies. Further, our Caliph's mother, may she live long and flourish, favored her own black African troops as her protectors and installed them in the palace.

It is true that Uncle Sahl was content to play them one against the other so that no one military faction might gain too much power. The Berbers and the Badawi, the Turks and the Africans, it seems that everyone but Arabs serves the Caliph. Al-Mustansir's court is a rainbow of colors and peoples and religions.

Everyone serves our Caliph, and the glory of the Fatimid rule is that it, in turn, serves everyone.

The Turks surrounded Uncle Sahl on his daily walk from his home to the palace. After they murdered him, they left his corpse and went into the parade ground between the eastern and the western palaces. They say that there were 20,000 Turkish troops massed there. The people of the city grew frightened at this display of raw power and feared for the Caliph. The other troops began to wonder if there would be civil war and who, then, they might favor.

Al-Mustansir sent a messenger to those Turkish troops who asked of them, "Are you loyal to the Commander of the Faithful, Sultan of the Isma'ili, Imam of the Mosque of al-Hakim, Scion of the Fatimid Dynasty, the Glorious al-Mustansir?"

The Turkish troops replied, "We are his obedient servants. But we have committed an offense against him."

The Caliph sent a reply, "Go now to your homes in peace."

Thus did the Caliph restore peace and order with the cost of only one life, that of our uncle Abu Saad, may he rest in Eden. Of course his brother Abu Nasr was both bereft and terrified. Abu Nasr sent a gift of 200,000 Maghrebi dinars to the Caliph's treasury, for Abu Nasr feared for his life. But the Caliph sent the money back with a messenger who brought him words of condolence for his loss. The Caliph wrote in his own hand, "Abu Saad was like my very own brother, and so I mourn with you over this irreplaceable loss. May Allah comfort you and your community."

To assure the Jewish community that he had firm control over his Turks, the Caliph appointed David HaLevi ben Isaac, of the Karaite Community of Scripture, to become the head of taxes for the Caliphal treasury. The Commander of the Faithful announced this at a ceremony to perfume the Nilometer, which was recently instituted to bring a fertile crop. This appointment assuaged both the Rabbanites and Karaites, for they had feared with the death of Sahl Abu Saad, pbu'h, there would be a loss of influence in the court. Everyone was satisfied that this murder was an unfortunate consequence of Abu Saad's having wielded too much power, that is to say, an almost random incident. But then Abu Nasr al-Tustari was assassinated, too! May I be atonement for both their graves.

Thus our most illustrious clan has met terrible violence. Despite the murder of these two patrons of the Jewish community, no one here wishes to make any untoward protest. Everyone fears that there could be reprisals if the Jews are too visible. The Caliph has once again sent assurances of our safety, this time through David HaLevi. It is ironic that the chief tax collector is suddenly everyone's friend. Yet I fear that those outside the Jewish community will resent the tax man, for how could they not? If that resentment ever comes to a boil, there will be no Sahl Abu Saad, may he be remembered for blessings, to protect us.

As for me, I spend my days in rabbinic study. I am unable to engage in trading, lest my well known associations as a member of the house of al-Tustari put me in danger. I believe I am safe, so long as I make it clear to all that I have no ambition beyond Torah study. As Rabbenu Nissim knows, this is no mean ambition. My teacher Rabbenu Ephraim reminded me that my time in the Caliph's court has to come to an end, but that Torah never ends.

He recalled the story in the Talmud about the time when the Sanhedrin had removed its leader because he had publicly insulted one of the senior sages. The Sanhedrin wished to appoint an interim leader, and they settled upon Rabbi Elazar ben Azariah, for he was wise, rich, and came from good lineage. Rabbi Elazar took counsel with his household before he accepted the honor of being the interim First, leader of the Great Sanhedrin. That wise woman told him, "It is good to drink from the exquisite goblet, which may be smashed tomorrow." And so Rabbi Elazar ben Azariah became Head of the Sanhedrin. Later, he ceded his power back to the previous Head, but always had the honor of preaching one Sabbath each month.

I have had my time of honor with our uncles in the Caliph's court. Now, I return to full time study in the academy. The present danger is really a blessing in disguise. To master the traditions of the rabbinic masters requires single-minded devotion. My funds here are sufficient for me and my household, praised be God day by day. But we no longer have any special protection for our caravans against the attacks of the Banu Hillal and Banu Sulaim. I pray that you are able to get along without the trade between Fustat and Kairawan. If we can send a boat now and again, it must suffice. In the meanwhile, we must live from our investments and our savings. I put my trust in God.

Here in Fustat there is a Kairawan trader who got his start here under Abu Nasr al-Tustari, pbu'h. In truth, this man's success was the product of the good will of Abu Nasr and of the Taherti family, whom you know in Kairawan. For a long time he managed the trading between them. We have already done some business with him. Now that Abu Nasr is gone, may he rest in Eden, this fellow is rapidly taking his place as a leading trader in Fustat. His name is Nehorai ben Nissim. He always jokes with me that he is no relation to my illustrious brother-in-law.

Nehorai ben Nissim has become influential, for he is close partners with Abu'l-Qasim Abd al-Rahman, a Muslim who maintains close connections with the Caliph's court. Abd al-Rahman is a good fellow and the Jews of Fustat trust him. More to the point, Nehorai not only can be trusted, but we can count upon him. He has become the mainstay of the rabbinic congregations here during these hard times. With Uncle Sahl Abu Saad and Abu Nasr gone, peace be upon them, Nehorai has given generously to the Jerusalem and the Babylonian rabbinic synagogues.

Nehorai continues to ply his trade, despite the difficulty of sending caravans. I do not know what secret arrangements he and Abd al-Rahman have made with the Badawi, but so far their caravans have remained unharmed. Perhaps we can yet partner with them on some ventures. In the meanwhile, I put my faith in God and in Nehorai ben Nissim. This son of Nissim will see to it that my letter gets to my brother-in-law Nissim ibn Shaheen and to his wife. My blessings and warmest wishes to your household.

From al-Iskander ibn Dunash HaCohen in Fustat, with the help of God.

From Nissim in Granada
to Karimah in Kairawan, Summer, 1049

To Karimah bint Dunash HaCohen, wife of Nissim ben Yakov ibn Shaheen, in Kairawan, with the help of God. From her husband Nissim, Second and Father of the Court in Kairawan, writing from Granada, in the name of the Merciful.

To my household, with praises to the One Who created all things for His glory. May Zion rejoice in her children. And may the dearly beloved delight, as the One Who formed us was delighted with that first couple in Eden. Praise be to God, Who has brought joy to the groom and to his bride.

Praises to my new son-in-law, Yehosef ben Shmuel ibn Naghrela. Praises to my daughter's new father-in-law, Shmuel ibn Naghrela, the Nagid and Wazir of Granada. And praises to the bride herself, Ghazal bint Nissim ibn Yakov ibn Shaheen, who is now wife to Yosef ibn Shmuel ibn Naghrela. I am so happy that we journeyed to Granada. I am so honored to join my family with the family of the Nagid Shmuel, may his household be praised and his offspring bear fruit like the orchards of paradise. This is a most fortuitous union for our family.

Karimah, I am drunk with joy at the wedding of my Ghazal. I only wish you could have journeyed through the mountains with us here. But the journey had its dangers and you had to look after our interests in Kairawan. Without your willingness to see to our home there, we could not have come here. And you do know that a wedding such as this is mostly an affair for the men of the academy and the court, the henna ceremony of the bride notwithstanding.

Ghazal was treated to constant poetry. The courtiers here never tired of singing a *Ghazzal*, for that is what they call their verses, to our Ghazal. I will share some of the poetry with you, since Shmuel and his protege Solomon ibn Gabirol wrote some verses for the wedding festivities. Many are the intellectuals of Shmuel the Nagid's academy. He invited rabbis and scholars from far and wide to the wedding. On Shabbat afternoon the sermon was given by a fabulous preacher named Moses, who comes from the Franj from a place called Narbonne. This Moses the Preacher attached himself to me and we had many excellent conversations. He is familiar with all of the rabbinic lore from east and west. But he insisted I relate all of the stories I knew. He had heard parts of my Delightful Compendium of Consolation, but complained that the work only circulated in Arabic. He begged me to commission someone to render the collection of the stories back into the original Hebrew and Aramaic so the scholars of Ashkenaz can read it. Of course, I was most flattered by his attentions.

This Moses seems unduly preoccupied with worry about the Christians of Ashkenaz. He claims that they have pretensions to retake the Holy Land from the Muslims. I find it hard to believe that anyone could think of dislodging the Islamic armies which protect the mosques of al-Kuds. But Moses says that these Christians are alert to the discord between the Sunni and the Shia, and they will try to exploit that weakness to their own military advantage. If what Moses says is true, our brethren in Jerusalem are in for hard times yet again.

Here in Granada it is hard to believe such worries exist. Everything in Rabbenu Shmuel the Nagid's court is so opulent. The wedding was fabulous, and Ghazal tells me that the women's ceremonies were very much to her liking. There was every kind of food imaginable, and it was served on shining silver platters in rooms hung with the most exquisite tapestries. The architecture of Shmuel's inner-court is open and airy. The walls have a reddish, rosy hue. There are fountains fed by waters which the Nagid has diverted from the river.

Below his palatial residence, on the other side of the river, is a new bath-house with star-shaped holes in the ceiling to vent the hot air and humidity. It is so amusing to be in the dark room and look up and appear to see the vault of heaven. For the most part, though, we bathed at Shmuel's residence where he has installed private baths in his gardens. These gardens are quite extensive and Shmuel has opened them to the public, to benefit the general life of Granada. I have heard it said that Rabbenu Shmuel has built this palace for Yehosef, my son-in-law!

The poet Solomon ibn Gabirol has described it in a beautiful *Ghazzal*, of which I, of course, can only remember fragments. I know that my Ghazal can recite it right off, having heard it only once. I suppose you, too, would have remembered it immediately or would have written down the words right away, so we could savor the verses later. Here are the fragments of the poem describing the palace which I can remember now,

A castle stood atop the sweet pastoral soil
Firm built with hardy rock
The walls had width of fortresses
But galleries with balustrades were decked around
The inner walls adorned with bas relief
Adjoined the alabaster floors which shimmered in the sun.
Windows, countless, shone forth from above
With gates and doors of ivory placed between them.
A pool burbled forth its waters so serene,
Like Solomon's sea, which adorned the Holy Sanctuary.

There were other lines of poetry about the gardens of the palace and the statues of lions that were found there. I am sorry I cannot remember them all, dear Karimah, but the imagery of ibn Gabirol gives you a hint of the riches of our new relative Rabbenu Shmuel ibn Naghrela.

Before I share any more of the poetry, I want to report one moment of dismay, which I pray to God our Ghazal did not overhear. Young Yehosef the groom had been told by his father that he was to be married into a prominent North African rabbinic family. Shmuel had emphasized our lineage and our connections to the Gaons of Iraq and the Land of Israel. I imagine that Shmuel had also prepared his son by reporting to him of our many years of doing business together and the ships and caravans we control. I even think that Rabbenu Shmuel had told the boy about Ghazal's prodigious memory and her quick facility with the give and take of the rabbinic academy. Apparently, however, he neglected to describe Ghazal physically, which might be just as well. When Yehosef first spied Ghazal he audibly whispered, "But she's a dwarf!"

Well, it is true that she is very small and has that big head. But we, who know and love her, cease to see her deformities and see, instead, the lovely person who she is within. Of course Rabbenu Shmuel immediately silenced his son, but the breach of etiquette was egregious, for this was a groom speaking of his bride to be! I am certain that those who did not hear him hiss the words learned of it immediately in any case, through the rumor and gossip. As our sages say, "The evil tongue slays three: the one who speaks ill, the one of whom it is spoken, and the one who hears it."

Solomon ibn Gabirol stepped into the breach and covered up for this gaffe by reciting a wedding poem, a dialogue between the bride and her best friend. It speaks of the bride's longing for the groom and her friend's lack of awareness of who the beloved might be. It did not escape the crowd that the groom is described as a stag that has fled. Still, the poem was well received and I know that Ghazal was thrilled to find herself the subject of one of ibn Gabirol's justly famous poems. It went like this:

The gate which was long closed, arise and swing it wide,
The stag that long had fled, now send him to his bride.
To lie between my breasts, asleep there to abide
His goodly scent upon my skin shall glide.
O sweet mouthed friend, how shall I take your side
And send to you the one for whom you've sighed?

He is so ruddy faced and darkly eyed,
Anoint my lover, friend, he is my pride.

So this young Solomon ibn Gabirol is quick witted, talented, and quite the diplomat. I confess I had a moment of wishing that he was to be the one to marry Ghazal instead of Yehosef. I do love Shmuel the Nagid, I count him like a member of the family—well, now he is a member of the family. But his son is spoiled by all the riches and the finery. He is arrogant and I am concerned that he might not treat my Ghazal properly. Oh, I suppose that every father must fret so. But you know how very special Ghazal is, and I think that she should have someone special as a groom.

That is not to say that Yosef is not without his good points. He is well spoken, handsome, and wholly at ease within the Andalusian court. He moves with equal aplomb among the rabbis and the courtiers, as does his illustrious father. It is no small matter to be the son of the Nagid and Wazir, as we have learned from the letters of your brother in Fustat. Yet your brother al-Iskander retains diffidence and an enthusiasm for rabbinic learning which the Nagid's son does not readily display. I do not think he appreciates how learned his new wife is.

I wonder if this will ever be more than a marriage of convenience for the young prince Yehosef. Karimah, do you think I may have made a mistake in agreeing to this betrothal without first thoroughly knowing the groom? It never occurred to me to even think that a son of Shmuel the Nagid could be a less than perfect match for my Ghazal. I never imagined that the boy might think himself too good for her, for how could anyone be too good for Ghazal? I pray that in due time the two of them will find the goodly partnership which you and I have found.

Forgive me for speaking my concerns so baldly. You know that I am an anxious father who wants only the very best for his daughter. I long for the day that I might dandle a grandchild on my knees. If nothing else, I have assured Ghazal's safety from the troubles in Kairawan. You know, despite my focus on

Burton L. Visotzky

this engagement and marriage, I am not blind to what happens beyond the walls of Kairawan. While I have been here I have been making arrangements for the boys of the academy to find positions in Sefarad.

There are one or two boys who are comfortable enough in Hebrew that I have also made some arrangements with Moses the Preacher to send them to Narbonne. While they might not have the luxury of speaking Arabic there, at least I know that they could get along in the Jewish community. It would put them out of harm's way, should that day ever, God forbid, come upon us in Kairawan. It pains me to deplete the academy in this way when the danger is still so far off. But you are right to remind me of the storm clouds on the horizon and I would be derelict if I were not to use this golden opportunity to make arrangements for my students. As Hillel used to say, "If I am not for me, then who is for me? And if I am only for myself alone, than what am I? And if not now, when?"

Dear help-mate, from whom with God's blessings I have merited only to have help and never been checked by your opposition; it has been a very long time since we have been apart at such a distance for so long a time. I would like my household to know how very much Ghazal's father misses and esteems her stepmother. I can think of no better way for that woman, so dear to me, to know my thoughts about her than to share the poem which Shmuel the Nagid composed for his son's marriage to my daughter. He might well have been writing of my own longings for my household.

The winter months no longer tarry,
The autumn season's long been buried,
The doves have to the trees returned,
Their coos resound throughout their aerie...
Come into my garden where,
The scent of roses, gusts do ferry.
And drink a toast among the buds,
While song-birds chirp the season merry.
The wine pours forth, like tears are carried,
Down distant lover's cheeks like cherries.

From Nissim berav Yakov, peace be upon him, ibn Shaheen, Father of the Bride, in Granada with God's bountiful blessings.

Chapter Sixteen
Late Summer 1052 – Summer 1058

From Karimah in Kairawan,
to al-Iskander in Fustat, Late Summer, 1052

My dear Abu Husayn, my brother al-Iskander ibn Dunash. I pray that this letter finds you and your household well and that your studies continue to bring you honor in the Jerusalemite community of Fustat. I hear from the rabbis here that you have not only become a member of the rabbinic Court of Fustat, but that you are respected by the Iraqi as well as the Palestinian Jews. I am always proud to hear such news of your accomplishments.

I hope you continue your ties with our Karaite Community there. I know it would be easy for you to go over to the Rabbanites entirely. I hear that in the Land of Israel there is bad blood between the Karaites and the Rabbanites; and that the leaders of the two communities have put one another under ban. I do not believe we can afford such pettiness these days and I pray you have no part of it. You have always boasted that you could be a master of both Jewish traditions.

I was copying a commentary on the verse of Proverbs which said, "May your fount be blessed and may you rejoice in the wife of your youth." The Midrash comments, "Blessed is he who learned Torah when he was young, for it is better to attend to the Torah which you suckled as a lad and which brings you merit, than to cleave to an alien bosom which may lead you to sin." I know that this comment originally was meant to tell rabbinic scholars not to study the teachings of the Karaites. But I think it is also appropriate as a reminder not to abandon our Karaite teachings. I do not mean, God forbid, that the teachings of the rabbis will lead you to sin. Just that you should remember the teachings and Torah we learned as children in our father's house. Now that it is you alone who carries on the family of al-Tustari, you must take care not to wholly assimilate to the ways of the Rabbanites. We have family traditions which must be preserved. I put my trust in you, al-Iskander.

Speaking of family, we get letters from Ghazal with almost every caravan or shipment that makes it here from Granada. It is as though she has never left Kairawan, so constant is her complaining. I do not understand how a person living in a palace can find so much fault with the world. On the other hand, I suspect there is some truth to her complaints that Yehosef ben Shmuel ibn Naghrela does

Burton L. Visotzky

not give her his attention. She complains that he is unceasingly flitting off with other women and even with young men. I know that sometimes in the courts of the Wazir such libertine behavior takes place, but I am hard pressed to think that the son of the Nagid could indulge in such promiscuity.

In any case, given how much the woman complains, I could not entirely blame young Yehosef if he took his pleasures elsewhere. I know I am being horrible and that I should not think such evil of my own step-daughter. I just pray that she does not end up being sent away by her husband. God forbid there should be such shame, and heaven forefend that she might ever return here to Kairawan. I would not wish her to be poisoning our household again and I would also fear for her safety. I know that Nissim's mind rests cooler knowing his daughter is far from harm's way.

The Zirids have abandoned Kairawan altogether. First they broke with the Caliph. Then the Caliph sent the Badawi against them. Now, the Zirids have fled to the fortress of al-Mahdia, leaving us here to fend for ourselves. The Banu Hilal and Banu Sulaim have broken through and taken the town of Gabbes and the coast near Jerba. As if this were not bad enough, Gabbes overlooks a natural pass through which virtually all of the caravans south must pass. I have heard that the Banu Sulaim force the caravaneers to drink goatskins full of warm salty water, which forces them to evacuate any gold they might have swallowed in hopes of saving something. Still, this is better than the Banu Hilal who simply kill all the members of a caravan and then disembowel every corpse in their hunt for gold.

All who lived in Gabbes have fled. The 300,000 palm trees of their oasis were simply abandoned. Not only the dates, but the olives and figs which grew among the palms were all taken by the Badawi. I hope their stomachs ache for months to come. Many of the townsfolk of Gabbes are now living in the huge caves which dot the countryside there. Unless they are cooking, in which case one can see the smoke rising, it is almost impossible to see there is a dwelling in the rock. I pray that the survivors of the Badawi onslaught remain safe there. I put my trust in God.

The Zirids, may God curse them, have retreated to the fortress which the Fatimids themselves built more than one hundred years ago. They built al-Mahdia and inhabited it until they conquered Fustat and build al-Kahira. I have no doubt that the Zirids will be quite safe there. That is, unless the Fatimids have revealed to the Banu Hilal the secret of the Berber tunnel which supposedly runs beneath the city. I do not know if what they say is true or not, but the story is appealing.

Long, long ago, before there were Fatimids, or even Shia and Sunnis, when the Muslims first came to conquer Afrikiya, Jews and Berbers lived here. The Queen of the Berbers was a Jewish woman, whom they called El-Kahina, for like us, she was from a priestly family. When the Muslims came to conquer, she challenged them to a battle in the old Roman amphitheatre of El Jem. The arena is immense and El-Kahina planned her last stand against the Muslim armies there. El-Kahina bombarded them with fish which she had fetched for her through the secret tunnel that went from El Jem all the way to the seashore of al-Mahdia. The amphitheater of El Jem still stands and it is one-and-a-half days' journey on camel from there to al-Mahdia. If there is a tunnel, it must have been built by Jinni. But if there is a tunnel, the Zirids will fall to the Banu Hilal and the Banu Sulaim, and that will be the end of them.

That will be the end of us some day, too. It is for this reason that Ghazal cannot return here. It is for this reason that Rabbenu Hananel and our master, Nissim, spend as much of their time making arrangements for their students to leave here as they do teaching them. It will be some time before the Badawi come this far north, whether to al-Mahdia or to Kairawan. But they will come. It may be two years, it may be five years. We would be fools, however, to believe that we can remain here yet another generation.

I suppose when the time comes we will go to Sousse, where we still have warehouses and wealth. We could escape by sea from there, if the navy of the Rum allows it. And Sousse has a wall and the Ribat-fortress to defend it. But even Sousse will not last forever against the Badawi, not if they besiege it. Then we shall be like Jerusalem, which fell under siege to the armies of Rome. In the meanwhile, we grieve for Kairawan as Jeremiah once did for the Holy City in his Lamentations, "See how she sits desolate, the city once great with people now is like a widow."

From his sister Karimah, wife of Rabbenu Nissim, Second and Father of the Court of Kairawan, which is Jerusalem of the Maghreb. To her brother Rabbi al-Iskander ibn Dunash HaCohen, in Fustat. With the assistance of Heaven, in the caravan of Nehorai ben Nissim, God willing.

From Karimah in Kairawan, to al-Iskander in Fustat, Spring, 1056

To Rabbi al-Iskander ibn Dunash HaCohen, may his light shine forth, member of the Court of the Jerusalemites at Fustat, Misr.

From his sister, wife to Rabbenu Nissim Gaon, Head of the academy of Kairawan, Master of the Maghreb and Light of the World, in the name of the Merciful.

To my brother Abu Husayn, Rabbi al-Iskander ibn Dunash, peace be upon him, HaCohen, in the court of Rabbenu Ephraim, where Torah is renewed and made great. Blessed is the True Judge, my brother, for I write you of the death of our old friend and teacher Rabbenu Hananel ben Hushiel, late First and Head of the academy here in Kairawan. I do not know how to begin to count this loss, for Rabbenu Hananel was both a friend and a master teacher to me and to my master Nissim.

We have spent the last week attending the seven days of mourning at Rabbenu Hananel's home. Those boys who remain in Kairawan at the academy were there, of course. What impressed me was how his students who are elsewhere in the Maghreb braved the dangers and arrived during the week to show their respects to their late master and his household. Of course, Hananel's daughters all returned from abroad with their husbands; but they came, wept, and are leaving again as soon as possible. It is simply too dangerous to remain here, for they fear they will not get out before the Badawi onslaught.

It was most curious to hear the elders and even Hananel's wife in her grief, refer to him as Elhanan, the name that he was called when he was much younger. Letters have begun arriving from the Holy Land, from Sefarad, even from the Rum, extolling the master's greatness. He was such a generous man, al-Iskander. I remember so fondly how he hosted me when I first arrived in Kairawan more than twenty years ago. It may have been at Hananel's table, seated with his household, that I first raised my eyes to see Rabbenu Nissim before me. How little I knew of life back then.

In deference to Rabbenu Hananel's memory, all of the eulogies were delivered in Hebrew and then published, so the rabbis who corresponded with him could read them without having to read Arabic. I was honored to copy many of the eulogies, it seemed the least I could do. He was my teacher, too.

Poor Nissim lived in Hananel's shadow all his life; first as a disciple of Hananel's father, then as Second to Hananel. Despite this, I know that Nissim never had a bad word to say about our master Hananel. He loved him like a brother, yet revered him as a master and teacher. Rabbenu Hananel did not talk a lot, but when he spoke, his words were golden. He always spoke to the point, never with any hint of rhetorical flourish. He valued directness and believed in saying little and doing much.

His family was wonderful, all of those girls who were my students, and then my friends and companions. When Hananel realized he was nearing his death, he requested to be buried here in Kairawan, next to his father's grave. He said he wanted to rest for eternity with his two masters, Rabbenu Hushiel and Rabbenu Yakov ibn Shaheen. We were very touched that he counted Nissim's father to be among those he revered. Nissim nevertheless suggested that we could arrange for him to be buried in the Holy Land. Rabbenu Nissim is fond of the tradition that those who are buried in the Land of Israel gain immediate atonement for their sins.

Rabbenu Hananel, ever the scholar, replied that his sins, please God, were few. And, he recalled that the very text that suggested that the Holy Land brings atonement for sin, also suggests that in the messianic future God will have the ministering angels bring the righteous through underground tunnels from the Diaspora back to the Holy Land, where they will have atonement and resurrection. So Rabbenu Hananel insisted that he be buried with his father and prayed that this would ensure that people should always know that Jews had flourished in Kairawan.

When Hananel died, Nissim was heartbroken. I know how much Nissim loved Hananel, but I could sense that he was upset over something more. It took me a long time, but finally our master admitted to me that he is fearful that he will bury Hananel in the cemetery here with Rabbenu Hushiel and with Nissim's own father Rabbenu Yakov ibn Shaheen; and then have to abandon all of them if the Badawi overwhelm the city walls. Nissim was so upset by this possibility that I had to hold him, and he rocked in my arms as though his father had died all over again. Finally, the poor man admitted what had left him so bereft was this: Rabbenu Hananel and he were born in the same year.

I confess I had no idea. I had always assumed that Rabbenu Hananel was older than my Nissim; I never really thought about it. Perhaps it was because Hananel was so terse. Perhaps it was because Hananel had so many children. Perhaps it was because Hananel was First when Nissim was always his Second. It never occurred to me that they were the same age. But I think I understand what it is that frightens Rabbenu Nissim so much. He fears that if Rabbenu Hananel can die, then he, Nissim, is also mortal.

Nissim is now 66 years old. Compared to Rabbenu Hai Gaon, may he rest in Eden, Nissim still is a youngster. But now Hananel, his contemporary, has gone to his reward. I fear Nissim thinks it will not be very long until he joins him in the Good Resting Place. I tease Rabbenu Nissim and remind him that I am but 43, and that I expect him to be my master for many years to come. He smiles at me, yet he is distracted by the Angel of Death hovering nearby.

In any case, there is little time for moping about. No sooner was the period of the seven days finished than the elders of the court and the academy unanimously elected Rabbenu Nissim to be First and Head of the Academy. They also voted that he should remain as Father of the Court in Kairawan, a position traditionally given to the Second. Times being what they are, the elders preferred stability and leadership to tradition.

Rabbenu Abu al-Maali was named Second. His wife Mulaah tells me she is terrified that her husband will feel he must remain in Kairawan until the bitter end, now that he has been named as Second. I know that she is angry that he is not also to be Father of the Court, but her fear is also real. Mulaah has long been a friend to me and she shares with me everything that is in her heart. I do not think she is aware of being angry or jealous that Nissim retained the title which she thought should be her husband's; only that she is worried, as we all are, for her family's safety. It is times like these that I am glad that Nissim and I never had offspring; otherwise I should be troubled unto death with worry if they were here with us.

We have had little time or desire to celebrate Rabbenu Nissim's elevation to Head. They voted him the titles Master of the Maghreb, Light of the World, and Head of the Academy. The students all call him Gaon now, despite his protests. But there is little joy in it for our Master, for the adulation comes as the result of the death of his friend and teacher. I suppose that is how it always must be. It is as Ecclesiastes teaches, "One generation goes, another comes. That which will happen, already was. There is nothing new under the sun." I hate to agree with that Book when it says, "All is vanity." Still, it teaches us that "more learning brings more sorrow," and that surely is the way of the world.

From his sister, wife of Rabbenu Nissim Gaon, Head of the Academy and Father of the Court in Kairawan, may his light shine forth; with the help of God, in Whom we put our trust.

From Nehorai ben Nissim in Sousse, to al-Iskander in Fustat, Late Summer, 1056

To Rabbi al-Iskander ibn Dunash HaCohen, at the court of the Jerusalemites in Fustat, Misr.

From Nehorai ben Nissim, member of the council of the community of the Holy Land in Fustat, and trustee of the synagogue of the Babylonians there, writing from Sousse, Afrikiya, in the name of the Merciful.

To Abu Husayn, my colleague and teacher Rabbi al-Iskander ibn Dunash HaCohen, peace and an abundance of blessings, from me in Sousse. I am here on business, and have much to report to you about your family, your family's business interests, and our revered master, Light of the World, Rabbenu Nissim Gaon, may God shine upon him, for we live among the Gentiles under his wing.

Our master and his household, your sister, are here in Sousse, having left Kairawan one month ago. It was wise of them to do so, for the city is vulnerable to attack by the Banu Hilal and the entire interior is under their control. Sousse remains free for now because of its fortifications and sea access. Our master and your sister are busy, engaged in surveying what goods are in the warehouses they control, shipping and selling what they can, and attending to the well-being of the remaining students from the Kairawan academy.

I am pleased to report that the warehouses in Sousse remain full, both from products acquired some time ago and from the shipping we are able to do even now. There will be no lack of income for our master Nissim Gaon or for your family. Further, I am empowered by the Kairawan branch of your family to bring to you, by hand upon my arrival back in Fustat, funds for you and your household, as well as funds for your academy. Our master's wife was quite particular in pointing out that any business I transacted in her interest was also in your interest. I am honored to be so trusted and will act as your agent in all matters.

It was painful to me that our master, Rabbenu Nissim Gaon, served as First and Head of the Academy of Kairawan for only three short months. His chief task, even then, was dismantling the academy and sending the students to safety. It must have been a bitter end for him to have to abandon the city of his fathers, but it was undoubtedly the correct decision. The final day the academy was in session was not a study day, but rather the 9th day of Av, when we joined together one last time to commemorate the destruction of the Jerusalem Temple.

As was our custom, we all sat in the dust and read the mournful words of Jeremiah's Scroll of Lamentations. After the morning service, Rabbenu Nissim gave a brief homily. When he finished, he sent the boys to their homes to prepare for the caravan to leave Kairawan. We left that same evening, under the cover of darkness. Our master preached about the calamities which have befallen the Jews on the 9th of Av. He recalled that it was on that same day that the generation of the wilderness, who had left Egypt with our master Moses, heard from God the sentence passed upon them for their lack of faith: they would not enter the Holy Land. Rabbenu Nissim recalled with tears the destruction of Betar and the wholesale slaughter of the rebels against Rome, who made their last stand there. He reminded us that when we rebelled against the Rum, they literally plowed up Jerusalem, so that not one home or synagogue remained; all that was left was the Western Wall of the Holy Temple. He concluded his words of Torah by quoting a story from the Babylonian Talmud. I will repeat it here, for it explains something your revered brother-in-law did when we all left the rabbinic academy of Kairawan for the last time.

It is said that when the First Temple neared destruction, the young boys who were the flower of the priesthood gathered together in groups. They held the keys to the Holy Temple in their hands and climbed to the roof of the Sacred Sanctuary. They said to God, "Master of the Universe, since we have not merited being faithful caretakers of Your House, we return the keys unto You."

With that, those boys threw the keys upward to the Heavens. As it were, a hand reached down from Heaven and took those keys. Then the young priests threw themselves from the roof of the Temple and fell into the flames consuming it.

This was the story that Rabbenu Nissim Gaon preached in his final sermon in the academy of Kairawan. After we all had left, our master carefully locked the doors of the academy and fiercely threw the keys upward. He did not wait to see where or if they landed.

When we first arrived in Sousse, our master took seriously ill. Many in the community despaired of his life and had already given up on him. But God did not ignore our prayers, and our master began to recover. The life of Rabbenu Nissim Gaon means progress for our people, observance of our law, and the renewal of our faith here in Sousse. The blow of leaving Kairawan is still sore. I do not know that we could have endured the loss of our great master, Light of the World.

His illness delayed a project we had long urged upon him. I was able to procure 27 quires of parchment so that he may make approved copies of his works and send them to Fustat, Baghdad, and Jerusalem for safekeeping. Unfortunately, there is only one copyist here, and he also serves as the teacher of reading and writing for the Jewish children of Sousse. Your sister, may God bless her and keep her, volunteered to assist with the copying, since she reads Rabbenu Nissim's hand with fluency and can communicate with him directly regarding his intentions for unclear passages.

The work is proceeding apace. I had planned to send you certified copies of the *Delightful Compendium*, the Talmud Commentaries, and our Master's *Key to the Locks of the Talmud*, which opens all of the cross references within the Talmudic literature and is a great boon to have when studying from a book. We also have made copies of all of his legal responsa and his notes for a history of rabbinic tradition. Rabbenu Nissim Gaon himself issued the *ijaza* verifying the accuracy of the copies, and asked that we also copy the Talmud commentaries of our master Rabbenu Hananel ben Hushiel, may the memory of the righteous be blessed.

All of these works are now copied and verified. We were prepared to send them with the next shipment to Damietta, but we decided it was too dangerous to risk losing them at sea. Instead, I am sending them by caravan, as part of a very large camel train heading to Fustat by the northern route. It should be safe from the Badawi and other brigands, God willing.

When these works arrive in your hands you must write to me here and inform me. I pray this will happen long before I return to Fustat, for it is my intention to remain here in Sousse until the close of shipping to ensure that we can make the best profits we can during these times of hardship. The more profit, the more charity. The more flour, the more Torah!

Please be sure that when the books arrive you have paper copies made for your own library. I wish the parchment to be in the academy, for it will hold up better during frequent usage. But I feel that the family of our master should also have a copy, even in Fustat. This way I will know that there are works of our master in Sousse and in Fustat. God willing, those manuscripts we left behind in Kairawan will survive until the Jews can return there. I undertake to pay all of the copying costs, please do not spare paper.

I have taken the liberty of including one more work for you and our colleagues at the Jerusalemite academy in Fustat. It is my gift to the academy. It is the first part of what will be, God willing, a many volume treatise by a promising young scholar in the Rum. He was a disciple of Moses the Preacher of Narbonne, and now the boy is working on an alphabetical listing of all of the words of the Talmud and other rabbinic literature. This fellow, Rabbi Nathan ben Yehiel, is including examples of each word's uses as part of each definition he is listing. Although he is but twenty-one, he already is supervising many older scholars in the work of collecting texts and comparing manuscripts for his dictionary. Some of Rabbenu Nissim's disciples have gone there to work with him. We trust they will be safe in the great city of Rome. I am certain that Rabbi Nathan ben Yehiel's work will be useful and popular in the academy in Fustat.

With praise to God for our life day by day and for the survival of our master Rabbenu Nissim Gaon, Head of all the rabbis and Light of the World. From his faithful disciple Nehorai ben Nissim, here in Sousse.

From Nissim and Karimah in Sousse, to al-Iskander in Fustat, Spring, 1057

To my honored brother-in-law, peace and greetings from your colleague Nissim ibn Shaheen and from your sister, who is writing this in her own hand. Would that we had good news to write to you, but as we say: God's name be blessed whether the news be good or bad. So, we put our trust in God, He is our Rock and Redeemer in Whom there is no blemish.

To start with the good, what little there may be: shipping is open on the Great Sea and we are partners in a variety of ventures which will insure a steady income stream in and out of the port of Sousse. I, Nissim, First and Head of the Kairawan academy, am asking your permission to undertake a project with the profits which God has bountifully bestowed upon us. I propose that we make a *Waqf*, and that this pious foundation be funded with one-third of the annual revenues from our trading ventures. Our household will take a third, your household will take a third, and the remaining third will be for our *Waqf*. It will be the mission of this *Waqf* to distribute these funds in equal measure to the disciples of the Kairawan academy and to your Jerusalemite students in Fustat.

We have long been informally supporting your disciples there, and you are aware that we have done the same for our boys in Kairawan. Now that we no longer have any illusions that we shall be returning to Kairawan from our current "exile," I wish to be sure to offer stipends of support for my students, whom the current circumstances have forced to be scattered far and wide. I will undertake to send them their funds in the various locales where they currently reside.

As for the Jerusalemites in Fustat, I will send you the funds directly so that you, your father-in-law, and Rabbenu Ephraim ben Shemariah can jointly determine appropriate distribution. You should use the funds as you see fit, whether as stipends for the individual students, or for the poor of the community, or for the synagogue's upkeep. That is your decision and we here have complete faith in you.

Since you are an equal partner to us in our business ventures, you have a say in approving it. As we are running the shipping for the time being from Sousse, we shall administer the initial funding of the *Waqf*. It will be easier to do this from Zirid territories as they will tax us at a much lower rate than in Fustat. As soon as you signal your assent, we will begin the transfer of funds for both the Kairawan and the Fustat disciples.

The reasons I wish to formalize this arrangement are three pieces of bad news. The first came from Kairawan. From the time that we fled from there, we had hoped that we might return and recover those things we had left behind. Recently, the rumors that the Banu Hilal and the Banu Sulaim had sacked the city were confirmed for us in an odd fashion.

Here in Sousse we were offered for purchase a copy of the commentary I, Nissim ibn Yakov ibn Shaheen, had written on the Babylonian Talmud tractate 'Eruvin. As if this were not odd enough to begin with, the volume was a fair copy that was well preserved and written in Karimah's own hand! We were being asked to buy a volume of my own commentary which I had dictated to my wife in our own household. This was clear evidence that our properties and the academy had been looted, and that the books there were now circulating as salable items.

I suppose I should be grateful that they did not simply burn the books. I have heard disturbing tales from my colleagues in Ashkenaz that there have been instances of zealous Christians burning Jewish books there. I assume this is a passing disturbance, but I know that books and even rabbis have been burnt. Long ago the evil Romans wrapped Rabbi Hanina ben Teradyon in a Torah scroll when they burnt him at the stake. When his disciples called out to him, "Rabbi, what do you see?" Rabbi Hanina ben Teradyon said to them, "The scroll burns, but the letters of the Torah ascend to heaven, returning to God Who gave them."

That is the first piece of bad news. The rest of the news only gets worse, so I have told our master Nissim that I will complete the letter to you and that he should return to his studies and find consolation in the words of Torah. It is all for the best that your sister writes this to you, for you will understand that Rabbenu Nissim cannot easily talk of what has befallen us.

Our master Rabbenu Shmuel ibn Naghrela, Nagid and Wazir of Granada, has been called to his eternal rest. I do not have to tell you how heavily this loss weighs upon Nissim. Shmuel the Nagid was a true friend to us; he supported the academy in Kairawan very generously and supported Nissim before we became married. Perhaps Rabbenu Shmuel's greatest gift to us was that he arranged the marriage of his son Yehosef to our Ghazal. I will tell you more of that later. It is enough to appreciate how much Nissim's mind was put at rest to have Ghazal away from Kairawan and safe in al-Andalus. The greatest sign of how safe Granada is for the Jews is this: even with Shmuel's death, the Jewish community there flourishes. Yehosef has been appointed Nagid in his father's stead.

Before I tell you more of Yehosef, I still must sing his father's praises. I will not pretend to tell you how great a Jewish scholar and legalist he was, for you know his works on those matters far better than I. I will tell you that I found his poetry moving, and even divine. God's presence lurks in the lines of his poetry. His synagogue liturgies are recited by Jews throughout the Maghreb for good reason. He moved our souls.

But he also wrote love poetry and drinking poetry of the type that the gentiles sing in the taverns. His wit tended to be cynical, but I always forgave him for two reasons. The first was that Rabbenu Shmuel truly saw the world as it was. Perhaps that is cynicism, but I also think it to be truth. Secondly, Rabbenu Shmuel HaLevi ibn Naghrela, peace be upon him, was both the Nagid and the Wazir of Granada. One cannot be involved in the politics of a city for any length of time without gaining the perspective of Ecclesiastes, that "all things are tiresome."

So my beloved master Nissim is deeply mourning the loss of his friend, patron, teacher, and student, to whom he was related through the marriage of Shmuel's son to our daughter, Ghazal. Alas, for that is the third piece of bad news and is a personal disaster. Shortly after the formal period of mourning for Rabbenu Shmuel the Nagid ended, and Yehosef HaLevi ben Shmuel ibn Naghrela was named to be the new Nagid, that boy repudiated Ghazal. It is as though he was waiting for his father to die before he could divorce her. I suppose we should be grateful that he waited as long as he did. They were not married even ten years, but he used the fact that they had no offspring as his excuse.

Ghazal complains that of course they had no offspring; he refused to be a man with her. She claims that he slept with any one and anything but her. She whines that he never called her by name and would speak of her as though she were not in the room, calling her "dwarf" and "midget" and "gnome."

Against my wishes Nissim has begged her to come to us in Sousse. She has written back, thank God, that she has no life with us and that Sousse is not Kairawan. She prefers to stay in al-Andalus and has found a small Jewish community near Granada where she can teach reading and writing to the children. That community, I have heard, has appealed to Yehosef the Nagid for support, which he has sent to supplement the lump-sum divorce settlement he gave to her. She is not lacking for funds, only love.

Rabbenu Nissim, may God watch over him, is depressed and ill. But he continues to write to his students every day, especially now that they are dispersed all over the world. Not a day goes by that we do not send or receive letters from al-Andalus, from the Maghreb, from Misr, from the Holy Land, from the Rum, from Constantinople, from Baghdad, even from India! Despite all of our troubles, we are able to see that the world is a good place, and that God is a beneficent Creator.

So, dear brother, we get along here in Sousse as best we can. I have our master Nissim to care for. I copy his works and write his letters. I still fear that the Badawi are not done with their battles and that Sousse, too, will someday fall. Until that time, I try to live by the commandments, for as Ecclesiastes says at the end of his book, "When all is said and done, fear God and observe His commandments, for that is the sum of man."

From Nissim in al-Mahdia, to al-Iskander in Fustat, Summer, 1058

To Rabbenu al-Iskander ibn Dunash HaCohen, member of the Court of the Jerusalemites. May God be his protector, helper, shepherd, and friend, in Fustat, Misr, if God wills it.

From Nissim ibn Yakov, pbu'h, ibn Shaheen, from here in al-Mahdia, in the name of the Merciful.

Blessed be the True Judge.

My dear Abu Husayn, disciple in Torah, brother-in-law, al-Iskander ben Dunash HaCohen al-Tustari, I am writing to you about a matter heavy on my heart. Our darling Karimah is gone! I almost cannot believe that your sister is no longer with us, she who was my helpmate for more than 20 years. The years that Karimah and I spent together, God be praised, were half of her life, if I calculate correctly. And now my dear darling Karimah, so aptly was she named, is no longer at my side.

I am writing to you from the fortress in al-Mahdia, where I have come following the attacks of the Banu Hilal upon the port of Sousse. We were able to hold out in Sousse last year when the winter came upon us, for although the Banu Hilal had massed outside the walls, the weather prevented them from attacking us for many months. Further, the rains allowed us to collect fresh water in abundance. Inside the walls of Sousse, everything appeared as normal. Trade continued, for the Badawi brigands had no sea-going vessels to speak of and ships were able to dock at port. Spring came and those fiends began to undermine the walls. We had very few illusions about the fate that awaited us if they were to breach the city.

Karimah and I had made sure long before this to send away the boys of the academy. Nevertheless, we wished to protect our interests in the city and spent much of the Spring alternately reinforcing the walls of the Ribat of Sousse and shipping goods out as fast as the port could bear the traffic. Just a few weeks ago, we took with us what remained. First we traveled by boat to Monastir where we could find safety in the Ribat of Harthema. That fortress has stood for two hundred fifty years and when the Badawi raiders came north they bypassed it, well aware of its reputation for impregnability. We spent the night there and arranged our belongings on a small, fast, camel caravan, which we rode south along the coast toward al-Mahdia. We calculated we would be safe upon our arrival, for the Zirids have heavily fortified the Ribat here and it is their last bastion against both the Badawi outlaws and their Fatimid masters.

We left the Ribat in Monastir while it was still dark. It was our wish to leave the city unobserved and to be well on the road south before sunrise. You will appreciate the danger we felt when I tell you that I recited the morning prayers while still on camel-back, for we did not wish to delay by stopping to dismount. Awkward though it may have been, my prayers were earnest. Nevertheless, God did not answer them, for when we passed Rass Dimass, we spied a Banu Hilal raiding party in the distance. They were sure to attack on the narrows which extend down the coast line. On one side was the Great Sea and on the other a large lake.

Karimah ordered the caravaneers to bring the camels into a tight circle that hugged the shore of the Great Sea. I asked her why she did this, for I worried that the Badawi could force our caravan into the briny water. But Karimah explained that the camels could sit quite firmly on the sand of the sea shore, and if the Banu Hilal attacked, she wished them to have the disadvantage of the rising sun in their eyes. The cameleers did as she commanded but they were terrified as we had not one warrior among us. We all stayed inside the circle of camels, our only protection from the coming assault.

One of the caravaneers suggested that we place the bundles we had loaded on the outside of the circle, so that the goods might form a bulwark against the attack. If nothing else, perhaps the Badawi would be satisfied with our goods and leave us in peace. But Karimah was adamant that the camels remain evenly loaded. She explained that if the Badawi met resistance at the early stages of their attack, they might leave us for easier prey. She demanded that our caravan be ready to ride to al-Mahdia at full gallop upon her command. To anticipate this eventuality, the camels had to remain saddled. However, Karimah did counsel us to lighten our loads. This we accomplished; heavy and non-essential items were put to the side in such a way that they would not impede the camels when the time came to flee.

Karimah energetically emptied the bales on her own camel. I could not see clearly what she was doing, for I had my own load to look after. I trusted that her experience supervising the caravans we sent out over the years gave her wisdom for just such times of danger. We put our trust in one another and in God Almighty. The preparations were almost finished when the Badawi raiders reined their horses down upon our caravan.

Karimah had explained that the Banu Hilal would first ride in a circle around us, shouting and clanging their swords to frighten us as much as possible. Because she had prepared us, it was actually reassuring rather than terrifying when her predictions proved sound. But none of us were prepared for what Karimah herself did as the Banu Hilal began their wild ride to encircle us.

Dear al-Iskander, may I never have a moment's consolation if I did not witness with my own eyes what I am about to tell you. As those brigands rode close, Karimah brandished her ceremonial sword and leapt from our circle directly into the path of the outlaw leader astride his horse. She stood in such a way that the sun was to her back, and that evil man could only see her as a shadow. It was enough for that villain to draw his sword and raise it high against her. Before he could bring down his blade, however, one brave-hearted caravaneer leapt forth to stand between Karimah and that depraved Badawi swordsman. With one swing of his sword, the Banu Hilal raider cut down our man. Our camel driver had been unarmed and was trampled beneath the hooves of the beast of that despicable pirate.

The Banu Hilal scum then reared his horse and turned so that he could attack my dear Karimah. As he brought down his sword towards her, I turned my head away against my will. I did not wish to see the blow fall upon my beloved wife, however I wanted to be a witness to her martyrdom in God's holy name. In that blink of an eye, Karimah lifted her own sword, still in its sheath, and parried the blow downward in such a way that she was able to grab that devil's sleeve. The motion of her scabbard combined with her tug on his sleeve to bring him off his horse and on to the ground.

Before he could rise, Karimah unsheathed her two-pronged sword and advanced upon him. He leapt up towards her and again raised his sword to my wife. I stood and watched, unable to move or turn away, transfixed as by a basilisk. I confess to you in mortal shame, and I pray that you will forgive me this terrible sin, it never occurred to me to move to defend her. Yet before that brigand's sword could fall upon my beloved, she stepped forward and cut that evil man's arm from his body. Then, by Heaven, she ran to his horse and leapt upon it. I was astounded, for I never thought I would see a Jew on horseback, let alone a woman.

Karimah leaned close to us and shouted that it was time to mount and ride towards al-Mahdia. She shouted to me that she would stand against them as Rabbi Yehuda ben Baba had stood against the Romans. This did not please me, for that saint stood firm like an unmovable stone against the Roman soldiers so that his students could escape to safety. Our sages teach that the Romans did not move him from there until they had driven three hundred javelins into him and his body resembled a sieve.

Karimah left us no choice but to mount and ride, for she had maneuvered the horse she had taken between us and the Banu Hilal raiders. The camels, as they always seem to do, took forever unfolding themselves to rise. But we were able to bring them to their feet and whip them southward.

All the while, I watched in amazement as Karimah rode this way and that, keeping the Banu Hilal at bay by ruthlessly threatening to cut them down with every new wave of her sword. I could see the Badawi pointing at the sword, no doubt warning one another to avoid its lethal blade. Karimah shouted at them and they yelled back. I could not make out the words, for she was facing away from us at some distance. Whatever threats she issued were very effective, the Banu Hilal refrained from attacking. I can only surmise that with their leader dead, they had become unnerved.

Our camels galloped away from this stand-off, staying so close to one another that the sand kicked up by the camels' hooves fell upon us. It was all I could do to stay in the saddle. One hand held the saddle, the other hand whipped the beast, the mouth prayed to God, the eyes wept. The last words I heard Karimah cry to us were those of our master Hillel the Elder. She screamed at me in Aramaic, "*Zil! Zil Gmor!* Go! Go, Study!"

Our camels arrived at the tunnel into the citadel of al-Mahdia by late afternoon. We entered filthy, hungry, and abject; but alive. I waited up all night at the city gate to greet Karimah upon her return. I waited the next day, and the next. Brother-in-law, I waited seven days and Karimah did not arrive at al-Mahdia.

A month has since passed and the sages here, whom I respect, tell me that I must consider her as one lost at sea. This current time of terror, they say, indicates that we should despair of her life. They tell me to rend my garments and sit for the seven days of mourning. They tell me that others, too, have suffered such losses.

Al-Iskander, behold, I am almost 70 years of age. In all these years I have put my trust in God and never abandoned hope. I lost my first wife, peace be upon her. Karimah and I lost our son, may he rest in Eden. Ghazal has been repudiated and lives far off, I shall never see her again. My academy is destroyed, and Kairawan is finished. Now Karimah, may I be atonement for her, is gone. Yet I will not despair. I put my trust in God. I complete this letter to you with praise for God, Creator of the world.

Author's Postscript

This book is a work of fiction. It is an historical novel, if that is not too much of an oxymoron. Yet it is precisely the blurred line between fact and fiction that I wished to explore here. My ideal was what Horace long ago commended for the writer, "so skillfully does he invent, so skillfully does he blend facts and fiction, that the middle is not discordant with the beginning, nor the end with the middle" (*The Art of Poetry*, #150).

The narrative world of rabbinic story telling, particularly those didactic tales which the ancient rabbis told about one another, has long been taken as historic fact rather than as fiction. By the time we come to the eleventh century, the era of Rabbenu Nissim, rabbinic legend gives way to historical documents. That treasure trove, the Cairo Geniza, has yielded a seemingly endless supply of historians' data.

This efflorescence of texts and documents seemed like a good conceit for my tale. Some of the material in this novel can be found in the Geniza. Following Rabbenu Nissim's lead, virtually all of the rabbis' stories retold here are actually found in extant rabbinic literature. Rabbenu Nissim, Rabbenu Hananel, Rabbenu Shmuel the Nagid, and their colleagues actually lived in North Africa, Spain, the Land of Israel, and Iraq in the eleventh century. But Karimah, al-Iskander, and Abu Sin are entirely products of my own imagination.

We know that Rabbenu Nissim had a dwarfish daughter who was married to Yehosef, son of Shmuel the Nagid. We know he repudiated her. Otherwise we know nothing about her, not even her name. We also know that Nissim had a father-in-law (or, perhaps, a son-in-law) named Dunash. The latter is otherwise a cipher. The family of al-Tustari were quite real, and Abu Saad and Shmuel the Nagid did each serve as the vizier (or Wazir, as I call it in the novel) of their respective countries. I leave any further sorting of fact from fiction to graduate students and their ilk.

The original text of Rabbenu Nissim's *Delightful Compendium of Consolation* circulated in both Arabic and Hebrew throughout the Middle Ages. English readers can consult the scholarly translation by Prof. William Brinner, *An Elegant Composition Concerning Relief After Adversity*, based on an Arabic manuscript. All of the poetry I translated in this volume is authentic. Readers will be inspired, as was I, by the elegant renderings of Raymond P. Scheindlin in his two annotated collections, *The Gazelle*, and *Wine, Women, & Death*. Many of Karimah's adventures mirror those in the *Arabian Nights*. I have consulted Sir Richard Burton's

translations, as well as his *Personal Narrative of a Pilgrimage to al-Madinah &
Mecca*, and his *Book of the Sword*.

The mother-lode of information on Jewish society in this period remains S. D.
Goitein's magisterial five-volume study, *A Mediterranean Society*, which I consulted
daily. His collection of *Letters of Medieval Jewish Traders* is also very informative.
Details about the parades and costumes of the Fatimid empire were culled from
Prof. Paula Sanders' book, *Ritual, Politics, and The City in Fatimid Cairo*. I am
grateful that the late Prof. Goitein's student, Prof. Mark R. Cohen of Princeton
University, read the manuscript of this book with a discerning eye. He has saved
me from many errors of fact, large and small. I am also grateful to Prof. Avigdor
Shinan, Pamela Eddy, Elisheva Urbas, and Rabbis Julie Schonfeld, Jeni Fried-
man, and Phil Lieberman for careful reading and editorial commentary. Special
thanks to Larry and Eve for playing Shifra and Pua to the book.

My first reader and editor, may her light shine ever brightly, is my wife, Sandy.
I thank God daily for her gracious presence in my life.

According to Prof. Goitein's translation of a letter to the trader Nehorai ben
Nissim, our master Rabbenu Nissim Gaon died in the city of al-Mahdia in mid-
August, 1062. May his memory be a blessing.

BV
New York, Passover, 5767
April, 2007

Notes On Sources

CHAPTER ONE

Letters written in Fustat were dated according to the old Seleucid calendar, beginning in 312 B.C.E. Hence this letter would have been written in the Fall (September/October) of the year **1031 C.E.** Letters from Kairawan, on the other hand, were reckoned in *Anno Mundi* (since the creation of the world), as is the Jewish calendar to this very day. We use dating according to the Common Era (B.C.E. = B.C. and C.E. = A.D.). For the remaining documents the C.E. date and an abbreviated salutation will be employed. The **Karaites** were a Jewish sectarian group who flourished during this period. Although they distinguished themselves from rabbinic Jews, there was regular interaction between these denominations of the Egyptian Jewish community. **Dunash** is from the Persian town of Tustar, and is related to the powerful Karaite **al-Tustari** clan. Nissim refers to him by his Arabic *kunya*, or "nickname": Abi Skander, the father of al-Iskander. In Kairawanese pronounciation, the normative *abu* is prounounced and written: *abi*. **Rum** is their pronounciation of the city Rome. The term refers to anywhere in Christian Europe and the broader Byzantine Empire.

Karimah's letter greets her brother with Numbers 6:26. **Skandi** is a diminutive of **al-Iskander**, itself an arabization of the name Alexander. The name she gives herself, **Wuhshah**, would translate to English as the name, Desireé.

King Shahriar and **Shahrazad** are, of course, characters from the frame-tale of the *1001 Nights*. Lady Badr, who disguises herself in her husband's clothing and passes as **Kamar al-Zaman** is also found in the *1001 Nights*. Readers should note that Karimah's description of the making of the **saddle** bears close resemblance to another story in the *Nights*, from "The Fourth Voyage of Sindbad."

The explanation regarding the **"stick injury"** is found in the Babylonian Talmud (henceforth, B.T.) Ketubot 11b. **Rabbenu Gershom** of Mainz, a Franco-German authority of the day, had issued a universal ban against anyone who would read another's mail without permission. The story of the **death of Rabbi Meir's sons** is found in the *Midrash to Proverbs*, chapter 31. The Scriptural quote is Prov. 31:10. The story of the death of **Rabban Yohanan ben Zakkai's son** is found in *The Fathers According to Rabbi Nathan* (*Avot D'Rabbi Nathan*), chapter 14.

CHAPTER TWO

Nissim is elaborate in his **salute to Dunash**. See Num. 6:24-25 for a paraphrase of the priestly blessing—appropriate for Dunash who is a "Cohen," i.e. tracing his lineage to the priestly caste.

Nissim on **gossip: Destroys three** – see *Midrash Leviticus Rabbah* 26:2, **Fingers like pegs** – see B.T. Ketubot 5b. **Death of Moses** – *Midrash to Proverbs*, chapter 14. **Beroka and clowns** – B.T. Taʿanit 22a. The **song** that Karimah refers to was sung after crossing the Reed Sea and is found in Exod. 15. The **wells** are probably biblical Marah or Elim, see Exod. 15:23-27. **Pillar of cloud** – see Exod. 14:19. **Feiran** – see Num. 10:12. **Quail** – see Num. 11:31ff. The story of **Abu Hasan** is found in the *1001 Nights*.

The hierarchical scheme "**Second, First**" was not used in Kairawan. It was a prerogative of the Babylonian academies. I have imported the scheme to Kairawan for fictional purposes.

The story of **Aqiba and Rachel**, as well as the story of the **daughter of Hakinai**, are in the B.T. Ketubot 62b. **Ben Kalba Savu**a and **Ben Tzitzit HaKesset**'s name derivations are in the B.T. Gittin 56a The story of **Martha bat Boethius** also is found in Gittin 56a. The detail of bribery is from B.T. Yoma 18a, with some added explanation. Medieval commentaries distinguish between the Martha of King Yannai's day and the latter Martha. The verse **Rabban Yohanan** quotes as his eulogy is Deut. 28:56, which continues rather starkly, "she shall begrudge her husband and her son and her daughter the very afterbirth that issues from between her legs and the babies she bears; for she will eat them in secret for want of all food." The passage refers to the curses that will befall the Jews if they stray from God's covenant.

"**Winter is past…**" – a verse from Song of Songs 2:11-12 indicating that Hannukah season (winter) is past and Purim (Spring) has arrived. The **rain maker** stories are in the B.T. Taʿanit 19b-20a, 23a.

Ibn Nagrhela, also known as Shmuel HaNagid, served as Wazir to the Caliph of Granada. The exact date and occasion for the poem is unknown.

CHAPTER THREE

The poem is by the famous tenth century poet Dunash **ibn Labrat**. In the late twentieth century, during renovations to the library at St. Katherine's monastery at the foot of Mt. Sinai, the monks there broke through a wall and discovered there some manuscripts of poetry in Hebrew. The "**Travel…**" poem is from the *1001 Nights*. The adventure at **Mt. Sinai** includes reference to **Moses** on the mountain top from Deut. 4:11. **Elijah** is in I Kings 19. **Beams of light** may be found in Exod. 34:29-35. The **well of Moses** is at Exod. 2:16-17. "**A Man's gift…**" – verse from Prov. 18:16 often associated with charitable contributions to rabbinic academies. **Wool and linen** – the prohibition is found in Lev. 19:19. The **Nahum stories** are in the B.T. Taʿanit 21a. The good Pharaoh and the evil Pharaoh "who knew not Joseph" are recorded in Gen. 41 and Exod. 1f. **Potiphar's wife** is from Gen. 39. **Ayla** is modern Eilat.

The imagery of the **flood at Sinai** is primarily from the "Song at the Sea," Exod. 15. The Psalms quote is Ps. 93:3-4. Nissim's diary quotes: **"Fine of figure,"** is from Gen. 29:17, there describing Rachel. **"Wife of his youth,"** is found in Prov. 5:18. Abraham's bedding of Hagar, the Egyptian handmaid of his wife Sarah, resulted in the birth of Ishmael, eponymous ancestor of the Arab Muslims; see Gen. 16. **Sarah** subsequently banned her, over Abraham's objection.

Rabbenu Gershom of Mainz, mentioned above, issued a ban against polygyny throughout Ashkenaz, that is, Franco-German Jewry. The phrase **"man-of-Scripture"** is the self-designation of the Karaite sectarians. For **rebuke,** see *Leviticus Rabbah* 25:1. The quote about **God and stories** at the end of the diary excerpt is from the *Sifre* "Ekev."

CHAPTER FOUR

In his deliberations about announcing **Mulaah's** engagement, Nissim engages in classical rabbinic reasoning regarding the permissibility of certain actions on the second day of a festival – a holiday only observed in the Diaspora by rabbinic decree. In the Holy Land, only one day of the festival was observed, as was also the case among the Karaites, who did not accept the authority of such rabbinic enactments. Nissim follows the rabbinic injunction, however, toward leniency in interpretation — a tacit admission of the weaker force of the rabbinic enactment. For the equation of the parting of the **waters of the Red Sea** with the matching of brides and grooms, see *Midrash Leviticus Rabbah* 8:1.

The story of Rabbi **Meir's sister-in-law** is in the B.T. Avoda Zarah 17b-18a. The story of the **fringes** is in the B.T. Menahot 44a.

"The winter has ended" – a quote from Song of Songs 2:11-13. The **festival of Giving of the Torah** is the biblical holiday of Pentecost, reckoned by the rabbis as the 50th day after the first day of Passover.

Ecclesiastes 7:28 – the misogynistic verse which follows is Eccles. 7:26.

Rav's wife in the B.T. Yebamot 63a-b. Ben Sirah 42:9-10 is quoted in the introduction to the story of **Yohani bat Ratibi,** which is from the B.T. Sotah 22a. The maxim of **Rabbi Eliezer** is from the Mishnah Sotah 3:4.

Laban and Hazeroth and di-Zahav – see: Deut. 1:1.

Angel Jibril cooled the flames – a story reported in the Quran. The story of the **builder's wedges** is told in the Kalilah and Dimnah, where the victim is a monkey.

Pigeon's blood substituting for virgin's blood is recounted in the tale of Kamar al-Zaman in the *1001 Nights*.

CHAPTER FIVE

The description of the shopping spree is very similar to that in the story of "The **Porter** and the Three Ladies," found in the *1001 Nights*. The story of the theft of the **golden dog-food bowl** that follows is also found in the *1001 Nights*. Abu Sin refers to Karimah with the mocking title, **Sittuna**, which means "little lady" or "missy." He also refers to her as Miss Desiree', in Arabic: **Sitt Wuhshah**. Karimah cites **Song of Songs** verse 8:2. **Tomb of Haroun** – the Arabs believe that Aaron is buried on the highest hill of Petra/Raqim. **The philosopher** – known in the West as Avicenna.

Bugio and Wadjina Karimah transliterates into Arabic the Latin terms: "*Pugio*," and "*Vagina*." The names of the sword thrusts which she lists below are found some centuries later in the work of Shaykh Nefzaoui called *The Perfumed Garden for the Soul's Recreation*, which is a manual of erotica. The Arabic terms mean: "liberator," "striker," and "strong-headed," respectively. In *The Perfumed Garden*, these are among the various terms for the penis.

The story of the "**Greedy Thief**" may have its origins in the *Midrash Ecclesiastes Rabbah*, chapter 1. "**The Parable of the Fox**" is in *Ecclesiastes Rabbah*, chapter 5, and is also found in *Aesop's Fables*. The "**Tale of the Butcher**" which follows "The Fox Fable" is found in a margin of the Oxford manuscript of *Midrash Tanhuma*.

The "**mournful season**" cited in the heading to this letter refers to the Hebrew month of Av, traditionally a period of mourning for the destruction of the Jerusalem Temple – first by the Babylonians in 587 B.C.E., and then again by Rome in 70 C.E. The tales Nissim quotes here are found in the B.T. Gittin 55b-56b, with the phrase "*Vive Domini Imperator*," transliterated in a parallel to the story in *Lamentations Rabbah*. The story of **Aqiba's laughter** is in the B.T. Makkot 24b, with a somewhat different ending. The fragmentary **marriage contract** dates include both the *Anno Mundi* used at Kairawan, as well as the Seleucid calendar, commonly used throughout the Muslim world and in Fustat, as well. Finally, in a nostalgic touch not uncommon at Jewish weddings, the year is given according to the time elapsed from the destruction of the Temple by the Romans in 70 of the Common Era. The date of 15 Av was auspicious among the Jews as early as the second century, and is mentioned as such in the Mishnah. It falls late summer, usually mid-August.

In addition to the exchange of vows, it was common for the bride to list her trousseau, which remained her private property throughout the marriage, even though her husband could benefit from any profit from these items. In listing the items it is specified that **a dinar equals one dinar,** as it was the practice for less fortunate families to artificially inflate the value of the items listed in the contract for the sake of the public ceremony.

Finally, stipulations for each of them are listed: he essentially limits himself to her alone, while she agrees to remain in Kairawan. It should be recalled that her family originates in Fustat.

The bride price in rabbinic contracts was virtually always **200 *zuz*,** a nominal sum stemming back to Talmudic times in Sassanian Iraq. The marriage contract is written in Aramaic, rather than Judeo-Arabic. The writing of a Jewish marriage contract in Aramaic remains custom to this very day.

In the heading of the letter Nissim refers to Dunash as **"businessman and philanthropist,"** both terms are transliterated into Arabic from the borrowed Greek: *pragmatatos, philanthropos.* These Greek loan words were not uncommon in the Byzantine and North African Jewish communities. Nissim further employs biblical imagery from the Song of Songs. During the month of **Elul** the **ram's horn** is sounded each morning in the synagogue in anticipation of the Jewish New Year, on which it is sounded at length many times. Elul is the month preceding the Jewish New Year, which usually falls in mid-to-late September.

The story of **Resh Laqish** is in the B.T. Bava Metzia 84a. The story about **Rabbi Yohanan and Ilfa** is in the B.T. Ta'anit 21a.

CHAPTER SIX

Raqim is called Petra today. The **city of black stone** is from a tale in the *1001 Nights*, called "The Porter and the Three Ladies."

"The Man who had Two Children" – a tale told in *Midrash Leviticus Rabbah* 37:2. Hoshanna Rabba is the penultimate day of the seven day Sukkot festival. On Sukkot, Jews ritually employ citrons, palm fronds, myrtle and willow branches.

The collection of **sea stories** is found in the B.T. Bava Bathra 73a-74a. **"Jonah's Tale"** is found in *Pirke Rabbi Eliezer*, chapter 10. The sign of Abraham is, of course, circumcision. "The Tale of the **Four Captives,**" a putative explanation of how rabbinic influence extended from Byzantium throughout the Mediterranean world, is from the twelfth-century *Book of Tradition* by Abraham ibn Daud.

The story of **Hatim al-Tayy** is from the *1001 Nights*.

Three precious gifts – found at the end of *Pirke Rabbi Eliezer*, chapter 3. The quotes there are Prov. 3:19-20, and Isa. 11:2. Below, Nissim tells a story from *Genesis Rabbah* 6:5. The verse quoted is Isa. 43:16.

CHAPTER SEVEN

Dunash begins his letter to his wife and son by invoking the benediction for **resurrection of the dead** – in this case, himself, after his long absence from sight. **"The Lord is just"** – quoted from Ps. 145:17. **"Find comfort"** is found in Isa. 40:1. The **stubborn and rebellious child** is found in Deut. 21:18-21.

"**Charity...death**" – Prov. 10:2, which reads in full, "The treasuries of evil-doing are no avail, but righteousness saves one from death." The term for "righteousness" (*tzedakkah*) was used in the Jewish community to refer to the giving of charity. Nowhere is it implied that charity atones for causing the death of another. "**Your servant was careful...**" – Ps. 19:12-14, which in the original is addressed to God. **Abban Yudan** – this story and the following tales of charity are in *Midrash Leviticus Rabbah,* chapter 5. The repeated biblical quote is from Prov. 18:16. The final story about **Tarphon** is in *Midrash Leviticus Rabbah* 34:16. The verses he quotes are Ps. 112:9 and Isa. 58:12.

"**Jerusalem with mountains**" Ps. 125:2. "**Blessed is He...Who resurrects the dead**" – Dunash here first invokes the benediction for those saved from peril, followed by verses from the sailor's prayer in the book of Jonah 2:3-7. At the end he recites the benediction for the resurrection of the dead, which is recited by those who have been out of touch with one another for a very long time. "**Vomited...**" – Nissim quotes from the biblical book of Jonah, first in the heading to the letter ("vomited"), see Jonah 2:11; and again ("deliverance") from Jonah 2:10. The last quote ("death...life") is Jonah 4:8. "**Great act of love**" – A quote from the Mishnah, *Chapters of the Fathers.* "**Overturned the table**" – B.T. Nedarim 20b. "**Torah is cure**" – Nissim first quotes from the *Midrash Tanhuma,* "Yitro" #8, and follows with a quote from the *Midrash to Psalms* 24:3.

Korah and his band – see Num. 16.

CHAPTER EIGHT

The **magnetic mountains** story is found in the *1001 Nights,* in the "Third Kalandar's Tale."

Hillel legends are from the B.T. Shabbat 31a. The verse quoted in the first tale is Eccles. 11:10. **Alif, Ba, Jimm, Dal** – the opening letters of the Hebrew alphabet, but in Arabic pronounciation. "**God bless you and keep you**" – The letter opens with a citation from the priestly benediction, Num. 6:24ff., appropriate for a member of the priestly clan. This is followed by a parody of the words of Isa. 2:3, "**Torah**...from Zion and **Word**...from Jerusalem."

Camphor – a description of the tapping of camphor can be found in the *1001 Nights,* among the "Voyages of Sindbad the Sailor." **Bab Ali** – *Bab,* in Arabic, means "gate," or "entrance." This story and the next are adapted from the famous tale in the *1001 Nights.* "**Sixty philosophers**" – This story is from the B.T. Bekhorot 8b-9a. Etiquette demands attendance at a circumcision, hence they cannot refuse him. The last phrase ("eyesight ... blind") is an Arabic folk saying. **Clever in Athens** – these tales are from *Midrash Lamentations Rabbah,* chapter 1. **Nissim's appeal letter** – Nissim closes his appeal with quotations from Isa. 57-58, which is the prophetic selection for Yom Kippur. His final appeal ("Reply, Here I am") has inverted the words of the prophet who imagined the Jews calling to God, and God thus replying.

CHAPTER NINE
"Honor" is from Deut. 5:16. "**Mother bird**" is found in Deut. 22:7. The tale of Rabbi Elisha is in the *Talmud of the Land of Israel, Hagiga*, chapter 2. **Rabbi Meir** asks about Prov. 6:26. This story which follows about **Elisha's grave** is from the *Midrash to Proverbs* on that verse. "**Lay down**" – Ruth 3:13.

Eliezer, Yohanan ben Zakkai, *Shma'*, etc – These are three elementary entry points into the rabbinic world. The *Shma'* includes rabbinic blessings to be said both before and after the recitation of three biblical passages from Deut. 6, Deut. 11, and Num. 16. The thanksgiving blessing after meals consists of a number of paragraphs thanking God for daily sustenance. The daily prayers are centered on the Eighteen Blessings recited three times a day. This legend is from *The Fathers According to Rabbi Nathan*, version B. **The oven of Okhnai** – This story is in the B.T. Bava Metzia 59b. The verse quoted by Rabbi Joshua is Deut. 30:11-12. The quote from Exod. 23:2 reads in context: "you shall NOT follow the majority to do wrong." **Eliezer on his deathbed** – This story is in the B.T. Sanhedrin 68a. The verse of eulogy is from II Kings 2:12.

CHAPTER TEN
The boy with the Book of Genesis – The motif of the sleepless king is found in the biblical Book of Esther. Nissim draws this story from Seder Eliahu Zuta. The king's quote is found in both the Quran and in the rabbinic liturgy, cf. Gen. 14:19.

Atonement and Leviticus – *Midrash Leviticus Rabbah*, chapter 7. The stories of Sabbath observance are from the B.T. Shabbat 119a, while the story of Rav Huna and his neighbor are from the B.T. Ta'anit 21b.

Epitropos – a Greek loan word, found in Arabic and Hebrew documents. It refers to a warden or steward who acted on behalf of minors or women as their agent in transactions in the male business world. **Elhanan/Hananel** – There is a current debate among historians as to whether Hananel and Elhanan are two distinct figures, or the same person. This book assumes that these are two ways of referring to the same historical personage. **Wife as millstone** – Nissim here refers to a discussion in the B.T. Kiddushin 29b. The story of the **woman with the sword** which follows is an adaptation of the story of Judith and Holofernes found in the biblical Apocrypha. **God writing Torah with calligraphy** – from the B.T. Menahot 29b. **Mamzer** – the product of a forbidden marriage and legally not considered part of the Jewish community. **"Good Resting Place"** – the euphemism of choice among the Karaites for the grave. The term is found on their early medieval tombstones.

CHAPTER ELEVEN

Rabbi and maidservant – from the B.T. Eruvin 53b. The story about Rabbi and **the Emperor Antoninus** is in the B.T. Avodah Zara 10 a-b. Nissim's commentary to Tractate Eruvin is one of the few extant Talmud commentaries we have from his pen. **Marry daughter to a scholar** – B.T. Pesahim 49b.

Blessing the tree – B.T. Ta'anit 5b. **Disciples and Students of Torah** – B.T. Berachot 7a and following. **Honi's alienation** – B.T. Ta'anit 23a.

Ezekiel quote – chapter 44. **Leviticus** commandment – chapter 21.

CHAPTER TWELVE

Sarah's laughter and the angels' not telling the truth – see Gen. 18:12-13. This text is often cited by the rabbis to show there are higher values than absolute truth telling; see, e.g., *Midrash Genesis Rabbah* 48:18 and *Midrash Leviticus Rabbah* 9:9. **Stolen purses** – B.T. Yoma 83b. **Elazar ben Durdaya** – B.T. Avoda Zara 17a. **Parable** – from the B.T. Yoma 86a. The biblical quote is Jer.3:22.

The **death of Samuel the prophet** is recorded in I Sam. 25:1, but no age of death is given there. Rabbinic tradition holds that Samuel was fifty-two upon his death: see B.T. Mo'ed Qatan 28a. The quote from the sages (**"strive to be the man"**) is from the *Chapters of the Fathers*. **Hananel's Commentary** is to the B.T. Mo'ed Qatan 20a-b.

CHAPTER THIRTEEN

God's anger at Ninevites – see *Pirke Rabbi Eliezer*, chapter 10. **A good woman** – B.T. Yebamot 63b. The Scriptural citation is from Prov. 18:22. **Marriage contract** – he opening quotes are from the Bible: ("Jerusalem") Ps. 137:6, ("beloved") Song of Songs 2:16, ("found") Song 3:4, ("captured") Song 4:9, ("bone") Gen. 2:23.

Seeing your face – Nissim paraphrases Gen. 33:10, when Jacob reunites with his brother Esau after a 20 year absence. Below ("took poor me"), Nissim paraphrases Ps. 113:7-8.

Student stung by wasp – Al-Iskander's story is found in the B.T. Mo'ed Qatan 17a.

CHAPTER FOURTEEN
Sound of silence – Al-Iskander quotes from I Kings 19, when God appears to the prophet Elijah at Mount Horev. The Talmud tale is found in B.T. Berakhot 58a.

Ibn Sina and Aristo – refers to Avicenna's (=ibn Sina) famous teachings about the writings of Aristotle. **Mind and Body** – From the *Mekhilta deRabbi Ishmael, Tractate Shira* chapter 2, and also in *Leviticus Rabbah* 4:5.

When a sage dies – The law is from the B.T. Mo'ed Qatan 22b. Below he cites traditions from folio 25b there, as well as from the *Tosefta Sota* 15:2-5.

Waqf – a term still used today by Muslims to denote a building site under the supervision of an accredited "pious foundation." **9th day of Sha'ban in the year 429** – that is May 17, 1038. For this document see Norman Stillman, *The Jews of Arab Lands* (Philadelphia, 1979) 189-191.

Red heifer – According to Num. chapter 19, the Red Heifer was used in the purification ceremony for ritual unfitness due to contact with a corpse. Without the Red Heifer, all Jews would be in a state of severe impurity, hence the high value of the red cow, which had to meet very exacting standards.

Give birth before she travails – see Isa. 66:7.

CHAPTER FIFTEEN
Ten-fold curse – *Avot D'Rabbi Nathan*, version A, chapter 1. **Elijah and circumcision** – Mal. 3:1 and 3:24. Most translations would read Mal. 3:1 as "the angel of the covenant" instead of her "messenger of circumcision." Karimah follows *Midrash Pirqe Rabbi Eliezer*, chapter 29, where the custom of Elijah's attendance at circumcisions is first mentioned in rabbinic literature.

Pbu'h – This is a scribal abbreviation for "peace be upon him," a phrase written out in full in most of these letters, but elsewhere in the Geniza literature commonly abbreviated.

Gog and Magog – This is a reference to the chaos and war that will ensue as a precursor to messianic times. See Ezek. 38-39.

Plastered cistern, overflowing fountain – see *Pirke Avot*, chapter 2, where two separate disciples of Rabban Yohanan ben Zakkai are described by these metaphors for good memory and originality. **The exquisite goblet** – This story is recounted in B.T. Berakhot 27b.

May Zion rejoice…bride and groom – Rabbenu Nissim here paraphrases the praises to God found in the seven wedding benedictions which are part of the rabbinic Jewish marriage ceremony.

CHAPTER SIXTEEN

Wife of your youth – from the *Midrash to Proverbs* 5:18-20.

Underground tunnels – see the *Midrash to Proverbs* 17:1. **Flower of the priesthood** – Nehorai quotes from the B.T. Ta'anit 29a. The five disasters of the **9th of Av** are reported in the Mishnah to that chapter of Talmud.

The scroll burns…but the letters ascend – From *Midrash Elah Ezkerah*. **Rabbi Yehuda ben Baba** – The martyr's legend is also in *Midrash Elah Ezkerah*. **I complete this letter to you** – Medieval scribes traditionally ended a manuscript with *Tam venishlam shevakh le'El borei olam.* – "I complete this with praise for God, Creator of the world."

Glossary

Abu/Abi – "father of"

Abu Sina – the Muslim philosopher Avicenna

Afrikiya – also Ifrikiya, refers to Africa, specifically what is modern Tunisia

Al-Ahlil – lit., "liberator," a sword thrust

Al-Andalus – Southern Spain, Muslim territory

Al-Aqsa – Ancient mosque in Jerusalem

Al-Azhar – great mosque in Cairo and seat of Shiite (now Sunni) learning

Al-Deukkak – lit., "striker," a sword thrust

Al-Jar – small port of Hijaz

Al-Kahira – Cairo, lit., "the victorious," built by Shiite Fatimids to celebrate their conquest of Egypt

Al-Mahdia – fortress town on Tunisian coast

Al-Manakha – market outside al-Medinah

Al-Medinah – city of Muhammad, a Holy City of Islam

Al-Quds – lit., "the Holy," Jerusalem

Alexandria – great port-city west of Cairo

Alif Ba Jimm Dal – first letters of Alphabet in Arabic pronunciation

Amalfi – western coastal town of Southern Italy

Antalya – coastal town of Turkey

Antoninus – Roman emperor

Aristo – Arabic name of Aristotle

Ashkenaz – Christian Europe, Franco-Germany

Av – summer month of Hebrew calendar, the first nine days of which are devoted to mourning the destruction of the First and Second Temples of Jerusalem

Aya Sufia – Hagia Sofia, the immense domed Church of Constantinople

Ayla – now called Eilat, on Israel's southern tip

Bab – Aramaic/Arabic: gateway

Bab Al-Shami – northern gate of city

Bab-Al-Ambari – gate of al-Medinah

Badawi – bedouins

Baghdad – capital of Eastern Sunni Empire

Baksheesh – petty bribe

Banu Hilal – Bedouin warrior tribe

Banu Sulaim – Bedouin warrior tribe

Banu Ziri – the Zirid tribe

Barouta – name of a holy well in Kairawan

Bat – daughter of

Ben – son of

Ben Sirah – an apocryphal book of the Bible

Berav – son of rabbi

Berber – western tribes of North Africa, distinct from Arabs

Bint – daughter of

Bir Abbas – well on west coast of Saudi Arabia

Bir Barouta – the well of Barouta in Kairawan, which according to Muslim legend, connects to the well of Zamzam in Mecca

Bir Said – well on west coast of Saudi Arabia

Bosphorus – neck of the Sea that separates Europe from Asia, outside Constantinople

Bugio – Latin for "sword," or "dagger," in Arabic pronunciation

Bukhara – Asian city in modern Uzbekistan

Buqalamun – a shimmering cloth

Caesarea – coastal port town in Holy Land

Caliph – head of Islamic nation

Ceuta – North African port city closest to Spain

City of the Dead – Cairo's Muslim cemetery

Cohen – a member of the priestly clan of Jews, tracing lineage back to biblical times

Constantinople – Istanbul, a Byzantine capital

Coptic – Egyptian Christian

Cyrenaica – North African city

Damascus – capital of Syria

Damietta – Egyptian port town

Daphne of Antioch – a suburb of Antioch, major city in Eastern Turkey, north of Holy Land

Dhimmi – protected People of the Book who have rights, but second-class status under Islam

Diaspora – lit., "dispersion," refers to Jewish settlements outside the Holy Land

Dinar – standard monetary unit of trade

Di-Zahav – biblical city of Sinai listed in Deuteronomy as a place of Israelite wanderings

Dirhem – a monetary unit, smaller than dinar

Diwan – a couch, divan

Dome of the Rock – ancient mosque in Jerusalem, built over Rock from which Muslims say the Prophet ascended to heaven and where Jews say Isaac was offered in sacrifice

Duomo – a cathedral, so named for its "dome"

Ed-Dommar – lit., "strong headed," a sword thrust

El Jem – Tunisian town with immense Coliseum remaining from Roman times

El-Kahina – lit., "the priestess," legendary queen of Berber tribes

Elijah – biblical prophet whom the rabbis believe never died and who visits them

Elul – name of Hebrew month in late summer, traditionally a time of repentance for Jews

Emir – a Muslim ruler

Epitropos – a legal representative, usually a man fronting for a woman in a business or real estate transaction

Exile – refers to Jewish settlements outside the Holy Land

Fayyum – Egypt just south of greater Cairo

Fez – major town of Western North Africa, now Morocco

Franj – lit., "the French," refers to Europeans

Fustat – old Cairo, now at South end of Cairo's urban sprawl, home to Jews, Copts, and Sunni Muslims

Gabbes – palm oasis in Tunisia

Gaon/Gaonim – lit., "genius," title for head of Talmudic academy from Babylonia

Gaza – coastal area on southern Mediterranean coast of Roman Palestine

Geniza – a used book depository containing sacred and even secular texts

Ghadir Khumm – Muslim festival commemorating the appointment of Ali by the Prophet

Ghazzal – an Arabic metric poem

Giza – outside of Cairo, the plain of the pyramids

Gog and Magog – the war of the Apocalypse, preceding advent of Messianic era

Golden Horn – tributary that divides city of Constantinople

Granada – southern town in Spain's al-Andalus

Ha-cohen – a member of the priestly clan of Jews, tracing lineage back to Biblical times

Hadith – a Muslim oral tradition about the Prophet and his circle

Hajj – pilgrimage to Mecca

Hannukah – rabbinic (non-biblical) winter festival of light

Har Nebo – mountain in trans-Jordan where Moses died

Haram Al-Sharif – lit., "the beautiful sanctuary," refers to Mecca or the Temple Mount in Jerusalem

Haroun – Aaron

Harthema – fortress city on Tunisian coast

Hatzeroth – biblical city of Sinai listed in Deuteronomy as a place of Israelite wanderings

Hellespont – narrows leading through Greek Islands to Turkey and Constantinople

Hijaz – west coast of Saudi Arabia, containing al-Medinah and Mecca

Hind - India

Hoshanna Rabba – final day of Sukkot harvest festival, an auspicious time

Ibn – son of

Ihram – garment worn during the Hajj

Ijaza – certificate of authenticity

Imam – An Islamic preacher/teacher

In-sh-allah – God willing (Arabic)

Isa – Jesus

Isfahan – Asian city in Persia

Isma'ili – a.k.a. Fatimid

Ismael/Hagar – see: *Genesis*, Chapters 16-17, and 21; the son and concubine of Abraham, whom Arabs see as ancestors of Arab tribes and Islam

Iwan – a palace of the Fatimid Caliph

Jaffa – port city of Holy Land, a.k.a. Yaffo

Jambiyya – small, curved dagger

Jebel Mousa – Mt. Sinai

Jerba – island off Tunisian coast

Jibril – the angel Gabriel, in Muslim sources

Jinn – genie

Kairawan – lit., "caravan," city in central Tunisia, built away from the coast to avoid pirates; staging ground for caravans heading east to Cairo and west to al-Maghreb (the western portion of North Africa)

Kalilah and Dimnah – collection of animal fables

Karaite – a non-rabbinic Jew, gives allegiance to Bible alone

Khaybar – one of the towns of Wadi al-Qura

Khutba – the Friday public sermon in a mosque

Kiddushin – tractate of Mishnah and Talmud

Kosher – generally means, "okay;" fit to eat according to rabbinic law

Kunya – a nickname

Kutama – a Berber warrior tribe

Laban – biblical city of Sinai listed in Deuteronomy as a place of Israelite wanderings

Lateen – a triangular sail

Mabruk – Arabic blessing of congratulations

Madressa – a Quranic school, the term is also used by Arabic speaking Jews for their own Torah and Talmudic academies

Maghreb – The West (i.e. western North Africa)

Makroud – sweet date cookies made with semolina

Malaga – Spanish port city

Malikite – school of Islamic thought; opposed Fatimid rulers

Mameluke – a slave class who served the caliph

Mamzer – one who cannot marry into rabbinic community due to an unacceptable parental marriage

Maryam – Miriam or Mary

Mazal Tov – Hebrew blessing of congratulations

Mecca – the Holy City of Islam, place where Muslims make Hajj (pilgrimage)

Messina – city in Sicily

Midrash – rabbinic interpretation of Bible

Minyan – a prayer quorum of ten adult males

Mishnah – a six part compendium of rabbinic law; basis of Talmud

Misr – Egypt, often Cairo

Mo'ed Qatan – tractate of Mishnah and Talmud

Moab – Biblical trans-Jordan

Monastir – fortress city on Tunisian coast

Mosque of Omar – see: Dome of the Rock

Nagid – leader of Sefarad's Jewish community

Neft – naphtha, a fuel

Nil – indigo dye

Nilometer – on the Nile Island of Roda, in Cairo, a measure of the height of the Nile to predict drought, good crops, or flooding

Pbu'h – Peace Be Upon Him (usually refers to The Prophet Muhammad)

Pentecost – Shavout, the rabbinic festival that begins 50 days after Passover, and celebrates the giving of the Torah/Law at Mt. Sinai

Pharos – The great light-house of Alexandria, a wonder of the ancient world

Phaselis – small, ancient coastal town of Turkey

Pumbeditha – city in Iraq, center of great Talmudic academy

Purim – spring holiday celebrating victory of Queen Esther

Qabbes – palm oasis in Tunisia

Qadi – an Islamic judge

Rav – rabbi

Ramle – town in Holy Land to the west of Jerusalem

Raqim – now called Petra in Jordan

Rass Dimass – Tunisian town situated between a large lake and Mediterranean coast

Ribat – a fortress

Rum – Rome, but refers to all lands under Byzantine Christianity

Samaritans – an early breakaway group from Judaism, traces their separation from rabbinic Judaism back to biblical times

Samarkand – Asian city in modern Uzbekistan

Sanhedrin – Greek loan word for Temple and rabbinic era supreme tribunal

Sea Of Mamara – Sea bordering Constantinople

Sefarad – lands of the Muslim west, the Iberian peninsula

Seljuk – Turkish homelands

Sh'aban – name of month in Islamic calendar

Shami Synagogue – the synagogue that followed the rite of the Land of Israel

Shaykh – sheikh, an honorific

Shiur Qoma – a form of rabbinic mystical speculation which measures God's body

Sidi Uqba – early Muslim general who established Kairawan and its Great Mosque

Sikilia – Sicily

Sin – the Sinai peninsula

Sitt/Sittuna – Miss, or Ma'am

Sivan – Hebrew month in late spring

Souk – bazaar

Sousse – major coastal town in Tunisia

Sukkot – Biblical fall harvest festival

Sultan – the ruler of Muslim lands

Sunna – Islamic law

Sura – city in Iraq, center of great Talmudic academy

Talmud – multivolume compendium of rabbinic law and lore

Taanit – tractate of Mishnah and Talmud

Tammuz – Hebrew month in summer

Taymah – one of the towns of Wadi al-Qura

Tiberius – town in northern Holy Land

Tobruk – North African city

Torah – the Five Books of Moses, but more broadly, all of the Bible and rabbinic teaching

Tripolitana – North African city

Umm – "mother of"

Vive Domine Imperator – Latin for "Long live the Emperor!"

Wadi Tur – a locale in the Sinai

Wadi Al-Qura – Jewish town locale in Hijaz

Wadjaina – Latin for "scabbard," or "sheath," in Arabic pronunciation

Waqf – a Muslim pious foundation and/or the buildings or funds it controls

Wazir – advisor to caliph, second-in-command

Wuhshah – lit., "desirable," a woman's name

Yaffo – a.k.a. Jaffa

Yavneh – Roman Jamnia, a garrison town west of Jerusalem

Zamzam – well of Mecca

Zil Gmor – Aramaic for, "Go study"

Zirids – anti-Fatimid tribe from Kairawan

Zuz – Aramaic: a small coin of the eastern Roman Empire

Reading Group Discussion Guide

WARNING!
This book should be read before perusing these questions, some of which contain "spoilers"

1) This story is told in the form of letters because many of the documents found in the Cairo Genizah, the store room for discarded Hebrew documents, were letters (as well as lists, contracts, and other artifacts of daily life). To whom does Karimah seem to write her most truthful letters? Of all the letter writers in the book, whose perspective seems most accurate? Whose perspective seems to be the least reliable?

2) Karimah uncovers an old family secret. What effect does this have on her? On her brother? Why did Karimah's parents not divulge the truth of Karimah's mother's family to their children? Might the story have gone differently if Karimah's parents had not kept this secret? In raising children, which is more important, truth or discipline? Why?

3) In what way does Karimah's resiliency and flexibility reflect her parents? In what way does al-Iskander's steadfastness reflect those same parents?

4) Karimah comes from a very distinguished family, the al-Tustaris. They are wealthy and politically well-connected. How might Karimah's family background and upbringing have affected her choices?

5) What do you make of Karimah's character? Is Karimah a heroine or an anti-heroine?

6) How might Karimah's life have been a different had her own child survived?

7) How would you characterize relations between the Karaites and the Rabbanites? What about the Jewish and Muslim relations? What about the Sunnis and the Shiites? How have relations between the various groups changed since the Middle Ages?

8) Karimah finds herself in several different "worlds." Is there one place, or identification, that seems to fit her best?

9) Karimah's sense of adventure and independence often leads her to take on the guise of a man. How might the story have gone if Karimah had been the son and al-Iskander had been the daughter?

10) How do you feel about Karimah's choices? Is she the good Jewish girl or is she a thrill-seeking cutthroat?

11) What were the implications of Karimah's father teaching her to read? How do you think he felt about it afterwards?

12) The author engages in what is called "intertexting," that is, playing two stories off one another. One example from the book is the juxtaposition of the ancient rabbinic story of "4 things God hates" with the scene of Karimah and Ismail in the tent. What is the effect of the placement of these stories? What are some other examples of intertexting in this book?

13) What do you make of the steady interplay between the stories of ancient rabbinic Midrash and those of the Arabian Nights? What is the effect of juxtaposing these stories?

14) Many of the rabbis in the story – Nissim, Hananel, Shumuel HaNagid – were real people and we are here encountering them in a book of fiction. Is there a comparison to be made to the ancient rabbinic legends about Rabbi Akiba, R. Yohanan, R. Meir, and others, which appear in this book?

15) The last chapter is open to differing interpretations. What do you think happens to Karimah at the end of the book? What leads you to come to your conclusion? How does your view of the book's ending relate to your understanding of Karimah's character? Why do you think the author chose an ambiguous ending to the tale?

16) The Delightful Compendium is a book within a book. The stories there are bound by the frame-tale of Karimah's disappearance, like the famous frame-tale of Shahrazad in the Arabian Nights. What do you make of the many other "books" within this book?

17) This is a historical novel. Do you find more Truth in history or in story?

Burton L. Visotzky

Author Burton Visotzky tries to make himself available for book groups, whether through personal appearances, telephone conference calls or email exchanges.

Interested groups can email him at buvisotzky@BenYehudaPress.com.
Information about the author's scheduled appearances can be found at www.benyehudapress.com/authors/Visotzky.html and BookTour.com.

About the Author

Burton L. Visotzky is the Appleman Professor of Midrash and Interreligious Studies at the Jewish Theological Seminary, where he was ordained as a rabbi in 1977. He is the author of nine books, including: *Reading the Book: Making the Bible a Timeless Text* (1991), *The Genesis of Ethics* (1996), *From Mesopotamia to Modernity: Ten Introductions to Jewish History and Literature* (1999), and a scholarly translation of *The Midrash on Proverbs* (1992).

With Bill Moyers, he developed ten hours of television for PBS on the book of Genesis, serving as consultant and a featured on-screen participant. The series, "Genesis: A Living Conversation," premiered in October, 1996. Visotzky was also a consultant to Jeffrey Katzenberg of DreamWorks for their 1998 film, "Prince of Egypt".

Rabbi Visotzky is active as a lecturer and scholar-in-residence throughout North America, Europe, and Israel. He is married to attorney Sandra Edelman. They make their home in New York City.

He is active in Jewish/Christian/Muslim dialogue in such cities as Rome, Cairo, and Doha, Qatar; testifying to his desire to promote the kind of Jewish-Muslim harmony that prevails throughout much of this novel.

Following almost two years of scholarly research and travel to the countries described in the book, Rabbi Visotzky began writing the novel in the summer of 2001, completing the first draft in December, 2001. A DELIGHTFUL COMPENDIUM OF CONSOLATION, a book about Jews and Muslims living in harmony, now stands as his reaction to the fateful day that took place in the middle of its writing.

Photo: Leora Visotzky

Jewish Women of the 20th Century: fiction from Ben Yehuda Press

HANNE GOLDSCHMIDT. Nicolette Maleckar draws upon her experiences in post-war Berlin in telling the story of Hanne, a brave-hearted waif who must find a way to begin her life in the rubble of a shattered world. Hanne's story is a delightful rendering of the first blush of love in an impossible time.

The Lilac Tree: A Novel of Love in the Ruins of Berlin, 1945 by Nicolette Maleckar.

BESSIE SAINER. Exiled to Siberia at age 12 for her brothers' anti-czarist activities, at 25 Bessie loses her husband and baby girl to the ravages of civil war in revolutionary Russia.

In America, she remains a "troublemaker," fighting Nazi hoodlums, going undergound to flee McCarthyite persecution, and nearly loses her beloved daughter amidst the civil rights struggles of the 1960s.

Narrating this novel at age 88, Bessie is still making trouble and still making jokes.

This is a profoundly optimistic novel about a remarkable heroine—a rebel, a lover, a mother, a grandmother, a nurse, a Jew, and an extraordinary human being.

"It will grip you from beginning to end," says *Hadassah Magazine.*

"A remarkable first novel," says *The Nation.*

Bessie: A Novel of Love and Revolution by Lawrence Bush

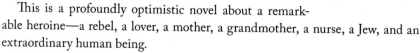

For more information, or to purchase these and other titles, visit your favorite bookstore or
http://www.BenYehudaPress.com

Jewish Women of the 20th Century: non-fiction from Ben Yehuda Press

Rifka Rosenwein. The daughter of Holocaust survivors, journalist Rifka Rosenwein chronicled her suburban, soccer-mom life in the back of *The Jewish Week* for seven years.

In 2001, Rifka's world was changed forever; first by the events of September 11th, and then, in a more personal blow, her diagnosis of terminal cancer. She died in 2003 at the age of 42.

Even when she discusses her life as being lived on "cancer time," her columns are a death-defying celebration of life. Reading her essays, you can see your own friends, your parents, your children, your co-workers, your spouse... and yourself.

"A treasure trove of wisdom from one of American Judaism's most beloved and lamented voices," says *Publishers Weekly*.

Life in the Present Tense: Reflections on Faith and Family by Rifka Rosenwein.

Dorothy Epstein. Growing up in the immigrant communities of New York, Dorothy Epstein entered the workforce during the worst part of the Depression. The child of activists herself, Dorothy had been loathe to follow in their overburdened, impoverished footsteps.

However, fate intervened, and Dorothy soon became radicalized and spent most of her life working for the advancement of labor unions and human rights. She died in 2006 at the age of 92.

"A really wonderful record of a life and its times," says Brian Lehrer of WNYC public radio.

A Song of Social Significance: Memoirs of an Activist by Dorothy Epstein.

For more information, or to purchase these and other titles, visit your favorite bookstore or
http://www.BenYehudaPress.com

Printed in the United States
201521BV00003B/1-90/A